CHARLEMONT

Darley fecit.

CHARLEMONT

OR

THE PRIDE OF THE VILLAGE

A TALE OF KENTUCKY

By W. GILMORE SIMMS, Esq.

"Nor will I be secure,
In any confidence of mine own strength,
For such security is oft the mother
Of negligence, and that, the occasion
Of unremedy'd ruin." *Microcosmus*—THO. NABBES.

AMS PRESS
NEW YORK

Reprinted from the edition of 1866, New York
First AMS EDITION published 1970
Manufactured in the United States of America

International Standard Book Number: 0-404-06008-0

Library of Congress Catalog Card Number: 78-119150

AMS PRESS, INC.
NEW YORK, N.Y. 10003

TO THE

HON. JAMES HALL,

OF CINCINNATI:

AS ONE OF THE ABLEST OF OUR LITERARY PIONEERS;
A GENUINE REPRESENTATIVE OF THE GREAT WEST;

WHOSE WRITINGS

EQUALLY ILLUSTRATE HER HISTORY AND GENIUS:

this story of "CHARLEMONT," and its Sequel "BEAUCHAMPE,"
are respectfully inscribed by

THEIR AUTHOR.

WOODLANDS, S. C.
December, 1855.

ADVERTISEMENT.

THE domestic legend which follows, is founded upon actual events of comparatively recent occurrence in the state
of Kentucky. However strange the facts may appear in
the sequel—however in conflict with what are usually supposed to be the sensibilities and characteristics of woman
—they are yet unquestionably true; most of them having
been conclusively established, by the best testimony, before
a court of justice. Very terrible, indeed, was the tragedy
to which they conducted—one that startled the whole
country when it took place, and the mournful interest of
which will long be remembered. More on this subject
need not be mentioned here. The narrative, it is hoped,
will satisfy all the curiosity of the reader. It has been
very carefully prepared from and according to the evidence;
the art of the romancer being held in close subjection to
the historical authorities. I have furnished only the necessary details which would fill such blanks in the story as
are of domestic character; taking care that these should
accord, in all cases, with the despotic facts. In respect to
these, I have seldom appealed to invention. It is in the
delineation and development of character, only, that I have
made free to furnish scenes, such as appeared to me calculated to perfect the portraits, and the better to reconcile

the reader to real occurrences, which, in their original na-
kedness, however unquestionably true, might incur the risk
of being thought improbabilities.

The reflections which will be most likely to arise from
the perusal of such a history, lead us to a consideration of
the social characteristics of the time and region, and to a
consideration of the facility with which access to society
is afforded by the manners and habits of our forest population. It is in all newly-settled countries, as among the
rustic population of most nations, that the absence of the
compensative resources of wealth leads to a singular and
unreserved freedom among the people. In this way, society
endeavors to find equivalents for those means of enjoyment
which a wealthy people may procure from travel, from
luxury, from the arts, and the thousand comforts of a well-
provided homestead. The population of a frontier country,
lacking such resources, scattered over a large territory,
and meeting infrequently, feel the lack of social intercourse ;
and this lack tends to break down most of the barriers
which a strict convention usually establishes for the protection, not only of sex and caste, but of its own tastes and
prejudices. Lacking the resources of superior wealth, population, and civilization, the frontier people are naturally
required to throw the doors open as widely as possible, in
order to obtain that intercourse with their fellows which is,
perhaps, the first great craving of humanity. As a matter
of necessity, there is little discrimination exercised in the
admission of their guests. A specious outside, agreeable
manners, cleverness and good humor, will soon make their
way into confidence, without requiring other guaranties for
the moral of the stranger. The people are naturally frank
and hospitable ; for the simple reason that these qualities

of character are essential for procuring them that intercourse which they crave. The habits are accessible, the
restraints few, the sympathies are genial, active, easily
aroused, and very confiding. It follows, naturally, that
they are frequently wronged and outraged, and just as naturally that their resentments are keen, eager, and vindictive. The self-esteem, if not watchful, is revengeful; and
society sanctions promptly the fierce redress — that wild
justice of revenge — which punishes without appeal to law,
with its own right hand, the treacherous guest who has
abused the unsuspecting confidence which welcomed him
to a seat upon the sacred hearth. In this brief portrait
of the *morale* of society, upon our frontiers, you will find
the *materiel* from which this story has been drawn, and its
justification, as a correct delineation of border life in one
of its more settled phases in the new states. The social
description of Charlemont exhibits, perhaps, a *third* advance in our forest civilization, from the original settlement.

It is not less the characteristic of these regions to exhibit
the passions and the talents of the people in equal and
wonderful saliency. We are accordingly struck with two
classes of social facts, which do not often arrest the attention in old communities. We see, for example, the most
singular combination of simplicity and sagacity in the same
person; simplicity in conventional respects, and sagacity
in all that affects the absolute and real in life, nature and
the human sensibilities. The rude man, easily imposed
upon, in his faith, fierce as an outlaw in his conflicts with
men, will be yet exquisitely alive to the nicest consciousness
of woman; will as delicately appreciate her instincts and
sensibilities, as if love and poetry had been his only tutors

1*

from the first, and had mainly addressed their labors to this one object of the higher heart, education ; and in due degree with the tenderness with which he will regard the sex, will be the vindictive ferocity with which — even though no kinsman — he will pursue the offender who has dared to outrage them in the case of any individual. In due degree as his faith is easy will his revenges be extreme. In due degree as he is slow to suspect the wrong-doer, will be the tenacity of his pursuit when the offender requires punishment. He seems to throw wide his heart and habitation, but you must beware how you trespass upon the securities of either.

The other is a mental characteristic which leads to frequent surprises among strangers from the distant cities. It consists in the wonderful inequality between his mental and social development. The same person who will be regarded as a boor in good society, will yet exhibit a rapidity and profundity of thought and intelligence — a depth and soundness of judgment — an acuteness in discrimination — a logical accuracy, and critical analysis, such as mere good society rarely shows, and such as books almost as rarely teach. There will be a deficiency of refinement, taste, art — all that the polished world values so highly — and which it seems to cherish and encourage to the partial repudiation of the more essential properties of intellect. However surprising this characteristic may appear, it may yet be easily accounted for by the very simplicity of a training which results in great directness and force of character — a frank heartiness of aim and object — a truthfulness of object which suffers the thoughts to turn neither to the right hand nor to the left, but to press forward decisively to the one object — a determined will, and a restless instinct—which, conscious of the deficiencies of wealth and position, is yet perpetually seeking to supply them from the resources within its reach. These characteristics will be found illustrated in the present legend, an object which it somewhat contemplates, apart from the mere story with which they are interwoven.

A few words more in respect to our heroine, Margaret Cooper. It is our hope and belief, that she will be found a real character by most of our readers. She is drawn from the life, and with a severe regard to the absolute features of the original. In these days of "strong-minded women," even more certainly than when the portrait was first taken, the identity of the sketch with its original will be sure of recognition. Her character and career will illustrate most of the mistakes which are made by that ambitious class, among the gentler sex, who are now seeking so earnestly to pass out from that province of humiliation to which the sex has been circumscribed from the first moment of recorded history. What she will gain by the motion, if successful, might very well be left to time, were it not that the proposed change in her condition threatens fatally some of her own and the best securities of humanity. We may admit, and cheerfully do so, that she might, with propriety, be allowed some additional legal privileges of a domestic sort. But the great object of attainment, which is the more serious need of the sex—her own more full development as a responsible being—seems mainly to depend upon herself, and upon self-education. The great first duty of woman is in her becoming the mother of men; and this duty implies her proper capacity for the education and training of the young. To fit her properly for this duty, her education should become more elevated, and more severe in degree with its elevation. But the argument is one of too grave, too intricate, and excursive a character, to be attempted here. It belongs to a very different connection. It is enough, in this place, to say that Margaret Cooper possesses just the sort of endowment to make a woman anxious to pass the guardian boundaries which hedge in her sex — her danger corresponds with her desires. Her securities, with such endowments, and such a nature, can only be found in a strict and appropriate education, such as woman seldom receives anywhere, and less, perhaps, in this country than in any other. To train fully the feminine mind, without in any degree impairing her susceptibilities and sensibilities, seems at once the necessity and the difficulty of the subject. Her very influence over man lies in her sensibilities. It will be to her a perilous fall from pride of place, and power, when, goaded by an insane ambition, in the extreme development of her mere intellect, she shall forfeit a single one of these securities of her sex.

CHARLEMONT.

CHAPTER I.

THE SCENE.

THE stormy and rugged winds of March were overblown
—the first fresh smiling days of April had come at last—
the days of sunshine and shower, of fitful breezes, the breath
of blossoms, and the newly-awakened song of birds. Spring
was there in all the green and glory of her youth, and the
bosom of Kentucky heaved with the prolific burden of the
season. She had come, and her messengers were everywhere, and everywhere busy. The birds bore her gladsome
tidings to

> " Alley green,
> Dingle or bushy dell of each wild wood,
> And every bosky bourn from side to side—"

nor were the lately-trodden and seared grasses of the forests left unnoted ; and the humbled flower of the wayside
sprang up at her summons. Like some loyal and devoted
people, gathered to hail the approach of a long-exiled and
well-beloved sovereign, they crowded upon the path over
which she came, and yielded themselves with gladness at
her feet. The mingled songs and sounds of their rejoicing
might be heard, and far-off murmurs of gratulation, rising
from the distant hollows, or coming faintly over the hill-

tops, in accents not the less pleasing because they were the less distinct. That lovely presence which makes every land blossom, and every living thing rejoice, met, in the happy region in which we meet her now, a double tribute of honor and rejoicing.

The " dark and bloody ground," by which mournful epithets Kentucky was originally known to the Anglo-American, was dark and bloody no longer. The savage had disappeared from its green forests for ever, and no longer profaned with slaughter, and his unholy whoop of death, its broad and beautiful abodes. A newer race had succeeded; and the wilderness, fulfilling the better destinies of earth, had begun to blossom like the rose. Conquest had fenced in its sterile borders with a wall of fearless men, and peace slept everywhere in security among its green recesses. Stirring industry — the perpetual conqueror — made the woods resound with the echoes of his biting axe and ringing hammer. Smiling villages rose in cheerful white, in place of the crumbling and smoky cabins of the hunter. High and becoming purposes of social life and thoughtful enterprise superseded that eating and painful decay, which has terminated in the annihilation of the red man; and which, among every people, must always result from their refusal to exercise, according to the decree of experience, no less than Providence, their limbs and sinews in tasks of well-directed and continual labor.

A great nation urging on a sleepless war against sloth and feebleness, is one of the noblest of human spectacles. This warfare was rapidly and hourly changing the monotony and dreary aspects of rock and forest. Under the creative hands of art, temples of magnificence rose where the pines had fallen. Long and lovely vistas were opened through the dark and hitherto impervious thickets. The city sprang up beside the river, while hamlets, filled with active hope and cheerful industry, crowded upon the verdant hill-side, and clustered among innumerable valleys.

Grace began to seek out the homes of toil, and taste supplied their decorations. A purer form of religion hallowed the forest-homes of the red-man, while expelling for ever the rude divinities of his worship; and throughout the land, an advent of moral loveliness seemed approaching, not less grateful to the affections and the mind, than was the beauty of the infant April, to the eye and the heart of the wanderer.

But something was still wanting to complete the harmonies of nature, in the scene upon which we are about to enter. Though the savage had for ever departed from its limits, the blessings of a perfect civilization were not yet secured to the new and flourishing regions of Kentucky. Its morals were still in that fermenting condition which invariably distinguishes the settlement of every new country by a various and foreign people. At the distant period of which we write, the population of Kentucky had not yet become sufficiently stationary to have made their domestic gods secure, or to have fixed the proper lines and limits regulating social intercourse and attaching precise standards to human conduct. The habits and passions of the first settlers—those fearless pioneers who had struggled foot to foot with the Indian, and lived in a kindred state of barbarity with him, had not yet ceased to have influence over the numerous race which followed them. That moral amalgam which we call society, and which recognises a mutual and perfectly equal condition of dependence, and a common necessity, as the great cementing principles of the human family, had not yet taken place; and it was still too much the custom, in that otherwise lovely region, for the wild man to revenge his own wrong, and the strong man to commit a greater with impunity. The repose of social order was not yet secured to the great mass, covering with its wing, as with a sky that never knew a cloud, the sweet homes and secure possessions of the unwarlike. The fierce robber sometimes smote the peaceful traveller upon the highway, and the wily assassin of reputation, within the limits of the city barrier, not unfrequently plucked the sweetest rose that ever adorned the virgin bosom of innocence, and triumphed, without censure, in the unhallowed spoliation.

But sometimes there came an avenger;—and the highway robber fell before the unexpected patriot; and the virgin was avenged by the yet beardless hero, for the wrong of her cruel seducer. The story which we have to tell, is of times and of actions such as these. It is a melancholy narrative—the more melancholy, as it is most certainly true. It will not be told in vain, if the crime which it describes in proper colors, and the vengeance by which it was followed, and which it equally records, shall secure the innocent from harm, and discourage the incipient wrongdoer from his base designs.

CHAPTER II.

THE TRAVELLERS.

LET the traveller stand with us on the top of this rugged eminence, and look down upon the scene below. Around us, the hills gather in groups on every side, a family cluster, each of which wears the same general likeness to that on which we stand, yet there is no monotony in their aspect. The axe has not yet deprived them of a single tree, and they rise up, covered with the honored growth of a thousand summers. But they seem not half so venerable. They wear, in this invigorating season, all the green, fresh features of youth and spring. The leaves cover the rugged limbs which sustain them, with so much ease and grace, as if for the first time they were so green and glossy, and as if the impression should be made more certain and complete, the gusty wind of March has scattered abroad and borne afar, all the yellow garments of the vanished winter. The wild flowers begin to flaunt their blue and crimson draperies about us, as if conscious that they are borne upon the bosom of undecaying beauty; and the spot so marked and hallowed by each charming variety of bud and blossom, would seem to have been a selected dwelling for the queenly Spring herself.

Man, mindful of those tastes and sensibilities which in great part constitute his claim to superiority over the brute, has not been indifferent to the beauties of the place. In the winding hollows of these hills, beginning at our feet, you see the first signs of as lovely a little hamlet as ever promised peace to the weary and the discontent. This is the village of Charlemont.

A dozen snug and smiling cottages seem to have been dropped in this natural cup, as if by a spell of magic. They appear, each of them, to fill a fitted place—not equally distant from, but equally near each other. Though distinguished, each by an individual feature, there is yet no great dissimilarity among them. All are small, and none of them distinguished by architectural pretension. They are now quite as flourishing as when first built, and their number has had no increase since the village was first settled. Speculation has not made it populous and prosperous, by destroying its repose, stifling its charities, and abridging the sedate habits and comforts of its people. The houses, though constructed after the fashion of the country, of heavy and ill-squared logs, roughly hewn, and hastily thrown together, perhaps by unpractised hands, are yet made cheerful by that tidy industry which is always sure to make them comfortable also. Trim hedges that run beside slender white palings, surround and separate them from each other. Sometimes, as you see, festoons of graceful flowers, and waving blossoms, distinguish one dwelling from the rest, declaring its possession of some fair tenant, whose hand and fancy have kept equal progress with habitual industry ; at the same time, some of them appear entirely without the little garden of flowers and vegetables, which glimmers and glitters in the rear or front of the greater number.

Such was Charlemont, at the date of our narrative. But the traveller would vainly look, now, to find the place as we describe it. The garden is no longer green with fruits and flowers—the festoons no longer grace the lowly portals—the white palings are down and blackening in the gloomy mould—the roofs have fallen, and silence dwells lonely among the ruins,—the only inhabitant of the place It has no longer a human occupant.

"Something ails it now—the spot is cursed."

Why this fate has fallen upon so sweet an abiding place—
why the villagers should have deserted a spot, so quiet and
so beautiful—it does not fall within our present purpose to
inquire. It was most probably abandoned—not because of
the unfruitfulness of the soil, or the unhealthiness of the
climate—for but few places on the bosom of the earth, may
be found either more fertile, more beautiful, or more health-
ful—but in compliance with that feverish restlessness of
mood—that sleepless discontent of temper, which, perhaps,
more than any other quality, is the moral failing in the
character of the Anglo-American. The roving desires of
his ancestor, which brought him across the waters, have
been transmitted without diminution—nay, with large increase—to the son. The creatures of a new condition of
things, and new necessities, our people will follow out their
destiny. The restless energies which distinguish them,
are, perhaps, the contemplated characteristics which Providence has assigned them, in order that they may the
more effectually and soon, bring into the use and occupation
of a yet mightier people, the wilderness of that new world
in which their fortunes have been cast. Generation is but
the pioneer of generation, and the children of millions,
more gigantic and powerful than ourselves, shall yet smile
to behold, how feeble was the stroke made by our axe upon
the towering trees of their inheritance.

It was probably because of this characteristic of our people, that Charlemont came in time to be deserted. The
inhabitants were one day surprised with tidings of more
attractive regions in yet deeper forests, and grew dissatisfied
with their beautiful and secluded valley. Such is the ready
access to the American mind, in its excitable state, of
novelty and sudden impulse, that there needs but few suggestions to persuade the forester to draw stakes, and re-
move his tents, where the signs seem to be more numerous
of sweeter waters and more prolific fields. For a time,
change has the power which nature does not often exer-

cise; and under its freshness, the waters *do* seem sweeter, and the stores of the wilderness, the wild-honey and the locust, *do* seem more abundant to the lip and eye.

Where our cottagers went, and under what delusion, are utterly unknown to us; nor is it important to our narrative that we should inquire. Our knowledge of them is only desirable, while they were in the flourishing condition in which they have been seen. It is our trust that the novelty which seduced them from their homes, did not fail them in its promises—that they may never have found, in all their wanderings, a less lovely abiding-place, than that which they abandoned. But change has its bitter, as well as its sweet, and the fear is strong that the cottagers of Charlemont, in the weary hours, when life's winter is approaching, will still and vainly sigh after the once-despised enjoyments of their deserted hamlet.

It was toward the close of one of those bright, tearful days in April, of which we have briefly spoken, when a couple of travellers on horseback, ascended the last hill looking down upon Charlemont. One of these travellers had passed the middle period of life; the other was, perhaps, just about to enter upon its heavy responsibilities, and more active duties. The first wore the countenance of one who had borne many sorrows, and borne them with that resignation, which, while it proves the wisdom of the sufferer, is at the same time, calculated to increase his benevolence. The expression of his eye, was full of kindness and benignity, while that of his mouth, with equal force, was indicative of a melancholy, as constant as it was gentle and unobtrusive. A feeble smile played over his lips while he spoke, that increased the sadness which it softened; as the faint glimmer of the evening sunlight, upon the yellow leaves of autumn, heightens the solemn tones in the rich coloring of the still decaying forest.

The face of his companion, in many of its features, was in direct contrast with his own. It was well formed, and, to the casual glance, seemed no less handsome than intellectual. There was much in it to win the regard of the young and superficial. An eye that sparkled with fire, a mouth that glowed with animation — cheeks warmly colored, and a contour full of vivacity, seemed to denote properties of mind and heart equally valuable and attractive. Still, a keen observer would have found something sinister, in the upward glancing of the eye, at intervals, from the half-closed lids ; and, at such moments, there was a curling contempt upon the lips, which seemed to denote a cynical and sarcastic turn of mind. A restless movement of the same features seemed equally significant of caprice of character, and a flexibility of moral ; while the chin narrowed too suddenly and became too sharp at the extremity, to persuade a thorough physiognomist, that the owner could be either very noble in his aims, or very generous in his sentiments. But as these outward tokens can not well be considered authority in the work of judgment, let events, which speak for themselves, determine the true character of our travellers.

They had reached the table land of the heights which looked down upon Charlemont, at a moment when the beauty of the scene could scarcely fail to impress itself upon the most indifferent observer. The elder of the travellers, who happened to be in advance, was immediately arrested by it ; and, staying the progress of his horse, with hand lifted above his eye, looked around him with a delight which expressed itself in an abrupt ejaculation, and brought his companion to his side. The sun had just reached that point in his descent, which enabled him to level a shaft of rosy light from the pinnacle of the opposite hill, into the valley below, where it rested among the roofs of two of the cottages, which arose directly in its path. The occupants of these two cottages had come forth, as it were, in answer to the summons ; and old and young, to the number of ten or a dozen persons, had met, in the winding pathway be-

tween, which led through the valley, and in front of every
cottage which it contained. The elder of the cottagers sat
upon the huge trunk of a tree, which had been felled beside
the road, for the greater convenience of the traveller; and
with eyes turned in the direction of the hill on which the
sunlight had sunk and appeared to slumber, seemed to enjoy the vision with no less pleasure than our senior travel
ler. Two tall damsels of sixteen, accompanied by a young
man something older, were strolling off in the direction of
the woods; while five or six chubby girls and boys were
making the echoes leap and dance along the hills, in the
clamorous delight which they felt in their innocent but stirring exercises. The whole scene was warmed with the equal
brightness of the natural and the human sun. Beauty was
in the sky, and its semblance, at least, was on the earth.
God was in the heavens, and in his presence could there be
other than peace and harmony among men!

"How beautiful!" exclaimed the elder of our travellers —
"could anything be more so! How pure, how peaceful!
See, Warham how soft, how spirit-like, that light lies along
the hill-side, and how distinct, yet how delicate, is the train
which glides from it down the valley, even to the white
dwellings at its bottom, from which it seems to shrink and
tremble as if half conscious of intrusion. And yet the
picture below is kindred with it. That, now, is a scene
that I delight in — it is a constant picture in my mind.
There is peace in that valley, if there be peace anywhere
on earth. The old men sit before the door, and contemplate with mingled feelings of pride and pleasure, the vigorous growth of their children. They behold in them their
own immortality, even upon earth. The young will preserve their memories, and transmit their names to other
children yet unborn; and how must such a reflection reconcile them to their own time of departure, not unfitly
shown in the last smiles of that sunlight, which they are so
soon about to lose. Like him, they look with benevolence

and love upon the world from which they will soon depart."

"Take my word for it, uncle, they will postpone their departure to the last possible moment, and, so far from looking with smiles upon what they are about to leave for ever, they will leave it with very great reluctance, and in monstrous bad humor. As for regarding their children with any such notions as those you dwell upon with such poetical raptures, they will infinitely prefer transmitting for themselves their names and qualities to the very end of the chapter. Ask any one of them the question now, and he will tell you that an immortality, each, in his own wigwam, and with his weight of years and infirmity upon him, would satisfy all his expectations. If they look at the vigor of their young, it is to recollect that they themselves once were so, and to repine at the recollection. Take my word for it, there is not a dad among them, that does not envy his own son the excellence of his limbs, and the long time of exercise and enjoyment which they seemingly assure him."

"Impossible!" exclaimed the elder of the two travellers. "Impossible! I should be sorry to think as you do. But you, Warham, can not understand these things. You are an habitual unbeliever—the most unfortunate of all mankind."

"The most fortunate, rather. I have but few burdens of credulity to carry. The stars be blessed, my articles of faith are neither very many nor very cumbrous. I should be sorry if my clients were so few."

"I should be sorry, Warham, if I had so little feeling as yourself."

"And I should be still more sorry, uncle, if I had half so much. Why, sir, yours is in such excess, that you continually mistake the joys and sorrows of other people for your own. You laugh and weep with them alternately; and, until all's done and over, you never seem to discover

that the business was none of yours;—that you had none
of the pleasure which made you laugh, and might have been
spared all the unnecessary suffering which moved your
tears. 'Pon my soul, sir, you pass a most unprofitable life."

"You mistake, Warham, I have shared both; and my
profits have been equally great from both sources. My
susceptibility has been an exceeding great gain to me, and
has quickened all my senses. There is a joy of grief, you
know, according to Ossian."

"Nay, if you quote Ossian, uncle, I give you up. I
don't believe in Ossian, and his raving stuff always sickens
me."

"I sometimes think, Warham," said the uncle, good naturedly, "that Providence has denied you some of the more
human faculties. Nay, I fear that you are partially deficient in some of the senses. Do you see that sunlight to
which I point—there, on the hill-side, a sort of rosy haze,
which seems to me eminently beautiful?"

"Yes, sir; and, if you will suffer me, I will get out of
its reach as quickly as possible. I have been half blinded
by it ever since you found it so beautiful. Sunlight is, I
think, of very little importance to professional men, unless
as a substitute for candles, and then it should come over the
left shoulder, if you would not have it endanger the sight.
Nay, I will go farther, and confess that it is better than
candlelight, and certainly far less expensive. Shall we go
forward, sir?"

"Warham," said the uncle, with increasing gravity, "I
should be sorry to believe that a habit of speech so irreve-
rential, springs from anything but an ambition for saying
smart things, and strange things, which are not always
smart. It would give me great pain to think that you
were devoid of any of those sensibilities which soften the
hearts of other men, and lead them to generous impulses."

"Nay, be not harsh, uncle. You should know me better.
I trust my sensibilities, and senses too, may be sufficient

for all proper purposes, when the proper time comes for their employment; but I can't flame up at every sunbeam, and grow enthusiastic in the contemplation of Bill Johnson's cottage, and Richard Higgins's hedgerow. A turnip-patch never yet could waken my enthusiasm, and I do believe, sir—I confess it with some shame and a slight misgiving, lest my admissions should give you pain—that my fancy has never been half so greatly enkindled by Carthula, of the bending spear, or Morven of the winds, as by the sedate and homely aspect of an ordinary dish of eggs and bacon, hot from the flaming frying-pan of some worthy housewife."

The uncle simply looked upon the speaker, but without answering. He was probably quite too much accustomed to his modes of thought and speech to be so much surprised as annoyed by what he said. Perhaps, too, his own benevolence of spirit interfered to save the nephew from that harsher rebuke which his judgment might yet have very well disposed him to bestow.

Following the course of the latter in silence, he descended into the valley, and soon made his way among the sweet little cottages at its foot. An interchange of courtesies between the travellers and the villagers whose presence had given occasion to some portion of the previous dialogue, in which the manner of the younger traveller was civil, and that of the elder kind; and the two continued on their journey, though not without being compelled to refuse sundry invitations, given with true patriarchal hospitality, to remain among the quiet abodes through which they passed.

As cottage after cottage unfolded itself to their eyes, along the winding avenue, the proprietors appeared at door and window, and, with the simple freedoms of rural life, welcomed the strangers with a smile, a nod, and sometimes, when sufficiently nigh, a friendly word of salutation, but

2

without having the effect of arresting their onward progress.
Yet many a backward glance was sent by the elder of the
travellers, whose eyes, beaming with satisfaction, sufficiently declared the delight which he received from the
contemplation of so many of the mingled graces of physical
and moral nature. His loitering steps drew from his young
companion an occasional remark, which, to ears less benevolent and unsuspecting than than those of the senior, might
have been deemed a sarcasm; and more than once the lips
of .the nephew had curled with contemptuous smiles, as he
watched the yearning glances of his uncle on each side of
the avenue, as they wended slowly through it.

At the end of the village, and at the foot of the opposite
hills, they encountered a group of young people of both
sexes, whose bursts of merriment were suddenly restrained
as they emerged unexpectedly into sight. The girls had
been sitting upon the grassy mead, with the young men before them; but they started to their feet at the sound of
strange steps, and the look of strange faces. Charlemont,
it must be remembered, was not in the thoroughfare of
common travel. If visited at all by strangers, it was most
usually by those only who came with a single purpose.
Nothing, therefore could have been more calculated to surprise a community so insulated, than that they should
attract, but not arrest the traveller. The natural surprise
which the young people felt, when unexpectedly encountered in their rustic sports, was naturally increased by this
unusual circumstance, and they looked after the departing
forms of the wayfarers with a wonder and curiosity that
kept them for some time silent. The elder of the two,
meanwhile—one of whose habits of mind was always to
give instantaneous utterance to the feeling which was uppermost—dilated, without heeding the sneers of his nephew,
upon the apparent happiness which they witnessed.

"Here, you see, Warham, is a pleasure which the great
city never knows:—the free intercourse of the sexes in all

those natural exercises which give health to the body, grace to the movement, and vivacity to the manners."

"The health will do well enough," replied the skeptic, "but save me from the grace of Hob and Hinney; and as for their manners—did I hear you correctly, uncle, when you spoke of their manners?"

"Surely, you did. I have always regarded the natural manners which belong to the life of the forester, as being infinitely more noble, as well as more graceful, than those of the citizen. Where did you ever see a tradesman whose bearing was not mean compared with that of the hunter?"

"Ay, but these are no hunters, and scarcely foresters. I see not a single Nimrod among the lads; and as for the lasses, even your eyes, indulgent as they usually are, will scarcely venture to insist that I shall behold one nymph among them worthy to tie the shoe-latchets of Diana. The manners of the hunter are those of an elastic savage; but these lads shear sheep, raise hogs for the slaughter-pen, and seldom perform a nobler feat than felling a bullock. They have none of the elasticity which, coupled with strength, makes the grace of the man; and they walk as if perpetually in the faith that their corn-rows and pota-toe-hills were between their legs."

"Did you note the young woman in the crimson bodv Warham? Was she not majestically made?"

"It struck me she would weigh against any two of the company."

"She is rather heavy, I grant you, but her carriage, Warham!"

"Would carry weight—nothing more."

"There was one little girl, just rising into womanhood; —you must admit that she had a very lovely face, and her form—"

"My dear uncle, what is it that you will not desire me to believe? You are sadly given to proselytism, and take

infinite pains to compel me to see with eyes that never do
their owner so much wrong, as when they reject the aid of
spectacles. How much would Charlemont and its inhabitants differ to your sight, were you only to take your green
spectacles from the shagreen case in which they do no
duty. But if you are resolved, in order to seem youthful, to
let your age go unprovided with the means of seeing as
youth would see, at least suffer me to enjoy the natural privileges of twenty-five. When, like you, my hairs whiten,
and my eyes grow feeble, ten to one, I shall think with you
that every third woodman is an Apollo, and every other
peasant-girl is a Venus, whom——"

The words of the speaker ceased—cut short by the sudden appearance of a form and face, the beauty and dignity
of which silenced the skeptic, and made him doubtful, for
the moment, whether he had not in reality reached that
period of confused and confounding vision, which, as he
alleged to be the case with his uncle, loses all power of
discrimination. A maiden stood before him—tall, erect,
majestic—beautiful after no ordinary standard of beauty.
She was a brunette, with large dark eyes, which, though
bright, seemed dark with excess of bright—and had a
depth of expression which thrilled instantly through the
bosom of the spectator. A single glance did she bestow
upon the travellers, while she acknowledged, by a slight
courtesy, the respectful bow which they made her. They
drew up their horses as with mutual instinct, but she passed
them quickly, courtesying a second time as she did so, and,
in another moment a turn of the road concealed her from
the eyes of the travellers.

"What say you to that, Warham?" demanded the senior
exultingly.

"A Diana, in truth; but, uncle, we find her not among
the rest. *She* is none of your cottagers. *She* is of another
world and element. She is no Charlemonter."

And, as he spoke, the younger traveller looked back with

straining eyes to catch another glance of the vanished object, but in vain.

"You deserve never to see a lovely woman again, Warham, for your skepticism."

"But I will have a second look at her, uncle, though the skies fall," answered the young man, as, wheeling his horse round, he deliberately galloped back to the bend in the avenue, by which she had been hidden from his view.

He had scarcely reached the desired point, when he suddenly recoiled to find the object of his pursuit standing motionless just beyond, with eyes averted to the backward path— her glance consequently encountering his own, the very moment when he discovered her. A deep crimson, visible even where he stood, suffused her cheeks when she beheld him; and without acknowledging the second bow which the traveller made, she somewhat haughtily averted her head with a suddenness which shook her long and raven tresses entirely free of the net-work which confined them.

"A proud gipsy!" muttered the youth as he rode back to his uncle—"just such a spirit as I should like to tame." He took especial care, however, that this sentiment did not reach the ears of his senior.

"Well?" said the latter, inquiringly, at his approach.

"I am right after all, uncle:—the wench is no better than the rest. A heavy bulk that seemed dignified only because she is too fat for levity. She walks like a blind plough-horse in a broken pasture, up and down, over and over; with a gait as rigid and deliberate as if she trod among the hot cinders, and had corns on all her toes. She took us so by surprise that if we had not thought her beautiful we must have thought her ugly, and the chances are equal, that, on a second meeting, we shall both think her so. I shall, I'm certain, and you must, provided you give your eyes the benefit, and your nose the burden of your green specs."

" Impossible ! I can scarce believe it, Warham," replied
the senior. " I thought her very beautiful."

" I shall never rely on your judgment again ;—nay, uncle,
I am almost inclined to suspect your taste."

" Well, let them be beautiful or ugly, still I should think
the same of the beauty of this village."

" While the sun shines it may be tolerable ; but, uncle,
in wet bad weather—it must become a mere pond, it lies
so completely in the hollow of the hills."

" There is reason in that, Warham."

" And yet, even as a pond, it would have its advantages
—it would be famous for duck-raising."

" Pshaw ! you are worse than a Mahometan."

" Something of a just comparison, uncle, though scarcely
aimed," said the other ; " like Mahomet, you know, I doubt
the possession of souls by women."

" Yet if these of Charlemont have not souls, they have
no small share of happiness on earth. I never heard more
happy laughter from human lips than from theirs. They
must be happy."

" I doubt that also," was the reply. " See you not,
uncle, that to nine or ten women there are but three lads ?
Where the disproportion is so great among the sexes, and
where it is so unfavorable to the weaker, women never can
be happy. Their whole lives will be lives of turmoil,
jealousy, and pulling of caps. Nay, eyes shall not be secure under such circumstances ; and Nan's fingers shall
be in Doll's hair, and Doll's claws in Nanny's cheeks,
whenever it shall so happen, that Tom Jenkins shall incline
to Nan, or John Dobbins to Doll. Such a disparity between the sexes is one of the most fruitful causes of domestic war."

" Warham, where do you think to go when you die ?"

" Where there shall be no great inequality in the population. Believe me, uncle, though I am sometimes disposed to think with Mahomet, and deny the possession of

souls to the sex, I also incline to believe, with other more charitable teachers — however difficult it may be to reconcile the two philosophies — that there will be no lack of them in either world."

"Hush, hush, Warham," was the mild rebuke of the senior; "you go too far — you are irreverent. As for this maiden, I still think her very beautiful — of a high and noble kind of beauty. My eyes may be bad; — indeed I am willing to admit they are none of the best; but I feel certain that they cannot so far deceive me, when we consider how nigh we were to her."

"The matter deserves inquiry, uncle, if it were only to satisfy your faith; — suppose we ride back, both of us, and see for ourselves — closely, and with the aid of the green spectacles? Not that I care to see farther — not that I have any doubts — but I wish you to be convinced in this case, if only to make you sensible of the frequent injustice to which your indulgence of judgment, subjects the critical fastidiousness of mine. What say you; shall we wheel about?"

"Why, you are mad, surely. It is now sunset, and we have a good eight miles before we get to Holme's Station."

"But we can sleep in Charlemont to-night. A night in this earthly Eden——"

"And run the risk of losing our company? Oh, no, most worthy nephew. They will start at dawn to-morrow."

"We can soon come up with 'em."

"Perhaps not, and the risk is considerable. Travelling to the Mississippi is no such small matter at any time, and, in these times it is only with a multitude, that there is safety. The murder of old Whiteford, is a sufficient warning not to go alone with more gold than lead in one's pocket. We are two, it is true, but better ten than two. You are a brave fellow enough, Warham, I doubt not; but a shot will dispose of you, and after that I should be an easy victim. I could wink and hold out my iron as well as the best of you, but I prefer to escape the necessity. Let us mend our pace. We are burning daylight.''

The nephew, with an air of some impatience, which, however, escaped the eyes of the senior, sent his horse forward by a sharp application of his spur, though looking back the while, with a glance of reluctance, which strongly disagreed with the sentiments which he expressed. Indeed, with both the travellers, the impression made by the little village of Charlemont was such that the subject seemed nowise displeasing to either, and furnished the chief staple of conversation between them, as they rode the remaining eight miles of their journey. The old man's heart had been subdued and won by the sweet air of peace which seemed to overspread and hallow the soft landscape, and the smiling cottages which made it human. The laughing maidens with their bright eyes and cheering accents, gave vivacity to its milder charms. We have heard from the lips of the younger traveller, that these attractions had failed to captivate his fancy. We may believe of this as we please. It is very probable that he had, in considerable part, spoken nothing but the truth. He was too much of a mocker;— one of those worldlings who derive their pleasures from circumstances of higher conventional attraction. He had no feeling for natural romance. His *penchant*, was decidedly for the artificial existence of city life ;. and the sneers which he had been heard to express at the humble joys of rustic life, its tastes, and characteristics, were, in truth, only such as he really felt. But, even in his case, there was an evident disposition to know something more of Charlemont. He was really willing to return. He renewed the same subject of conversation, when it happened to flag, with obvious eagerness ; and, though his language was still studiedly disparaging, a more deeply penetrating judgment than that of his uncle, would have seen that the little village, slightly as he professed to esteem it, was yet an object of thought and interest in his eyes.   Of the sources of this new interest time must inform us.

"Well, well, Warham," at length exclaimed the uncle, in a tone that seemed meant to close the discussion of a topic which his nephew now appeared mischievously bent to thrust upon him, "you will return to Kentucky in the fall.   Take Charlemont in your route.   Stop a week there. It will do you no harm.   Possibly you may procure some clients — may, indeed, include it in your tour of practice — at all events, you will not be unprofitably employed if you come to see the village and the people with *my* eyes, which, I doubt not, you will in time."

"In time, perhaps, I may.   It is well that you do not insist upon any hurried convictions.   Were I at your years, uncle mine," continued the other irreverently, "I should no doubt see with your eyes, and possibly feel with your desires.   Then, no doubt, I shall acquire a taste for warm-ingpans and nightcaps — shall look for landscapes rather than lands — shall see nothing but innocence among the young, and resignation and religion among the old; and fancy, in every aged pair of bumpkins that I see, a Darby and Joan, with perpetual peace at their fireside, though they may both happen to lie there drunk on apple-brandy. Between caudle-cups and 'John Anderson, my Jo-John,' it is my hope to pass the evening of my days with a tolerable grace, and leave behind me some comely representatives, who shall take up the burden of the ditty where I leave off. On this head be sure you shall have no cause to complain of me.   I shall be no Malthusian, as you certainly have shown yourself.   It is the strangest thing to me, uncle, that, with all your *spoken* rapture for the sex, you should never have thought of securing for yourself at least one among the crowd which you so indiscriminately admire. Surely, a gentleman of your personal attractions — attractions which seem resolute to cling to you to the last — could not have found much difficulty in procuring the damsel he

2*

desired! And when, too, your enthusiasm for the sex is
known, one would think it only necessary that you should
fling your handkerchief, to have it greedily grappled by the
fairest of the herd. How is it, uncle—how have you
escaped from them—from yourself?"

"Pshaw, Warham, you are a fool!" exclaimed the senior,
riding forward with increasing speed. The words were
spoken good naturedly, but the youth had touched a spot,
scarcely yet thoroughly scarred over, in the old man's bosom: and memories, not less painful because they had been
hidden so long, were instantly wakened into fresh and cruel
activity.

It will not diminish the offence of the nephew in the mind
of the reader, when he is told that the youth was not ignorant of the particular tenderness of his relative in this respect. The gentle nature of the latter, alone, rescued him
from the well-merited reproach of suffering his habitual levity of mood to prevail in reference to one whom even he
himself was disposed to honor. But few words passed between the two, ere they reached the place of appointment.
The careless reference of the youth had made the thoughts
of the senior active at the expense of his observation. His
eyes were now turned inward; and the landscape, and the
evening sun, which streamed over and hallowed it with a
tender beauty to the last, was as completely hidden from his
vision, as if a veil had been drawn above his sight. The
retrospect, indeed, is ever the old man's landscape; and
perhaps, even had he not been so unkindly driven back to
its survey, our aged traveller would have been reminded of
the past in the momently-deepening shadows which the evening gathered around his path. Twilight is the cherished
season for sad memories, even as the midnight is supposed
to be that of guilty ghosts; and nothing, surely, can be
more fitting than that the shadows of former hopes should
revisit us in those hours when the face of nature itself
seems darkening into gloom.

It was night before the wayfarers reached the appointed baiting place. There they found their company—a sort of little caravan, such as is frequent in the history of western emigration—already assembled, and the supper awaiting them. Let us leave them to its enjoyment, and return once more to the village of Charlemont.

CHAPTER III.

THE STRONG-MINDED WOMAN.

THE young maiden last met by our travellers, and whose appearance had so favorably impressed them, had not been altogether uninfluenced by the encounter. Her spirit was of a musing and perhaps somewhat moody character, and the little adventure related in our last chapter, had awakened in her mind a train of vague and purposeless thought, from which she did not strive to disengage herself. She ceased to pursue the direct path back to Charlemont, the moment she had persuaded herself that the strangers had continued on their way; and turning from the beaten track, she strolled aside, following the route of a brooklet, the windings of which, as it led her forward, were completely hidden from the intrusive glance of any casual wayfarer. The prattle of the little stream as it wound upon its sleepless journey, contributed still more to strengthen the musings of those vagrant fancies that filled the maiden's thoughts.

She sat down upon the prostrate trunk of a tree, and surrendered herself for a while to their control. Her thoughts were probably of a kind which, to a certain extent, are commended to every maiden. Among them, perpetually rose an image of the bold and handsome stranger, whose impudence, in turning back in pursuit of her, was somewhat qualified by the complimentary curiosity which such conduct manifested. Predominant even over this image, however, was the conviction of isolation which she felt where she was, and the still more painful conviction, that the future was without promise. Such thoughts and apprehensions may be natural enough to all young persons of active, earnest nature, not permitted to perform; but in the bosom of Margaret Cooper they were particularly so. Her mind was of a masculine and commanding character, and was ill-satisfied with her position and prospect in Charlemont. A quiet, obscure village, such as that we have described, held forth no promise for a spirit so proud, impatient, and ambitious as hers. She knew the whole extent of knowledge which it contained, and all its acquisitions and resources — she had sounded its depths, and traced all its shallows. The young-women kept no pace with her own progress — they were good, silly girls enough — a chattering, playful set, whom small sports could easily satisfy, and who seemed to have no care, and scarce a hope, beyond the hilly limits of their homestead; and as for the young men — they were only suited to the girls, such as they were, and could never meet the demand of such an intellect as hers.

This lofty self-estimate, which was in some sense just, necessarily gave a tone to her language and a coloring to all her thoughts, such as good sense and amiability should equally strive to suppress and conceal — unless, as in the case of Margaret Cooper, the individual herself was without due consciousness of their presence. It had the effect of discouraging and driving from her side many a good-natured damsel, who would have loved to condole with her, and might have been a pleasant companion. The young women regarded her with some dislike in consequence of her self-imposed isolation — and the young men with some apprehension. Her very knowledge of books, which infinitely surpassed that of all her sex within the limits of Charlemont, was also an object of some alarm. It had been her fortune, whether well or ill may be a question, to inherit from her father a collection, not well chosen, upon which her mind had preyed with an appetite as insatiate as it was undiscriminating. They had taught her many things, but among these neither wisdom nor patience was included;—and one of the worst lessons which she had learned, and which they had contributed in some respects to teach, was discontent with her condition—a discontent which saddened, if it did not embitter, her present life, while it left the aspects of the future painfully doubtful, even to her own eye.

She was fatherless, and had been already taught some of those rude lessons which painfully teach dependence; but such lessons, which to most others would have brought submission, only provoked her to resistance. Her natural impetuosity of disposition, strengthened by her mother's idolatrous indulgence, increased the haughtiness of her character; and when, to these influences, we add that her surviving parent was poor, and suffered from privations which were unfelt by many of their neighbors, it may be easily conceived that a temper and mind such as we have described those of Margaret Cooper—ardent, commanding, and impatient—hourly found occasion, even in the secluded village where she dwelt, for the exercise of moods equally adverse to propriety and happiness. Isolated from the world by circumstances, she doubly exiled herself from its social indulgences, by the tyrannical sway of a superior will, strengthened and stimulated by an excitable and ever feverish blood; and, as we find her now, wandering sad and sternly by the brookside, afar from the sports and humbler sources of happiness, which gentler moods left open to the rest, so might she customarily be found, at all hours, when it was not absolutely due to appearances that she should be seen among the crowd.

We will not now seek to pursue her musings and trace them out to their conclusions, nor will it be necessary that we should do more than indicate their character. That they were sad and solemn as usual — perhaps humbling — may be gathered from the fact that a big tear might have been seen, long gathering in her eye; — the next moment she brushed off the intruder with an impatience of gesture, that plainly showed how much her proud spirit resented any such intrusion. The tear dispersed the images which had filled her contemplative mood, and rising from her sylvan seat, she prepared to move forward, when a voice calling at some little distance, drew her attention. Giving a hasty glance in the direction of the sound, she beheld a young man making his way through the woods, and approaching her with rapid footsteps. His evident desire to reach her, did not, however, prompt her to any pause in her own progress ; but, as if satisfied with the single glance which she gave him, and indifferent utterly to his object, she continued on her way, nor stopped for an instant, nor again looked back, until his salutation, immediately behind her, compelled her attention and answer.

"Margaret — Miss Cooper!" said the speaker, who was a young rustic, probably twenty or twenty-one years of age, of tall, good person, a handsome face, which was smooth, though of dark complexion, and lightened by an eye of more than ordinary size and intelligence. His tones were those of one whose sensibilities were fine and active, and it would not have called for much keen observation to have seen that his manner, in approaching and addressing the maiden, was marked with some little trepidation. She, on the contrary, seemed too familiar with his homage, or too well satisfied of his inferiority, to deign much attention to his advances. She answered his salutation coldly, and was preparing to move forward, when his words again called for her reluctant notice.

"I have looked for you, Margaret, full an hour. Mother sent me after you to beg that you will come there this evening. Old Jenks has come up from the river, and brought a store of fine things — there's a fiddle for Ned, and Jason Lightner has a flute, and I — I have a small lot of books, Margaret, that I think will please you."

" I thank you, William Hinkley, and thank your mother, but I can not come this evening."

" But why not, Margaret ? — your mother's coming — she promised for you too, but I thought you might not get home soon enough to see her, and so I came out to seek you."

" I am very sorry you took so much trouble, William, for I can not come this evening."

" But why not, Margaret ? You have no other promise to go elsewhere have you ?"

" None," was the indifferent reply.

" Then — but, perhaps, you are not well, Margaret ?"

" I am quite well, I thank you, William Hinkley, but I don't feel like going out this evening. I am not in the humor."

Already, in the little village of Charlemont, Margaret Cooper was one of the few who were permitted to indulge in humors, and William Hinkley learned the reason assigned for her refusal, with an expression of regret and disappointment, if not of reproach. An estoppel, which would have been so conclusive in the case of a city courtier, was not sufficient, however, to satisfy the more frank and direct rustic, and he proceeded with some new suggestions, in the hope to change her determination.

" But you'll be so lonesome at home, Margaret, when your mother's with us. She'll be gone before you can get back, and——"

" I'm never lonesome, William, at least I'm never so well content or so happy as when I'm alone," was the self-satisfactory reply.

" But that's so strange, Margaret. It's so strange that you should be different from everybody else. I often wonder at it, Margaret ; for I know none of the other girls but love to be where there's a fiddle, and where there's pleasant company. It's so pleasant to be where everybody's pleased ; and then, Margaret, where one can talk so well as you, and of so many subjects, it's a greater wonder still that you should not like to be among the rest."

"I do not, however, William," was the answer in more softened tones. There was something in this speech of her lover, that found its way through the only accessible avenues of her nature. It was a truth, which she often repeated to herself with congratulatory pride, that she had few feelings or desires in common with the crowd.

"It is my misfortune," she continued, "to care very little for the pastimes you speak of; and as for the company, I've no doubt it will be very pleasant for those who go, but to me it will afford very little pleasure. Your mother must therefore excuse me, William:—I should be a very dull person among the rest."

"She will be so very sorry, Margaret—and Ned, whose new fiddle has just come, and Jason Lightner, with his flute. They all spoke of you and look for you above all, to hear them this evening. They will be so disappointed."

William Hinkley spoke nothing of his own disappointment, but it was visible enough in his blank countenance, and sufficiently audible in the undisguised faltering of his accents.

"I do not think they will be so much disappointed, William Hinkley. They have no reason to be, as they have no right to look for me in particular. I have very little acquaintance with the young men you speak of."

"Why, Margaret, they live alongside of you—and I'm sure you've met them a thousand times in company," was the response of the youth, uttered in tones more earnest than any he had yet employed in the dialogue, and with something of surprise in his accents.

"Perhaps so; but that makes them no intimates of mine, William Hinkley. They may be very good young men, and, indeed, so far as I know, they really are; but that makes no difference. We find our acquaintances and our intimates among those who are congenial, who somewhat resemble us in spirit, feeling, and understanding."

"Ah, Margaret!" said her rustic companion with a sigh, which amply testified to the humility of his own self-estimate, and of the decline of his hope which came with it — "ah, Margaret, if that be the rule, where are you going to find friends and intimates in Charlemont?"

"Where!" was the single word spoken by the haughty maiden, as her eye wandered off to the cold tops of the distant hills along which the latest rays of falling sunlight, faint and failing, as they fell, imparted a hue, which though bright, still as it failed to warm, left an expression of October sadness to the scene, that fitly harmonized with the chilling mood under which she had spoken throughout the interview.

"I don't think, Margaret," continued the lover, finding courage as he continued, "that such a rule is a good one. I know it can't be a good one for happiness. There's many a person that never will meet his or her match in this world, in learning and understanding — and if they won't look on other persons with kindness, because they are not altogether equal to them, why there's a chance that they'll always be solitary and sad. It's a real blessing, I believe, to have great sense, but I don't see, that because one has great sense, that one should not think well and kindly of those who have little, provided they be good, and are willing to be friendly. Now, a good heart seems to be the very best thing that nature can give us; and I know, Margaret, that there's no two better hearts in all Charlemont — perhaps in all the world, though I won't say that — than cousin Ned Hinkley, and Jason Lightner, and——"

"I don't deny their merits and their virtues, and their goodness of heart, William Hinkley," was the answer of the maiden — "I only say that the possession of these qualities gives them no right to claim my sympathies or affection. These claims are only founded upon congeniality of character and mind, and without this congeniality, there can be no proper, no lasting intimacy between persons. They no doubt, will find friends between whom and themselves, this congeniality exists. I, on the other hand, must be permitted to find mine, after my own ideas, and as I best can. But if I do not — the want of them gives me no great concern. I find company enough, and friends enough, even in these woods, to satisfy the desires of my heart at present; I am not anxious to extend my acquaintance or increase the number of my intimates."

William Hinkley, who had become somewhat warmed by the argument, could have pursued the discussion somewhat further; but the tones and manner of his companion, to say nothing of her words, counselled him to forbear. Still, he was not disposed altogether to give up his attempts to secure her presence for the evening party.

"But if you don't come for the company, Margaret, recollect the music. Even if Ned Hinkley was a perfect fool, which he is not, and Jason Lightner were no better, — nobody can say that they are not good musicians. Old Squire Bee says there's not in all Kentucky a better violinist than Ned, and Jason's flute is the sweetest sound that ear ever listened to along these hills. If you don't care anything for the players, Margaret, I'm sure you can't be indifferent to their music; and I know they are anything but indifferent to what you may think about it. They will play ten times as well if you are there; and I'm sure, Margaret, I shall be the last" — here the tone of the speaker's voice audibly faltered — " I shall be the very last to think it sweet if you are not there."

But the words and faltering accents of the lover equally failed in subduing the inflexible, perverse mood of the haughty maiden. Her cold denial was repeated; and with looks that did not fail to speak the disappointment of William Hinkley, he attended her back to the village. Their progress was marked by coldness on the one hand, and decided sadness on the other. The conversation was carried on in monosyllables only, on the part of Margaret, while timidity and a painful hesitancy marked the language of her attendant. But a single passage may be remembered of all that was said between the two, ere they separated at the door of the widow Cooper.

" Did you see the two strangers, Margaret, that passed through Charlemont this afternoon ?"

The cheeks of the maiden became instantly flushed, and the rapid utterance of her reply in the affirmative, denoted an emotion which the jealous instincts of the lover readily perceived. A cold chill, on the instant, pervaded the veins of the youth ; and that night he did not hear, any more than Margaret Cooper, the music of his friends. He was present all the time and he answered their inquiries as usual ; but his thoughts were very far distant, and somehow or other, they perpetually mingled up the image of the young traveller, whom he too had seen, with that of the proud woman, whom he was not yet sure that he unprofitably worshipped.

CHAPTER IV.

SIMPLICITY AND THE SERPENT.

THE mirth and music of Charlemont were enjoyed by others, but not by Margaret Cooper. The resolution not to share in the pleasures of the young around her, which she showed to her rustic lover, was a resolution firmly persevered in throughout the long summer which followed. Her wayward mood shut out from her contemplation the only sunshine of the place; and her heart, brooding over the remote, if not the impossible, denied itself those joys which were equally available and nigh. Her lonesome walks became longer in the forests, and later each evening grew the hour of her return to the village. Her solitude daily increased, as the youth who really loved her with all the ardency of a first passion, and who regarded her at the same time with no little veneration for those superior gifts of mind and education which, it was the general conviction in Charlemont, that she possessed, became, at length, discouraged in a pursuit which hitherto had found nothing but coldness and repulse. Not that he ceased to love — nay, he did not cease entirely to hope. What lover ever did? He fondly ascribed to the object of his affections a waywardness of humor, which he fancied would pass away after a season, and leave her mind to the influence of a more sober and wholesome judgment. Perhaps, too, like many other youth in like circumstances, he did not always see or feel the caprice of which he was the victim. But for this fortunate blindness, many a fair damsel would lose her conquest quite as suddenly as it was made.

But the summer passed away, and the forest put on the sere and sombre robes of autumn, and yet no visible change — none at least more favorable to the wishes of William Hinkley — took place in the character and conduct of the maiden. Her mind, on the contrary, seemed to take something of its hue from the cold sad tones of the forest. The serious depth of expression in her dark eyes seemed to deepen yet more, and become yet more concentrated — their glance acquired a yet keener intentness — an inflexibility of direction — which suffered them seldom to turn aside from those moody contemplations, which had made her, for a long time, infinitely prefer to gaze upon the rocks, and woods, and waters, than upon the warm and wooing features of humanity.

At distance the youth watched and sometimes followed her, and when, with occasional boldness, he would draw nigh to her secret wanderings, a cold fear filled his heart, and he shrunk back with all the doubt and dread of some guilty trespasser. But his doubt, and we may add, his dread also, was soon to cease entirely, in the complete conviction of his hopelessness. The day and the fate were approaching, in the person of one, to whom a natural instinct had already taught him to look with apprehension, and whose very first appearance had inspired him with antipathy.

What a strange prescience, in some respects, has the devoted and watchful heart that loves! William Hinkley, had seen but for a single instant, the face of that young traveller, who has already been introduced to us, and that instant was enough to awaken his dislike — nay, more, his hostility. Yet no villager in Charlemont but would have told you, that, of all the village, William Hinkley was the most gentle, the most generous — the very last to be moved by bad passions, by jealousy or hate.

The youth whom we have seen going down with his uncle to the great valley of the Mississippi, was now upon his return. He was now unaccompanied by the benignant senior with whom we first made his acquaintance. He had simply attended the old bachelor, from whom he had considerable expectations, to his plantation, in requital of the spring visit which the latter had paid to his relatives in Kentucky; and having spent the summer in the southwest, was about to resume his residence, and the profession of the law, in that state. We have seen that, however he might have succeeded in disguising his true feelings from his uncle, he was not unmoved by the encounter with Margaret Cooper, on the edge of the village. He now remembered the casual suggestion of the senior, which concluded their discussion on the subject of her beauty; and he resolved to go aside from his direct path, and take Charlemont in the route of his return. Not that he himself needed a second glance to convince him of that loveliness which, in his wilfulness, he yet denied. He was free to acknowledge to himself that Margaret Cooper was one of the noblest and most impressive beauties he had ever seen. The very scorn that spoke in all her features, the imperious fires that kindled in her eyes, were better calculated than any more gentle expressions, to impose upon one who was apt to be skeptical on the subject of ordinary beauties. The confidence and consciousness of superiority, which too plainly spoke out in the features of Margaret, seemed to deny to his mind the privilege of doubting or discussing her charms — a privilege upon which no one could have been more apt to insist than himself. This seeming denial, while it suggested to him ideas of novelty, provoked his curiosity and kindled his pride. The haughty glance with which she encountered his second approach, aroused his vanity, and a latent desire arose in his heart, to overcome one who had shown herself so premature in her defiance. We will not venture to assert that the young traveller had

formed any very deliberate designs of conquest, but, it may
be said, as well here as elsewhere, that his self-esteem was
great; and accustomed to easy conquests among the sex,
in the region where he dwelt, it was only necessary to in-
flame his vanity, to stimulate him to the exercise of all his
arts.

It was about noon, on one of those bright, balmy days,
early in October, when "the bridal of the earth and sky,"
in the language of the good old Herbert, is going on —
when, the summer heats subdued, there is yet nothing
either cold, or repulsive in the atmosphere; and the soft
breathing from the southwest has just power enough to
stir the flowers and disperse their scents; that our young
traveller was joined in his progress towards Charlemont,
by a person mounted like himself and pursuing a similar
direction.

At the first glance the youth distinguished him as one
of the homely forest preachers of the methodist persuasion,
who are the chief agents and pioneers of religion in most
of the western woods. His plain, unstudied garments all
of black, rigid and unfashionable; his pale, demure features,
and the general humility of his air and gesture, left our
young skeptic little reason to doubt of this; and when the
other expressed his satisfaction at meeting with a companion at last, after a long and weary ride without one, the
tone of his expressions, the use of biblical phraseology, and
the monotonous solemnity of his tones, reduced the doubts
of the youth to absolute certainty. At first, with the habitual levity of the young and skeptical, he congratulated himself upon an encounter which promised to afford him a good
subject for quizzing; but a moment's reflection counselled
him to a more worldly policy, and he restrained his natural
impulse in order that he might first sound the depths of the
preacher, and learn in what respect he might be made subservient to his own purposes. He had already learned
from the latter that he was on his way to Charlemont,

of which place he seemed to have some knowledge; and
the youth, in an instant, conceived the possibility of making
him useful in procuring for himself a favorable introduction
to the place. With this thought, he assumed the grave
aspect and deliberate enunciation of his companion, expressed himself equally gratified to meet with a person
who, if he did not much mistake, was a divine, and concluded his address by the utterance of one of those pious commonplaces which are of sufficiently easy acquisition, and
which at once secured him the unscrupulous confidence of
his companion.

"Truly, it gladdens me, sir," said the holy man in reply,
"to meet with one, as a fellow-traveller in these lonesome
ways, who hath a knowledge of God's grace and the blessings which he daily sheddeth, even as the falling of the
dews, upon a benighted land. It is my lot, and I repine
not that such it is, to be for ever a wayfarer, in the desert
where there are but few fountains to refresh the spirit.
When I say desert, young gentleman, I speak not in the
literal language of the world, for truly it were a most
sinful denial of God's bounty were I to say, looking round
upon the mighty forests through which I pass, and upon
the rich soil over which I travel, that my way lies not
through a country covered, thrice covered, with the best
worldly bounties of the Lord. But it is a moral desert
which my speech would signify. The soul of man is here
lacking the blessed fountains of the truth—the mind of
man here lacketh the holy and joy-shedding lights of the
spirit; and it rejoiceth me, therefore, when I meet with
one, like thyself, in whose language I find a proof that thou
hast neither heard the word with idle ears, nor treasured it
in thy memory with unapplying mind. May I ask of thee,
my young friend, who thou art, and by what name I shall
call thee?—not for the satisfaction of an idle curiosity, to
know either thy profession or thy private concerns, but that
I may the better speak to thee in our conference hereafter.

3

Thou hast rightly conjectured as to my calling—and my own name, which is one unknown to most even in these forests, is John Cross—I come of a family in North Carolina, which still abide in that state, by the waters of the river Haw. Perhaps, if thou hast ever travelled in those parts, thou hast happened upon some of my kindred, which are very numerous."

"I have never, reverend sir, travelled in those parts," said the youth, with commendable gravity, " but I have heard of the Cross family, which I believe, as you say, to be very numerous—both male and female."

"Yea, I have brothers and sisters an equal number; I have aunts and uncles a store, and it has been the blessing of God so to multiply and increase every member thereof, that each of my brothers, in turn, hath a goodly flock, in testimony of his favors. I, alone, of all my kindred, have neither wife nor child, and I seem as one set apart for other ties, and other purposes."

"Ah, sir," returned the other, quickly, and with a slyness of expression which escaped the direct and unsuspecting mind of the preacher, " but if you are denied the blessings which are theirs, you have your part in the great family of the world. If you have neither wife nor child of your own loins, yet, I trust, you have an abiding interest in the wives and children of all other men."

"I were but an unworthy teacher of the blessed word, had I not," was the simple answer. " Verily, all that I teach are my children ; there is not one crying to me for help, to whom I do not hasten with the speed of a father flying to bring succor to his young. I trust in God, that I have not made a difference between them ; that I heed not one to the forfeit or suffering of the other ; and for this impartial spirit toward the flock intrusted to my charge, do I pray, as well as for the needful strength of body and soul, through which my duties are to be done. But thou hast not yet spoken thy name, or my ears have failed to receive it."

There was some little hesitation on the part of the youth before he answered this second application ; and a less unheeding observer than his fellow-traveller, might have noticed an increasing warmth of hue upon his cheek, while he was uttering his reply :—

"I am called Alfred Stevens," he replied at length, the color increasing upon his cheek even after the words were spoken. But they were spoken. The falsehood was registered against him beyond recall, though, of course, without startling the doubts or suspicions of his companion.

"Alfred Stevens ; there are many Stevenses : I have known several and sundry. There is a worthy family of that name by the waters of the Dan."

"You will find them, I suspect, from Dan to Beersheba," responded the youth with a resumption of his former levity.

"Truly, it may be so. The name is of good repute. But what is thy calling, Alfred Stevens ? Methinks at thy age thou shouldst have one."

"So I have, reverend sir," replied the other ; "my call ing heretofore has been that of the law. But it likes me not, and I think soon to give it up."

"Thou wilt take to some other then. What other hast thou chosen ; or art thou like those unhappy youths, by far too many in our blessed country, whom fortune hath hurt by her gifts, and beguiled into idleness and sloth ?"

"Nay, not so, reverend sir ; the gifts of fortune have been somewhat sparing in my case, and I am even now conferring with my own thoughts whether or not to take to schoolkeeping. Nay, perhaps, I should incline to something better, if I could succeed in persuading myself of my own worthiness in a vocation which, more than all others, demands a pure mind with a becoming zeal. The law consorts not with my desires — it teaches selfishness, rather than self-denial ; and I have already found that some of its duties demand the blindness and the silence of that best teacher from within, the watchful and unsleeping conscience."

"Thou hast said rightly, Alfred Stevens; I have long thought that the profession of the law hardeneth the heart, and blindeth the conscience. Thou wilt do well to leave it, as a craft that leads to sin, and makes the exercise of sin a duty; and if, as I rightly understand thee, thou lookest to the gospel as that higher vocation for which thy spirit yearneth, then would I say to thee, arise, and gird up thy loins; advance and falter not; — the field is open, and though the victory brings thee no worldly profit, and but little worldly honor, yet the reward is eternal, and the interest thereof, unlike the money which thou puttest out to usury in the hands of men, never fails to be paid, at the very hour of its due, from the unfailing treasury of Heaven. Verily, I rejoice, Alfred Stevens, that I have met with thee to-day. I had feared that the day had been lost to that goodly labor, to which all my days have been given for seventeen years, come the first sabbath in the next November. But what thou hast said, awakens hope in my soul that such will not be the case. Let not my counsels fail thee, Alfred; — let thy zeal warm; let thy spirit work within thee, and thy words kindle, in the service of the Lord. How it will rejoice me to see thee taking up the scrip and the staff and setting forth for the wildernesses of the Mississippi, of Arkansas, and Texas, far beyond; — bringing the wild man of the frontier, and the red savage, into the blessed fold and constant company of the Lord Jesus, to whom all praise!"

"It were indeed a glorious service," responded the young stranger — whom we shall proceed, hereafter, to designate by the name by which he has called himself. He spoke musingly, and with a gravity that was singularly inflexible — "it were indeed a glorious service. Let me see, there were thousands of miles to traverse before one might reach the lower Arkansas; and I reckon, Mr. Cross, the roads

are mighty bad after you pass the Mississippi — nay, even
in the Mississippi, through a part of which territory I have
gone only this last summer, there is a sad want of cause-
ways, and the bridges are exceedingly out of repair.   There
is one section of near a hundred miles, which lies between
the bluffs of Ashibiloxi, and the far creek of Catahoula, that
was a shame and reproach to the country and the people
thereof.   What, then, must be the condition of the Texas
territory, beyond ? and, if I err not, the Cumanchees are a
race rather given to destroy than to build up.   The chance
is that the traveller in their country might have to swim
his horse over most of the watercourses, and where he found
a bridge, it were perhaps a perilous risk to cross it.   Even
then he might ride fifty miles a day, before he should see
the smokes which would be a sign of supper that night."

"The greater the glory — the greater the glory, Alfred
Stevens.   The toil and the peril, the pain and the privation,
in a good cause, increase the merit of the performance in
the eyes of the Lord.   What matters the roads and the
bridges, the length of the way, or the sometimes lack of
those comforts of the flesh, which are craved only at the
expense of the spirit, and to the great delay of our day of
conquest.   These wants are the infirmities of the human,
which dissipate and disappear, the more few they become,
and the less pressing in their complaint.   Shake thyself
loose from them, Alfred Stevens, and thy way henceforth
is perfect freedom."

"Alas! this is my very weakness, Mr. Cross : — it was
because of these very infirmities, that I had doubt of my
own worthiness to take up the better vocation which is yet
my desire.   I am sadly given to hunger and thirst toward
noon and evening ; and the travel of a long day makes me
so weary at night, that I should say but a hurried grace before meal, and make an even more hurried supper after it.
Nay, I have not yet been able to divest myself of a habit
which I acquired in my boyhood ; and I need at times,

throughout the day, a mouthful of something stronger than mere animal food, to sustain the fainting and feeble flesh, and keep my frame from utter exhaustion. I dare not go upon the road, even for the brief journey of a single day, without providing myself beforehand with a supply of a certain beverage, such as is even now contained within this vessel, and which is infallible against sinking of the the spirits, faintings of the frame, disordered nerves, and even against flatulence and indigestion. If, at any time, thou shouldst suffer from one or the other of these infirmities, Mr. Cross, be sure there is no better medicine for their cure than this."

The speaker drew from his bosom a little flask, such as is sufficiently well known to most western travellers, which he held on high, and which, to the unsuspecting eyes of the preacher, contained a couple of gills or more of a liquid of very innocent complexion.

"Verily, Alfred Stevens, I do myself suffer from some of the weaknesses of which thou hast spoken. The sinking of the spirits, and the faintness of the frame, are but too often the enemies that keep me back from the plough when I would thereto set my hand; and that same flatulence—"

"A most frequent disorder in a region where greens and collards form the largest dishes on the tables of the people," interrupted Stevens, but without changing a muscle of his countenance.

"I do believe as thou say'st, Alfred Stevens, that the disorder comes in great part from that cause, though, still, I have my doubts if it be not a sort of wind-melancholy, to which people, who preach aloud are greatly subject. It is in my case almost always associated with a sort of hoarseness, and the nerves of my frame twitch grievously at the same periods. If this medicine of thine be sovereign against so cruel an affliction, I would crave of thee such knowledge as would enable me to get a large supply of it, that I may overcome a weakness, which, as I tell thee, oftentimes impairs my ministry, and sometimes makes me wholly incapable of fervent preaching. Let me smell of it, I pray thee."

"Nay, taste of it, sir — it is just about the time when I find it beneficial to partake of it, as a medicine for my own weakness, and I doubt not, it will have a powerful effect also upon you. A single draught has been found to relieve the worst case of flatulence and colic."

"From colic too, I am also a great sufferer," said the preacher as he took the flask in his hand, and proceeded to draw the stopper.

"That is also the child of collards," said Stevens, as he watched with a quiet and unmoved countenance the proceedings of his simple companion, who finding some difficulty in drawing the cork, handed it back to the youth. The latter, more practised, was more successful, and now returned the open bottle to the preacher.

"Take from it first, the dose which relieves thee, Alfred Stevens, that I may know how much will avail in my own case;" and he watched curiously, while Stevens, applying the flask to his lips, drew from it a draught, which, in western experience of benefits, would have been accounted a very moderate potion. This done, he handed it back to his companion, who, about to follow his example, asked. him :—

"And by what name, Alfred Stevens, do they call this medicine, the goodly effect of which thou holdst to be so great?"

Stevens did not immediately reply — not until the preacher had applied the bottle to his mouth, and he could see by the distension of his throat, that he had imbibed a taste. at least, of the highly-lauded medicine. The utterance then, of the single word — "Brandy" — was productive of an effect no less ludicrous in the sight of the youth, than it was distressing to the mind of his worthy companion. The descending liquor was ejected with desperate effort from the throat which it had fairly entered — the flask flung from his hands — and with choking and gurgling accents, start-ling eyes, and reddening visage, John Cross turned full upon his fellow-traveller, vainly trying to repeat, with the accompanying horror of expression which he felt, the single spellword, which had produced an effect so powerful.

"Bran — bran — brandy! — Alfred Stevens! — thou hast given me poison — the soul's poison — the devil's liquor — liquor distilled in the vessels of eternal sin.   Wherefore hast thou done this ?   Dost thou not know "——

"Know — know what, Mr. Cross?" replied Stevens, with all the astonishment which he could possibly throw into his air, as he descended from his horse with all haste to recover his flask, and save its remaining contents from loss.

" Call me not mister — call me plain John Cross," replied the preacher — in the midst of a second fit of choking, the result of his vain effort to disgorge that portion of the per-nicious liquid which had irretrievably descended into his bowels.   With a surprise admirably affected, Stevens ap-proached him.

" My dear sir — what troubles you ? — what can be the matter ?   What have I done ?   What is it you fear ?"

" That infernal draught — that liquor — I have swallow-ed of it a.mouthful.   I feel it in me.   The sin be upon thy head, Alfred Stevens — why did you not tell me, before I drank, that it was the soul's poison ? — the poison that slays more than the sword or the pestilence ; — the liquor of the devil, distilled in the vessels of sin — and sent among men for the destruction of the soul!   I feel it now within me, and it burns — it burns like the fires of damnation.   Is there no water nigh that I may quench my thirst ? — Show me, Alfred Stevens, show me where the cool waters lie, that I may put out these raging flames."

" There is a branch, if I mistake not, just above us on the

road — I think I see it glistening among the leaves. Let us ride toward it, sir, and it will relieve you."

"Ah, Alfred Stevens, why have you served me thus? Why did you not tell me?"

Repeated groans accompanied this apostrophe, and marked every step in the progress of the preacher to the little rivulet which trickled across the road. John Cross, descended with the rapidity of one whose hope hangs upon a minute, and dreads its loss, as equal to the loss of life. He straddled the stream and thrust his lips into the water, drawing up a quantity sufficient, in the estimation of Stevens, to have effectually neutralized the entire contents of his flask.

"Blessed water! Blessed water! Holiest beverage! Thou art the creation of the Lord, and, next to the waters of eternal life, his best gift to undiscerning man. I drink of thee, and I am faint no longer. I rise up, strong and refreshed! Ah, my young friend, Alfred Stevens, I trust thou didst not mean me harm in giving me that poisonous liquor?"

"Far from it, sir, I rather thought to do you a great benefit"

"How couldst thou think to do me benefit by proffering such poison to my lips? nay, wherefore dost thou thyself carry it with thee, and why dost thou drink of it, as if it were something not hurtful as well to the body as the soul? Take my counsel, I pray thee, Alfred Stevens, and cast it behind thee for ever. Look not after it when thou dost so, with an eye of regret lest thou forfeit the merit of thy self-denial. If thou wouldst pursue the higher vocation of the brethren, thou must seek for the needful strength from a better and purer spirit. But what unhappy teacher could have persuaded thee to an indulgence which the good men of all the churches agree to regard as so deadly?"

"Nay, Mr. Cross——"

"John Cross, I pray thee; do I not call thee Alfred

3*

Stevens? — Mr. is a speech of worldly fashion, and becomes not one who should put the world and its fashions behind him."

Stevens found it more difficult to comply with this one requisition of the preacher, than to pursue a long game of artful and complex scheming. He evaded the difficulty by dropping the name entirely.

" You are too severe upon brandy, and upon those who use it. Nay, I am not sure, but you do injustice to those who make it. So far from its manufacturers being such as you call them, we have unquestionable proof that they are very worthy people of a distant but a Christian country; and surely you will not deny that we should find a medicine for our hurts, and a remedy for our complaints, in a liquor which, perhaps, it might be sinful to use as an ordinary beverage. Doctors, who have the care of human life, and whose business and desire it is to preserve it, nevertheless do sometimes administer poisons to their patients, which poisons, though deadly at other times, will, in certain diseases and certain conditions of disease, prove of only and great good."

" Impossible! I believe it not! I believe not in the good of brandy. It is hurtful — it is deadly. It has slain its thousands and its tens of thousands — it is worse than the sword and the summer pestilence. Many a man have I known to perish from strong drink. In my own parts, upon the river Haw, in North Carolina state, I have known many. Nay, wherefore should I spare the truth, Alfred Stevens? — the very father of my own life, Ezekiel Cross, perished miserably from this burning water of sin. I will not hear thee speak of it again; and if thou wouldst have me think of thee with favor, as one hopeful of the service of the brethren, cast the accursed beverage of Satan from thy hands."

The youth, without a word, deliberately emptied the contents of his vessel upon the sands, and the garrulous

lips of the preacher poured forth as great a flood of speech
in congratulation, as he had hitherto bestowed in homily.
The good, unsuspecting man, did not perceive that the
liquor thus thrown away, was very small in quantity, and
that his companion, when the flask was emptied, quietly
restored it to his bosom.   John Cross had obtained a seeming victory, and did not care to examine its details.

CHAPTER V.

THE SERPENT IN THE GARDEN.

THE concession made by Stevens, and which had produced an effect so gratifying upon his companion, was one
that involved no sacrifices. The animal appetite of the
young lawyer was, in truth, comparatively speaking, indifferent to the commodity which he discarded; and even
had it been otherwise, still he was one of those selfish, cool
and calculating persons, who seem by nature to be perfectly able to subdue the claims of the blood, with great ease,
whenever any human or social policy would appear to
render it advisable. The greatest concession which he
made in the transaction, was in his so readily subscribing
to that false logic of the day, which reasons against the
use of the gifts of Providence, because a diseased moral,
and a failing education, among men, sometimes result in
their abuse.

The imperfections of a mode of reasoning so utterly
illogical, were as obvious to the mind of the young lawyer
as to anybody else; and the compliance which he exhibited to a requisition which his own sense readily assured him
was as foolish as it was presumptuous, was as degrading
to his moral character from the hypocrisy which it declared, as it was happy in reference to the small policy by
which he had been governed. The unsuspecting preacher
did not perceive the scornful sneer which curled his lips
and flashed his eyes, by which his own vanity still asserted

itself through the whole proceeding; or he would not have been so sure that the mantle of grace which he deemed to have surely fallen upon the shoulders of his companion, was sufficiently large and sound, to cover the multitude of sins which it yet enabled the wearer, so far, to conceal. Regarding him with all the favor which one is apt to feel for the person whom he has plucked as a brand from the burning, the soul of John Cross warmed to the young sinner; and it required no great effort of the wily Stevens to win from him the history, not only of all its own secrets and secret hopes — for these were of but small value in the eyes of the worldling — but of all those matters which belonged to the little village to which they were trending, and the unwritten lives of every dweller in that happy community.

With all the adroit and circumspect art of the lawyer, sifting the testimony of the unconscious witness, and worming from his custody those minor details which seem to the uninitiated so perfectly unimportant to the great matter immediately in hand — Stevens now propounded his direct inquiry, and now dropped his seemingly unconsidered insinuation, by which he drew from the preacher as much as he cared to know of the rustic lads and lasses of Charlemont. It does not concern our narrative to render the details thus unfolded to the stranger. And we will content ourselves, as did the younger of the travellers, who placed himself with hearty good will at the disposal of the holy man.

"You shall find for me a place of lodging, Mr. Cross, while it shall suit me to stay in Charlemont. You have a knowledge of the people, and of the world, which I possess not; and it will be better that I should give myself up to your guidance. I know that you will not bring me to the dwelling of persons not in good repute; and, perhaps, I need not remind you that my worldly means are small — I must be at little charge wherever I stop."

"Ah, Brother Stevens, worldly goods and worldly wealth

are no more needed in Charlemont, than they are necessary
to the service of the blessed Redeemer. With an empty
scrip is thy service blest;—God sees the pure heart through
the threadbare garment. I have friends in Charlemont
who will be too happy to receive thee in the name of the
Lord, without money and without price."

The pride of Stevens, which had not shrunk from hypocrisy and falsehood, yet recoiled at a suggestion which involved the idea of his pecuniary dependence upon strangers,
and he replied accordingly; though he still disguised his
objections under the precious appearance of a becoming
moral scruple.

"It will not become me, Mr. Cross, to burden the brethren of the church for that hospitality which is only due
to brethren."

"But thou art in the way of grace — the light is shining
upon thee — the door is open, and already the voice of the
Bridegroom is calling from within. Thou wilt become a
burning and a shining light — and the brethren of the
church will rejoice to hail thee among its chosen. Shall
they hold back their hand when thou art even on the threshold?"

"But, Mr. Cross——"

"Call me not Mr., I pray thee. Call me plain John
Cross, if it please thee not yet to apply to me that sweeter
term of loving kindness which the flock of God are happy
to use in speech one to another. If thou wilt call me
Brother Cross, my heart shall acknowledge the bonds between us, and my tongue shall make answer to thine, in
like fashion. Oh, Alfred Stevens, may the light shine soon
upon thine eyes, that thou may'st know for a truth how
pleasant it is for brethren to dwell together in the peace of
of the Lord, and according to his law. I will, with God's
grace, bring thee to this perfect knowledge, for I see the
way clear because of the humility which thou hast already
shown, and thy yielding to the counsels of the teacher.

As for what thou sayest about charges to the brethren, let that give thee no concern. Thou shalt lodge with old Brother Hinkley, who is the pattern of good things and of holiness in Charlemont. His house is more like unto the tent of the patriarch pitched upon the plain, than the house of the dweller among the cities. No lock fastens its doors against the stranger; and the heart of the aged man is even more open than the doorway of his dwelling. He standeth in the entrance like one looking out for him that cometh, and his first word to the messenger of God, is 'welcome!' Thou shalt soon see the truth of what I say to thee, for even now do we look down upon his house in the very midst of the village."

If the scruples of Stevens still continued to urge him against accepting the hospitality of the old patriarch of whom he had received a description at once just and agreeable, the recollection of the village-maiden whom he had gone aside from his direct path of travel, and made some even greater departures from the truth, to see, determined him at length to waive them; particularly when he ascertained from his fellow-traveller that he knew of nobody in Charlemont who accommodated strangers for money.

Stevens was one of those persons who watch the progress of events, and he resolved, with a mental reservation — that seems strange enough in the case of one who had shown so little reluctance to say and do the thing which he could not maintain or defend — to avail himself of some means for requiting, to the uttermost farthing, the landlord, to whose hospitality he might be indebted during his stay in Charlemont.

Such are the contradictions of character which hourly detect and describe the mere worldling — the man lacking in all principle, but that which is subservient to his selfish policy. To accept money or money's worth from a stranger, seemed mean and humbling to one, who did not hesitate, in the promotion of a scheme, which had treachery for its object, to clothe himself in the garments of deception, and to make his appearance with a lie festering upon his lips. That evening, Alfred Stevens became, with his worthier companion, an inmate of the happy dwelling of William Hinkley, the elder—a venerable, white-headed father, whose whole life had made him worthy of a far higher eulogium than that which John Cross had pronounced upon him.

The delight of the family to see their reverend teacher was heartfelt and unreserved. A vigorous gripe of the hand, by the elder dragged him into the house, and a sentence of unusual length, from his better half, assured him of that welcome which the blunter action of her venerable husband had already sufficiently declared. Nor was the young adventurer who accompanied the preacher, suffered to remain long unconsidered. When John Cross had told them who he was, or rather when he had declared his spiritual hopes in him—which he did with wonderful unction, in a breath—the reception of old Hinkley, which had been hospitable enough before, became warm and benignant; and Brother Stevens already became the word of salutation, whenever the old people desired to distinguish their younger guest.

Brother Stevens, it may be said here, found no difficulty in maintaining the character he had assumed. He had, in high degree, the great art of the selfish man, and could, when his game required it, subdue with little effort, those emotions and impulses, which the frank and ardent spirit must speak out or die. He went into the house of the hospitable old man, and into the village of Charlemont, as if he had gone into the camp of an enemy. He was, indeed, a spy, seeking to discover, not the poverty, but the richness of the land. His mind, therefore, was like one who has clothed himself in armor, placed himself in waiting for the foe, and set all his sentinels on the watch. His caution measured every word ere it was spoken, every

look ere it was shown, every movement ere he suffered his
limbs to make it. The muscles of his face, were each put
under curb and chain—the smiles of the lip and the
glances of the eyes, were all subdued to precision, and
permitted to go forth, only under special guard and restric-
tion. In tone, look, and manner, he strove as nearly as he
might, to resemble the worthy but simple-minded man, who
had so readily found a worthy adherent and pupil in him;
and his efforts at deception might be held to be sufficiently
successful, if the frank confiding faith of the aged heads of
the Hinkley family be the fitting test of his experiment.

With them he was soon perfectly at home—his own carriage seemed to them wondrously becoming, and the approbation of John Cross was of itself conclusive. The
preacher was the oracle of the family, all of whom were
only too happy of his favor not to make large efforts to be
pleased with those he brought; and in a little while, sitting
about the friendly fireside, the whole party had become as
sociable as if they had been "hail fellow! well met," a
thousand years. Two young girls, children of a relative,
and nieces of the venerable elder, had already perched
themselves upon the knee of the stranger, and strove at
moments over his neck and shoulder, without heeding the
occasional sugary reproof of Dame Hinkley, which bade
them "let Brother Stevens be;" and, already had Brother
Stevens himself, ventured upon the use of sundry grave
saws from the holy volume, the fruit of early reading and
a retentive memory, which not a little helped to maintain
his novel pretensions in the mind of the brethren, and the
worthy teacher, John Cross himself. All things promised
a long duration to a friendship suddenly begun; when
William Hinkley, the younger, a youth already introduced
to the reader, made his appearance within the happy circle.
He wore a different aspect from all the rest as he recognised in the person of Brother Stevens, the handsome
stranger, his antipathy to whom, at a first glance, months

before, seemed almost to have the character of a warning instinct. A nearer glance did not serve to lessen his hostility.

Our traveller was to the eye of a lover, one, indeed, who promised dangerous rivalship, and an intrepid air of confidence which, even his assumed character could not enable him to disguise from the searching eyes of jealousy, contributed to strengthen the dislike of the youth for a person who seemed so perfectly sure of his ground. Still, William Hinkley behaved as a civil and well-bred youth might be expected to behave. He did not suffer his antipathy to put on the aspect of rudeness; he was grave and cold, but respectful; and though he did not " be-brother" the stranger, he yet studiously subdued his tones to mildness, when it became necessary, in the course of the evening meal, that he should address him. Few words, however, were exchanged between the parties. If Hinkley beheld an enemy to his heart's hopes in Stevens, the latter was sufficiently well-read in the human heart to discover quite as soon, that the rustic was prepared to see in himself any character but that of a friend. The unwillingness with which Hinkley heard his suggestions—the absence of all freedom and ease in his deportment, toward himself, so different from the manner of the youth when speaking or listening to all other persons; the occasional gleam of jealous inquiry and doubt within his eye, and the utter lack of all enthusiasm and warmth in his tones while he spoke to him, satisfied Stevens, that he, of all the household of his hospitable entertainers, if not actually suspicious of his true character, was the one whose suspicions were those most easily to be awakened, and who of all others, needed most to be guarded against. It will not increase our estimate of the wisdom of the stranger, to learn that, with this conviction, he should yet arrogate to himself a tone of superiority, while speaking in hearing of the youth.

This was shown in a manner that was particularly galling

to a high-spirited youth, and one whose prejudices were already awakened against the speaker. It was that of a paternal and patronizing senior, whose very gentleness and benignity of look and accent, seem to arise from a full conviction of the vast difference which exists between himself and his hearer. An indignity like this, which can not be resented, is one which the young mind feels always most anxious to resent. The very difficulties in the way of doing so, stimulates the desire. Such was the feeling of William Hinkley. With such a feeling it may be conjectured that opportunity was not long wanting, or might soon be made, for giving utterance to the suppressed fires of anger which were struggling in his heart. Days and weeks may elapse, but the antipathy will declare itself at last. It would be easier to lock up the mountain torrent after the breath of the tornado has torn away its rocky seals, than to stifle in the heart that hates, because of its love, the fierce fury which these united passions enkindle within it.

In the first hour of their first interview, William Hinkley and Alfred Stevens felt that they were mutual foes. In that little space of time, the former had but one thought, which, though it changed its aspect with each progressive moment, never for an instant changed its character. He panted with the hope of redressing himself for wrongs which he could not name; for injuries and indignities which he knew not how to describe. Stevens had neither done nor said anything which might be construed into an offence. And yet, nobody knew better than Stevens that he had been offensive. The worthy John Cross, in the simplicity of his nature, never dreamed of this, but, on the contrary, when our adventurer dilated in the fatherly manner already adverted to, he looked upon himself as particularly favored of Heaven, in falling upon a youth, as a pupil, of such unctuous moral delivery.

"Surely," he mused internally, "this is a becoming in

strument which I have found, for the prosecution of the
good work. He will bear the word like one sent forth to
conquer. He will bind and loose with a strong hand. He
will work wondrous things!"

Not unlike these were the calculations of old Hinkley,
as he hearkened to the reverend reasonings and the solemn
commonplaces of the stranger. Stevens, like most recent
converts, was the most uncompromising enemy of those
sins from which he professed to have achieved with difficulty his own narrow escape; and finding, from the atten-
tive ear of his audience, that he had made a favorable impression, he proceeded to manufacture for them his religious experience; an art which his general information,
and knowledge of the world enabled him to perform without much difficulty.

But the puritan declamation which pleased all the rest,
disgusted young Hinkley, and increased his dislike for the
declaimer. There was too much of the worldling in the
looks, dress, air, and manner of Stevens, to satisfy the rustic of his sincerity. Something of his doubts had their
source, without question, in the antipathy which he had
formed against him; but William Hinkley was not without
keen, quick, observing, and justly discriminating faculties,
and much of his conclusions were the due consequence of a
correct estimate of the peculiarities which we have named.
Stevens, he perceived, declared his experiences of religion,
with the air of one who expects the congratulations of his
audience. The humility which thinks only of the acquisition itself, as the very perfection of human conquest, was
wanting equally to his language and deportment. The very
details which he gave, were ostentatious; and the gracious
smiles which covered his lips as he concluded, were those
of the self-complacent person, who feels that he has just
been saying those good things, which, of necessity, must
command the applause of his hearers.

A decent pause of half an hour after the supper was finished, which was spent by the jealous youth in utter silence, and he then rose abruptly and hurried from the apartment, leaving the field entirely to his opponent. He proceeded to the house of his neighbor and cousin, Ned Hinkley, but without any hope of receiving comfort from his communion. Ned was a lively, thoughtless, light-hearted son of the soil, who was very slow to understand sorrows of any kind ; and least of all, those which lie in the fancy of a dreaming and a doubtful lover. At this moment, when the possession of a new violin absorbed all his thoughts, his mind was particularly obtuse on the subject of sentimental grievances, and the almost voluptuous delight which filled his eyes when William entered his chamber, entirely prevented him from seeing the heavy shadow which overhung the brows of the latter.

" What, back again, William ? Why, you're as changeable as the last suit of a green lizard. When I asked you to stop, and hear me play ' Cross-possum,' and ' Criss-cross,' off you went without giving me a civil answer. I've a mind now to put up the fiddle and send your ears to bed supperless. How would you like that, old fellow ? but I'll be good-natured. You shall have it, though you don't deserve it : she's in prime tune, and the tones — only hear that, Bill — there. Isn't she delicious ?"

And as the inconsiderate cousin poured out his warmest eulogy of the favorite instrument, his right hand flourished the bow in air, in a style that would have cheered the heart of Jean Crapaud himself, and then brought it over the cat-gut in a grand crash, that sounded as harshly in the ears of his morbid visiter, as if the two worlds had suddenly come together with steam-engine velocity. He clapped his hands upon the invaded organs, and with something like horror in his voice, cried out his expostulations.

" For heaven's sake, Ned, don't stun a body with your noise."

" Noise ! Did you say noise, Bill Hinkley — noise ?"

"Yes, noise," answered the other with some peevishness in his accents. The violinist looked at him incredulously, while he suffered the point of the fiddle-bow to sink on a line with the floor; then, after a moment's pause, he approached his companion, wearing in his face the while, an appearance of the most grave inquiry, and when sufficiently nigh, he suddenly brought the bow over the strings of the instrument, immediately in William's ears, with a sharp and emphatic movement, producing an effect to which the former annoying crash, might well have been thought a very gentle effusion. This was followed by an uncontrollable burst of laughter from the merry lips of the musician.

"There—that's what I call a noise, Bill. Sweet Sall *can* make a noise when I worry her into it; she's just like other women in that respect; she'll be sure to squall out if you don't touch her just in the right quarter. But the first time she did *not* go amiss, and as for stunning you—but what's the matter? Where's the wind now?"

"Nothing—only I don't want to be deafened with such a clatter."

"Something's wrong, Bill, I know it. You look now for all the world like a bottle of sour sop, with the cork out, and ready to boil over. As for Sall making a noise the first time, that's all a notion, and a very strange one. She was as sweet-spoken then as she was when you left me before supper. The last time, I confess, I made her squall out on purpose. But what of that? you are not the man to get angry with a little fun!"

"No, I'm not angry with you, Ned—I am not angry with anybody; but just now, I would rather *not* hear the fiddle. Put it up."

"There!" said the other good-naturedly, as he placed the favorite instrument in its immemorial case in the corner. "There; and now Bill, untie the pack, and let's see the sort of wolf-cubs you've got to carry; for there's no two horns to a wild bull, if something hasn't gored you to-night."

" You're mistaken, Ned—quite mistaken—quite !"

" Deuse a bit ! I know you too well, Bill Hinkley, so it's no use to hush up now. Out with it, and don't be sparing, and if there's any harm to come, I'm here, just as ready to risk a cracked crown for you, as if the trouble was my own. I'd rather fiddle than fight, it's true ; but when there's any need for it, you know I can do one just as well as the other ; and can go to it with just as much good humor. So show us the quarrel."

" There's no quarrel, Ned," said the other, softened by the frank and ready feeling which his companion showed ; " but I'm very foolish in some things, and don't know how it is. I'm not apt to take dislikes, but there's a man come to our house with John Cross, this evening, that I somehow dislike very much."

" A man ! What's he like ? Anything like Joe Richards ? That was a fellow that I hated mightily. I never longed to lick any man but Joe Richards, and him I longed to lick three times, though you know I never got at him more than twice. It's a great pity he got drowned, for I owe him a third licking, and don't feel altogether right, since I know no sort of way to pay it. But if this man's anything like Joe, it may be just the same if I give it to *him*. Now——"

" He's nothing like Richards," said the other. " He's a taller and better-looking man."

" If he's nothing like Joe, what do you want to lick him for ?" said the single-minded musician, with a surprise in his manner, which was mingled with something like rebuke.

" I have expressed no such wish, Ned ; you are too hasty ; and if I did wish to whip him, I don't think I should trouble you or any man to help me. If I could not do it myself, I should give it up as a bad job, without calling in assistants."

" Oh, you're a spunky fellow—a real colt for hard riding," retorted the other with a good-natured mock in his tones and looks ; " but if you don't want to lick the fellow, how comes it you dislike him ? It seems to me if a chap behaved so as to make me dislike him, it wouldn't be an easy matter to keep my hands off him. I'd teach him how to put me into a bad humor, or I'd never touch violin again."

"This man's a parson, I believe."

"A parson — that's a difficulty. It is not altogether right to lick parsons, because they're not counted fighting people. But there's a mighty many on 'em that licking would help. No wonder you dislike the fellow, though if he comes with John Cross, he shouldn't be altogether so bad. Now, John Cross *is* a good man. He's good, and he's good-humored. He don't try to set people's teeth on edge against all the pleasant things of this world, and he can laugh, and talk, and sing, like other people. Many's the time he's asked me, of his own mouth, to play the violin ; and I've seen his little eyes caper again, when sweet Sall talked out her funniest. If it was not so late, I'd go over now and give him a reel or two, and then I could take a look at this strange chap, that's set your grinders against each other."

The fiddler looked earnestly at the instrument in the corner, his features plainly denoting his anxiety to resume the occupation which his friends coming had so inopportunely interrupted. William Hinkley saw the looks of his cousin, and divined the cause.

"You shall play. for me, Ned," he remarked ; "you shall give me that old highland-reel that you learned from Scotch Geordie. It will put me out of my bad humor, I think, and we can go to bed quietly. I've come to sleep with you to-night."

"You're a good fellow, Bill ; I knew that you couldn't stand it long, if Sweet Sall kept a still tongue in her head. That reel's the very thing to drive away bad humors, though there's another that I learnt from John Blodget, the boat-man, that sounds to me the merriest and comicalest thing in the world. It goes——," and here the fiddle was put in requisition to produce the required sounds : and having got *carte blanche*, our enthusiastic performer, without weariness, went through his whole collection, without once perceiving that his comical and merry tunes had entirely failed to change the grave, and even gloomy expression which still mantled the face of his companion. It was only when in his exhaustion he set down the instrument, that he became conscious of William Hinkley's continued discomposure.

"Why, Bill, the trouble has given you a bigger bite than I thought for. What words did you have with the preacher?"

"None: I don't know that he is a preacher. He speaks only as if he was trying to become one."

"What, you hadn't any difference — no quarrel?"

"None."

"And it's only to-night that you've seen him for the first time?"

A flush passed over the grave features of William Hinkley as he heard this question, and it was with a hesitating manner and faltering accents, that he contrived to tell his cousin of the brief glimpse which he had of the same stranger several months before, on that occasion, when, in the emotion of Margaret Cooper, replying to a similar question, he first felt the incipient seed of jealousy planted within his bosom. But this latter incident he forbore to reveal to the inquirer; and Ned Hinkley, though certainly endowed by nature with sufficient skill to draw forth the very soul of music from the instrument on which he played, had no similar power upon the secret soul of the person whom he partially examined.

"But 'tis very strange how you should take offence at a man you've seen so little; though I have heard before this of people taking dislikes at other people the first moment they set eyes on 'em. Now, I'm not a person of that sort, unless it was in the case of Joe Richards; and him I took a sort of grudge at from the first beginning. But even then there was a sort of reason for it; for, at the beginning, when Joe came down upon us here in Charle-

4

mont, he was for riding over people's necks, without so much as asking, ' by your leave.' He had a way about him that vexed me, though we did not change a word."

" And it's that very way that this person has that I don't like," said William Hinkley. " He talks as if he made you, and when you talk, he smiles as if he thought you were the very worst work that ever went out of his hands. Then, if he has to say anything, be it ever so trifling, he says it just as if he was telling you that the world was to come to an end the day after to-morrow."

" Just the same with Joe Richards. I never could get at him but twice ; though I give him then a mighty smart hammering ; and if he hadn't got under the broadhorn and got drowned ; — but this fellow ?"

" You'll see him at church to-morrow. I shouldn't wonder if he preaches ; for John Cross was at him about it before I came away. What's worse, the old man's been asking him to live with us."

" What, here in Charlemont ?"

" Yes."

" I'll be sure to lick him then, if he's anything like Joe Richards. But what's to make him live in Charlemont ? Is he to be a preacher for us ?"

" Perhaps so, but I couldn't understand all, for I came in while they were at it, and left home before they were done. I'm sure if he stays there I shall not. I shall leave nome, for I really dislike to meet him."

" You shall stay with me, Bill, and we'll have Sall at all hours," was the hearty speech of the cousin, as he threw his arms around the neck of his morose companion, and dragged him gently toward the adjoining apartment, which formed his chamber. " To-morrow," he continued, " as you say, we'll see this chap, and if he's anything like Joe Richards—" The doubled fist of the speaker, and his threatening visage, completed the sentence with which this present conference and chapter may very well conclude

CHAPTER VI.

THE TOAD ON THE ALTAR.

THE next day was the sabbath. John Cross had timed his arrival at the village with a due reference to his duties, and after a minute calculation of days and distances, so that his spiritual manna might be distributed in equal proportions among his hungering flock. His arrival made itself felt accordingly, not simply in Charlemont, but throughout the surrounding country for a circuit of ten miles or more. There was a large and hopeful gathering of all sorts and sexes, white and black, old and young. Charlemont had a very pretty little church of its own; but one, and that, with more true Christianity than is found commonly in this world of pretence and little tolerance, was open to preachers of all denominations. The word of God, among these simple folks, was quite too important to make them scruple at receiving it from the lips of either Geneva, Rome, or Canterbury. The church stood out among the hills at a little distance from, but in sight of the village; a small, neat Grecian-like temple, glimmering white and saintlike through solemn-visaged groves, and gaudy green foliage. The old trees about it were all kept neatly trimmed, the brush pruned away and cleared up, and a smooth sweet sward, lawnlike, surrounded it, such as children love to skip and scramble over, and older children rest at length upon, in pairs, talking over their sweet silly affections.

Surrounded by an admiring crowd, each of whom had his

respectful salutation, we see our friend John Cross toward noon approaching the sacred dwelling. Truly he was the most simple, fraternal of all God's creatures. He had a good word for this, an affectionate inquiry for that, a benevolent smile, and a kind pressure of the hand for all. He was a man to do good, for everybody saw that he thought for others before himself, and sincerity and earnestness constitute, with the necessary degree of talent, the grand secrets for making successful teachers in every department.

Though a simple, unsophisticated, unsuspecting creature, John Cross was a man of very excellent natural endowments. He chose for his text a passage of the Scriptures which admitted of a direct practical application to the concerns of the people, their daily wants, their pressing interests, moral, human, and social. He was thus enabled to preach a discourse which sent home many of his congregation much wiser than they came, if only in reference to their homely duties of farmstead and family. John Cross was none of those sorry and self-constituted representatives of our eternal interests, who deluge us with a vain, worthless declamation, proving that virtue is a very good thing, religion a very commendable virtue, and a liberal contribution to the church-box at the close of the sermon one of the most decided proofs that we have this virtue in perfection. Nay, it is somewhat doubtful, indeed, if he ever once alluded to the state of his own scrip and the treasury of the church. His faith, sincere, spontaneous, ardent, left him in very little doubt that the Lord will provide, for is he not called "JEHOVAH-JIREH?" — and his faith was strengthened and confirmed by the experience of his whole life. But then John Cross had few wants — few, almost none! In this respect he resembled the first apostles. The necessities of life once cared for, never was mortal man more thoroughly independent of the world. He was not one of those fine preachers who, dealing out counsels of self-denial, in grave saws and solemn maxims, with wondrous grim visage and a most slow, lugubrious shaking of the head — are yet always religiously careful to secure the warmest seat by the fire-side, and the best buttered bun on table. He taught no doctrine which he did not practise; and as for consideration — that test at once of the religionist and the gentleman — he was as humbly solicitous of the claims and feelings of others, as the lovely and lowly child to whom reverence has been well taught as the true beginning, equally of politeness and religion.

Before going into church he urged his *protégé*, Stevens, to consent to share in the ceremonies of the service as a layman; but there was still some saving virtue in the young man, which made him resolute in refusing to do so. Perhaps, his refusal was dictated by a policy like that which had governed him so far already; which made him reluctant to commit himself to a degree which might increase very much the hazards of detection. He feared, indeed, the restraints which the unequivocal adoption of the profession would impose upon him, fettering somewhat the freedom of his intercourse with the young of both sexes, and, consequently, opposing an almost insurmountable barrier to the prevailing object which had brought him to the village. Whatever may have been the feelings or motives which governed him, they, at least, saved him from an act which would have grievously aggravated his already large offence against truth and propriety. He declined, in language of the old hypocrisy. He did not feel justified in taking up the cross — he felt that he was not yet worthy; and, among the members of a church, which takes largely into account the momentary impulses and impressions of the professor, the plea was considered a sufficiently legitimate one.

But though Stevens forbore to commit himself openly in the cause which he professed a desire to espouse, he was yet sufficiently heedful to maintain all those externals of devotion which a serious believer would be apt to exhibit. He could be a good actor of a part, and in this lay his best talent.   He had that saving wisdom of the worldling, which is too often estimated beyond its worth, called cunning; and the frequent successes of which produces that worst of all the diseases that ever impaired the value of true greatness — conceit.   Alfred Stevens fancied that he could do everything, and this fancy produced in him the appearance of a courage which his moral nature never possessed.   He had the audacity which results from presumption, not the wholesome strength which comes from the conscious possession of a right purpose.   But a truce to our metaphysics.

Never did saint wear the aspect of such supernatural devotion.   He knelt with the first, groaned audibly at intervals, and when his face became visible, his eyes were strained in upward glances, so that the spectator could behold little more in their orbs than a sea of white.

"Oh! what a blessed young man!" said Mrs. Quackenbosh.

"How I wish it was he that was to preach for us to-day," responded that gem from the antique, Miss Polly Entwistle, who had joined every church in Kentucky in turn, without having been made a spouse in either.

"How handsome he is!" simpered Miss Julia Evergreen — a damsel of seventeen, upon whom the bilious eyes of Miss Entwistle were cast with such an expression as the devil is said to put on when suddenly soused in holy water.

"Handsome is that handsome does!" was the commentary of a venerable cormorant to whom Brother Cross had always appeared the special and accepted agent of heaven.

"I wish Brother Cross would get him to pray only.   I wonder if he believes in the new-light doctrine?" purred one of the ancient tabbies of the conventicle.

"The new light is but the old darkness, Sister Widgeon," responded an old farmer of sixty four, who had divided his time so equally between the plough and the prayer-book, that his body had grown as crooked as the one, while his mind was bewildered with as many doctrines as ever worried all sense out of the other.

We shall not suffer these to divert us, any more than Stevens permitted their speculations upon his person and religion to affect his devotion. He looked neither to the right nor to the left while entering the church, or engaging in the ceremonies. No errant glances were permitted to betray to the audience a mind wandering from the obvious duties before it; and yet Alfred Stevens knew just as well that every eye in the congregation was fixed upon him, as that he was himself there; and among those eyes, his own keen glance had already discovered those of that one for whom all these labors of hypocrisy were undertaken.

Margaret Cooper sat on the opposite side of the church, but the line of vision was uninterrupted between them, and when — though very unfrequently — Stevens suffered his gaze to rest upon her form, it was with a sudden look of pleased abstraction, as if, in spite of himself, his mind was irresistibly drawn away from all recollection of its immediate duties.

If a word is sufficient for the wise, a look answers an equal purpose with the vain. Margaret Cooper left the church that morning with a pleased conviction that the handsome stranger had already paid his devotion to her charms. There was yet another passion to be gratified. The restless ambition of her foolish heart whispered to her momently; that if her person had done so much, what might she not hope to achieve when the treasures of her mind were known. She had long since made the comparison of her own intellect with that of every other maiden in the village, and she flattered herself that before many days, the young stranger should make it too. Her vain heart was rapidly preparing to smooth the path of the enemy and make his conquests easy.

But it was not the women only, by whom the deportment of Alfred Stevens was so closely watched. The eyes of suspicion and jealousy were upon him. The two young men whose interview formed the conclusion of our last chapter, scanned his conduct and carriage with sufficient keenness of scrutiny.

"I'll tell you what, Bill Hinkley," said his cousin, "this fellow, to my thinking, is a very great rascal."

"What makes you think so?" demanded the former, with slow, dissatisfied accents; "he seems to pray very earnestly."

"That's the very reason I think him a rascal. His praying seems to me very unnatural. Here, he's a perfect stranger in the place, yet he never shows any curiosity to see the people. He never once looks around him. He walks to the church with his eye cast upon the ground, and sometimes he squints to this side and sometimes to that, but he seems to do it slyly, and seems to take pains that nobody should see him doing it. All this might answer for an old man, who — believes that everything is vanity — as, indeed, everything must seem to old people; but to a young fellow, full of blood, who eats well, drinks well, sleeps well, and should naturally have a hankering after a young girl, all this is against nature. Now, what's against nature is wrong, and there's wrong at the bottom of it. Youth is the time to laugh, dance, sing, play on the violin, and always have a sweetheart when it can find one. If you can't get a beauty take a brown; and if Mary won't smile, Susan will. But always have a sweetheart; always be ready for fun and frolic; that's the way for the young, and when they don't take these ways, it's unnatural — there's something wrong about it, and I'm suspicious of *that* person. Now, I just have this notion of the young stranger. He's after no good. I reckon he's like a hundred others; too lazy to go to work, he goes to preaching, and learns in the first sermon to beg hard for the missionaries. I'll lick him,

Bill, to a certainty, if he gives me the littlest end of an opportunity."

"Pshaw, Ned, don't think of such a thing. You are quite too fond of licking people."

"Deuse a bit. It does 'em good. Look you, this chap is monstrous like Joe Richards. I'll have to lick him on that account."

"You're mad. Ned; talk of whipping a preacher."

"He's no preacher yet," said the other, "but if I lick him he may become one."

"No matter, he's never offended you."

"Ay, but he will. I see it in the fellow's looks. I never was mistaken in a fellow's looks in all my life."

"Wait till he does offend you then."

"Well, I'm willing to do that, for I know the time will come. I'm always sure, when I first see a man, to know whether I'll have to flog him or not. There's a something that tells me so. Isn't that very singular, Bill?"

"No! you form a prejudice against a man, fancy that you ought to whip him, and then never rest till you've done so. You'll find your match some day."

"What! you think some other chap will fancy he ought to whip me? Well—maybe so. But this ain't the fellow to do that."

"He's a stout man, and I reckon strong. Besides, Ned, he's very handsome."

"Handsome! Lord, Bill, what a taste you have? How can a man be called handsome that never altogether opens his eyes, except when he turns up the whites until you'd think he'd never be able to get the balls back to their proper place? Then, what a chin he has—as sharp as a pitchfork, and who but a girl child would fancy a man with his hair combed sleek like a woman's on each side of his ears, with big whiskers at the same time that looks for all the world like the brush of a seven years running fox.

4*

Handsome! If my pup 'Dragon' was only half so much like a beast, I'd plump him into the horsepond!"

It is probable that Ned Hinkley did not altogether think of the stranger as he expressed himself. But he saw how deep a hold his appearance had taken, in an adverse way, upon the mind and feelings of his relative and friend, and his rude, but well-meant endeavors were intended to console his companion, after his own fashion, by the exhibition of a certain degree of sympathy.

His efforts, however well intended, did not produce any serious effect. William Hinkley, though he forbore the subject, and every expression which might indicate either soreness or apprehension, was still the victim of that presentiment which had touched him on the very first appearance of the stranger. He felt more than ever apprehensive on the score of his misplaced affections. While his cousin had been watching the stranger, *his* eyes had been fixed upon those of Margaret Cooper, and his fears were increased and strengthened, as he perceived that she was quite too much absorbed in other thoughts and objects to behold for an instant the close espionage which he maintained upon her person. His heart sunk within him, as he beheld how bold was her look, and how undisguised the admiration which it expressed for the handsome stranger.

" You will go home with me, William ?" said the cousin.

The other hesitated.

" I think," said he, after a moment's pause, " I should rather go to my own home. It is a sort of weakness to let a stranger drive a man off from his own family, and though I somehow dislike this person's looks, and am very sorry that John Cross brought him to our house, yet I shouldn't let a prejudice which seems to have no good foundation take such possession of my mind. I will go home, Ned, and see — perhaps I may come to like the stranger more when I know him better."

" You'll never like him. I see it in the fellow's eye; but

just as you please about going home. You're right in one
thing—never to give up your own dunghill, so long as you
can get room on it for a fair fling with your enemy. Besides, you can see better, by going home, what the chap's
after. I don't see why he should come here to learn to
preach. We can't support a preacher. We don't want
one. He could just as well have learned his business,
where he came from."

With these words the cousins separated.

"Now," said Ned Hinkley as he took his own way
homeward, in a deeper fit of abstraction than was altogether
usual with him, " now will Bill Hinkley beat about the bush
without bouncing through it, until it's too late to do anything. He's mealy-mouthed with the woman, and mealy-
mouthed with the man, and mealy-mouthed with everybody.
—quite too soft-hearted and too easy to get on. Here's a
stranger nobody knows, just like some crow from another
corn-field, that'll pick up his provisions from under his very
nose, and he doing nothing to hinder until there's no use in
trying. If I don't push in and help him, he'll not help
himself. As for Margaret Cooper, dang it, I'll court her
for him myself. If he's afraid to pop the question, I ain't ;
though I'll have to be mighty careful about the words I use,
or she'll be thinking I come on my own hook ; and that
would be a mighty scary sort of business all round the
house. Then this stranger. If anybody can look through a
stranger here in Charlemont, I reckon I'm that man. I
suspect him already. I think he's after no good with his
great religioning ; and I'll tie such a pair of eyes to his
heels, that his understanding will never be entirely out of
my sight. I'll find him out if anybody can. But I wont
lick him till I do. That wouldn't be altogether right, considering he's to be a parson, though I doubt he'll never
make ore."

And thus, with a head filled with cares of a fashion
altogether new, the sturdy young Kentuckian moved home-

ward with a degree of abstraction in his countenance which
was not among the smallest wonders of the day and place
in the estimation of his friends and neighbors.

Meanwhile, the work of mischief was in full progress.
Everybody knows the degree of familiarity which exists
among all classes in a country-village, particularly when
the parties are brought together under the social and stimulating influences of religion. It was natural that the pastor, long known and well beloved, should be surrounded by
his flock as he descended from the pulpit. The old ladies
always have a saving interest in his presence, and they
pave the way for the young ones. Alfred Stevens, as the
protégé of John Cross, naturally attended his footsteps,
and was introduced by him to the little congregation, which
had mostly remained to do honor to the preacher. Of
these, not last, nor least, was the widow Cooper; and, un-
reluctant by her side, though in silence, and not without a
degree of emotion, which she yet was able to conceal, stood
her fair but proud-hearted daughter.

Margaret, alas! Margaret stood there with a heart more
proud, yet more humble, than ever. Proud in the consciousness of a new conquest—humble in the feeling that
this conquest had not been made, but at the expense of some
portion of her own independence. Hitherto, her suitors
had awakened no other feeling in her heart but vanity.
Now, she felt no longer able to sail on, " imperial arbitress,"
smiling at woes which she could inflict, but never share.
That instinct, which, in the heart of young Hinkley had
produced fear, if not antipathy, had been as active in her
case, though with a very different result. The first glimpse
which she had of the handsome stranger, months before,
had impressed her with a singular emotion; and now that
he was returned, she could not divest herself of the thought
that his return was a consequence of that one glimpse.

With a keener judgment than belonged to her neighbors,
she too had some suspicions that religion was scarcely the

prevailing motive which had brought the youth back to their little village; for how could she reconcile with his present demure gravity and devout profession, the daring which he had shown in riding back to behold her a second time? That such had been his motive she divined by her own feeling of curiosity, and the instincts of vanity were prompt enough to believe that this was motive sufficient to bring him back once more, and under the guise of a character, which would the readiest secure an easy entrance to society. Pleased with the fancy that she herself was the object sought, she did not perceive how enormous was the sort of deception which the stranger had employed to attain the end desired. With all her intellect she had not the wisdom to suspect that he who could so readily practise so bold an hypocrisy, was capable of the worst performances; and when their names were mentioned, and his eyes were permitted to meet and mingle their glances with hers, she was conscious of nothing farther than a fluttering sentiment of pleasure, which was amply declared to the stranger, in the flash of animation which spoke openly in her countenance; eye speaking to lip and cheek, and these, in turn, responding with a kindred sentiment to the already tell-tale eye.

William Hinkley, from a little distance, beheld this meeting. He had lingered with the curiosity which belongs to the natural apprehension of the lover. He saw them approach—nay, fancied he beheld the mutual expression of their sympathizing eyes, and he turned away, and hurried homeward, with the feeling of a heart already overborne, and defrauded in all its hopes and expectations. The flowers were threatened with blight in his Eden: but he did not conjecture, poor fellow, that a serpent had indeed entered it!

CHAPTER VII.

THE GOOD YOUNG MAN IN MEDITATION.

PERHAPS, it may be assumed, with tolerable safety, that no first villany is ever entirely deliberate. There is something in events to give it direction — something to egg it on — to point out time, place, and opportunity. Of course, it is to be understood that the actor is one, in the first place, wanting in the moral sense. What we simply mean to affirm is, that the particular, single act, is, in few instances, deliberately meditated from the beginning. We very much incline to think that some one event, which we ordinarily refer to the chapter of accidents, has first set the mind to work upon schemes, which would otherwise, perhaps, never be thought of at all. Thus, we find persons who continue very good people, as the world goes, until middle age, or even seniority; then, suddenly breaking out into some enormous offence against decency and society, which startles the whole pious neighborhood. Folks start up, with outstretched hands and staring eyes, and cry aloud: —

"Lord bless us, who would have thought so good a man could be so bad!"

He, poor devil, never fancied it himself, till he became so, and it was quite too late to alter his arrangements. Perhaps his neighbors may have had some share in making him so. Pious persons are very frequently reduced to these straits by having the temptation forced too much upon them. Flesh and blood can not always withstand the provocation of earthly delicacies, even where the spirit is a

tolerably stout one ; and of the inadequacy of the mind,
always to contend with the inclinations of the flesh, have
we not a caution in that injunction of Holy Book which
warns us to fly from temptation ?   But lame people can not
fly, and he is most certainly lame who halts upon mere feet
of circumstances.   Such people are always in danger.

Now, Alfred Stevens, properly brought up, from the beginning, at some theological seminary, would have been—
though in moral respects pretty much the same person—yet
in the eye of the world a far less criminal man.   Not that
his desires would have been a jot more innocent, but they
would have taken a different direction.   Instead of the
recklessness of course, such as seems to have distinguished
the conduct of our present subject—instead of his loose
indulgences — his smart, licentious speeches — the sheep's-
eye glances, right and left, which he was but too prone to
bestow, without prudence or precaution, whenever he walked
among the fair sisters—he, the said Alfred, would have
taken counsel of a more worldly policy, which is yet popu-
larly considered a more pious one.   He would have kept
his eyes from wandering to and fro ; he would have held
his blood in subjection.   Patient as a fox on a long scent
in autumn, he would have kept himself lean and circumspect, until, through the help of lugubrious prayer and lantern visage, he could have beguiled into matrimony some
one feminine member of the flock — not always fair — whose
worldly goods would have sufficed in full atonement for all
those circumspect, self-imposed restraints, which we find
usually so well rewarded.   But Alfred Stevens was not a
man of this pious temper.   It is evident, from his present
course, that he had some inkling of the *modus operandi;*
but all his knowledge fell short of that saving wisdom which
would have defrauded the social world of one of its moral
earthquakes, and possibly deprived the survivors of the
present moral story — for moral it is, though our hero is
not exactly so.

It would be doing our subject and our theory equal injustice if we were to suppose that he had any fixed purpose,
known to himself, when he borrowed the professional garment, and began to talk with the worthy John Cross in the
language of theology, and with the tongue of a hypocrite.
He designed to visit Charlemont—that was all—as he had
really been impressed by the commanding figure and noble
expression of beauty of that young damsel whom he had
encountered by the roadside. Even this impression, however, would have been suffered to escape from his mind,
had it not been so perfectly convenient to revisit the spot,
on his return to his usual place of residence. During the
summer, Charlemont and its rustic attractions had been the
frequent subject of a conversation, running into discussion,
between himself and the amiable old man, his uncle. The
latter repeatedly urged upon his nephew to make the visit;
fondly conceiving that a nearer acquaintance with the pleasant spot which had so won upon his own affections, would
be productive of a like effect upon his nephew. Alas, how
little did he know the mischief he was doing!

In the very idleness of mood—with just that degree of
curiosity which prompts one to turn about and look a second time—Alfred Stevens resumed the route which included
Charlemont. But the devil had, by this time, found his
way into the meditations of the youth, and lay lurking, unknown to himself, perhaps, at the bottom of this same curiosity. The look of pride and defiance which Margaret
Cooper had betrayed, when the bold youth rode back to
steal a second glance at her matchless person, was equiva-
lent to an equally bold challenge; and his vanity hastily
picked up the gauntlet which hers had thrown down. He
wished to see the damsel again—to see if she *was* so beautiful—if she did, indeed, possess that intellectual strength
and vivacity which flashed out so suddenly and with so
much splendor from beneath her long, dark eye-lashes!

In this mood he met with John Cross; and the simplicity

of that worthy creature offered another challenge, not less
provoking than the former, to the levity and love of mischief which also actively predominated in the bosom of the
youth. Fond of a malicious sort of fun, and ever on the
look-out for subjects of quizzing, it was in compliance with
a purely habitual movement of his mind that he conjured
up that false, glozing story of his religious inclinations,
which had so easily imposed upon the unsuspecting preacher. Never was proceeding less premeditated, or so completely the result of an after-thought, than this; and now
that it had proved so perfectly successful—now that he
found himself admitted into the very heart of the little village, and into the bosoms of the people—he began, for the
first time, to feel the awkwardness of the situation in which
he had placed himself, and the responsibilities, if not dangers, to which it subjected him. To play the part of a
mere preacher—to talk glibly, and with proper unction,
in the stereotype phraseology of the profession—was no
difficult matter to a clever young lawyer of the West, having a due share of the gift of gab, and almost as profoundly
familiar with scripture quotation as Henry Clay himself.
But there was something awkward in the idea of detection,
and he was not unaware of those summary dangers which
are likely to follow, in those wild frontier regions, from the
discovery of so doubtful a personage as "Bro' Wolf" in
the clothing of a more innocent animal. Chief-Justice
Lynch is a sacred authority in those parts; and, in such a
case as his, Alfred Stevens did not doubt that the church
itself would feel it only becoming to provide another sort
of garment for the offender, which, whether pleasant or not,
would at least be likely to stick more closely, and prove
less comfortably warm.

But, once in, there was no help but to play out the game
as it had been begun. Villagers are seldom very sagacious
people, and elegant strangers are quite too much esteemed
among them to make them very particular in knowing the

whys and wherefores about them—whence they come, what they do, and whither they propose to go. Stevens had only to preserve his countenance and a due degree of caution, and the rest was easy. He had no reason to suppose himself an object of suspicion to anybody; and should he become so, nothing was more easy than to take his departure with sufficient promptness, and without unnecessarily soliciting the prayers of the church in behalf of the hurried traveller! At all events, he could lose nothing by the visit: perhaps something might be gained.

What was that something? Behold him in his chamber, preparing to ask and to answer this question for himself. The sabbath-day is finally over. He has been almost the lion of the day. We say almost, for the worthy John Cross could not easily be deprived, by any rivalry, of the loyal regards of his old parishioners. But, though the latter had most friends, the stranger, Alfred Stevens, had had most followers. All were anxious to know him—the young, in particular, maidens and men; and the grave old dames would have given their last remaining teeth, bone or waxen, to have heard him discourse. There was so much sense and solemnity in his profound, devout looks! he has been made known to them all; he has shaken hands with many. But he has exchanged the speech of sympathy and feeling with but one only—and that one!—

Of her he thinks in his chamber—his quiet, snug, little chamber—a mere closet, looking out upon a long garden-slip, in which he sees, without much heeding them, long lanes of culinary cabbage, and tracts of other growing and decaying vegetation, in which his interest is quite too small to make it needful that he should even ask its separate names. His chin rests upon his hands with an air of meditation; and gradually his thoughts rise up in soliloquy, which is suffered to invade no ear but ours :—

"Well! who'd have thought it? a parson!—devilish good, indeed! How it will tell at Murkey's! What a metamorphose! if it don't stagger 'em, nothing will! It's the best thing I've done yet! I shall have to do it over a hundred times, and must get up a sermon or two before-hand. and swear that I preached them—and, egad! I may have to do it yet before I'm done—ha! ha! ha!"

The laughter was a quiet chuckle, not to be heard by vulgar ears; it subsided in the gorges of his throat. The idea of really getting up a sermon tickled him. He mut-tered over texts, all that he could remember; and pro-ceeded to turn over the phrases for an introduction, such as, unctuous with good things in high degree, he fancied would be particularly commendable to his unsuspecting hearers. Alfred Stevens had no small talent for imitation. He derived a quiet sort of pleasure, on the present occa-sion, from its indulgence.

"I should have made a famous parson, and, if all trades fail, may yet. But, now that I am here, what's to come of it? It's not so hard to put on a long face, and prose in scripture dialect; but, *cui bono?* Let me see—hem! The girl is pretty, devilish pretty—with such an eye, and looks so! There's soul in the wench—life—and a passion that speaks out in every glance and movement. A very Cressid, with a cross of Corinne! Should she be like her of Troy? At all events, it can do no harm to see what she's made of!

"But I must manage warily. I have something to lose in the business. Frankfort is but fifty miles from Charle-mont—fifty miles—and there's Ellisland, but fourteen. Fourteen!—an easy afternoon ride. That way it must be done. Ellisland shall be my post-town. I can gallop there in an afternoon, drop and receive my letters, and be back by a round-about which shall effectually baffle inquiry. A week or two will be enough. I shall see, by that time, what can be done with her; though still, cautiously, Parson Ste-vens!—cautiously."

The farther cogitations of Stevens were subordinate to these, but of the same family complexion. They were such as to keep him wakeful. The Bible which had been placed upon his table, by the considerate providence of his hostess, lay there unopened; though, more than once, he lifted the cover of the sacred volume, letting it fall again suddenly, as if with a shrinking consciousness that such thoughts as at that moment filled his mind were scarcely consistent with the employment, in any degree, of such a companion. Finally, he undressed and went to bed. The hour had become very late.

"Good young man," muttered worthy Mrs. Hinkley to her drowsy spouse, in the apartment below, as she heard the movements of her guest—"good young man, he's just now going to bed. He's been studying all this while. I reckon Brother Cross has been sound this hour."

The light from Stevens's window glimmered out over the cabbage-garden, and was seen by many an ancient dame as she prepared for her own slumbers.

"Good young man," said they all with one accord. "I reckon he's at the Bible now. Oh! he'll be a blessed laborer in the vineyard, I promise you, when Brother Cross is taken."

"If it were not for the cursed bore of keeping up the farce beyond the possibility of keeping up the fun, such a rig as this would be incomparably pleasant; but"—yawning—"that's the devil! I get monstrous tired of a joke that needs dry nursing!"

Such were the last muttered words of Parson Stevens before he yielded himself up to his slumbers. Good young man—charitable old ladies—gullible enough, if not charitable! But the professions need such people, and we must not quarrel with them!

CHAPTER VIII.

PAROCHIAL PERFORMANCES.

THE poor, conceited blackguards of this ungracious earth have a fancy that there must be huge confusion and a mighty bobbery in nature, corresponding with that which is for ever going on in their own little spheres. If we have a toothache, we look for a change of weather; our rheumatism is a sure sign that God has made his arrangements to give us a slapping rain; and, should the white bull or the brown heifer die, look out for hail, or thunderstorm, at least, as a forerunner of the event. Nothing less can possibly console or satisfy us for such a most unaccountable, not to say unnatural and unwarrantable, a dispensation. The poets have ministered largely to this vanity on the part of mankind. Shakspere is constantly at it, and Ben Jonson, and all the dramatists. Not a butcher, in the whole long line of the butchering Cæsars, from Augustus down, but, according to them, died in a sort of gloom-glory, resulting from the explosion of innumerable stars and rockets, and the apparitions of as many comets! "Gorgons, and hydras, and chimeras dire," invariably announce the coming stroke of fate; and five or seven moons of a night have suddenly arisen to warn some miserable sublunarian that orders had been issued that there should be no moon for him that quarter, or, in military and more precise phrase, that he should have no "quarters" during that moon. Even our venerable and stern old puritan saint, Milton—

he who was blessed with the blindness of his earthly eye, that he should be more perfectly enabled to contemplate the Deity within—has given way to this superstition when he subjects universal nature to an earthquake because Adam's wife followed the counsels of the snake.

A pretty condition of things it would be, if stars, suns, and systems, were to shoot madly from their spheres on such occasions! Well might the devil laugh if such were the case! How he would chuckle to behold globes and seas, and empires, fall into such irreverend antics because some poor earthling, be he kingling or common sodling, goes into desuetude, either by the operation of natural laws, or the sharp application of steel or shot! Verily, it makes precious little difference to the Great Reaper, by what process we finally become harvested. He is sure of us, though no graves gape, no stars fall, no comets rush out, like young colts from their stables, flinging their tails into the faces of the more sober and pacific brotherhood of lights. But, denied the satisfaction of chuckling at such sights as these, his satanic majesty chuckles not the less at the human vanity which looks for them. Nay, he himself is very likely to suggest this vanity. It is one of his forms of temptation —one of his manoeuvres; and we take leave, by way of warning, to hint to those worthy people, who judge of tomorrow's providence by the corns of their great toe, or their periodical lumbago, or the shooting of their warts, or the pricking of their palms, that it is in truth the devil which is at the bottom of all this, and that the Deity has nothing to do in the business. It is the devil instilling his vanities into the human heart, in that form which he thinks least likely to prove offensive, or rouse suspicion. The devil is most active in your affairs, Mrs. Thompson, the moment you imagine that there must be a revolution on your account in the universal laws of nature. At such a moment your best policy will be to have blood let, take physic, and go with all diligence to your prayers.

There was no sort of warning on the part of the natural
to the moral world, on the day when Alfred Stevens set
forth with the worthy John Cross, to visit the flock of the
latter. There was not a lovelier morning in the whole
calendar. The sun was alone in heaven, without a cloud;
and on earth, the people in and about Charlemont, having
been to church only the day before, necessarily made their
appearance everywhere with petticoats and pantaloons tolerably clean and unrumpled. Cabbages had not yet been
frost-bitten. Autumn had dressed up her children in the
garments of beauty, preparatory to their funeral. There
was a good crop of grain that year, and hogs were brisk,
and cattle lively, and all "looking-up," in the language of
the prices current. This was long before the time when
Mr. M—— made his famous gammon speeches; but the
people had a presentiment of what was coming, and to
crown the eventful anticipations of the season, there was
quite a freshet in Salt river. The signs were all and everywhere favorable. Speculation was beginning to chink his
money-bags; three hundred new banks, as many railways,
were about to be established; old things were about to fleet
and disappear; all things were becoming new; and the
serpent entered Charlemont, and made his way among the
people thereof, without any signs of combustion, or overthrow, or earthquake.

Everybody has some tolerable idea of what the visitation
of a parson is, to the members of his flock. In the big
cities he comes one day, and the quarterly collector the
next. He sits down with the "gude wife" in a corner to
themselves, and he speaks to her in precisely the same low
tones which cunning lovers are apt to use. If he knows
any one art better than another, it is that of finding his
way to the affections of the female part of his flock. A
subdued tone of voice betrays a certain deference for the
party addressed. The lady is pleased with such a prelimi-
nary. She is flattered again by the pains he takes in behalf

of her eternal interests; she is pretty sure he takes no such pains with any of her neighbors. It is a sign that he thinks her soul the most becoming little soul in the flock, and when he goes away, she looks after him and sighs, and thinks him the most blessed soul of a parson. The next week she is the first to get up a subscription which she heads with her own name in connection with a sum realized by stinting her son of his gingerbread money, in order to make this excellent parson a life-member of the "Zion African Bible and Missionary Society, for disseminating the Word among the Heathen." The same fifty dollars so appropriated, would have provided fuel for a month to the starving poor of her own parish.

But Brother Cross gets no such windfalls. It is probable that he never heard of such a thing, and that if he did, he would unhesitatingly cry out, "Humbug," at the first intimation of it. Besides, his voice was not capable of that modulation which a young lover, or a city parson can give it. Accustomed to cry aloud and spare not, he usually spoke as if there were some marrow in his bones, and some vigor in his wind-bags. When he came to see the good wife of his congregation, he gave her a hearty shake of the hand, congratulated her as he found her at her spinning-wheel; spoke with a hearty approbation, if he saw that her children were civil and cleanly; if otherwise, he blazed out with proper boldness, by telling her that all her praying and groaning, would avail nothing for her soul's safety, so long as Jackey's breeches were unclean; and that the mother of a rude and dirty child, was as sure of damnation, as if she never prayed at all. He had no scruples about speaking the truth. He never looked about him for the gentle, easy phrases, by which to distinguish the conduct which he was compelled to condemn. He knew not only that the truth must be spoken, and be spoken by him, if by anybody, but that there is no language too strong — perhaps none quite strong enough — for the utterance of the truth. But it must not be supposed, that John Cross was in any respect an intolerant, or sour man. He was no hypocrite, and did not, therefore, need to clothe his features in the vinegar costume of that numerous class. His limbs were put into no such rigid fetters as too often denote the unnatural restraints which such persons have imposed upon their inner minds. He could laugh and sing with the merriest, and though he did not absolutely shake a leg himself, yet none rejoiced more than he, when Ned Hinkley's fiddle summoned the village to this primitive exercise.

"Now, Alfred Stevens," said he, the breakfast being over, "what say'st thou to a visit with me among my people. Some of them know thee already; they will all be rejoiced to see thee. I will show thee how they live, and if thou shouldst continue to feel within thee, the growing of that good seed whose quickening thou hast declared to me, it will be well that thou shouldst begin early to practise the calling which may so shortly become thine own. Here mightest thou live a space, toiling in thy spiritual studies, until the brethren should deem thee ripe for thy office; meanwhile, thy knowledge of the people with whom thou livest, and their knowledge of thee, would be matter of equal comfort and consolation, I trust, to thee as to them."

Alfred Stevens expressed himself pleased with the arrangement. Indeed, he desired nothing else.

"But shall we see all of them?" he demanded. The arch-hypocrite began to fear that his curiosity would be compelled to pay a heavy penalty to dullness.

"The flock is small," said John Cross. "A day will suffice, but I shall remain three days in Charlemont, and some I will see to-day, and some to-morrow, and some on the day after, which is Wednesday."

"Taken in moderate doses," murmured Stevens to himself, "one may stand it."

He declared himself in readiness, and the twain set

5

forth. The outward behavior of Stevens was very exemplary. He had that morning contrived to alter his costume
in some respects to suit the situation of affairs. For example, he had adopted that slavish affectation which seems
to insist that a preacher of God should always wear a
white cravat, so constructed and worn as to hide the tips
of his shirt collar. If they wore none, they would look
infinitely more noble, and we may add, never suffer from
bronchitis. In his deportment, Stevens was quite as sanc-
tified as heart could wish. He spoke always deliberately,
and with great unction. If he had to say "cheese and
mousetrap," he would look very solemn, shake his head
with great gravity and slowness, and then deliberately and
equally emphasizing every syllable, would roll forth the
enormous sentence with all the conscious dignity of an
ancient oracle. That "cheese and mousetrap," so spoken,
acquired in the ears of the hearer, a degree of importance
and signification, which it confounded them to think they
had never perceived before in the same felicitous colloca-
tion of syllables. John Cross was not without his vanities.
Who is? Vanity is quite as natural as any other of our
endowments. It is a guaranty for amiability. A vain
man is always a conciliatory one. He is kind to others,
because the approbation of others is a strong desire in his
mind. Accordingly, even vanity is not wholly evil. It has
its uses.

John Cross had his share, and Alfred Stevens soon discovered that he ministered to it in no small degree. The
good old preacher took to himself the credit of having
effected his conversion, so far as it had gone. It was his
hand that had plucked the brand from the burning. He
spoke freely of his *protégé*, as well before his face as behind his back. In his presence he dwelt upon the holy
importance of his calling; to others he dilated upon the
importance of securing for the church a young man of so
much talent, yet of so much devotion : qualities not always

united, it would seem, among the churchlings of modern times.

Alfred Stevens seemed to promise great honor to his teacher. That cunning which is the wisdom of the world-ling, and which he possessed in a very surprising degree, enabled him to adopt a course of conduct, look, and remark, which amply satisfied the exactions of the scrupulous, and secured the unhesitating confidence of those who were of a more yielding nature. He soon caught the phraseology of his companion, and avoiding his intensity, was less likely to offend his hearers. His manner was better subdued to the social tone of ordinary life, his voice lacked the sharp twang of the backwoods man; and, unlike John Cross, he was able to modulate it to those undertones, which, as we have before intimated, are so agreeable from the lips of young lovers and fashionable preachers. At all events, John Cross himself, was something more than satisfied with his pupil, and took considerable pains to show him off. He was a sort of living and speaking monument of the good man's religious prowess.

It does not need that we should follow the two into all the abodes which they were compelled to visit. The reader would scarcely conceal his yawns though Stevens did. Enough, that a very unctuous business was made of it that morning. Many an old lady was refreshed with the spir-itual beverage bestowed in sufficient quantity to last for another quarter; while many a young one rejoiced in the countenance of so promising a shepherd as appeared under the name of Alfred Stevens. But the latter thought of the one damsel only. He said many pleasant things to those whom he did see; but his mind ran only upon one. He began to apprehend that she might be among the flock who were destined to wait for the second or last day's vis-itation; when, to his great relief, John Cross called his attention to the dwelling of the widow Cooper, to whom they were fast approaching.

Stevens remarked that the dwelling had very much the appearance of poverty — he did not fail to perceive that it lacked the flower-garden in front which distinguished the greater number of the cottages in Charlemont; and there was an appearance of coldness and loneliness about its externals which impressed itself very strongly upon his thoughts, and seemed to speak unfavorably for the taste of the inmates. One is apt to associate the love of flowers with sweetness and gentleness of disposition, and such a passion would seem as natural, as it certainly would be becoming, to a young lady of taste and sensibility. But the sign is a very doubtful one. Taste and gentleness may satisfy themselves with other objects. A passion for books is very apt to exclude a very active passion for flowers, and it will be found, I suspect, that these persons who are most remarkable for the cultivation of flowers are least sensible to the charms of letters. It seems monstrous, indeed, that a human being should expend hours and days in the nursing and tendance of such stupid beauties as plants and flowers, when earth is filled with so many lovelier objects that come to us commended by the superior sympathies which belong to humanity. Our cities are filled with the sweetest orphans — flowers destined to be immortal ; angels in form, that might be angels in spirit — that must be, whether for good or evil — whom we never cultivate — whom we suffer to escape our tendance, and leave to the most pitiable ignorance, and the most wretched emergencies of want. The life that is wasted upon dahlias, must, *prima facie*, be the life of one heartless and insensible, and most probably, brutish in a high degree.

But Alfred Stevens had very little time for further reflection. They were at the door of the cottage. Never did the widow Cooper receive her parson in more tidy trim, and with an expression of less qualified delight. She brought forth the best chair, brushed the deerskin-seat with her apron, and having adjusted the old man to her own satisfaction as well as his, she prepared to do a like office for the young one. Having seated them fairly, and smoothed her apron, and gone through the usual preliminaries, and placed herself a little aloof, on a third seat, and rubbed her hands, and struggled into a brief pause in her brisk action, she allowed her tongue to do the office for which her whole soul was impatient.

"Oh, Brother Cross, what a searching sermon you gave us yesterday. You stirred the hearts of everybody, I warrant you, as you stirred up mine. We've been a needing it for a precious long time, I tell you; and there's no knowing what more's a wanting to make us sensible to the evil that's in us. I know from myself what it is, and I guess from the doings of others. We're none of us perfect, that's certain; but it's no harm to say that some's more and some's not so perfect as others. There's a difference in sin, Brother Cross, I'm a thinking, and I'd like you to explain why, and what's the difference. One won't have so much, and one will have more; one will take a longer spell of preaching, and half the quantity will be a dose to work another out clean, entire. I'm not boastful for myself, Brother Cross, but I do say, I'd give up in despair if I thought it took half so much to do me, as it would take for a person like that Mrs. Thackeray."

"Sister Cooper," said brother Cross, rebukingly, "beware of the temptation to vain-glory. Be not like the Pharisee, disdainful of the publican. To be too well pleased with one's self is to be displeasing to the Lord."

"Oh, Brother Cross, don't be thinking that I'm over and above satisfied with the goodness that's in me. I know I'm not so good. I have a great deal of evil; but then it seems to me there's a difference in good and a difference in evil. One has most of one and one has most of another. None of us have much good, and all of us have a great deal of sin. God help me, for I need his help—I have my own

share ; but as for that Mrs. Thackeray, she's as full of wickedness as an an egg's full of meat."

"It is not the part of Christianity, Sister Cooper," said
John Cross mildly, "to look into our neighbors' accounts
and make comparisons between their doings and our own.
We can only do so at great risk of making a false reckon-
ing. Besides, Sister Cooper, it is business enough on our
hands, if we see to our own short-comings. As for Mrs.
Thackeray, I have no doubt she's no better than the rest
of us, and we are all, as you said before, children of suffering, and prone to sin as certain as that the sparks fly upward. We must only watch and pray without ceasing,
particularly that we may not deceive ourselves with the
most dangerous sin of being too sure of our own works.
The good deeds that we boast of so much in our earthly
day will shrivel and shrink up at the last account to so small
a size that the best of us, through shame and confusion,
will be only too ready to call upon the rocks and hills to
cover us. We are very weak and foolish all, Sister Cooper.
We can't believe ourselves too weak, or too mean, or too
sinful. To believe this with all our hearts, and to try to
be better with all our strength, is the true labor of religion.
God send it to us, in all its sweetness and perfection, so
that we may fight the good fight without ceasing."

"But if you could only hear of the doings of Mrs. Thackeray, Brother Cross, you'd see how needful it would be to
put forth all your strength to bring her back to the right
path."

"The Lord will know. None of us can hide our evil
from the eyes of the Lord. I will strive with our sister,
when I seek her, which will be this very noon, but it is of
yourself, Sister Cooper, and your daughter Margaret, that I
would speak. Where is she that I see her not?"

This was the question that made our *quasi* hierophant
look up with a far greater degree of interest than he had
felt in the long and random twattle to which he had been

compelled to listen. Where was she — that fair daughter? He was impatient for the answer. But he was not long detained in suspense. Next to her neighbors there was no subject of whom the mother so loved to speak as the daughter, and the daughter's excellences.

"Ah! she is up-stairs, at her books, as usual. She does so love them books, Brother Cross, I'm afraid it'll do harm to her health. She cares for nothing half so well. Morning, noon, and night, all the same, you find her poring over them; and even when she goes out to ramble, she must have a book, and she wants no other company. For my part I can't see what she finds in them to love so; for except to put a body to sleep I never could see the use they were to any person yet."

"Books are of two kinds," said Brother Cross gravely. "They are useful or hurtful. The useful kinds are good, the hurtful kinds are bad. The Holy Bible is the first book, and the only book, as I reckon it will be the book that'll live longest. The 'Life of Whitefield' is a good book, and I can recommend the sermons of that good man, Brother Peter Cummins, that preached when I was a lad, all along through the back parts of North Carolina, into South Carolina and Georgia. I can't say that he came as far back into the west as these parts; but he was a most faithful shepherd. There was a book of his sermons printed for the benefit of his widow and children. He died, like that blessed man, John Rogers, that we see in the primer-books, leaving a wife with eleven children and one at the breast. His sermons are very precious reading. One of them in particular, on the Grace of God, is a very falling of manna in the wilderness. It freshens the soul, and throws light upon the dark places in the wilderness. Ah! if only such books were printed, what a precious world for poor souls it would be. But they print a great many bad books now-a-days."

The natural love of mischief which prevailed in the bosom of Alfred Stevens now prompted him to take part in the conversation at this happy moment. The opportunity was a tempting one.

"The printers," said he, "are generally very bad men. They call themselves devils, and take young lads and bring them up to their business under that name!"

The old lady threw up her hands, and John Cross, to whom this intelligence was wholly new, inquired with a sort of awe-struck gravity —

"Can this be true, Alfred Stevens? Is this possible?"

"The fact, sir. They go by no other name among themselves; and you may suppose, if they are not ashamed of the name, they are not unwilling to perform the doings of the devil. Indeed, they are busy doing his business from morning to night — and night to morning. They don't stop for the sabbath. They work on Sunday the same as any other day, and if they take any rest at all it is on Saturday, which would show them to be a kind of Jews."

"Good Lord deliver us!" ejaculated the widow.

"Where, O! where?" exclaimed the Brother Cross with similar earnestness. The game was too pleasant for Alfred Stevens. He pursued it.

"In such cities," he continued, "as New York and Philadelphia, thousands of these persons are kept in constant employ sending forth those books of falsehood and folly which fill the hearts of the young with vain imaginings, and mislead the footsteps of the unwary. In one of these establishments, four persons preside, who are considered brothers; but they are brothers in sin only, and are by some supposed to be no other. They have called themselves after the names of saints and holy men; even the names of the thrice blessed apostles, John and James, have been in this fashion abused; but if it be true that the spirits of evil may even in our day as of old embody themselves in mortal shape for the better enthralling and destruction of mankind, then should I prefer to believe that these persons were no other than the evil demons who ruled in Ashdod and Assyria.

Such is their perseverance in evil — such their busy industry, which keeps a thousand authors (which is but another name for priests and prophets) constantly at work to frame cunning falsehoods and curious devices, and winning fancies, which when printed and made into books, turn the heads of the young and unwary, and blind the soul to the wrath which is to come."

The uplifted hands of the widow Cooper still attested her wonder.

"Lord save us!" she exclaimed, "I should not think it strange if Sister Thackeray had some of these very books. Do ask, Brother Cross, when you go to see her. She speaks much of books, and I see her reading them whenever I look in at the back window."

John Cross did not seem to give any heed to the remark of the old woman. There was a theological point involved in one of the remarks of Alfred Stevens which he evidently regarded as of the first importance.

"What you say, Alfred Stevens, is very new and very strange to me, and I should think from what I already know of the evil which is sometimes put in printed books, that there was indeed a spirit of malice at work in this way, to help the progress and the conquests of Satan among our blind and feeble race. But I am not prepared to believe that God has left it to Satan to devise so fearful a scheme for prosecuting his evil designs as that of making the demons of Ashdod and Assyria take the names of mortal men, while seeming to follow mortal occupations. It would be fearful tidings for our poor race were this so. But if so, is it not seen that there is a difference in the shapes of these persons. If either of these brothers who blasphemously call themselves John and James, after the manner of the apostles, shall be in very truth and certainty that Dagon of the Philistines whom Jehovah smote before his altar, will he not be made fishlike from the waist downward, and will this not be seen by his followers and some of the thousands whom he daily

5*

perverts to his evil purposes and so leads to eternal destruction ?"

"It may be that it is permitted to such a demon to put on what shape he thinks proper," replied Stevens; "but even if it is not, yet this would not be the subject of any difference — it would scarcely prevent the prosecution of this evil purpose. You are to remember, Mr. Cross—"

"John Cross — plain John Cross, Alfred Stevens," was the interruption of the preacher.

"You are to remember," Stevens resumed, "that when the heart is full of sin, the eyes are full of blindness. The people who believe in these evil beings are incapable of seeing their deformities."

"That is true — a sad truth."

"And, again," continued Stevens, "there are devices of mere mortal art, by which the deformities and defects of an individual may be concealed. One of these brothers, I am told, is never to be seen except seated in one position at the same desk, and this desk is so constructed, as to hide his lower limbs in great part, while still enabling him to prosecute his nefarious work."

"It's clear enough, Brother Cross," exclaimed the widow Cooper, now thoroughly convinced — "it's clear enough that there's something that he wants to hide. Lord help us! but these things are terrible."

"To the weak and the wicked, Sister Cooper, they are, as you say, terrible, and hence the need that we should have our lamps trimmed and lighted, for the same light which brings us to the sight of the Holy of Holies, shows us the shape of hatefulness, the black and crouching form of Satan, with nothing to conceal his deformity. Brother Stevens has well said that when the heart is full of sin, the eyes are full of blindness; and so we may say that when the heart is full of godliness, the eyes are full of seeing. You can not blind them with devilish arts. You can not delude them as to the true forms of Satan, let him take any shape.

The eye of godliness sees clean through the mask of sin, as the light of the sun pierces the. thickest cloud, and brings day after the darkest night."

" Oh! what a blessed thing to hear you say so."

" More blessed to believe, Sister Cooper, and believing, to pray with all your heart for this same eye of godliness. But we should not only pray but work. Working for God is the best sort of prayer. We must do something in his behalf: and this reminds me, Sister Cooper, that if there is so much evil spread abroad in these books, we should look heedfully into the character of such as fall into the hands of the young and the unmindful of our flock."

" That is very true; that is just what I was thinking of, Brother Cross. You can not look too close, I'm thinking into such books as you'll find at the house of Widow Thackeray. I can give a pretty 'cute guess where she gets all that sort of talk, that seems so natural at the end of her tongue."

" Verily, I will speak with Sister Thackeray on this subject," responded the pastor — " but your own books, Sister Cooper, and those of your daughter Margaret — if it is convenient, I should prefer to examine them now while I am here."

" What! Margaret's books! examine Margaret's books!"

" Even so, while I am present and while Brother Stevens is here, also, to give me his helping counsel in the way of judgment."

" Why, bless us, Brother Cross, you don't suppose that my daughter Margaret would keep any but the properest books? she's too sensible, I can tell you, for that. She's no books but the best; none, I'll warrant you, like them you'll find at Widow Thackeray's. She's not to be put off with bad books. She goes through 'em with a glance of the eye. Ah! she's too smart to be caught by the contrivances of those devils, though in place of four brothers there was four thousand of 'em. No, no! let her alone for that — she's a match for the best of 'em."

"But as Brother Stevens said," continued John Cross, "where sin gets into the heart, the eye is blinded to the truth. Now——"

"Her eye's not blinded, Brother Cross, I can tell you. They can't cheat her with their books. She has none but the very best. I'll answer for them. None of them ever did me any harm; and I reckon none of them 'll ever hurt her. But I'm mistaken, if you don't have a real burning when you get to Mrs. Thackeray's."

"But, Sister Cooper——" commenced the preacher.

"Yes, Brother Cross," replied the dame.

"Books, as I said before, are of two kinds."

"Yes, I know — good and bad — I only wonder there's no indifferent ones among 'em," replied the lady.

"They should be examined for the benefit of the young and ignorant."

"Oh, yes, and for more besides, for Mrs. Thackeray's not young, that's clear enough; and I know there's a good many things that she's not ignorant of. She's precious knowing about many things that don't do her much good; and if the books could unlearn her, I'd say for one let her keep 'em. But as for looking at Margaret's books — why, Brother Cross, you surely know Margaret?"

The preacher answered meekly, but negatively.

"Ain't she about the smartest girl you ever met with?" continued the mother.

"God has certainly blessed her with many gifts," was the reply, "but where the trust is great, the responsibility is great also."

"Don't she know it?"

"I trust she does, Sister Cooper."

"You may trust every bit of it. She's got the smartness, the same as it is in books——"

"But the gift of talents, Sister Cooper, is a dangerous gift."

"I don't see, Brother Cross, how good things that come from God can be dangerous things."

"If I could see the books, Sister Cooper;—I say not that they are evil——"

John Cross began in tones that denoted something like despair; certainly dissatisfaction was in them, when Alfred Stevens, who had long since tired of what was going on, heard a light footfall behind him. He turned his eyes and beheld the fair maiden, herself, the propriety of whose reading was under discussion, standing in the doorway. It appeared that she had gathered from what had reached her ears, some knowledge of what was going on, for a smile of ineffable scorn curled her classic and nobly-chiselled mouth, while her brow was the index to a very haughty volume. In turning, Alfred Stevens betrayed to her the playful smile upon his own lips—their eyes met, and that single glance established a certain understanding between them.

Her coming did not avail to stifle the subject of discussion. John Cross was too resolute in the prosecution of his supposed duty, to give up the cause he had once undertaken. He had all the inveteracy of the stout old puritan. The usual introduction over and he resumed, though he now addressed himself to the daughter rather than the mother. She scarcely heard him to the end.

"The books were my father's, Mr. Cross; they are valuable to me on that account. They are dear to me on their own. They are almost my only companions, and though I believe you would find nothing in them which might be held detrimental, yet I must confess, if there were, I should be sorry to be made acquainted with the fact. I have not yet discovered it myself, and should be loath to have it shown by another."

"But you will let me see them, Margaret?"

"Yes, sir, whenever you please. I can have no objection to that, but if by seeing them you only desire an opportunity to say what I shall read and what not, I can only tell you that your labor will be taken in vain. Indeed, the evil

is already done. I have not a volume which I have not
read repeatedly."

It is needless to add that Brother Cross was compelled
to forego his book examination at the widow Cooper's,
though strongly recommended there to press it at Widow
Thackeray's. Alfred Stevens was a mute observer during
the interview, which did not last very long after the appearance of Margaret. He was confirmed in all his previous
impressions of her beauty, nor did the brevity of the conference prevent him from perceiving her intense self-esteem,
which under certain influences of temperament is only another name for vanity. Besides they had exchanged glances
which were volumes, rendering unnecessary much future
explanation. She had seen that he was secretly laughing
at the simple preacher, and that was a source of sympathy
between them. She was very much in the habit of doing
the same thing. He, on the other hand, was very well satisfied that the daughter of such a mother must be perverse
and vain; and he was moralist enough to know that there
is no heart so accessible to the tempter as the proud and
wilful heart. But few words had passed between them,
but those were expressive, and they both parted, with the
firm conviction that they must necessarily meet again.

CHAPTER IX.

HOW THE TOAD GRINS UPON THE ALTAR.

SHALL we go the rounds with our pastor? Shall we look in upon him at Mrs. Thackeray's, while, obeying the suggestion of the widow Cooper, he purges her library of twenty volumes, casting out the devils and setting up the true gods? It is scarcely necessary. Enough to know that, under his expurgatorial finger, our beloved and bosom friend, William Shakspere, was the first to suffer. Plays! The one word was enough. Some lying histories were permitted to escape. The name of history saved them! Robinson Crusoe was preserved as a true narrative; and Swift's Tale of a Tub escaped, as it was assumed (there being no time to read any of the books, and in this respect John Cross showed himself much more of a professional critic than he conjectured) to be a treatise on one branch of the cooperage business, and so, important to domestic mechanics in a new country. The reader will remember the manner in which the library of the knight of La Mancha was disposed of. He would err, however, if he supposed that John Cross dismissed the books from the window, or did anything farther than simply to open the eyes of Mrs. Thackeray to the bad quality of some of the company she kept. That sagacious lady did not think it worth while to dispute the *ipse dixit* of a teacher so single-minded, if not sagacious. She bowed respectfully to all his suggestions, promised no longer to bestow her smiles on the undeserving—a promise

of no small importance when it is remembered that, at thirty-
three, Mrs. Thackeray was for the first time a widow — and
that night she might have been seen laughing heartily with
Mesdames Ford and Quickly at the amorous pertinacity of
the baffled knight of Eastcheap.

Under the paternal wing of John Cross, Alfred Stevens
obtained the desired *entrée* into the bosom of the flock.
He was everywhere admitted with gladness — everywhere
welcomed as to a home ; and the unsophisticated old teacher
by whose agency this was effected, congratulated his congregation and himself, on leaving the village, that he had
left in it a person so full of grace, and one who, with the
blessing of God, was so likely to bring about the birth of
grace in others.   The good old man bestowed long and
repeated counsels upon his neophyte.   The course of study
which he prescribed was very simple.   The Bible was the
Alpha and the Omega — it was the essential whole.   It
would be well to read other books if they could be had —
Clarke and Wesley were, of course, spoken of — but they
could be done without.   The word of God was in the one
volume, and it needed no help from commentators to win
its way and suffice the hungering and thirsting soul.

" If you could lay hands upon the book of sermons written by Brother Peter Cummins, which his wife had printed,
I'm thinking it would serve, next to God's own blessed
word, to put you in the right way.   It's been a great helping to me, Alfred Stevens, that same book of sermons ; and
I reckon it's because it's so good a book that it's not printed now.   I don't see it much about.   But I'll get you one
if I can, and bring or send it to you, soon enough to help
you to the wisdom that you're a seeking after.   If it only
wakes the spirit in you as it did in me — if it only stirs you
up with the spirit of divine love — you'll find it easy enough
to understand the teachings of the holy volume.   All things
become clear in that blessed light.   By its help you read,
and by its working you inwardly digest all the needful

learning.   The Lord be with you, Alfred Stevens, and bring
to perfect ripening your present undertaking."

"Amen!" was the solemn response of the hypocrite, but
we need not say what an irreverent and unholy thought lay
at the bottom of his mind in making this ejaculation.

Before the departure of John Cross, the latter had made
terms with Squire Hinkley for the board and lodging of
Brother Stevens and his horse.   Hinkley would have preferred taking nothing, considering the praiseworthy purpose of the supposed theological student ; but Stevens
shrunk from receiving such an obligation with a feeling of
pride, which yet had no scruples at practising so wretched
an imposture.   He insisted upon making compensation, or
upon leaving the house ; and, not to incur this risk, Hinkley consented to receive a weekly sum in payment ; but the
charge was considerably smaller, as we may suppose, than
it would have been had the lodger simply appeared as an
inoffensive traveller, practising no fraud and making no
professions of religion.

Having effected all these arrangements, to his own satisfaction and seemingly that of all others, John Cross departed once more into the wilderness on his single-hearted
ministry of love.   A sturdy and an honest worker was he
in the tabernacle, with a right mind if not a very wise one ;
and doing more good in his generation, and after the fashion of his strength, than is often permitted to the stall-fed
doctors of his vocation.

The reader will suppose that the old man has been already gone some seven days.   Meanwhile, the young student has fairly made himself at home in Charlemont.   He
has a snug room, entirely to himself, at Squire Hinkley's,
and, by the excellent care of the worthy dame, it is provided with the best bedding and the finest furniture.   Her
own hands sweep it clean, morning and night, for the incipient parson ; she makes up the bed, and, in customary
phrase, puts it in all respects to rights.   His wants are an-

ticipated, his slightest suggestion met with the most prompt consideration; and John Cross himself, humble and unexacting as he was, might have felt some little twinges of mortal envy could he have known that his *protégé* promised to become a much greater favorite than himself.

This, indeed, seemed very likely to be the case. A good young man in the sight of the ladies is always a more attractive person than a good old man. Dame Hinkley, though no longer young herself, remembered that she had been so, and preserved all her sympathies, in consequence, for young people. She thought Alfred Stevens so handsome, and he smiled so sweetly, and he spoke so gently, and, in short, so great had been his progress in the affections of his hostess in the brief space of a single week, that we are constrained to confess ourselves rejoiced that she herself was an old woman, as well on her own account as on that of her worthy spouse.

Her good man was very well satisfied, whether from confidence or indifference, that such should be the case. Her attentions to the young stranger probably diverted them from himself. But not so with William Hinkley — the son. We have already had some glimpses of the character of this young man. We may now add that the short week's residence of Stevens in Charlemont had increased the soreness at his heart. In that week he had seen fairly established that intimacy between his rival and the lady of his love which seemed to give the death-blow to any pretensions of his. He had seen them meet; had seen them go forth together; beheld their mutual eyes, and, turning his own inward, saw how deeply his heart was concerned in the probable sympathies of theirs. Then, to turn to his own habitation, and to behold *that*, mother and all, devoted to the same absolute stranger; to pass unheeded in the presence of those whom he best loved — over whom natural ties gave him inalienable rights; to feel himself put aside for one only known of yesterday; to look with yearning, and meet eyes only of disregard and indifference! Such being the suggestions of his jealous and suffering nature, it is surely no matter of wonder that the youth grew melan-choly and abstracted.

Our adventurer was snugly seated in the little but select chamber which had been given him in the house of Squire Hinkley. A table, neatly spread with a cotton cover, stood before him: a travelling-portfolio was opened beneath his hand, with a broad sheet of paper, already well written over, and waiting nothing but his signature, and perhaps the postscript. He was absorbed unusually in his cogita-tions, and nibbled into bits the feathery end of the gray goosequill of which he had been making such excellent use. While he meditates, unseeing, we will use the liberty of an old acquaintance to scan the letter—for such it is—which he·has been writing. Perhaps we shall gather from it some matters which it may concern us yet to know:—

"DEAR BARNABAS: The strangest adventure—positively the very strangest—that ever happened to a son of Murkey's, will keep me from the embraces of the brethren a few weeks longer. I am benighted, bewildered, taken with art-magic, transmuted, *transmogrified,* not myself nor yet another, but, as they say in Mississippi, 'a sort of betweenity.' Fancy me suddenly become a convert to the bluest presbyterian-ism, as our late excellent brother Woodford became, when he found that he could not get Moll Parkinson on any other terms—and your guess will not be very far from the true one. I am suddenly touched with conviction. I have seen a light on my way from Tarsus. The scales have fallen from my eyes. I have seen the wickedness of my ways, and yours too, you dog; and, having resolved on my own repentance, I am taking lessons which shall enable me to effect yours. Precious deal of salt will it need for that! Salt river will fall, while its value rises. But the glory of the thing—think of that, my boy! What a triumph it will

be to revolutionize Murkey's!—to turn out the drinkers,
and smokers, and money-changers; to say, 'Hem! my
brethren, let us pay no more taxes to sin in this place!'
There shall be no more cakes and ale. Ginger shall have
no heat i' the mouth there; and, in place of smoking meats
and tobacco, give you nothing but smoking methodism!
Won't that be a sight and a triumph which shall stir the
dry bones in our valley—ay, and bones not so dry? There
shall be a quaking of the flesh in sundry places. Flam will
perish in the first fit of consternation; and if Joe Burke's
sides do not run into sop and jelly, through the mere humor of the thing, then prophecy is out of its element quite.

"Seriously, you dog, I have become a theological student! Don't you see proofs of my progress in my unctuous phraseology. I was taken suddenly upon the highway—a brand plucked from the burning—and to be stuck
up on high, still lighted, however, as a sort of lantern and
lighthouse to other wayfarers—wandering rogues like
yourself, who need some better lights than your own if it
only be to show you how to sin decently. I am professedly
a convert to the true faith, though which that is, I think,
has not well been determined among you at Murkey's, or,
indeed, anywhere else. I believe the *vox populi, vox Dei,*
still comprises the only wholesome decision which has yet
been made on the subject. The popular vote here declares
it to be methodism; with you it is baptism or presbyteri-
anism—which? I am a flexible student, however, and
when I meet you again at Murkey's, shall be prepared to
concur with the majority.

"But, in sober fact, I am a professor—actually recog
nised by my neighbors as one of the elect—set apart to
be and do mighty things. How I came so, will call for a
long story, which I defer to another occasion. Enough to
tell you that an accidental rencontre with a silly old
preacher (whose gullet I filled with raw brandy, which I
recommended to him, under another name, as a sovereign

remedy against flatulence, and which nearly strangled him, he took such a premeditated swallow), brought me into one of the loveliest little villages in all this western country, and there I saw many things—among others—a woman!—

"A woman!—that one word, you dog, will explain the mystery—will show you why I am thus transmuted, *transmogrified*, and in ' a state of betweenity.' Nothing less, I assure you, could make me disguise myself after the present fashion ; wear the sanctimonious and sour phiz which the common law of modern religion prescribes, and keep me much longer from the pleasanter communion of such glorious imps, as I suppose, are, even now, beginning to gather in the dingy smoke-room of our sovereign Murkey. But this woman, you will ask. Ay, ay, but you shall have no answer yet. It shall be enough for you that she is a queen of Sheba, after her own fashion. A proud, imperious, passionate creature—tall, really beautiful—and so majestic! You should see the flashing of her eyes to know what sort of a thing is moral lightning. Her face kindles up in an instant. She is an intensifier, and like most such, cursedly smart. Young too—scarce eighteen, I think ; queer too—almost tyrannical at times—but full of blood, of unregulated passions, moody, capricious, and, of course, easy game, if the sportsman knows anything of the habits of the bird. She is a country-girl, but no hoyden. Her intensity of character, her pride and great self-esteem, have made her a solitary. Unsophisticated in some respects, she is yet not to be surprised. In solitude, and a taste for it, she has acquired a sort of moral composure which makes her secure against surprise. I am really taken with the girl, and *could* love her, I tell you—nay, do love her—so long as love can keep himself—out of a state of bondage ! I do not think, at this moment, that I shall violate any of the laws of the conventicle, like small-witted Brother Woodford ; though, so far as the woman is concerned, I should leave it without argument to the free vote of all the Lads of Fancy that ever gather round Murkey's round table, if my justification for turning traitor, would not prove immeasurably more complete than his.

"So! so! There are bones enough for you to crunch, you professional bandog. I had not meant to tell you half so much. There is some danger that one may lose his game altogether, if he suffers his nose to point unnecessarily to the cover where it lies. I know what keen scents are in the club, some of which would be on my track in no time if they knew where to find me; but I shall baffle you, you villains. My post-town is fifty miles from the place where I pursue my theological studies; you are too wise to attempt a wild-goose chase. You may smack your chaps, Barney, with envy; bite them too if you please, and it will only whet my own sense of pleasure to fancy your confusion, and your hopeless denunciations in the club. I shall be back in time for term—meanwhile get the papers in readiness. Write to me at the post-town of Ellisland, and remember to address me as Alfred Stevens—nay, perhaps, you may even say, 'Rev. Alfred Stevens,' it will grace the externals of the document with a more unctuous aspect, and secure the recipient a more wholesome degree of respect. Send all my letters to this town under envelope with this direction. I wrote you twice from Somerville. Did I tell you that old Hunks has been deused liberal? I can laugh at the small terms, yet go to Murkey's and shine through the smoke with the best of you. I solicit the prayers of the Round Table.

"Faithfully, yours, &c."

So far our profligate had written to his brother profligate, when a tap was heard at the entrance of his chamber. Thrusting the written papers into his portfolio, he rose, and opening the door discovered his hostess at the entrance.

"I came, Brother Stevens," said the old lady, "if you

were not too busy in your studies, to have a little talk
with you, and to get your counsel upon a subject that a
little distresses me. But you look as if you were busy
now—"

"Not too busy, Mrs. Hinkley, to oblige you in this or in
any other respect," replied the guest with suitable suavity
of expression—"shall I attend you down stairs."

"Oh! no! it won't need," said she. "I'll take a seat
with you awhile. We shall be less liable to interruption
here."

Stevens scarcely repressed his smile, but the seniority
of the old lady made her proceedings very innocent, however much they might have been adverse to the rules. He
threw wide the door, and without more hesitation she followed him at once into the chamber.

CHAPTER X.

THE MOTHER'S GRIEFS.

THE business upon which Mrs. Hinkley sought the chamber of her guest was a very simple one, and easily expressed. Not that she expressed it in few words. That is scarcely possible at any time with an ancient lady. But the long story which she told, when compressed into intelligible form, related to her son William. She had some maternal fears on his account. The lad was a decided melancholic. His appetite was bad; his looks were thin and unhappy; he lacked the usual spirit of youth; he lacked his own usual spirit. What was the cause of the change which had come over him so suddenly, she could not divine. Her anxiety was for the remedy. She had consulted Brother Cross on the subject before he departed; but that good man, after a brief examination of the patient, had freely admitted his inability to say what was the matter with him, and what was proper for his cure. To the object of this solicitude himself, he had given much good counsel, concluding finally with a recommendation to read devoutly certain chapters in Job and Isaiah. It appears that William Hinkley submitted to all this scrutiny with exemplary fortitude, but gave no satisfactory answers to any of the questions asked him. He had no complaints, he denied any suffering; and expressed himself annoyed at the inquisition into his thoughts and feelings. This annoyance had been expressed, however, with the subdued tones and language of one habitually gentle and modest. Whenever he was approached on the subject, as the good old lady assured her guest, he shook off his questioners with no little haste, and took to the woods for the rest of the day. "That day," said she, "you needn't look for William Hinkley to his dinner."

Stevens had been struck with the deportment of this youth, which had seemed to him haughty and repulsive; and, as he fancied, characterized by some sentiment of hostility for himself. He was surprised therefore to learn from the old lady that the lad was remarkable for his gentleness.

"How long has he been in this way, Mrs. Hinkley?" he asked with some curiosity.

"Well now, Brother Stevens, I can't tell you. It's been growing on him for some time. I reckon it's a matter of more than four months since I first seen it; but it's only been a few weeks that I have spoken to him. Brother Cross spoke to him only Monday of last week. My old man don't seem to see so much of it; but I know there's a great change in him now from what there used to be. A mother's eye sees a great way farther into the hearts of her children, Brother Stevens, than any other persons; and I can see plainly that William is no more the same boy — no! nor nothing like it — that he once was. Why, once, he was all life, and good humor; could dance and sing with the merriest among them; and was always so good and kind, and loved to do whatever would please a body; and was always with somebody, or other, making merry, and planning the prettiest sports. Now, he don't sing, nor dance, nor play; when you see him, you 'most always see him alone. He goes by himself into the woods, and he'll be going over the hills all day, nobody with him, and never seeming to care about his food, and what's more strange, never looking at the books that he used to be so fond of."

"He has been fond of books, then — had he many?"

6

"Oh, yes, a whole drawer of them, and he used to get them besides from the schoolmaster, Mr. Calvert, a very good man that lives about half a mile from the village, and has a world of books. But now he neither gets books from other people nor reads what he's got. I'm dubious, Brother Stevens, that he's read too much for his own good. Something's not right here, I'm a thinking."

The good old lady touched her head with her finger and in this manner indicated her conjecture as to the seat of her son's disease. Stevens answered her encouragingly.

"I scarcely think, Mrs. Hinkley, that it can be anything so bad. The young man is at that age when a change naturally takes place in the mind and habits. He wants to go into the world, I suspect. He's probably tired of doing nothing. What is to be his business? It's high time that such a youth should have made a choice."

"That's true, Brother Stevens, but he's been the apple to our eyes, and we haven't been willing that he should take up any business that would carry him away from us. He's done a little farming about the country, but that took him away, and latterly he's kept pretty much at home, going over his books and studying, now one and now another, just as Mr. Calvert gave them to him."

"What studies did he pursue?"

"Well, I can't tell you. He was a good time at Latin, and then he wants to be a lawyer;—"

"A lawyer!"

"Yes, he had a great notion to be a lawyer and was at his books pretty hard for a good year, constant, day by day, until, as I said before, about four months ago, when I saw that he was growing thin, and that he had put down the books altogether, and had the change come over him just as I told you. You see how thin he is now. You'd scarce believe him to be the same person if you'd seen him then. Why his cheeks were as full and as red as roses, and his eye was always shining and laughing, and he had the liveliest step, and between him and Ned Hinkley, his cousin, what with flute and fiddle, they kept the house in a constant uproar, and we were all so happy. Now, it isn't once a month that we hear the sound of the fiddle in the house. He never sings, and he never dances, and he never plays, and what little he lets us see of him, is always so sad and so spiritless that I feel heartsick whenever I look upon him. Oh! Brother Stevens, if you could only find out what's the matter, and tell us what to do, it would be the most blessed kindness, and I'd never forget it, or forget you, to my dying day."

"Whatever I can do, Mrs. Hinkley, shall surely be done. I will see and speak with your son."

"Oh! do — that's a dear good sir. I'm sure if you only talk to him and advise him it will do him good."

"Without being so sure, ma'am, I will certainly try to please you. Though I think you see the matter with too serious eyes. Such changes are natural enough to young people, and to old ones too. But what may be your son's age."

"Nineteen last April."

"Quite a man for his years, Mrs. Hinkley."

"Isn't he?"

"He will do you credit yet."

"Ah! if I could believe so. But you'll speak to him, Brother Stevens? You'll try and bring all to rights?"

"Rely upon me to do what I can; — to do my best."

"Well, that's as much as any man can do, and I'm sure I'll be so happy — we shall all be so much indebted to you."

"Do not speak of it, my dear madam," said Stevens, bowing with profound deference as the old lady took her departure. She went off with light heart, having great faith in the powers of the holy man, and an equal faith in his sincerity.

"What a bore!" he muttered as he closed the door behind her. "This is one of the penalties, I suppose, which I must pay for my privileges. I shall be called upon to reform the morals and manners, and look into the petty cares of every chuckle-headed boor and boor's brat for ten miles round. See why boys reject their mush, and why the girls dislike to listen .to the exhortations of a mamma, who requires them to leave undone what she has done herself — and with sufficient reason too, if her own experience be not wholly profitless. Well, I must submit. There are advantages, however; I shall have other pupils to tutor, and it shall go hard with me if all the grapes prove sour where the vines are so various."

The student of divinity, after these conclusions, prepared to make his toilet. Very few of these students, in their extreme solicitude for the well being of the inner man, show themselves wholly regardless of their externals. Even mourning, it appears, requires to be disposed by a fashionable costumer. Though the garments to which the necessities of travel limited Brother Stevens were not various, they were yet select. The good young man had an affection for his person, which was such certainly as to deserve his care. On this occasion he was more than usually particular. He did not scruple to discard the white cravat. For this he substituted a handkerchief which had the prettiest sprig of lilac, on a ground of the most delicate lemon color. He consulted complexions, and his mirror determined him in favor of this pattern. Brother Stevens would not have worn it had he been summoned, in his new vocation, to preach or pray at the conventicle; nor would he have dreamed of anything but a black stock had his business been to address the democracy from the top of a cider-barrel. His habits, under such necessities, would have been made to correspond with the principles (Qu?) which such a situation more distinctly called for.

But the thoughts of our worthy brother ran upon other objects. He was thinking of Margaret Cooper. He was about to pay that damsel a visit. His progress, we may suppose, had not been inconsiderable when we are told that his present visit was one of previous arrangement. They were about to go forth on a ramble together — the woods were so wild and lovely — the rocks surrounding Charlemont were so very picturesque ; — there was the quietest tarn, a sort of basin in the bosom of the hills at a little distance, which she was to show him ; and there was the sweetest stream in the world, that meandered in the neighborhood ; and Brother Stevens so loved the picturesque — lakes embosomed in hills, and streams stealing through unbroken forests, and all so much the more devotedly, when he had such a companion as Margaret Cooper.

And Margaret Cooper ! — she the wild, the impassioned. A dreamer — a muse — filled with ambitious thoughts — proud, vain, aspiring after the vague, the unfathomable ! What was her joy, now that she could speak her whole soul, with all its passionate fullness, to understanding ears ! Stevens and herself had already spoken together. Her books had been his books. The glowing passages which she loved to repeat, were also the favorite passages in his memory. Over the burning and thrilling strains of Byron, the tender and spiritual of Shelley, the graceful and soft of Campbell, she loved to linger. They filled her thoughts. They made her thoughts. She felt that her true utterance lay in their language ; and this language, until now, had fallen dead and without fruit upon the dull ears of her companions in Charlemont. What was their fiddling and festivity to her ! What their tedious recreations by hillside or stream, when she had to depress her speech to the base levels of their unimaginative souls ! The loveliness of nature itself, unrepresented by the glowing hues of poetry, grew tame, if not offensive ; and when challenged to its contemplation by those to whom the muse was nothing, the fancy of the true observer grew chilled and heavy, and the scenes of beauty seemed prostituted in their glance.

We have all felt this. Nothing can more annoy the soul of taste or sensibility than to behold its favorite scene and subject fail in awakening others to that emotion which it has inspired in ourselves. We turn away in haste, lest the object of our worship should become degraded by a longer survey. Enthusiasm recoils at a denial of sympathy; and all the worth of our companion, in a thousand other respects, fails to reconcile us to his coldness and indifference.

That Alfred Stevens had taste and talent—that he was well read in the volumes which had been her favorite study, Margaret Cooper needed no long time to discover. She soon ascribed to him qualities and tastes which were beyond his nature. Deceived by his tact, she believed in his enthusiasm. He soon discovered *her* tastes; and she found equally soon that *his* were like her own. After this discovery, she gave him credit for other and more important possessions; and little dreamed that, while he responded to her glowing sentiments with others equally glowing— avowed the same love for the same authors, and concurred with her in the preference of the same passages—his feelings were as little susceptible of sympathy with hers as would have been those of the cold demon Mephistopheles! While her eye was flashing, her cheek flushed, her breast heaving with the burning thoughts and strains of the master to whom her beautiful lips were giving utterance, he was simply sensible to *her* beauty—to its strange, wild charms—and meditating thoughts from which the soul of true poetry recoils with the last feelings of aversion. Even the passion which he felt while he surveyed her, foreign as it was to those legitimate emotions which her ambition and her genius would equally have tended to inspire in any justly-minded nature, might well be considered frigid— regarded as the result of deliberate artifice—the true offspring of an habitual and base indulgence.

It was to meet this unsophisticated, impassioned, and confiding girl, that Alfred Stevens bestowed such particular pains on his costume. He felt its deficiencies, and, accordingly, the necessity of making the most of it; for, though he perfectly well knew that such a woman as Margaret Cooper would have been the very last to regard the mere garment in which a congenial nature is arrayed, yet he also well knew that the costume is not less indicative of the tastes than the wealth of the wearer. You will see thousands of persons, men and women, richly dressed, and but one will be *well* dressed: that one, most generally, will be the individual who is perhaps of all others possessed of the least resources for dress, other than those which dwell in the well-arranged mind, the well-disposing taste, and the happy, crowning fancy.

His tasks of the toilet were at length ended, and he was preparing to go forth. He was about to leave the chamber, had already placed his hand upon the latch of the door, when he heard the voice of his hostess, on the stairway, in seeming expostulation with her son He was about to forbear his purpose of departure until the parties had retired, when, remembering the solicitude of the lady, and thinking it would show that zeal in her service which he really could not entertain, he determined at once to join the young man, and begin with him that certain degree of intimacy without which it could scarcely be supposed that he could broach the subject of his personal affairs. He felt somewhat the awkwardness of this assumed duty, but then he recollected his vocation; he knew the paramount influence of the clergy upon all classes of persons in the West, and, with the conscious superiority derived from greater years and better education, he felt himself fortified in undertaking the paternal office which the fond, foolish mother had confided to his hands. Accordingly descending the stairs briskly, he joined the two at the entrance of the dwelling. The son was already on the outside; the mother stood in the doorway; and, as Stevens appeared and drew nigh, William Hinkley bowed, and turned away as if to withdraw.

"If you have no objections, Mr. Hinkley," said Stevens, "I will join you. You seem to be about to go my way."

The young man paused with an air of reluctance, muttered something which was not altogether intelligible, but which Stevens construed into assent, and the two set forth together — the good old matron giving a glance of gratitude to the benevolent young student which her son did not fail to note, while, at the same time, a sentence which evidently conveyed some motherly rebuke, was addressed to his already-irritated ears.

CHAPTER XI.

WRESTLING.

ALFRED STEVENS, as he walked behind his young companion, observed him with a more deliberate survey than he had yet taken. Hitherto, the young man had challenged but little of his scrutiny. He had simply noted him for a tall youth, yet in the green, who appeared of a sulky, retiring nature, and whose looks had seemed to him on one or more occasions to manifest something like distaste for himself. The complacency of Stevens, however, was too well grounded to be much disturbed by such an exhibition. Perhaps, indeed, he would have derived a malicious sort of satisfaction in making a presumptuous lad feel his inferiority. He had just that smallness of spirit which would find its triumph in the success of such a performance.

He now observed that the youth was well formed, tall, not ungraceful—with features of singular intelligence, though subdued to the verge of sadness. His face was pale and thin, his eyes were a little sunken, and his air, expression, and general outside, denoted a youth of keen sensibilities, who had suffered some disappointment.

In making this examination, Alfred Stevens was not awakened to any generous purposes. He designed, in reality, nothing more than to acquit himself of the duty he had undertaken with the smallest possible exertion. His own mind was one of that mediocre character which the

6*

heart never informs. His scrutiny, therefore, though it enabled him to perceive that the young man had qualities of worth, was not such as to prompt any real curiosity to examine further. A really superior mind would have been moved to look into these resources; and, without other motive than that of bringing a young, laboring, and ardent soul out of the meshes of a new and bewildering thought or situation, would have addressed himself to the task with that degree of solicitous earnestness which disarms prejudice and invites and wins confidence. But, with his first impression, that the whole business was a "bore," our benevolent young teacher determined on getting through with it with the least possible effort. He saw that the youth carried a book under his arm, the externals of which, so uniform and discouraging as they appear in every legal library, could not well be questioned as belonging to some such venerable receptacle of barbarous phrase and rigid authority. The circumstance afforded him an occasion to begin a conversation, the opening of which, with all his coolness, was a subject of some awkwardness.

"You seem a student like myself, Mr. Hinkley, and, if I mistake not from the appearance of your book, you are taking up the profession which I am about to lay down."

"This is a law-book, sir," said Hinkley, in accents which were rather meek than cold; "it is Blackstone."

"Ah! I thought as much. Have you been long a student?"

"I may scarcely consider myself one yet. I have read, sir, rather than studied."

"A good distinction, not often made. But, do you incline to law seriously?"

"Yes, sir—I know no occupation to which I so much incline."

"The law is a very arduous profession. It requires a rare union of industry, talent, and knowledge of mankind to be a good lawyer."

"I should think so, sir."

"Few succeed where thousands fail. Young men are very apt to mistake inclination for ability ; and to be a poor lawyer—"

"Is to be worse than poor—is to be despicable!" replied Hinkley with a half-smile, as he interrupted a speech which might have been construed into a very contemptuous commentary on his own pretensions. It would seem that the young man had so understood it. He continued thus :—

"It may be so with me, sir. It is not improbable that I deceive myself, and confound inclination with ability."

"Oh, pardon me, my dear young friend," said Stevens patronizingly ; "but I do not say so. I utter a mere generality. Of course, I can know nothing on the subject of your abilities. I should be glad to know. I should like to converse with you. But the law is very arduous, very exacting. It requires a good mind, and it requires the whole of it. There is no such thing as being a good lawyer from merely reading law. You can't bolt it as we do food in this country. We must chew upon it. It must be well digested. You seem to have the right notion on this subject. I should judge so from two things : the distinction which you made between the reader and the student ; and the fact that your appearance is that of the student. I am afraid, my young friend, that you overwork yourself. You look thin, and pale, and unhappy. You should be careful that your passion for study is not indulged in at the peril of your health."

The frame of the young man seemed to be suddenly agitated. His face was flushed, and a keen, quick, flash of anger seemed to lighten in his eyes as he looked up to the paternal counsellor and replied : —

"I thank you, sir, for your interest, but it is premature. I am not conscious that my health suffers from this or any other cause."

"Nay, my young friend, do not deceive yourself. You perhaps underrate your own industry. It is very difficult matter to decide how much we can do and how much we ought to do, in the way of study. No mere thinking can determine this matter for us. It can only be decided by being able to see what others do and can endure. In a little country village like this, one can not easily determine; and the difficulty may be increased somewhat by one's own conviction, of the immense deal that one has to learn. If you were to spend a year in some tolerably large community. Perhaps you meditate some such plan?"

"I do not, sir," was the cold reply.

"Indeed; and have you no desire that way?"

"None!"

"Very strange! at your time of life the natural desire is to go into the great world. Even the student fancies he can learn better there than he can anywhere else — and so he can."

"Indeed, sir: if I may be so bold to ask, why, with this opinion, have you left the great city to bury yourself in a miserable village like Charlemont?"

The question was so quickly put, and with so much apparent keenness, that Stevens found the tables suddenly reversed. But he was in nowise discomposed. He answered promptly.

"You forget," he said, "that I was speaking of very young men, of an ambitious temper, who were seeking to become lawyers. The student of divinity may very well be supposed to be one who would withdraw himself from the scene of ambition, strifes, vanities. and tumultuous passions."

"You speak, sir, as if there were a material difference in our years?" said Hinkley inquiringly.

"Perhaps it is less than in our experience, my young friend," was the answer of the other, betraying that quiet sense of superiority which would have been felt more gallingly by Hinkley had he been of a less modest nature. Still, it had the effect of arousing some of the animal in his blood, and he responded in a sentence which was not entirely without its sneer, though it probably passed without penetrating such a buff of self-esteem as guarded the sensibilities of our adventurer.

"You are fortunate sir, if, at your time of life, you have succeeded in withdrawing your thoughts and feelings, with your person, from such scenes of ambition as you speak of. But I fancy the passions dwell with us in the country as well as with the wiser people in the town; and I am not sure that there is any pursuit much more free from their intrusion than that of the law."

"Your remark exhibits penetration, Mr. Hinkley. I should not be surprised if you have chosen your profession properly. Still, I should counsel you not to overwork yourself. Bear with me, sir; I feel an interest in your behalf, and I must think you do so. Allow me to be something of a judge in this matter. You are aware, sir, that I too have been a lawyer."

The youth bowed stiffly.

"If I can lend you any assistance in your studies, I will do so. Let me arrange them for you, and portion out your time. I know something about that, and will save you from injuring your health. On this point you evidently need instruction. You are doing yourself hurt. Your appearance is matter of distress and apprehension to your parents."

"To my parents, sir?"

"Your mother, I mean! She spoke to me about you this very morning. She is distressed at some unaccountable changes which have taken place in your manners, your health, your personal appearance. Of course I can say nothing on the subject of the past, or of these changes; but I may be permitted to say that your present looks do not betoken health, and I have supposed this to be on account of your studies. I promised your good mother to confer with you, and counsel you, and if I can be of any help——

"You are very good, sir!"

The young man spoke bitterly. His gorge was rising. It was not easy to suppress his vexation with his mother, and the indignation which he felt at the supercilious approaches of the agent whom she had employed. Besides, his mind, not less than his feelings, was rising in vigor in due degree with the pressure put upon it.

"You are very good, sir, and I am very much obliged to you. I could have wished, however, that my mother had not given you this trouble, sir. She certainly must have been thinking of Mr. John Cross. She could scarcely have hoped that any good could have resulted to me, from the counsel of one who is so little older than myself."

This speech made our adventurer elevate his eyebrows. He absolutely stopped short to look upon the speaker. William Hinkley stopped short also. His eye encountered that of Stevens with an expression as full of defiance as firmness. His cheeks glowed with the generous indignation which filled his veins.

"This fellow has something in him after all," was the involuntary reflection that rose to the other's mind. The effect was, however, not very beneficial to his own manner. Instead of having the effect of impressing upon Stevens the necessity of working cautiously, the show of defiance which he saw tended to provoke and annoy him. The youth had displayed so much propriety in his anger, had been so moderate as well as firm, and had uttered his answer with so much dignity and correctness, that he felt himself rebuked. To be encountered by an unsophisticated boy, and foiled, though but for an instant—slightly estimated, though but by a youth, and him too, a mere rustic — was mortifying to the self-esteem that rather precipitately hurried to resent it."

"You take it seriously, Mr. Hinkley. But surely an

offer of service need not be mistaken. As for the trifling difference which may be in our years, that is perhaps nothing to the difference which may be in our experience, our knowledge of the world, our opportunities and studies."

" Surely, sir ; all these *may* be, but at all events we are not bound to assume their existence until it is shown."

" Oh, you are likely to prove an adept in the law, Mr. Hinkley."

" I trust, sir, that your progress may be as great in the church."

" Ha !—do I understand you ? There is war between us then ?" said Stevens, watching the animated and speaking countenance of William Hinkley with increasing curiosity.

" Ay, sir—there is !" was the spirited reply of the youth. " Let it be war ; I am the better pleased, sir, that you are the first to proclaim it."

" Very good," said Stevens, " be it so, if you will. At all events you can have no objection to say why it should be so."

" Do you ask, sir ?"

" Surely ; for I can not guess."

" You are less sagacious, then, than I had fancied you. You, scarce older than myself—a stranger among us— come to me in the language of a father, or a master, and without asking what I have of feeling, or what I lack of sense, undertake deliberately to wound the one, while insolently presuming to inform the other."

" At the request of your own mother !"

" Pshaw ! what man of sense or honesty would urge such a plea. Years, and long intimacy, and wisdom admitted to be superior, could alone justify the presumption."

The cheeks of Stevens became scalding hot.

" Young man !" he exclaimed, " there is something more than this !"

" What ! would it need more were our positions reversed ?"

demanded Hinkley with . promptness that surprised himself.

"Perhaps not! would you provoke me to personal violence?"

. "Ha! might I hope for that? surely you forget that you are a churchman?"

Stevens paused awhile before he answered. His eyes looked vacantly around him. By this time they had left the more thickly-settled parts of the village considerably behind them. But a few more dwellings lay along the path on which they were approaching. On the left, a gorge opened in the hills by which the valley was dotted, which seemed a pathway, and did indeed lead to one or more dwellings which were out of sight in the opposite valley. The region to which this pathway led was very secluded, and the eye of Stevens surveyed it for a few moments in silence. The words of Hinkley unquestionably conveyed a challenge. According to the practice of the country, *as a lawyer*, he would have been bound to have taken it as such. A moment was required for reflection. His former and present position caused a conflict in his mind. The last sentence of Hinkley, and a sudden glimpse which he just then caught of the residence of Margaret Cooper, determined his answer.

"I thank you, young man, for reminding me of my duties. You had nearly provoked the old passions and old practices into revival. I forgive you—you misunderstand me clearly. I know not how I have offended you, for my only purpose was to serve your mother and yourself. I may have done this unwisely. I will not attempt to prove that I have not. At all events, assured of my own motives, I leave you to yourself. You will probably ere long feel the injustice you have done me!"

He continued on his way, leaving William Hinkley almost rooted to the spot. The poor youth was actually stunned, not by what was said to him, but by the sudden consciousness of his own vehemence. He had expressed himself with a boldness and an energy of which neither himself nor his friend, until now, would have thought him capable. A moment's pause in the provocation, and the feelings which had goaded him on were taken with a revulsion quite as sudden. As he knew not well what he had said, so he fancied he had said everything precisely as the passionate thought had suggested it in his own mind. Already he began to blame himself—to feel that he had done wrong—that there had been nothing in the conduct or manner of Stevens, however unpleasant, to justify his own violence; and that the true secret of his anger was to be found in that instinctive hostility which he had felt for his rival from the first. The more he mused, the more he became humbled by his thoughts; and when he recollected the avowed profession of Stevens his shame increased. He felt how shocking it was to intimate to a sworn non-combatant the idea of a personal conflict. To what point of self-abasement his thoughts would have carried him, may only be conjectured; he might have hurried forward to overtake his antagonist with the distinct purpose of making the most ample apology; nay, more, such was the distinct thought which was now pressing upon his mind, when he was saved from this humiliation by perceiving that Stevens had already reached, and was about to enter the dwelling of Margaret Cooper. With this sight, every thought and feeling gave place to that of baffled love, and disappointed affection. With a bitter groan he turned up the gorge, and soon shut himself from sight of the now hateful habitation.

CHAPTER XII.

THE MASTER AND HIS PUPILS.

THE course of the young rustic was pursued for half a mile further till he came to a little cottage of which the eye could take no cognizance from any part of the village. It was embowelled in a glen of its own—a mere cup of the slightly-rising hills, and so encircled by foliage that it needed a very near approach of the stranger before he became aware of its existence. The structure was very small, a sort of square box with a cap upon it, and consisted of two rooms only on a ground floor, with a little lean-to or shed-room in the rear, intended for a kitchen. As you drew nigh and passed through the thick fringe of wood by which its approach was guarded, the space opened before you, and you found yourself in a sort of amphitheatre, of which the cottage was the centre. A few trees dotted this area, large and massive trees, and seemingly preserved for purposes of shade only. It was the quietest spot in the world, and inspired just that sort of feeling in the contemplative stranger which would be awakened by a ramble among the roofless ruins of the ancient abbey. It was a home for contemplation—in which one might easily forget the busy world without, and deliver himself up, without an effort, to the sweetly sad musings of the anchorite.

The place was occupied, however. A human heart beat within the humble shed, and there was a spirit, sheltered by its quiet, that mused many high thoughts, and dreamed in equal congratulation and self-reproach, of that busy world from which it was an exile. The visit of William Hinkley was not paid to the solitude. A venerable man, of large frame, and benignant aspect, sat beneath an aged tree, paternal in its appearance like himself. This person might be between fifty and sixty years of age. His hair, though very thick and vigorous, was as white as driven snow. But there were few wrinkles on his face, and his complexion was the clear red and white of a healthy and sanguine temperament. His brow was large and lofty. It had many more wrinkles than his face. There were two large horizontal seams upon it that denoted the exercise of a very busy thought. But the expression of his eye was that of the most unembarrassed benevolence and peace. It was subdued and sometimes sad, but then it had the sweetest, playfullest twinkle in the world. His mouth, which was small and beautifully formed, wore a similar expression. In short he was what we would call a hand-some old gentleman, whose appearance did not offend taste, and whose kind looks invited confidence. Nor would we mistake his character.

This person was the Mr. Calvert, the schoolmaster of the village, of whom Mrs. Hinkley spoke to Alfred Stevens in discussing the condition of her son. His tasks were over for the day. The light-hearted rabble whom he taught, released from his dominion which was not severe, were, by this time, scampering over the hills, as far from their usual place of restraint as the moderate strength of their legs could carry them. Though let loose, boys are not apt to feel their liberty in its prime and freshness, immediately in the neighborhood of the schoolhouse. The old gentleman left to himself, sat out in the open air, beneath a massive oak, the paternal stretching of whose venerable arms not unfrequently led to the employment of the shade below for carrying on the operations of the schoolhouse. There, squat on their haunches, the sturdy boys—germs of the finest peasantry in the world—surrounded their teacher in a group quite as pleasing as picturesque. The sway of the old man was paternal. His rod was rather a figurative than a real existence; and when driven to the use of the birch, the good man, consulting more tastes than one, employed the switch from the peach or some other odorous tree or shrub, in order to reconcile the lad, as well as he could, to the extraordinary application. He was one of those considerate persons, who disguise pills in gold-leaf, and if compelled, as a judge, to hang a gentleman, would decree that a rope of silk should carry out the painful requisitions of the laws.

Seated beneath his tree, in nearly the same spot and position in which he had dismissed his pupils, William Calvert pored over the pages of a volume as huge of size as it was musty of appearance. It was that pleasant book —quite as much romance as history—the "Knights of Malta," by our venerable father, Monsieur L'Abbe Vertot. Its dull, dim, yellow-looking pages—how yellow, dim, and dull-looking in comparison with more youthful works— had yet a life and soul which it is not easy to find in many of these latter. Its high wrought and elaborate pictures of strife, and toil, and bloodshed, grew vividly before the old man's eyes; and then, to help the illusion, were there not the portraits—mark me—the veritable portraits, engraved on copper, with all their titles, badges, and insignia, done to the life, of all those brave, grand, and famous masters of the order, by whom the deeds were enacted which he read, and who stared out upon his eyes, at every epoch, in full confirmation of the veracious narrative? No wonder that the old man became heedless of external objects. No wonder he forgot the noise of the retiring urchins, and the toils of the day, as, for the twentieth time, he glowed in the brave recital of the famous siege —the baffled fury of the Turk—the unshaken constancy and unremitted valor of the few but fearless defenders. The blood in his cheek might be seen hastening to and fro in accordance with the events of which he read. His eye was glowing—his pulse beating, and he half started from his seat, as, hearing a slight footstep, he turned to encounter the respectful homage of his former pupil, still his friend, our young acquaintance, William Hinkley.

The old man laid down his book upon the grass, extended his hand to his visiter, and leaning back against the tree, surrendered himself to a quiet chuckle in which there was the hesitancy of a little shame.

"You surprised me, William," he said; "when I read old Vertot, and such books, I feel myself a boy again. You must have seen my emotion. I really had got so warm, that I was about to start up and look for the weapons of war; and had you but come a moment later, you might have suffered an assault. As it was, I took you for a Turk—Solyman himself—and was beginning to ask myself whether I should attack you tooth and nail, having no other weapons, or propose terms of peace. Considering the severe losses which you—I mean his Turkish highness —had sustained, I fancied that you would not be disinclined to an arrangement just at this moment. But this very notion, at the same time, led me to the conclusion that I might end the struggle for ever by another blow. A moment later, my boy, and you might have been compelled to endure it for the Turk."

The youth smiled sadly as he replied: "I must borrow that book from you, sir, some of these days. I have often thought to do so, but I am afraid."

"Afraid of what, William?"

"That it will turn my head, sir, and make me dislike more difficult studies."

"It is a reasonable fear, my son; but there is no danger of this sort, if we will only take heed of one rule, and that is, to take such books as we take sweetmeats—in very small quantities at a time, and never to interfere with the main repast. I suspect that light reading—or reading which we usually call light, but which, as it concerns the fate of man in his most serious relations, his hopes, his affections, his heart, nay, his very people and nation—is scarcely less important than any other. I suspect that this sort of reading would be of great service to the student, by relieving the solemnity of more tedious and exacting studies, if taken sparingly and at allotted hours. The student usually finds a recreation of some kind. I would make books of this description his recreation. Many a thick-headed and sour parent has forced his son into a beer-shop, into the tastes for tobacco and consequently brandy, simply from denying him amusements which equally warm the blood and elevate the imagination. Studies which merely inform the head are very apt to endanger the heart. This is the reproach usually urged against the class of persons whom we call thorough lawyers. Their intense devotion to that narrow sphere of law which leaves out jury-pleading, is very apt to endanger the existence of feeling and imagination. The mere analysis of external principles begets a degree of moral indifference to all things else, which really impairs the intellect by depriving it of its highest sources of stimulus. Mathematicians suffer in the same way—become mere machines, and forfeit, in their concern for figures, all the social and most of the human characteristics. The mind is always enfeebled by any pursuit so single and absorbing in its aims as to leave out of exercise any of the moral faculties. That course of study is the only one to make a truly great man, which compels the mind to do all things of which it is capable."

"But how do you reconcile this, sir, with the opinion, so generally entertained, that no one man can serve two masters? Law, like the muse, is a jealous mistress. She is said to suffer no *lachesse* to escape with impunity."

"You mistake me. While I counsel one to go out of his profession for relief and recreation, I still counsel but the one pursuit. Men fail in their professions, not because they daily assign an hour to amusement, but because they halt in a perpetual struggle between some two leading objects. For example, nothing is more frequent in our country than to combine law and politics. Nothing is more apt to ruin the lawyer."

"Very true, sir. I now understand you. But I should think the great difficulty would be, in resorting to such pleasant books as this of Vertot for relief and recreation, that you could not cast him off when you please. The intoxication would continue even after the draught has been swallowed, and would thus interfere with the hours devoted to other employments."

"There is reason in that, William, and that, indeed, is the grand difficulty. But to show that a good scheme has its difficulties is not an argument for abandoning it."

"By no means, sir."

"The same individual whom Vertot might intoxicate, would most probably be intoxicated by more dangerous stimulants. Everything, however, depends upon the habits of self-control which a man has acquired in his boyhood. The habit of self-control is the only habit which makes mental power truly effective. The man who can not compel himself to do or to forbear, can never be much of a student. Students, if you observe, are generally dogged men —inflexible, plodding, persevering—among lawyers, those men whom you always find at their offices, and seldom see anywhere else. They own that mental habit which we call self-control, which supplies the deficiency in numerous instances of real talent. It is a power, and a mighty power, particularly in this country, where children are seldom taught it, and consequently grow up to be a sort of moral vanes that move with every change of wind, and never fix until they do so with their own rust. He who learns this power in boyhood will be very sure to master all his com anions."

The darker expression of sadness passed over the countenance of the ingenuous youth.

" I am afraid," said he, " that I shall never acquire this habit."

" Why so ?   In your very fear I see a hope."

" Alas! sir, I feel my own instability of character.   I feel myself the victim of a thousand plans and purposes, which change as soon and as often as they are made.   I am afraid, sir, I shall be nothing!"

" Do not despond, my son," said the old man sympathizingly.   " Your fear is natural to your age and temperament.   Most young men at your time of life feel numerous yearnings — the struggle of various qualities of mind, each striving in newly-born activity, and striving adversely. Your unhappiness arises from the refusal of these qualities to act together.   When they learn to co-operate, all will be easy.   Your strifes will be subdued; there will be a calm like that upon the sea when the storms subside."

" Ah! but when will that be ?   A long time yet.   It seems to me that the storm rather increases than subsides."

" It may seem so to you now, and yet, when the strife is greatest, the favorable change is at hand.   It needs but one thing to make all the conflicting qualities of one's mind cc-operate."

" What is that one thing, sir ?"

" An object!   As yet, you have none."

" None, sir!"

" None — or rather many — which is pretty much the same thing as having none."

" I am not sure, sir — but it seems to me, sir, that I have an object."

" Indeed, William! are you sure ?"

" I think so, sir."

" Well, name it."

"I have ambition, sir."

"Ah! that is a passion, not an object. Does your ambition point in one direction? Unless it does, it is objectless."

The youth was silent. The old man proceeded:—

"I am disposed to be severe with you, my son. There is no surer sign of feebleness than in the constant beginnings and the never performings of a mind. Know thyself, is the first lesson to learn. Is it not very childish to talk of having ambition, without knowing what to do with it? If we have ambition, it is given to us to work with. You come to me, and declare this ambition! We confer together. Your ambition seeks for utterance. You ask, 'What sort of utterance will suit an ambition such as mine?' To answer this question, we ask, 'What are your qualities?' Did you think, William, that I disparaged yours when I recommended the law to you as a profession?"

"No, sir! oh, no! Perhaps you overrated them. I am afraid so —I think so."

"No, William, unfortunately, you do not think about it. If you would suffer yourself to think, you would speak a different language."

"I can not think—I am too miserable to think!" exclaimed the youth in a burst of passion. The old man looked surprised. He gazed with a serious anxiety into the youth's face, and then addressed him:—

"Where have you been, William, for the last three weeks? In all that time I have not seen you."

A warm blush suffused the cheeks of the pupil. He did not immediately answer.

"Ask *me!*" exclaimed a voice from behind them, which they both instantly recognised as that of Ned Hinkley, the cousin of William. He had approached them, in the earnestness of their interview, without having disturbed them. The bold youth was habited in a rough woodman's dress. He wore a round jacket of homespun, and in his hand he

7

carried a couple of fishing-rods, which, with certain other implements, betrayed sufficiently the object of his present pursuit.

" Ask me !" said he. " I can tell you what he's been about better than anybody else."

" Well, Ned," said the old man, " what has it been ? I am afraid it is your fiddle that keeps him from his Blackstone."

" My fiddle, indeed ! If he would listen to my fiddle when she speaks out, he'd be wiser and better for it. Look at him, Mr. Calvert, and say whether it's book or fiddle that's likely to make him as lean as a March pickerel in the short space of three months. Only look at him, I say."

" Truly, William, I had not observed it before, but, as Ned says, you do look thin, and you tell me you are unhappy. Hard study might make you thin, but can not make you unhappy. What is it ?"

The more volatile and freespoken cousin answered for him.

" He's been shot, gran'pa, since you saw him last."

" Shot ?"

" Yes, shot !— *He thinks* mortally. I think not. A flesh wound to my thinking, that a few months more will cure."

" You have some joke at bottom, Edward," said the old man gravely.

" Joke, sir ! It's a tough joke that cudgels a plump lad into a lean one in a single season."

" What do you mean ?"

" I mean to use your own language, gran'pa. Among the lessons I got from you when you undertook to fill our heads with wisdom by applications of smartness to a very different place — among the books we sometimes read from was one of Master Ovid."

" Ha ! ha ! I see what you're after. I understand the shooting. So you think that the blind boy has hit William, eh ?"

" A flesh wound as I tell you ; but he thinks the bolt is

in his heart. I'm sure it can and will be plucked out, and no death will follow."

" Well! who's the maiden from whose eyes the arrow was barbed ?"

" Margaret Cooper."

" Ah! indeed!" said the old man gravely.

" Do not heed him," exclaimed William Hinkley; but the blush upon his cheeks, still increasing, spoke a different language.

" I would rather not heed him, William. The passions of persons so young as yourself are seldom of a permanent character. The attractions which win the boy seldom compensate the man. There is time enough for this, ten years hence, and love then will be far more rational."

" Ah, lud!—wait ten years at twenty. I can believe a great deal in the doctrine of young men's folly, but I can't go that. I'm in love myself."

" You!"

" Yes! I!—I'm hit too—and if you don't like it, why did you teach us Ovid and the rest? As for rational love, that's a new sort of thing that we never heard about before. Love was never expected to be rational. He's known the contrary. I've heard so ever since I was knee-high to the great picture of your Cupid that you showed us in your famous Dutch edition of Apuleius. The young unmarried men feel that it's irrational; the old married people tell us so in a grunt that proves the truth of what they say. But that don't alter the case. It's a sort of natural madness that makes one attack in every person's lifetime. I don't believe in repeated attacks. Some are bit worse than others; and some think themselves bit, and are mistaken. That's the case with William, and it's that that keeps him from your law-books and my fiddle. That makes him thin. He has a notion of Margaret Cooper, and she has none of him; and love that's all of one side is neither real nor rational. I don't believe it."

William Hinkley muttered something angrily in the ears of the speaker.

"Well, well!" said the impetuous cousin, "I don't want to make you vexed, and still less do I come here to talk such politics with you. What do you say to tickling a trout this afternoon? That's what I come for."

"It's too cool," said the old man.

"Not a bit. There's a wind from the south, and a cast of cloud is constantly growing between us and the sun. I think we shall do something—something better than talking about love, and law, where nobody's agreed. You, gran'pa, won't take the love; Bill Hinkley can't stomach the law, and the trout alone can bring about a reconciliation. Come, gran'pa, I'm resolved on getting your supper to-night, and you must go and see me do it."

"On one condition only, Ned."

"What's that, gran'pa?"

"That you both sup with me."

"Done for myself. What say you, Bill?"

The youth gave a sad assent, and the rattling youth proceeded:—

"The best cure of grief is eating. Love is a sort of pleasant grief. Many a case of affliction have I seen mended by a beefsteak. Fish is better. Get a lover to eat, rouse up his appetites, and, to the same extent, you lessen his affections. Hot suppers keep down the sensibilities; and, gran'pa, after ours, to-night, you shall have the fiddle. If I don't make her speak to you to-night, my name's Brag, and you need never again believe me."

And the good-humored youth, gathering up his canes, led the way to the hills, slowly followed by his two less elastic companions.

CHAPTER XIII.

THE HISTORY OF A FAILURE.

THE route, which conducted them over a range of gently-ascending hills, through groves tolerably thick, an uncleared woodland tract comprising every variety of pleasant foliage, at length brought them to a lonely tarn or lake, about a mile in circumference, nestled and crouching in the hollow of the hills, which, in some places sloped gently down to its margin, at others hung abruptly over its deep and pensive waters. A thick fringe of shrubs, water-grasses, and wild flowers, girdled its edges, and gave a dark and mysterious expression to its face. There were many beaten tracks, narrow paths for individual wayfarers on foot, which conducted down to favorite fishing-spots. These were found chiefly on those sides of the lake where the rocks were precipitous. Perched on a jutting eminence, and half shrouded in the bushes which clothed it, the silent fisherman took his place, while his fly was made to kiss the water in capricious evolutions, such as the experienced angler knows how to employ to beguile the wary victim from close cove, or gloomy hollow, or from beneath those decaying trunks of overthrown trees which have given his brood a shelter from immemorial time.

To one of these selected spots, Ned Hinkley proceeded, leaving his companions above, where, in shade themselves, and lying at ease upon the smooth turf, they could watch his successes, and at the same time enjoy the *coup d'œil*,

which was singularly beautiful, afforded by the whole surrounding expanse. The tarn, like the dark mysterious
dwelling of an Undine, was spread out before them with the
smoothness of glass, though untransparent, and shining beneath their eyes like a vast basin of the richest jet. A
thousand pretty changes along the upland slopes, or abrupt
hills which hemmed it in, gave it a singular aspect of variety which is seldom afforded by any scene very remarkable
for its stillness and seclusion. Opposite to the rock on
which Ned Hinkley was already crouching, the hill-slope to
the lake was singularly unbroken, and so gradual was the
ascent from the margin, that one was scarcely conscious of
his upward movement, until looking behind him, he saw how
far below lay the waters which he had lately left.

The pathway, which had been often trodden, was very
distinctly marked to the eyes of our two friends on the opposite elevation, and they could also perceive where the
same footpath extended on either hand a few yards from
the lake, so as to enable the wanderer to prolong his rambles, on either side, until reaching the foot of the abrupt
masses of rock which distinguished the opposite margin of
the basin. To ascend these, on that side, was a work of
toil, which none but the lover of the picturesque is often
found willing to encounter. Above, even to the eyes of our
friends, though they occupied an eminence, the skies seemed
circumscribed to the circumference of the lake and the hills
by which it was surrounded; and the appearance of the
whole region, therefore, was that of a complete amphitheatre, the lake being the floor, the hills the mighty pillars,
and the roof, the blue, bright, fretted canopy of heaven.

"I have missed you, my son, for some time past, and the
beauty of the picture reminds me of what your seeming neglect has made me lose. When I was a young man I would
have preferred to visit such a spot as this alone. But the
sense of desolation presses heavily upon an old man under
any circumstances; and he seeks for the company of the

young, as if to freshen, with sympathy and memory, the cheerlessness and decay which attends all his own thoughts and fancies. To come alone into the woods, even though the scene I look on be as fair as this, makes me moody and awakens gloomy imaginations ; and since you have been so long absent, I have taken to my books again, and given up the woods. Ah ! books, alone, never desert us ; never prove unfaithful ; never chide us ; never mock us, as even these woods do, with the memory of baffled hopes, and dreams of youth, gone, never to return again.

"I trust, my dear sir, you do not think me ungrateful. I have not wilfully neglected you. More than once I set out to visit you ; but my heart was so full — I was so very unhappy — that I had not the spirit for it. I felt that I should not be any company for you, and feared that I would only affect you with some of my own dullness."

"Nay, that should be no fear with you, my dear boy, for you should know that the very sorrows of youth, as they awaken the sympathies of age, provide it with the means of excitement. It is the misfortune of age that its interest is slow to kindle. Whatever excites the pulse, if not violently, is beneficial to the heart of the old man. But these sorrows of yours, my son — do you not call them by too strong a name ? I suspect they are nothing more than the discontents, the vague yearnings of the young and ardent nature, such as prompt enterprise and lead to nobleness. If you had them not, you would think of little else than how to squat with your cousin there, seeking to entrap your dinner ; nay, not so much — you would think only of the modes of cooking and the delight of eating the fish, and shrink from the toil of taking it. Do not deceive yourself. This sorrow which distresses you is possibly a beneficial sorrow. It is the hope which is in you to be something — to *do* something — for this *doing* is after all, and before all, the great object of living. The hope of the heart is always a discontent — most generally a wholesome discontent —

sometimes a noble discontent leading to nobleness. It is to be satisfied rather than nursed. You must do what it requires."

" I know not what it requires."

" Your *doing* then must be confined at present to finding out what that is."

" Alas! sir, it seems to me as if I could no more *think* than I can *do*."

" Very likely; — that is the case at present; and there are several reasons for this feebleness. The energies which have not yet been tasked, do not know well how to begin. You have been a favored boy. Your wants have been well provided for. Your parents have loved you only too much."

" Too much! Why, even now, I am met with cold looks and reproachful words, on account of this stranger, of whom nobody knows anything."

" Even so: suppose that to be the case, my son; still it does not alter the truth of what I say. You can not imagine that your parents prefer this stranger to yourself, unless you imagine them to have undergone a very sudden change of character. They have always treated you tenderly — too tenderly."

" Too tenderly, sir ?"

" Yes, William, too tenderly. Their tenderness has enfeebled you, and that is the reason you know not in what way to begin to dissipate your doubts, and apply your energies. If they reproach you, that is because they have some interest in you, and a right in you, which constitutes their interest. If they treat the stranger civilly, it is because he is a stranger."

" Ay, sir, but what if they give this stranger authority to question and to counsel me? Is not this a cruel indignity ?"

" Softly, William, softly! There is something at the bottom of this which I do not see, and which perhaps you do not see. If your parents employ a stranger to counsel you, it proves that something in your conduct leads them to think that you need counsel."

"That may be, sir; but why not give it themselves? why employ a person of whom nobody knows anything?"

"I infer from your tone, my son, rather than your words, that you have some dislike to this stranger.

"No, sir——" was the beginning of the young man's reply, but he stopped short with a guilty consciousness. A warm blush overspread his cheek, and he remained silent. The old man, without seeming to perceive the momentary interruption, or the confusion which followed it, proceeded in his commentary.

"There should be nothing, surely, to anger you in good counsel, spoken even by a stranger, my son; and even where the counsel be not good, if the motive be so, it requires our gratitude though it may not receive our adoption."

"I don't know, sir, but it seems to me very strange, and is very humiliating, that I should be required to submit to the instructions of one of whom we know nothing, and who is scarcely older than myself."

"It may be mortifying to your self-esteem, my son, but self-esteem, when too active, is compelled constantly to suffer this sort of mortification. It may be that one man shall not be older in actual years than another, yet be able to teach that other. Merely living, days and weeks and months, constitutes no right to wisdom; it is the crowding events and experience — the indefatigable industry — the living actively and well — that supply us with the materials for knowing and teaching. In comparison with millions of your own age, who have lived among men, and shared in their strifes and troubles, you would find yourself as feeble a child as ever yet needed the helping hand of counsel and guardianship; and this brings me back to what I said before. Your parents have treated you too tenderly.

They have done everything for you. You have done nothing for yourself. They provide for your wants, hearken to your complaints, nurture you in sickness, with a diseasing fondness, and so render you incapable. Hence it is, that, in the toils of manhood, you do not know how to begin. You lack courage and perseverance."

" Courage and perseverance!" was the surprised exclamation of the youth.

" Precisely, and lest I should offend you, my son, I must acknowledge to you beforehand, that this very deficiency was my own."

" Yours, sir? I can not think it. What! lack courage?"

" Exactly so!"

" Why, sir — did I not see you myself, when everybody else looked on with trembling and with terror, throw yourself in the way of Drummond's horses and save the poor boy from being dashed to pieces? There was surely no lack of courage there!"

" No! in that sense, my son, I labor under no deficiency. But this sort of courage is of the meanest kind. It is the courage of impulse, not of steadfastness. Hear me, William. You have more than once allowed the expression of a wonder to escape you, why a man, having such a passion for books and study, and with the appearance of mental resources, such as I am supposed to possess, should be content, retiring from the great city, to set up his habitation in this remote and obscure region. My chosen profession was the law; I was no unfaithful student. True, I had no parents to lament my wanderings and failures; but I did not wander. I studied closely, with a degree of diligence which seemed to surprise all my companions. I was ambitious — intensely ambitious. My head ran upon the strifes of the forum, its exciting contests of mind and soul — its troubles, its triumphs. This was my leading thought — it was my only passion. The boy-frenzies for women, which are prompted less by sentiment or judgment, than by feverish blood, troubled me little. Law was my mistress — took up all my time — absorbed all my devotion. I believe that I was a good lawyer — no pettifogger — the merely drilled creature who toils for his license, and toils for ever after solely for his petty gains, in the miserably petty arts of making gains for others, and eluding the snares set for his own feet by kindred spirits. As far as the teaching of this country could afford me the means and opportunity, I endeavored to procure a knowledge of universal law — its sources — its true objects — its just principles — its legitimate dicta. Mere authorities never satisfied me, unless, passing behind the black gowns, I could follow up the reasoning to the first fountains — the small original truths, the nicely discriminated requisitions of immutable justice — the clearly-defined and inevitable wants of a superior and prosperous society. Everything that could illustrate law as well as fortify it; every collateral aid, in the shape of history or moral truth, I gathered together, even as the dragoon whose chief agent is his sabre, yet takes care to provide himself with pistols, that may finish what the other weapon has begun. Nor did I content myself with the mere acquisition of the necessary knowledge. Knowing how much depends upon voice, manner and fluency, in obtaining success before a jury, I addressed myself to these particulars with equal industry. My voice, even now, has a compass which your unexercised lungs, though quite as good originally as mine, would fail entirely to contend with. I do not deceive myself, as I certainly do not seek to deceive you, when I say, that I acquired the happiest mastery over my person."

"Ah! sir — we see that now — that must have been the case!" said the youth interrupting him. The other continued, sadly smiling as he heard the eulogy which the youth meant to speak, the utterance of which was obviously from the heart.

"My voice was taught by various exercises to be slow

or rapid, soft or strong, harsh or musical, by the most sudden, yet unnoticeable transitions. I practised all the arts, which are recommended by elocutionists for this purpose, I rumbled my eloquence standing on the seashore, up to my middle in the breakers. I ran, roaring up steep hills —I stretched myself at length by the side of meandering brooks, or in slumberous forests of pine, and sought, by the merest whispers, to express myself with distinctness and melody. But there was something yet more requisite than these, and this was language. My labors to obtain all the arts of utterance did not seem less successful. I could dilate with singular fluency, with classical propriety, and great natural vigor of expression. I studied directness of expression by a frequent intercourse with men of business, and examined, with the nicest urgency, the particular characteristics of those of my own profession who were most remarkable for their plain, forcible speaking. I say nothing of my studies of such great masters in discourse and philosophy, as Milton, Shakspere, Homer, Lord Bacon, and the great English divines. As a model of pure English the Bible was a daily study of two hours; and from this noble well of vernacular eloquence, I gathered — so I fancied—no small portion of its quaint expressive vigor, its stern emphasis, its golden and choice phrases of illustration. Never did a young lawyer go into the forum more thoroughly clad in proof, or with a better armory as well for defence as attack."

"You did not fail, sir?" exclaimed the youth with a painful expression of eager anxiety upon his countenance.

"I did fail—fail altogether! In the first effort to speak, I fainted, and was carried lifeless from the court-room."

The old man covered his face with his hands, for a few moments, to conceal the expression of pain and mortification which memory continued to renew in utter despite of time. The young man's hand rested affectionately on his shoulder. A few moments sufficed to enable the former to renew his narrative.

"I was stunned but not crushed by this event. I knew my own resources. I recollected a similar anecdote of Sheridan; of his first attempt and wretched failure. I, too, felt that 'I had it in me,' and though I did not express, I made the same resolution, that 'I would bring it out.' But Sheridan and myself failed from different causes, though I did not understand this at that time. He had a degree of hardihood which I had not; and he utterly lacked my sensibilities. The very intenseness of my ambition; the extent of my expectation; the elevated estimate which I had made of my own profession; of its exactions; and, again, of what was expected from me; were all so many obstacles to my success. I did not so esteem them, then; and after renewing my studies in private, my exercises of expression and manner, and going through a harder course of drilling, I repeated the attempt to suffer a repetition of the failure. I did not again faint, but I was speechless. I not only lost the power of utterance, but I lost the corresponding faculty of sight. My eyes were completely dazed and confounded. The objects of sight around me were as crowded and confused as the far, dim ranges of figures, tribes upon tribes, and legions upon legions, which struggle in obscurity and distance, in any one of the begrimed and blurred pictures of Martin's Pandemonium. My second failure was a more enfeebling disaster than the first. The first procured me the sympathy of my audience, the last exposed me to its ridicule."

Again the old man paused. By this time, the youth had got one of his arms about the neck of the speaker, and had taken one of his hands within his grasp.

"Yours is a generous nature, William," said Mr. Calvert, "and I have not said to you, until to-day, how grateful your boyish sympathies have been to me from the first day when you became my pupil. It is my knowledge of these sympathies, and a desire to reward them, that prompts me to tell a story which still brings its pains to memory, and which would be given to no other ears than your own. I see that you are eager for the rest—for the wretched sequel."

"Oh, no! sir—do not tell me any more of it if it brings you pain. I confess I should like to know all, but—"

"You shall have it all, my son. My purpose would not be answered unless I finished the narrative. You will gather from it, very possibly, the moral which I could not. You will comprehend something better, the woful distinction between courage of the blood and courage of the brain; between the mere recklessness of brute impulse, and the steady valor of the soul—that valor, which, though it trembles, marches forward to the attack—recovers from its fainting, to retrieve its defeat; and glows with self-indignation because it has suffered the moment of victory to pass, without employing itself to secure the boon!—

"Shame, and a natural desire to retrieve myself, operated to make me renew my efforts. I need not go through the processes by which I endeavored to acquire the necessary degree of hardihood. In vain did I recall the fact that my competitors were notoriously persons far inferior to me in knowledge of the topics; far inferior in the capacity to analyze them; rude and coarse in expression; unfamiliar with the language—mere delvers and diggers in a science in which I secretly felt that I should be a master. In vain did I recall to mind the fact that I knew the community before which I was likely to speak; I knew its deficiencies; knew the inferiority of its idols, and could and should have no sort of fear of its criticism. But it was myself that I feared. I had mistaken the true censor. It was my own standards of judgment that distressed and made me tremble. It was what I expected of myself—what I thought should be expected of me—that made my weak soul recoil in terror from the conviction that I must fail in its endeavor to reach the point which my ambitious soul strove to attain. The fear, in such cases, produced the very disaster, from the anticipated dread of which it had arisen. I again failed — failed egregiously — failed utterly and for ever! I never again attempted the fearful trial. I gave up the contest, yielded the field to my inferiors, better-nerved, though inferior, and, with all my learning, all my eloquence, my voice, my manner; my resources of study, thought, and utterance, fled from sight — fled here — to bury myself in the wilderness, and descend to the less ambitious, but less dangerous vocation of schooling — I trust, to better uses — the minds of others. I had done nothing with my own."

" Oh, sir, do not say so. Though you may have failed in one department of human performance, you have succeeded in others. You have lost none of the knowledge which you then acquired. You possess all the gifts of eloquence, of manner, of voice, of education, of thought."

" But of what use, my son? Remember, we do not toil for these possessions to lock them up — to content ourselves, as the miserable miser, with the consciousness that we possess a treasure known to ourselves only — useless to all others as to ourselves! Learning, like love, like money, derives its true value from its circulation."

" And you circulate yours, my dear sir. What do we not owe you in Charlemont? What do I not owe you, over all ?"

" Love, my son — love only. Pay me that. Do not desert me in my old age. Do not leave me utterly alone !"

" I will not, sir — I never thought to do so."

" But," said the old man, " to resume. Why did I fail is still the question. Because I had not been taught those lessons of steady endurance in my youth which would have strengthened me against failure, and enable me finally to triumph. There is a rich significance in what we hear

of the Spartan boy, who never betrayed his uneasiness or
agony though the fox was tearing out his bowels. There
is a sort of moral roughening which boys should be made
to endure from the beginning, if the hope is ever entertained, to mature their minds to intellectual manhood. Our
American Indians prescribe the same laws, and in their
practice, very much resemble the ancient Spartans. To
bear fatigue, and starvation, and injury—exposure, wet,
privation, blows—but never to complain. Nothing betrays
so decidedly the lack of moral courage as the voice of
complaint. It is properly the language of woman. It
must not be your language. Do you understand me, William?"

"In part, sir, but I do not see how I could have helped
being what I am."

"Perhaps not, because few have control of their own
education. Your parents have been too tender of you.
They have not lessoned you in that proper hardihood which
leads to performance. That task is before yourself, and
you have shrunk from the first lessons."

"How, sir?"

"Instead of clinging to your Blackstone, you have allowed yourself to be seduced from its pages, by such attractions as usually delude boys. The eye and lip of a pretty
woman—a bright eye and a rosy cheek, have diverted you
from your duties."

"But do our duties deny us the indulgence of proper
sensibilities?"

"Certainly not—*proper* sensibilities, on the contrary,
prescribe our duties."

"But love, sir—is not love a proper sensibility?"

"In its place, it is. But you are a boy only. Do you
suppose that it was ever intended that you should entertain this passion before you had learned the art of providing your own food? Not so; and the proof of this is to
be found in the fact that the loves of boyhood are never of

a permanent character. No such passion can promote happiness if it is indulged before the character of the parties is formed. I now tell you that in five years from this time you will probably forget Miss Cooper."

"Never! never!"

"Well, well—I go farther in my prophecy. Allow me to suppose you successful in your suit, which I fancy can never be the case——"

"Why, sir, why?"

"Because she is not the girl for you; or rather, she does not think you the man for her!"

"But why do you think so, sir?"

"Because I know you both. There are circumstances of discrepancy between you which will prevent it, and even were you to be successful in your suit, which I am very sure will never be the case, you would be the most miserably-matched couple under the sun."

"Oh, sir, do not say so—do not. I can not think so, sir."

"You *will* not think so, I am certain. I am equally certain from what I know of you both, that you are secure from any such danger. It is not my object to pursue this reference, but let me ask you, William, looking at things in the most favorable light, has Margaret Cooper ever given you any encouragement?"

"I can not say that she has, sir, but——"

"Nay, has she not positively discouraged you? Does she not avoid you—treat you coldly when you meet—say little, and that little of a kind to denote—I will not say dislike—but pride, rather than love?"

The young man said nothing. The old one proceeded:—

"You are silent, and I am answered. I have long watched your intercourse with this damsel, and loving you as my own son, I have watched it with pain. She is not for you, William. She loves you not. I am sure of it. I can not mistake the signs. She seeks other qualities than such as you possess. She seeks meretricious qualities, and yours are substantial. She seeks the pomps of mind, rather than its subdued performances. She sees not, and can not see, your worth ; and whenever you propose to her, your suit will be rejected. You have not done so yet ?"

" No, sir — but I had hoped——"

" I am no enemy, believe me, William, when I implore you to discard your hope in that quarter. It will do you no hurt. Your heart will suffer no detriment, but be as whole and vigorous a few years hence — perhaps months — as if it had never suffered any disappointment."

" I wish I could think so, sir."

" And you would not wish that you could think so, if you were not already persuaded that your first wish is hopeless."

" But I am not hopeless, sir."

" Your cause is. But, promise me that you will not press your suit at present."

The young man was silent.

" You hesitate."

" I dare not promise."

" Ah, you are a foolish boy. Do you not see the rock on which you are about to split. You have never learned how to submit. This lesson of submission was that which made the Spartan boy famous. Here, you persist in your purpose, though your own secret convictions, as well as your friend's counsel, tell you that you strive against hope. You could not patiently submit to the counsel of this stranger, though he came directly from your parents, armed with authority to examine and to counsel."

" Submit to him ! I would sooner perish !" exclaimed the indignant youth.

" You will perish unless you learn this one lesson. But where now is your ambition, and what does it aim at ?"

The youth was silent.

" The idea of an ambitious youth, at twenty, giving up

book and candle, leaving his studies, and abandoning himself to despair, because his sweetheart won't be his sweetheart any longer, gives us a very queer idea of the sort of ambition which works in his breast."

"Don't, sir, don't, I pray you, speak any more in this manner."

"Nay, but, William, ask yourself. Is it not a queer idea?"

"Spare me, sir, if you love me."

"I do love you, and to show you that I do, I now recommend to you to propose to Margaret Cooper."

"What, sir, you do not think it utterly hopeless then?"

"Yes, I do."

"And you would have me expose myself to rejection?"

"Exactly so!"

"Really, sir, I do not understand you."

"Well, I will explain. Nothing short of rejection will possibly cure you of this malady; and it is of the last importance to your future career, that you should be freed as soon as possible from this sickly condition of thought and feeling — a condition in which your mind will do nothing, and in which your best days will be wasted. Blackstone can only hope to be taken up when you have done with her."

"Stay, sir — that is she below."

"Who?"

"Margaret——"

"Who is with her?"

"The stranger — this man, Stevens."

"Ha! your counsellor, that would be? Ah! William, you did not tell me all."

CHAPTER XIV.

THE ENTHUSIAST.

THE cheeks of the youth glowed. He felt how much he had suppressed in his conference with his venerable counsellor. Mr. Calvert did not press the topic, and the two remained silent, looking down, from the shaded spot where they lay, upon the progress of Margaret Cooper and her present attendant, Stevens. The eminence on which they rested was sufficiently lofty, as we have seen, to enable them, though themselves almost concealed from sight, to take in the entire scene, not only below but around them; and the old man, sharing now in the interest of his young companion, surveyed the progress of the new-comers with a keen sense of curiosity which, for a time, kept him silent. The emotions of William Hinkley were such as to deprive him of all desire for speech; and each, accordingly, found sufficient employment in brooding over his own awakened fancies. Even had they spoken in the ordinary tone of their voices, the sounds could not have reached the persons approaching on the opposite side. They drew nigh, evidently unconscious that the scene was occupied by any other than themselves. Ned Hinkley was half-shrouded in the shrubbery that environed the jutting crag upon which his form was crouched, and they were not yet sufficiently nigh to the tarn to perceive his projecting rod, and the gaudy fly which he kept skipping about upon the surface. The walk which they pursued was an ancient Indian footpath, which had without doubt conducted the red warriors, a thousand times before, to a spot of seclusion and refreshment after their long day's conflict on the "*dark and bloody ground.*" It was narrow and very winding, and had been made so in order to lessen the fatigue of an ascent which, though gradual enough, was yet considerable, and would have produced great weariness, finally, had the pathway been more direct.

The circuitousness of this route, which lay clear enough before the eyes of our two friends upon the eminence — crawling, as it did, up the woodland slopes with the sinuous course of a serpent — was yet visible to Ned Hinkley, on his lowlier perch, only at its starting-point, upon the very margin of the lake. He, accordingly, saw as little of the approaching persons as they had seen of him. They advanced slowly, and seemed to be mutually interested in their subject of conversation. The action of Stevens was animated. The air and attitude of Margaret Cooper was that of interest and attention. It was with something little short of agony that William Hinkley beheld them pause upon occasion, and confront each other as if the topic was of a nature to arrest the feet and demand the whole fixed attention of the hearer.

It will be conjectured that Alfred Stevens had pressed his opportunities with no little industry. Enough has been shown to account for the readiness of that reception which Margaret Cooper was prepared to give him. Her intelligence was keen, quick, and penetrating. She discovered at a glance, not his hypocrisy, but that his religious enthusiasm was not of a sort to become very tyrannical. The air of mischief which was expressed upon his face when the venerable John Cross proposed to purge her library of its obnoxious contents, commended him to her as a sort of ally; and the sympathy with herself, which such a conjecture promised, made her forgetful of the disingenuousness of his conduct if her suspicions were true. But there were some other particulars which, in her mind, tended to dissipate the distance between them. She recognised the individual. She remembered the bold, dashing youth, who, a few months before, had encountered her on the edge of the village, and, after they had parted, had ridden back to the spot where she still loitered, for a second look. To that very spot had she conducted him on their ramble that afternoon.

"Do you know this place, Mr. Stevens?" she demanded with an arch smile, sufficiently good-humored to convince the adventurer that, if she had any suspicions, they were not of a nature to endanger his hopes.

"Do I not!" he said, with an air of *empressement* which caused her to look down.

"I thought I recollected you," she said, a moment after.

"Ah! may I hope that I did not then offend you with my impertinence? But the truth is, I was so struck—pardon me if I say it—with the singular and striking difference between the group of damsels I had seen and *the one* —the surprise was so great—the pleasure so unlooked for—that—"

The eye of Margaret Cooper brightened, her cheek glowed, and her form rose somewhat proudly. The arch-hypocrite paused judiciously, and she spoke:—

"Nay, nay, Mr. Stevens, these fine speeches do not pass current. You would make the same upon occasion to any one of the said group of damsels, were you to be her escort."

"But I would scarcely ride back for a second look," he responded, in a subdued tone of voice, while looking with sad expressiveness into her eyes. These were cast down upon the instant, and the color upon her cheeks was heightened.

"Come," said she, making an effort, "there is nothing nere to interest us."

"Except memory," he replied ; "I shall never forget the spot."

She hurried forward, and he joined her. She had received the impression which he intended to convey, without declaring as much—namely, that his return to Charlemont had been prompted by that one glimpse which he had then had of her person. Still, that nothing should be left in doubt, he proceeded to confirm the impression by other suggestions :—

"You promise to show me a scene of strange beauty, but your whole village is beautiful, Miss Cooper. I remember how forcibly it struck me as I gained the ascent of the opposite hills coming in from the east. It was late in the day, the sun was almost setting, and his faintest but loveliest beams fell upon the cottages in the valley, and lay with a strange, quiet beauty among the grass-plats, and the flower-ranges, and upon the neat, white palings."

"It is beautiful," she said with a sigh, "but its beauty does not content me. It is too much beauty ; it is too soft ; for, though it has its rocks and huge trees, yet it lacks wildness and sublimity. The rocks are not sufficiently abrupt, the steeps not sufficiently great ; there are no chasms, no waterfalls—only purling brooks and quiet walks."

"I have felt this already," he replied ; "but there is yet a deficiency which you have not expressed, Miss Cooper."

"What is that?" she demanded.

"It is the moral want. You have no life here ; and that which would least content me would be this very repose— the absence of provocation — the strife — the triumph! These, I take it, are the deficiencies which you really feel when you speak of the want of crag, and chasm, and waterfall."

"You, too, are ambitious, then!" she said quickly ; "but how do you reconcile this feeling with your profession?"

She looked up, and caught his eye tenderly fixed upon her.

"Ah!" said he, "Miss Cooper, there are some situations in which we find it easy to reconcile all discrepancies."

If the language lacked explicitness, the look did not. He proceeded :—

"If I mistake not, Miss Cooper, you will be the last one to blame me for not having stifled my ambition, even at the calls of duty and profession."

"Blame you, sir? Far from it. I should think you very unfortunate indeed, if you could succeed in stifling ambition at any calls, nor do I exactly see how duty should require it."

"If I pursue the profession of the divine?" he answered hesitatingly.

"Yes—perhaps—but that is not certain?" There was some timidity in the utterance of this inquiry. He evaded it.

"I know not yet what I shall be," he replied with an air of self-reproach ; "I fear I have too much of this fiery ardor which we call ambition to settle down into the passive character of the preacher."

"Oh, do not, do not!" she exclaimed impetuously ; then, as if conscious of the impropriety, she stopped short in the sentence, while increasing her forward pace.

"What!" said he, "you think that would effectually stifle it?"

"Would it not—does it not in most men?"

"Perhaps ; but this depends upon the individual. Churchmen have a great power—the greatest in any country."

"Over babes and sucklings!" she said scornfully.

"And, through these, over the hearts of men and women."

"But these, too, are babes and sucklings—people to be scared by shadows—the victims of their own miserable fears and superstitions!"

"Nevertheless, these confer power. Where there is power, there is room for ambition. You recollect that churchmen have put their feet upon the necks of princes."

"Yes, but that was when there was one church only in Christendom. It was a monopoly, and consequently a tyranny. Now there are a thousand, always in conflict, and serving very happily to keep each other from mischief. They no longer put their feet on princes' necks, though I believe that the princes are no better off for this forbearance — there are others who do. But only fancy that this time was again, and think of the comical figure our worthy brother John Cross would make, mounting from such a noble horse-block!"

The idea was sufficiently pleasant to make Stevens laugh.

"I am afraid I shall have greater trouble in converting you, Miss Cooper, than any other of the flock in Charlemont. I doubt that your heart is stubborn — that you are an insensible!"

"I insensible!" she exclaimed, and with such a look! The expression of sarcasm had passed, as with the rapidity of a lightning-flash, from her beautiful lips; and a silent tear rose, tremulous and large, with the same instantaneous emotion, beneath her long, dark eyelashes. She said nothing more, but, with eyes cast down, went forward. Stevens was startled with the suddenness of these transitions. They proved, at least, how completely her mind was at the control of her blood. Hitherto, he had never met with a creature so liberally endowed by nature, who was, at the same time, so perfectly unsophisticated. The subject was gratifying as a study alone, even if it conferred no pleasure, and awakened no hopes.

"Do not mistake me," he exclaimed, hurrying after, "I had no purpose to impute to you any other insensibility except to that of the holy truths of religion."

She looked up and smiled archly. There was another transition from cloud to sunlight.

"What! are you so doubtful of your own ministry?"

"In your case, I am."

8

"Why?"

"You will force me to betake myself to studies more severe than any I have yet attempted."

She was flattered but she uttered a natural disclaimer.

"No, no! I am presumptuous. I trust you will teach me, Begin — do not hesitate — I will listen."

"To move you I must not come in the garments of methodism. That faith will never be yours."

"What faith shall it be?"

"That of catholicism. I must come armed with authority. I must carry the sword and keys of St. Peter. I must be sustained by all the pomps of that church of pomps and triumphs. My divine mission must speak through signs and symbols, through stately stole, pontifical ornaments, the tiara of religious state on the day of its most solemn ceremonial; and with these I must bring the word of power, born equally of intellect and soul, and my utterance must be in the language of divinest poesy!"

"Ah! you mistake! That last will be enough. Speak to me in poesy — let me hear that — and you will subdue me, I believe, to any faith that you teach. For I can not but believe the faith that is endowed with the faculty of poetic utterance."

"In truth it is a divine utterance — perhaps the only divine utterance. Would I had it for your sake."

"Oh! you must have it. I fancy I see it in some things that you have said. You read poetry, I am sure — I am sure you love it."

"I do! I know not anything that I love half so well."

"Then you write it?" she asked eagerly.

"No! the gift has been denied me."

She looked at him with eyes of regret.

"How unfortunate," she said.

"Doubly so, as the deficiency seems to disappoint you."

She did not seem to heed the flattery of this remark, nor did she appear to note the expression of face with which it was accompanied. Her feelings took the ascendency. She spoke out her uncommissioned thoughts and fancies musingly, as if without the knowledge of her will.

"I fancy that I could kneel down and worship the poet, and feel no shame, no humility. It is the only voice that enchants me — that leads me out from myself; that carries me where it pleases and finds for me companions in the solitude; songs in the storm; affections in the barren desert! Even here, it brings me friends and fellowships. How voiceless would be all these woods to me had it no voice speaking to, and in, my soul. Hoping nothing, and performing nothing here, it is my only consolation. It reconciles me to this wretched spot. It makes endurance tolerable. If it were not for this companionship — if I heard not this voice in my sorrows, soothing my desolation, I could freely die! — die here, beside this rock, without making a struggle to go forward, even to reach the stream that flows quietly beyond!"

She had stopped in her progress while this stream of enthusiasm poured from her lips. Her action was suited to her utterance. Unaccustomed to restraint — nay, accustomed only to pour herself forth to woods, and trees, and waters, she was scarcely conscious of the presence of any other companion, yet she looked even while she spoke, in the eyes of Stevens. He gazed on her with glances of unconcealed admiration. The unsophisticated nature which led her to express that enthusiasm which a state of conventional existence prompts us, through fear of ridicule, industriously to conceal, struck him with the sense of a new pleasure. The novelty alone had its charm; but there were other sources of delight. The natural grace and dignity of the enthusiastic girl, adapting to such words the appropriate action, gave to her beauty, which was now in its first bloom, all the glow which is derived from intellectual inspiration. Her whole person spoke. All was vital, spiritual, expressive, animated; and when the last word lingered

on her lips, Stevens could scarcely repress the impulse
which prompted him to clasp her in his embrace.

"Margaret!" he exclaimed—"Miss Cooper!—you are
yourself a poet!"

"No, no!" she murmured, rather than spoke;—"would
I were!—a dreamer only—a self-deluded dreamer."

"You can not deceive me!" he continued, "I see it in
your eyes, your action; I hear it in your words. I can not
be deceived. You are a poet—you will, and must be
one!"

"And if I were!" she said mournfully, "of what avail
would it be here? What heart in this wilderness would
be touched by song of mine? Whose ear could I soothe in
this cold and sterile hamlet? Where would be the temple
—who the worshippers—even were the priestess all that
her vanity would believe, or her prayers and toils might
make her? No, no! I am no poet; and if I were, better
that the flame should go out—vanish altogether in the
smoke of its own delusions—than burn with a feeble light,
unseen, untrimmed, unhonored—perhaps, beheld with the
scornful eye of vulgar and unappreciating ignorance!"

"Such is not your destiny, Margaret Cooper," replied
Stevens, using the freedom of address, perhaps unconsciously, which the familiarity of country life is sometimes
found to tolerate. "Such is not your destiny, Margaret.
The flame will not go out—it will be loved and worshipped!"

"Ah! never! what is here to justify such a hope—such
a dream?"

"Nothing *here;* but it was not of Charlemont I spoke.
The destiny which has endowed you with genius will not
leave it to be extinguished here. There will come a wor-
shipper, Margaret. There will come one, equally capable
to honor the priestess and to conduct her to befitting altars.
This is not your home, though it may have been your place
of trial and novitiate. Here, without the restraint of cold,

oppressive, social forms, your genius has ripened — your enthusiasm has been kindled into proper glow — your heart, and mind, and imagination, have kept equal pace to an equal maturity! Perhaps this was fortunate. Had you grown up in more polished and worldly circles, you would have been compelled to subdue the feelings and fancies which now make your ordinary language the language of a muse."

"Oh! speak not so, I implore you. I am afraid you mock me."

"No! on my soul, I do not. I think all that I say, More than that, I feel it, Margaret. Trust to me — confide in me — make me your friend! Believe me, I am not altogether what I seem."

An arch smile once more possessed her eyes.

"Ah! I could guess that! But sit you here. Here is a flower — a beautiful, small flower, with a dark blue eye. See it — how humbly it hides amid the grass. It is the last flower of the season. I know not its name. I am no botanist. but it is beautiful without a name, and it is the last flower of the season. Sit down on this rock, and I will sing you Moore's beautiful song, ''Tis the last of its kindred.'"

"Nay, sing me something of your own, Margaret."

"No, no! Don't speak of me, and mine, in the same breath with Moore. You will make me repent of having seen you. Sit down and be content with Moore, or go without your song altogether."

He obeyed her, and the romantic and enthusiastic girl, seating herself upon a fragment of rock beside the path, sang the delicate and sweet verses of the Irish poet, with a natural felicity of execution, which amply compensated for the absence of those Italian arts, which so frequently elevate the music at the expense of the sentiment. Stevens looked and listened, and half forgot himself in the breathlessness of his attention — his eye fastened with a gaze of absolute devotion on her features, until, having finished her song, she detected the expression of his face, and started, with blushing cheeks, to her feet.

"Oh! sweet!" he murmured as he offered to take her hand, but she darted forward, and following her, he found himself a few moments after, standing by her side, and looking down upon one of the loveliest lakes that ever slept in the embrace of jealous hills.

CHAPTER XV.

A CATASTROPHE.

"You disparage these scenes," said Stevens, after several moments had been given to the survey of that before him, "and yet you have drawn your inspiration from them —the fresh food which stimulates poetry and strengthens enthusiasm. Here you learned to be contemplative; and here, in solitude, was your genius nursed. Do not be ungrateful, Margaret—you owe to these very scenes all that you are, and all that you may become."

"Stay! before I answer. Do you see yon bird?"

"Where?"

"In the west—there!" she pointed with her fingers, catching his wrist unconsciously, at the same time, with the other hand, as if more certainly to direct his gaze.

"I see it—what bird is it?"

"An eagle! See how it soars and swings; effortless, as if supported by some external power!"

"Indeed—it seems small for an eagle."

"It is one nevertheless! There are thousands of them that roost among the hills in that quarter. I know the place thoroughly. The heights are the greatest that we have in the surrounding country. The distance from this spot is about five miles. He, no doubt, has some fish, or bird now within his talons, with which to feed his young. He will feed them, and they will grow strong, and will

finally use their own wings. Shall he continue to feed them
after that? Must they never seek their own food?"

"Surely they must."

"If these solitudes have nursed me, must they continue
to nurse me always? Must I never use the wings to which
they have given vigor? Must I never employ the sight to
which they have imparted vigilance? Must I never go forth,
and strive and soar, and make air, and earth, and sea, tribu-
tary to my wing and eye? Alas! I am a woman!—and her
name is weakness! You tell me of what I am, and of what
I may become. But what am I? I mock myself too often
with this question to believe all your fine speeches. And
what may I become? Alas! who can tell me that? I
know my strength, but I also know my weakness. I feel the
burning thoughts of my brain; I feel the yearning impulses
in my heart; but they bring nothing—they promise nothing—I feel the pang of constant denial. I feel that I can
be nothing!"

"Say not so, Margaret—think not so, I beseech you.
With your genius, your enthusiasm—your powers of expression—there is nothing, becoming in your sex, and
worthy of it, which you may not be."

"You can not deceive me! It might be so, if this were
Italy; there, where the very peasant burns with passion,
and breathes his feeblest and meanest thoughts and desires
in song. But here, they already call me mad! They look
on me as one doomed to Bedlam. They avoid me with
sentiments and looks of distrust, if not of fear; and when
I am looking into the cloud, striving to pierce, with dilating
eye its wild yellow flashing centres, they draw their flaxen-
headed infants to their breasts, and mutter their thanks to
God, that he has not, in a fit of wrath, made them to resemble me! If, forgetful of earth, and trees, and the
human stocks around me, I pour forth the language of the
great song-masters, they grin at my insanity—they hold
me incapable of reason, and declare, their ideas of what

that is, by asking who knows most of the dairy, the cabbage-patch, the spinning-wheel, the darning-needle—who can best wash Polly's or Patty's face and comb its head—can chop up sausage-meat the finest—make the lightest paste, and more economically dispense the sugar in serving up the tea! and these are what is expected of woman! These duties of the meanest slave! From her mind nothing is expected. Her enthusiasm terrifies, her energy offends, and if her taste is ever challenged, it is to the figures upon a quilt or in a flower-garden, where the passion seems to be to make flowers grow in stars, and hearts, and crescents. What has woman to expect where such are the laws; where such are the expectations from her? What am I to hope? I, who seem to be set apart—to feel nothing like the rest—to live in a different world—to dream of foreign things—to burn with a hope which to them is frenzy, and speak a language which they neither understand nor like! What can I be, in such a world? Nothing, nothing! I do not deceive myself. I can never hope to be anything."

Her enthusiasm hurried her forward. In spite of himself, Stevens was impressed. He ceased to think of his evil purposes in the superior thoughts which her wild, unregulated energy inspired. He scarcely wondered, indeed —if it were true—that her neighbors fancied her insane. The indignation of a powerful mind denied—denied justice —baffled in its aims—conscious of the importance of all its struggles against binding and blinding circumstances— is akin to insanity!—is apt to express itself in the defiant tones of a fierce and feverish frenzy.

"Margaret," said he, as she paused and waited for him, "you are not right in everything. You forget that your lonely little village of Charlemont, is not only not the world, but that it is not even an American world. America is not Italy, I grant you, nor likely soon to become so; but if you fancy there are not cities even in our country, where

8*

genius such as yours would be felt and worshipped, you are mistaken."

"Do you believe there are such?" she demanded incredulously.

"I *know* there are!"

"No! no! I know better. You can not deceive me. It can not be so. I know the sort of genius which is popular in those cities. It is the gentleman and lady genius. Look at their verses for example. I can show you thousands of such things that come to us here, from all quarters of the Union—verses written by nice people—people of small tastes and petty invention, who would not venture upon the utterance of a noble feeling, or a bold sentiment of originality, for fear of startling the fashionable nerves with the strong words which such a novelty would require. Consider, in the first place, how. conclusive it is of the feeblest sort of genius that these people should employ themselves, from morning to night, in spinning their small strains, scraps of verse, song, and sonnet, and invariably on such subjects of commonplace, as can not admit of originality, and do not therefore task reflection. Not an infant dies or is born, but is made the subject of verse; nay, its smiles and tears are put on record; its hobby-horse, and its infant ideas as they begin to bud and breathe aloud. Then comes the eternal strain about summer blooms and spring flowers; autumn's melancholy and winter's storms, until one sickens of the intolerable monotony. Such are the things that your great cities demand. Such things content them. Speak the fearless and always strange language of originality and strength, and you confound and terrify them."

"But, Margaret, these things are held at precisely the same value in the big cities as they are held by you here in Charlemont. The intelligent people smile—they do not applaud. If they encourage at all it is by silence."

"No! no! that you might say, if, unhappily, public

opinion did not express itself. The same magazines which bring us the verses bring us the criticism."

"That is to say, the editor puffs his contributors, and disparages those who are not. Look at the rival journal and you will find these denounced and another set praised and beplastered."

"Ah! and what would be my hope, my safety, in communities which tolerate these things; in which the number of just and sensible people is so small that they dare not speak, or can not influence those who have better courage? Where would be my triumphs? I, who would no more subscribe to the petty tyranny of conventional law, than to that baser despotism which is wielded by a mercenary editor, in the absence of a stern justice in the popular mind. Here I may pine to death—there, my heart would burst with its own convulsions."

"No! Margaret, no! It is because they have not the genius, that such small birds are let to sing. Let them but hear the true minstrel—let them but know that there is a muse, and how soon would the senseless twitter which they now tolerate be hushed in undisturbing silence. In the absence of better birds they bear with what they have. In the absence of the true muse they build no temple— they throng not to hear. Nay, even now, already, they look to the west for the minstrel and the muse—to these very woods. There is a tacit and universal feeling in the Atlantic country, that leads them to look with expectation to the Great West, for the genius whose song is to give us fame. 'When?' is the difficult—the only question. Ah! might I but say to them—'now'—the muse is already here!"

He took her hand—she did not withhold it; but her look was subdued—the fires had left her eyes—her whole frame trembled with the recoil of those feelings—the relaxation of those nerves—the tension of which we have endeavored feebly to display. Her cheek was no longer flushed but pale; her lips trembled—her voice was low and faint—only a broken and imperfect murmur; and her glance was cast upon the ground.

"You!" she exclaimed.

"Yes, I! Have I not said I am not altogether what i seem? Ah! I may not yet say more. But I am not without power, Margaret, in other and more powerful regions. I too have had my triumphs; I too can boast that the minds of other men hang for judgment upon the utterance of mine."

She looked upward to his glance with a stranger expression of timidity than her features had before exhibited. The form of Stevens had insensibly risen in seeming elevation as he spoke, and the expression of his face was that of a more human pride. He continued:—

"My voice is one of authority in circles where yours would be one of equal attraction and command. I can not promise you an Italian devotion, Margaret; our people, though sufficiently enthusiastic, are too sensible to ridicule to let the heart and blood speak out with such freedom as they use in the warmer regions of the South: but the homage will be more intellectual, more steady, and the fame more enduring. You must let your song be heard—you must give me the sweet privilege of making it known to ears whose very listening is fame."

"Ah!" she said, "what you say makes me feel how foolishly I have spoken. What is my song? what have I done? what am I? what have I to hope? I have done nothing—I am nothing! I have suffered, like a child, a miserable vanity to delude me, and I have poured into the ears of a stranger those ravings which I have hitherto uttered to the hills and forests. You laugh at me now—you must."

The paleness on her cheek was succeeded by the deepest flush of crimson. She withdrew her hand from his grasp.

"Laugh at you, Margaret! You have awakened my wonder. Struck with you when we first met—"

"Nay, no more of that, but let us follow these windings; they lead us to the tarn. It is the prettiest Indian path, and my favorite spot. Here I ramble morning and eve, and try to forget those vain imaginings and foolish strivings of thought which I have just inflicted upon you. The habit proved too much for my prudence, and I spoke as if you were not present. Possibly, had you not spoken in reply, I should have continued until now."

"Why did I speak?"

"Ah! it is better. I wish you had spoken sooner. But follow me quickly. The sunlight is now falling in a particular line which gives us the loveliest effect, shooting its rays through certain fissures of the rock, and making a perfect arrow-path along the water. You would fancy that Apollo had just dismissed a golden shaft from his quiver, so direct is the levelled light along the surface of the lake."

Speaking thus, they came in sight of the party on the opposite hills, as we have already shown—without, however, perceiving them in turn. It will be conjectured without difficulty that, with a nature so full of impulse, so excitable, as that of Margaret Cooper—particularly in the company of an adroit man like Stevens, whose purpose was to encourage her in that language and feeling of egotism which, while it was the most grateful exercise to herself, was that which most effectually served to blind her to his designs—her action was always animated, expressively adapting itself, not only to the words she uttered, but, even when she did not speak, to the feelings by which she was governed. It was the art of Stevens to say little except by suggestives. A single word, or brief sentence, from his lips, judiciously applied to her sentiments or situation, readily excited her to speech; and this utterance necessarily brought with it the secret of her soul, the desire of her heart, nay, the very

shape of the delusion which possessed it. The wily libertine, deliberate as the demon to which we have likened
him, could provoke the warmth which he did not share—
could stimulate the eloquence which he would not feel—
could coldly, like some Mephistopheles of science, subject
the golden-winged bird or butterfly to the torturous process
of examination, with a pin thrust through its vitals, and
gravely dilate on its properties, its rich plumage, and elaborate finish of detail, without giving heed to those writhings
which declared its agonies. It is not meant to be understood that Stevens found no pleasure himself in the display
of that wild, unschooled imagination which was the prevailing quality in the mind of Margaret Cooper. He was a
man of education and taste. He could be pleased as an
amateur; but he wanted the moral to be touched, and to
sympathize with a being so gifted and so feeble—so high
aiming, yet so liable to fall.

The ardor of Margaret Cooper, and the profound devotion which it was the policy of Stevens to display, necessarily established their acquaintance, in a very short time, on
the closest footing of familiarity. With a nature such as
hers, all that is wanted is sympathy—all that she craves
is sympathy—and, to win this, no toil is too great, no sufferance too severe; alas, how frequently do we see that no
penalty is too discouraging! But the confiding spirit never
looks for penalties, and seldom dreams of deceit.

What, then, were the emotions of William Hinkley as he
beheld the cordiality which distinguished the manner of
Margaret Cooper as she approached the edge of the lake
with her companion? In the space of a single week, this
stranger had made greater progress in her acquaintance
than *he* had been able to make in a period of years. The
problem which distressed him was beyond his power to
solve. His heart was very full; the moisture was already
in his eyes; and when he beheld the animated gestures of
the maid—when he saw her turn to her companion, and

meet his gaze without shrinking, while her own was fixed
in gratified contemplation—he scarcely restrained himself
from jumping to his feet. The old man saw his emotion.

"William," he said, "did I understand you that this
young stranger was a preacher?"

"No, sir, but he seeks to be one. He is studying for
the ministry, under Brother Cross."

"Brother Cross is a good man, and is scarcely likely to
have anything to do with any other than good men. I suppose he knows everything about the stranger?"

William Hinkley narrated all that was known on the subject in the village. In the innocence of his heart, Brother
Cross had described Alfred Stevens as a monument of his
own powers of conversion. Under God, he had been a
blessed instrument for plucking this brand from the burning. A modified account of the brandy-flask accompanied
the narrative. Whether it was that Mr. Calvert, who had
been a man of the world, saw something in the story itself,
and in the ludicrousness of the event, which awakened his
suspicions, or whether the carriage of Alfred Stevens, as
he walked with Margaret Cooper, was rather that of a
young gallant than a young student in theology, may admit
of question; but it was very certain that the suspicions of
the old gentleman were somewhat awakened.

Believing himself to be alone with his fair companion,
Alfred Stevens was not as scrupulous of the rigidity of manner which, if not actually prescribed to persons occupying
his professional position, is certainly expected from them;
and, by a thousand little acts of gallantry, he proved himself much more at home as a courtier and a ladies' man
than as one filled with the overflow of divine grace, and
thoughtful of nothing less than the serious earnest of his
own soul. His hand was promptly extended to assist the
progress of his fair companion—a service which was singularly unnecessary in the case of one to whom daily rambles, over hill and through forest, had imparted a most un-

feminine degree of vigor. Now he broke the branch away from before her path ; and now, stooping suddenly, he gathered for her the pale flower of autumn.

These little acts of courtesy, so natural to the gentleman, were anything but natural to one suddenly impressed with the ascetical temper of methodism. Highly becoming in both instances, they were yet strangely at variance with the straight-laced practices of the thoroughgoing Wesleyan, who sometimes fancies that the condition of souls is so desperate as to leave no time for good manners. Mr. Calvert had no fault to find with Stevens's civility, but there was certainly an inconsistency between his deportment now, and those characteristics which were to be predicated of the manner and mode of his very recent conversion. Besides, there was the story of the brandy-flask, in which Calvert saw much less of honor either to John Cross or his neophyte. But the old man did not express his doubts to his young friend, and they sat together, watching, in a silence only occasionally broken by a monosyllable, the progress of the unconscious couple below.

Meanwhile, our fisherman, occupying his lonely perch just above the stream, had been plying his vocation with all the silent diligence of one to the manner born. Once busy with his angle, and his world equally of thought and observation became confined to the stream before his eyes, and the victim before his imagination. Scarcely seen by his companions on the heights above, he had succeeded in taking several very fine fish ; and had his liberality been limited to the supper-table of his venerable friend Calvert, he would long before have given himself respite, and temporary immunity to the rest of the finny tribe remaining in the tarn. But Ned Hinkley thought of all his neighbors, not omitting the two rival widows, Mesdames Cooper and Thackeray.

Something too, there was in the sport, which, on the present occasion, beguiled him rather longer than his wont.

More than once had his eye detected, from the advantageous and jutting rock where he lay concealed, just above the water, the dark outlines of a fish, one of the largest he had ever seen in the lake, whose brown sides, and occasionally flashing fins, excited his imagination and offered a challenge to his skill, which provoked him into something like a feeling of personal hostility.

The fish moved slowly to and fro, not often in sight, but at such regularly-recurring periods as to keep up the exciting desire which his very first appearance had awakened in the mind of his enemy.

To Ned Hinkley he was the beau-ideal of the trout genius. He was certainly the hermit-trout of the tarn. Such coolness, such strength, such size, such an outline, and then such sagacity. That trout was a triton among his brethren. A sort of Dr. Johnson among fishes. Ned Hinkley could imagine—for on such subjects his imagination kindled—how like an oracle must be the words of such a trout, to his brethren, gathering in council in their deep-down hole—or driven by a shower under the cypress log— or in any other situation in which an oracle would be apt to say, looking around him with fierceness mingled with contempt, "Let no dog bark." Ned Hinkley could also fancy the contemplations of such a trout as he witnessed the efforts made to beguile him out of the water.

"Not to be caught by a fly like that, my lad !" and precisely as if the trout had spoken what was certainly whispered in his own mind, the fisherman silently changed his gilded, glittering figure on his hook for one of browner plumage—one of the autumn tribe of flies which stoop to the water from the overhanging trees, and glide off for twenty paces in the stream, to dart up again to the trees, in as many seconds, if not swallowed by some watchful fisher-trout, like the one then before the eyes of our companion.

Though his fancy had become excited, Ned Hinkley was

not impatient. With a cautious hand he conducted the fly
down the stream with the flickering, fidgety motion which
the real insect would have employed. The keen-nosed
trout turned with the movements of the fly, but philosophi-
cally kept aloof. Now he might be seen to sink, now to
rise, now he glided close under the rock where the angler
reclined, and, even in the very deep waters which were
there, which were consequently very dark, so great was the
size of the animal, that its brown outline was yet to be seen,
with its slightly-waving tail, and at moments the flash of its
glittering eye, as, inclining on its side, it glanced cunningly
upward through the water.

Again did Ned Hinkley consult his resources. Fly after
fly was taken from his box, and suffered to glide upon the
stream. The wary fish did not fail to bestow some degree
of attention upon each, but his regards were too deliberate
for the success of the angler, and he had almost began to
despair, when he observed a slight quivering movement in
the object of pursuit which usually prepares the good sportsman to expect his prey. The fins were laid aback. The
motion of the fish became steady ; a slight vibration of the
tail only was visible ; and in another moment he darted,
and was hooked.

Then came the struggle. Ned Hinkley had never met
with a more formidable prey. The reel was freely given,
but the strain was great upon shaft and line. There was
no such thing as contending. The trout had his way, and
went down and off, though it might have been observed that
the fisherman took good care to baffle his efforts to retreat
in the direction of the old log which had harbored him, and
the tangling alders, which might have been his safest places
of retreat. The fish carried a long stretch of line, but the
hook was still in his jaws, and this little annoyance soon
led him upon other courses. The line became relaxed, and
with this sign, Ned Hinkley began to amuse himself in
tiring his victim.

This required skill and promptness rather than strength.
The hermit-trout was led to and fro by a judicious turn of
wrist or elbow. His efforts had subsided to a few spasmodic struggles—an occasional struggle ending with a
shiver, and then he was brought to the surface. This was
followed by a last great convulsive effort, when his tail
churned the water into a little circle of foam, which disappeared the moment his struggles were over. But a few
seconds more were necessary to lift the prey into sight of
all the parties near to the lake. They had seen some of
the struggle, and had imagined the rest. Neither Margaret Cooper nor Stevens had suspected the presence of the
fisherman until drawn to the spot by this trial of strength.

"What a prodigious fish!" exclaimed Stevens; "can
we go to the spot?"

"Oh! easily—up the rocks on the left there is a path.
I know it well. I have traversed it often. Will you go?
The view is very fine from that quarter."

"Surely: but who is the fisherman?"

"Ned Hinkley, the nephew of the gentleman with whom
you stay. He is a hunter, fisherman, musician—everything. A lively, simple, but well-meaning young person. It
is something strange that his cousin William Hinkley is
not with him. They are usually inseparable."

And with these words she led the way for her companion following the edge of the lake until reaching the point
where the rocks seemed to form barriers to their further
progress, but which her agility and energy had long since
enabled her to overcome.

"A bold damsel!" said Calvert, as he viewed her progress. "She certainly does not intend to clamber over
that range of precipices. She will peril her life."

"No!" said William Hinkley; "she has done it often
to my great terror. I have been with her more than once
over the spot myself. She seems to me to have no fear,
and to delight in the most dangerous places."

" But her companion! If he's not a more active man than he seems he will hardly succeed so well."

William was silent, his eye watching with the keenest interest the progress of the two. In a few moments he started to his feet with some appearance of surprise.

" What's the matter ?" demanded Calvert.

" She does not seem as if she wished to ascend the rocks, but she's aiming to keep along the ledges that overhang the stream, so as to get where Ned is. That can hardly be done by the surest-footed, and most active. Many of the rocks are loose. The ledge is very narrow, and even where there is room for the feet there are such projections above as leave no room for the body. I will halloo to her, and tell her of the danger."

" If you halloo, you will increase the danger — you will alarm her," said the old man.

" It will be best to stop her now, in season, when she can go back. Stay for me, sir, I can run along on the heights so as to overlook them, and can then warn without alarming."

" Do so, my son, and hasten, for she seems bent on going forward. The preacher follows but slowly, and she stops for him. Away !"

The youth darted along the hill, pursuing something of a table-line which belonged to the equal elevation of the range of rock on which he stood. The rock was formed of successive and shelving ledges, at such intervals, however, as to make it no easy task — certainly no safe one — to drop from one to the other. The perch of Ned Hinkley, was a projection from the lowest of these ledges, running brokenly along the margin of the basin until lost in the forest slope over which Margaret Cooper had led her companion.

If it was a task to try the best vigor and agility — to say nothing of courage — of the ablest mountaineer, to ascend the abrupt ledges from below, aiming at the highest point of elevation — the attempt was still more startling to follow the lower ledges, some of which hung, loosened and tottering, just above the deepest parts of the lake. Yet, with that intrepidity which marked her character, this was the very task which Margaret Cooper had proposed to herself. William Hinkley had justly said that she did not seem to know fear; and when Stevens with the natural sense of caution which belongs to one to whom such performances are unusual, suggested to her that such a pathway seemed very dangerous——

"Dangerous !" she exclaimed, standing upon the merest pinnacle of a loosened fragment which rested on the very margin of the stream.

"Did you never perceive that there was a loveliness in danger which you scarcely felt to be half so great in any other object or situation. I love the dangerous. It seems to lift my soul, to make my heart bound with joy and the wildest delight. I know nothing so delightful as storm and thunder. I look, and see the tall trees shivering and going down with a roar, and feel that I could sing — sing aloud — and believe that there are voices, like mine, then singing through all the tempest. But there is no danger here. I have clambered up these ledges repeatedly — up to the very top. Here, you see, we have an even pathway along the edge. We have nothing to do but to set the foot down firmly."

But Stevens was not so sure, and his opinion on the beauties of the dangerous did not chime exactly with hers. Still, he did not lack for courage, and his pride did not suffer him to yield in a contest with a female. He gazed on her with increasing wonder. If he saw no loveliness in danger — he saw no little loveliness just then in her; and she might be said to personify danger to his eyes. Her tall, symmetrical, and commanding figure, perched on the trembling pinnacle of rock which sustained her, was as firm and erect as if she stood on the securest spot of land.

Nor was her position that of simple security and firmness. The grace of her attitude, her extended and gently waving arm as she spoke, denoted a confidence which could only have arisen from a perfect unconsciousness of danger. Her swan-like neck, with the face slightly turned back to him; the bright flashing eyes, and the smile of equal pride and dignity on her exquisitely-chiselled mouth; — all formed a picture for the artist's study, which almost served to divert the thoughts of Stevens from the feeling of danger which he expressed.

While he gazed, he heard a voice calling in tones of warning from above; and, at the sound, he perceived a change in the expression of Margaret Cooper's face, from confidence and pride, to scorn and contempt. At the same time she darted forward from rock to rock, with a sort of defying haste, which made him tremble for her safety, and left him incapable to follow. The call was repeated; and Stevens looked up, and recognised the person of the youth whom he had counselled that morning with such bad success.

If the progress of Margaret Cooper appeared dangerous in his sight, that of the young man was evidently more so. He was leaping, with the cool indifference of one who valued his life not a pin's fee, from ledge to ledge, down the long steppes which separated the several reaches of the rock formation. The space between was very considerable, the descent abrupt; the youth had no steadying pole to assist him, but flying rather than leaping, was now beheld in air, and in the next moment stood balancing himself with difficulty, but with success, and without seeming apprehension, on the pinnacle of rock below him. In this way he was approaching the lower ledge along which Margaret Cooper was hurrying as rapidly as fearlessly, and calling to her as he came, implored her to forbear a progress which was so full of danger.

Stevens fancied he had no reason to love the youth, but

he could not help admiring and envying his equal boldness and agility ; the muscular ease with which he flung himself from point to point, and his sure-footed descent upon the crags and fragments which trembled and tottered beneath the sudden and unaccustomed burden. Charitably wishing that, amid all his agility he might yet make a false step, and find an unexpected and rather cold bath in the lake below, Stevens now turned his eyes upon Margaret Cooper.

She did not answer the counsels of William Hinkley — certainly did not heed them : and, but for the increased impatience of her manner might be supposed not to have heard them. The space between herself and Stevens had increased meanwhile, and looking back, she waited for his approach. She stood on a heavy mass which jutted above the lake, and not six feet from the water. Her right foot was upon the stone, sustaining the whole weight of her person. Her left was advanced and lifted to another fragment which lay beyond. As she looked back she met the eyes of Stevens. Just then he saw the large fragment yield beneath her feet. She seemed suddenly conscious of it in the same moment, and sprung rapidly on that to which her left foot was already advanced. The impetus of this movement, sent the rock over which she had left. This disturbed the balance of that to which she had risen, and while the breath of the stranger hung suspended in the utterance of the meditated warning, the catastrophe had taken place. The stone shrank from beneath her, and, sinking with it, in another moment, she was hidden from sight in the still, deep waters of the lake.

CHAPTER XVI.

SOUSING A GURNET.

THE disappearance of Margaret Cooper was succeeded by a shriek from above — a single shriek — a cry of terror and despair; and in the same instant the form of William Hinkley might have been seen cleaving the air, with the boldness of a bird, secure always of his wing, and descending into the lake as nearly as it was possible for him to come, to the spot where she had sunk. Our cooler fisherman looked up to the abrupt eminence, just above his own head, from which his devoted cousin had sprung.

" By gemini!" he exclaimed with an air of serious apprehension, " if William Hinkley hasn't knocked his life out by that plunge he's more lucky than I think him. It's well the lake's deep enough in this quarter else he'd have tried the strength of hard head against harder rock below. But there's no time for such nice calculations! We can all swim — that's a comfort."

Thus speaking, he followed the example of his cousin, though more quietly, plunging off from his lowlier perch, and cleaving the water, headforemost, with as little commotion as a sullen stone would make sent directly downward to the deep. By this time, however, our former companion, Stevens, had done the same thing. Stevens was no coward, but he had no enthusiasm. He obeyed few impulses. His proceedings were all the result of calculation. He could swim as well as his neighbors. He had no apprehensions on that score; but he disliked cold water; and there was an involuntary shrug of the shoulder and shiver of the limbs before he committed himself to the water, which he did with all the deliberation of the cat, who, longing for fish, is yet unwilling to wet her own feet. His deliberation, and the nearness of his position to Margaret Cooper, were so far favorable to his design that he succeeded in finding her first. It must be understood that the events, which we have taken so much time to tell, occupied but a few seconds in the performance. Stevens was in the water quite as quickly as Ned Hinkley, and only not so soon as his more devoted and desperate cousin. If it was an advantage to him to come first in contact with the form of Margaret Cooper, it had nearly proved fatal to him also. In the moment when he encountered her, her outstretched and grasping arms, encircled his neck. They rose together, but he was nearly strangled, and but for the timely interposition of the two cousins, they must probably have both perished.

It was the fortune of our fisherman to relieve the maiden, whom he bore to the opposite shore with a coolness, a skill and spirit, which enabled him to save himself from her desperate but unconscious struggles, while supporting her with a degree of ease and strength which had been acquired while teaching some dozen of the village urchins how to practise an art in which he himself was reckoned a great proficient.

It was fortunate for Stevens that the charities of William Hinkley were more active and indulgent than his own, since, without the timely succor and aid which he afforded, that devout young gentleman would have been made to discontinue his studies very suddenly and have furnished a summary conclusion to this veracious narrative — a consummation which, if it be as devoutly wished by the reader as by the writer, will be a much greater source of annoyance to our publisher than it has proved already. Never had poor

9

mortal been compelled to drink, at one time, a greater
quantity of that celestial beverage, which the Reverend Mr.
Pierpont insists is the only liquor drunk at the hotels of
heaven.   We should be sorry to misrepresent that very
gentle gentleman, but we believe that this is substantially
his idea.   It was unfortunate for Stevens that, previously
to this, he had never been accustomed to drink much of this
beverage in its original strength anywhere.   He had been
too much in the habit of diluting it; and being very temperate always in his enjoyment of the creature comforts, he
had never taken it, even when thus diluted, except in very
moderate quantities.

In consequence of his former abstemiousness, the quantity which he now swallowed nearly strangled him.   He
was about to take his last draught with many wry faces,
when the timely arms of the two cousins, by no very sparing application of force withdrew him from the grasp of
the damsel; and without very well understanding the process, or any particulars of his extrication, he found himself
stretched upon the banks over which he had lately wandered, never dreaming of any such catastrophe; discharging
from his stomach by no effort of his own, a large quantity
of foreign ingredients — the ordinary effect, we are given
to understand, of every inordinate indulgence in strong
waters.

Our excellent old friend, Mr. Calvert, was soon upon the
spot, and while Ned Hinkley was despatched to the village
for assistance, he took himself the charge of recovering the
unconscious maiden.   Half-forgetting his hostility, William
Hinkley undertook the same good service to Stevens, who
really seemed to need succor much more than his fair companion.   While William Hinkley busied himself by rolling,
friction, fanning, and other practices, employed in such
cases, to bring his patient back to life, he could not forbear
an occasional glance to the spot where, at a little distance,
lay the object of his affections.

Her face was toward him, as she lay upon her side. Her head was supported on the lap of the old man. Her long hair hung dishevelled, of a more glossy black now when filled with water. Her eyes were shut, and the dark fringes of their lids lay like a pencil-streak across the pale, prominent orbs which they served to bind together. The glow of indignant pride with which she was wont to receive his approaches had all disappeared in the mortal struggle for life through which she had lately gone; and pure, as seemingly free from every passion, her pale beauties appeared to his doating eye the very perfection of human loveliness. Her breast now heaved convulsively—deep sighs poured their way through her parted lips. Her eyes alternately opened upon but shut against the light, and, finally, the exertions of the old man were rewarded as the golden gleam of expression began to relight and reillumine those features which seemed never to be without it.

She recovered her consciousness, started up, made an effort to rise, but, reeling with inability, sunk down again into the paternal grasp of the old man.

" Mr. Calvert!" she murmured.

" You are safe, my daughter," said the old man.

" But how did it happen?—where am I?"

" By the lake."

" Ah! I remember. I was drowning. I felt it all—the choking—the struggle—the water in my ears and eyes! It was a dreadful feeling. How did I come here? Who saved me?"

" Ned Hinkley brought you to land, but he was helped by his cousin William, who assisted the stranger."

" The stranger? ah! yes, I remember: but where is he?"

She looked around wildly and anxiously, and beholding William Hinkley at a little distance, busy with the still unconscious form of Stevens, a quick, fearful shudder passed over her frame. She almost crouched into the old man's arms as she asked, in husky accents—

"He is not dead—he lives?"

"I hope so.   He breathes."

She waited for no more, but, starting to her feet, she staggered to the spot where Stevens lay.   The old man would have prevented her.

"You are feeble; you will do yourself harm.   Better, if you are able to walk, hurry homeward with me, when you can change your clothes."

"Would you have me ungrateful?" she exclaimed; "shall I neglect him when he risked his life for me?"

There was a consciousness in her mind that it was not all gratitude which moved her, for the deathly paleness of her cheek was now succeeded by a warm blush which denoted a yet stronger and warmer emotion.   The keen eyes of William Hinkley understood the meaning of this significant but unsyllabling mode of utterance, and his eyes spoke the reproach to hers which his lips left unsaid:—

"Ah! did I not risk my life too, to prevent—to save? When would she feel such an interest in me? when would she look thus were my life at stake?"

"He will not be neglected," said the old man, gently endeavoring to restrain her.   Perhaps she would not have given much heed to the interruption, for hers was the strength of an unfettered will, one accustomed to have way, but that, at this moment, the eyes of Stevens unclosed and met her own.   His consciousness had returned, and, under the increasing expression in his looks, she sunk back, and permitted the old man to lead her along the homeward path.   More than once she looked back, but, with the assurance of Mr. Calvert that there was no more danger to be apprehended, she continued to advance; the worthy old man, as they went, seeking to divert her mind, by pleasant and choice anecdotes of which his memory had abundant stores, from dwelling upon the unpleasant and exciting event which had just taken place.

Margaret Cooper, whose habits previously had kept her

from much intimacy with the village sage, was insensibly taken by his gentleness, the purity of his taste, the choiceness of his expression, the extent of his resources. She wondered how a mind so full should have remained unknown to her so long—committing the error, very common to persons of strong will and determined self-esteem, of assuming that she should, as a matter of inevitable necessity, have known everything and everybody of which the knowledge is at all desirable.

In pleasant discourse he beguiled her progress, until Ned Hinkley was met returning with horses—the pathway did not admit of a vehicle, and the village had none less cumbrous than cart and wagon—on one of which she mounted, refusing all support or assistance; and when Mr. Calvert insisted upon walking beside her, she grasped the bough of a tree, broke off a switch, and, giving an arch but good-natured smile and nod to the old man, laid it smartly over the horse's flank, and in a few moments was out of sight.

"The girl is smart," said Calvert, as he followed her retreating form with his eye—"too smart! She speaks well—has evidently read. No wonder that William loves her; but she will never do for him. She has no humility. Pride is the demon in her heart. Pride will overthrow her. These woods spoil her. Solitude is the natural nurse of self-esteem, particularly where it is strong at first, and is coupled with anything like talent. Better for such a one if sickness, and strife, and suffering, had taken her at the cradle, and nursed her with the milk of self-denial, which is the only humility worth having. And yet, why should I speak of her, when the sting remains in my own soul—when I yet feel the pang of my feebleness and self-reproach? Alas! I should school none. The voice speaks to me ever, 'Old man, to thy prayers! Thy own knees are yet stubborn as thy neck!'"

Leaving him to the becoming abasement of that delusive self-comfort which ministers to our vain-glory, and which this good old man had so happily succeeded in rebuking, we will return to the spot where we left our other parties. Ned Hinkley had already joined them. With his horse he had providently brought a suit of his own clothes for the stranger, which, though made of homespun, and not of the most modern fashion, were yet warm and comfortable, and as Stevens was compelled to think, infinitely preferable to the chilly and dripping garments which he wore. A few moments, in the cover of the woods, sufficed the neophyte to make the alteration; while the two cousins, to whom the exigencies of forester and fisherman life were more familiar, prepared to walk the water out of their own habits, by giv· ing rapid circulation to their blood and limbs. While their preparations were in progress, however, Ned Hinkley could not deny himself the pleasure of discoursing at length on the subject of the late disaster.

"Stranger," he said, "I must tell you that you've had a souse in as fine a fishing-pond as you'll meet with from here to Salt river. I reckon, now, that while you were in, you never thought for a moment of the noble trout that inhabit it."

"I certainly did not," said the other.

"There, now! I could have sworn it. That a man should go with his eyes open into a country without ever asking what sort of folks lived there! Isn't it monstrous?"

"It certainly seems like a neglect of the first duty of a traveller," said Stevens good-humoredly; "let me not show myself heedless of another. Let me thank you, gentlemen, for saving my life. I believe I owe it to one or both of you."

"To him, not to me," said Ned Hinkley, pointing to his cousin. William was at a little distance, looking sullenly upon the two with eyes which, if dark and moody, seemed to denote a thought which was anywhere else but in the scene around him.

"He saved you, and I saved the woman. I wouldn't

have a woman drowned in this lake for all the houses in Charlemont."

" Ah! why ?"

" 'Twould spoil it for fishing for ever."

" Why would a woman do this more than a man ?"

" For a very good reason, my friend. Because the ghost of a woman talks, and a man's don't, they say. The ghost of a man says what it wants to say with its eyes ; a woman's with her tongue. You know there's nothing scares fish so much as one's talking."

" I have heard so. But is it so clear that there is such a difference between ghosts ? How is it known that the female does all the talking ?"

" Oh, that's beyond dispute. There's a case that we all know about—all here in Charlemont—the case of Joe Barney's millpond. Barney lost one of his children and one of his negroes in the pond—drowned as a judgment, they say, for fishing a Sunday. That didn't make any difference with the fish : you could catch them there just the same as before. But when old Mrs. Frey fell in, crossing the dam, the case was altered. You might sit there for hours and days, night and day, and bob till you were weary ; devil a bite after that! Now, what could make the difference but the tongue ? Mother Frey had a tongue of her own, I tell you. 'Twas going when she fell in, and I reckon's been going ever since. She was a sulphury, spiteful body, to be sure, and some said she poisoned the fish if she didn't scare them. To my thinking, 'twas the tongue."

Stevens had been something seduced from his gravity by the blunt humor and unexpected manner of Ned Hinkley ; besides, having been served, if not saved, by his hands, something, perhaps, of attention was due to what he had to say ; but he recollected the assumed character which he had to maintain—something doubtful, too, if he had not already impaired it in the sight and hearing of those who had come so opportunely but so unexpectedly to his relief.

He recovered his composure and dignity; forbore to smile at the story which might otherwise have provoked not only smile but corresponding answer; and, by the sudden coolness of his manner, tended to confirm in Ned Hinkley's bosom the half-formed hostility which the cause of his cousin had originally taught him to feel.

"I'll lick the conceit out of him yet!" he muttered, as Stevens, turning away, ascended to the spot where William Hinkley stood.

"I owe you thanks, Mr. Hinkley," he began.

The young man interrupted him.

"You owe me nothing, sir," he answered hastily, and prepared to turn away.

"You have saved my life, sir."

"I should have saved your dog's life, sir, in the same situation. I have done but an act of duty."

"But, Mr. Hinkley—"

"Your horse is ready for you, sir," said the young man, turning off abruptly, and darting up the sides of the hill, remote from the pathway, and burying himself in the contiguous forests.

"Strange!" exclaimed the neophyte — "this is very strange!"

"Not so strange, stranger, as that I should stand your groom, without being brought up to such a business for any man. Here's your nag, sir."

"I thank you—I would not willingly trespass," he replied, as he relieved our angler from his grasp upon the bridle.

"You're welcome without the thanks, stranger. I reckon you know the route you come. Up hill, follow the track to the top, take the left turn to the valley, then you'll see the houses, and can follow your own nose or your nag's Either's straight enough to carry you to his rack. You'll find your clothes at your boarding-house about the time that you'll get there."

"Nay, sir, I already owe you much. Let them not trouble you. I will take them myself."

"No, no, stranger!" was the reply of our fisherman, as he stooped down and busied himself in making the garments into a compact bundle; "I'm not the man to leave off without doing the thing I begin to do. I sometimes do more than I bargain for—sometimes lick a man soundly when I set out only to tweak his nose; but I make it a sort of Christian law never to do less. You may reckon to find your clothes home by the time you get there. There's your road."

"A regular pair of cubs!" muttered the horseman, as he ascended the hill.

"To purse up his mouth as if I was giving him root-drink, when I was telling him about Mother Frey's spoiling the fish! Let him take care—he may get the vinegar next time, and not the fish!"

And, with these characteristic commentaries, the parties separated for the time.

9*

CHAPTER XVII.

PHILOSOPHY OF FIGHTING.

" You're not a fighter, Bill Hinkley, and that's about the worst fault that I can find against you."

Such was the beginning of a dialogue between the cousins some three days after the affair which was narrated in our last chapter. The two young men were at the house of the speaker, or rather at his mother's house; where, a favorite and only son, he had almost supreme dominion. He was putting his violin in tune, and the sentences were spoken at intervals with the discordant scraps of sound which were necessarily elicited by this unavoidable musical operation. These sounds might be said to form a running accompaniment for the dialogue, and, considering the sombre mood of the person addressed, they were, perhaps, far more congenial than any more euphonious strains would have been.

" Not a fighter !" said the other ; " why, what do you mean ?"

" Why, just what I say — you are not a fighter. You love reading, and fiddling, and fishing sometimes, and sometimes dancing, and hunting, and swimming ; but I'm pretty certain you don't love fighting. You needn't contradict, Bill — I've been thinking the matter over ; and I'm sure of it. I recollect every battle or scrape you ever were in, from the time we went to old Chandler's, and I tell you, you're not a fighter — you don't love fighting !"

This was concluded with a tremendous scrape over the strings, which seemed to say as well as scrape could speak —" There can be no mistake on the subject—I've said it."

" If I knew exactly what you were driving at," said the other, " perhaps I might answer you. I never pretended to be a fighter ; and as for loving it, as I love eating, drinking, books, fiddling, and dancing, why that needs no answer. Of course I do not, and I don't know who does."

" There it is. I told you. I knew it. You'd sooner do almost anything than fight."

" If you mean that I would submit to insult," said the more peaceable cousin, with some displeasure in his tones and countenance, " sooner than resent it, you are very much mistaken. It wouldn't be advisable even for you to try the experiment."

" Poh, poh, Bill, you know for that matter that it wouldn't take much trying. I'd lick you as easily now as I did when we were boys together."

" We are boys no longer," said the other gravely.

" I'm as much a boy as ever, so far as the licking capacity calls for boyhood. I've pretty much the same spirit now that I had then, and ten times the same strength and activity. But don't look so blue. I'm not going to try my strength and spirit and activity on you. And don't suppose, Bill Hinkley, that I mean to say you're anything of a coward, or that you'd submit to any open insult; but still I do say, you're not only not fond of fighting, but you're just not as much inclined that way as you should be."

" Indeed ! what more would you have ? Do you not say that I would not submit to insult ?—that I show the proper degree of courage in such cases ?"

" Not the *proper* degree. That's the very question. You're not quick enough. You wait for the first blow. You don't step out to meet the enemy. You look for him to come to you."

" Surely! I look upon fighting as brutal — to be waited for, not sought — to be resorted to only in compliance with necessity — to be avoided to the last!"

" No such thing — all a mistake. Fighting and the desire to get on the shoulders of our neighbors is a natural passion. We see that every day. The biggest boy licks the one just below him, he whips the next, and so down, and there's not one that don't lick somebody and don't stand licked himself — for the master licks the biggest. The desire to fight and flog is natural, and this being the case, it stands to reason that we must lick our neighbor or he'll be sure to lick us."

" Pshaw! you speak like a boy yet. This is schoolhouse philosophy."

" And very good philosophy too. I'm thinking the schoolhouse and the play-ground is pretty much a sort of world to itself. It's no bad show of what the world without is; and one of its first lessons and that which I think the truest, is the necessity of having a trial of strength with every new-comer; until we learn where he's to stand in the ranks, number one or number nothing. You see there just the same passions, though, perhaps, on a small scale, that we afterward find to act upon the big world of manhood. There, we fight for gingerbread, for marbles, top and ball; not unfrequently because we venture to look at our neighbor's sweetheart; and sometimes, quite as often, for the love of the thing and to know where the spirit and the sinew are. Well, isn't that just what the big world does after us? As men, we fight for bigger playthings, for pounds, where before we fought for pence — for gold where before we fought for coppers — for command of a country instead of a schoolyard; for our wives instead of sweethearts, and through sheer deviltry and the love of the thing, when there's nothing else to fight about, just the same as we did in boyhood."

" But even were you to prove, and I to admit, that it is

so, just as you say, that would not prove the practice to be a jot more proper, or a jot less brutal."

"Begging your pardon, Bill, it proves it to be right and proper, and accordingly, if brutal, a becoming brutality. If this is the natural disposition of boys and men, don't you see that this schoolboy licking and fighting is a necessary part of one's moral education? It learns one to use his strength, his limbs and sinews, as he may be compelled to use them, in self-defence, in every future day of his life. You know very well what follows a boy at school who doesn't show himself ready to bung up his neighbor's eye the moment he sees it at a cross-twinkle. He gets his own bunged up. Well, it's just the same thing when he gets to be a man. If you have a dispute with your enemy, I don't say that you shouldn't reason with him, but I do say that your reasoning will have very little effect upon him unless he sees that you are able and willing to write it in black and blue upon his sheepskin. And what better way could you find to show him *that*, unless by giving him word and blow, the blow first, as being the most impressive argument?"

"You must have been dreaming of these subjects last night," said the grave cousin—"you seem to have them unusually well cut and dried."

"I haven't been dreaming about it, Bill, but I confess I've been thinking about it very seriously all night, and considering all the arguments that I thought you would make use of against it. I haven't quite done with my discussion, which I took up entirely for your benefit."

"Indeed! you are quite philanthropic before breakfast; but let us hear you?"

"You talk of the brutality of fighting—now in what does that brutality consist? Is it not in breaking noses, kicking shins, bunging up eyes, and making one's neighbor feel uncomfortable in thigh, and back, and arms, and face, and skin, and indeed, everywhere, where a big fist or a cowhide shoe may plant a buffet or a bruise ?"

" Quite a definition, Ned."

" I'm glad you think so : for if it's brutal in the boy to do so to his schoolmate, is it less so for the schoolmaster to do the same thing to the boy that's under his charge ? He bruises my skin, makes my thighs, and arms, and back, and legs, and face, and hands, ache, and if my definition be a correct one, he is quite as brutal as the boys who do the same thing to one another."

" He does it because the boys deserve it, and in order to make them obedient and active."

" And when did a boy not deserve a flogging when he gets licked by his companion ?" demanded the other triumphantly—" and don't the licking make him obedient, and don't the kicking make him active ? By gemini, I've seen more activity from one chap's legs under the quick application of another's feet, than I think anything else could produce, unless it were feet made expressly for such a purpose and worked by a steam-engine. That might make them move something faster, but I reckon there would be no need in such a case of any such improvement."

" What are you driving at, Ned Hinkley ? This is by far the longest argument, I think, that you've ever undertaken. You must be moved by some very serious considerations."

" I am, and you'll see what I'm driving at after a little while. I'm not fond of arguing, you know, but I look upon the fighting principle as a matter to be known and believed in, and I wish to make clear to you my reasons for believing in it myself. You don't suppose I'd put down the fiddle for a talk at any time if the subject was not a serious one ?"

" Give way — you have the line."

" About the brutality of fighting then, there's another

thing to be said. Fighting produces good feeling — that is to say supposing one party fairly to have licked another."

" Indeed — that's new."

" And true too, Bill Hinkley. It cures the sulks. It lets off steam. It's like a thunderstorm that comes once in a while, and drives away the clouds, and clears the skies until all's blue again."

" Black and blue."

" No! what was black becomes blue. Chaps that have been growling at each other for weeks and months lose their bad blood—"

" From the nostrils !"

" Yes, from the nostrils. It's a sort of natural channel, and runs freely from that quarter. The one crows and the other runs and there's an end of the scrape and the sulks. The weaker chap, feeling his weakness, ceases to be impudent; the stronger, having his power acknowledged, becomes the protector of the weak. Each party falls into his place, and so far from the licking producing bad feeling it produces good feeling and good humor; and I conclude that one half of the trouble in the world, the squabbles between man and man, woman and woman, boy and boy — nay, between rival nations — is simply because your false and foolish notions of brutality and philanthropy keep them from coming to the scratch as soon as they should. They hang off, growling and grumbling, and blackguarding, and blaspheming, when, if they would only take hold, and come to an earnest grapple, the odds would soon show themselves — broken heads and noses would follow — the bad blood would run, and as soon as each party found his level, the one being finally on his back, peace would ensue, and there would be good humor for ever after, or at least until the blood thickened again. I think there's reason in my notion. I was thinking it over half the night. I've thought of it oftentimes before. I've never yet seen the argument that's strong enough to tumble it."

"Your views are certainly novel, Ned, if not sound.
You will excuse me if I do not undertake to dispute them
this morning. I give in, therefore, and you may congratulate yourself upon having gained a triumph if not a convert?"

"Stop, stop, William Hinkley: you don't suppose I've
done all this talking only to make a convert or to gain a
triumph?"

"Why, that's your object in fighting, why not in arguing?"

"Well, that's the object of most persons when they dispute, I know; but it is not mine. I wish to make a practical application of my doctrine."

"Indeed! who do you mean to fight now?"

"It's not for me to fight, it's for you."

"Me!"

"Yes; you have the preference by rights, though if you
don't — and I'm rather sorry to think, as I told you at the
start, that the only fault I had to find with you is that you're
not a fighter — I must take your place and settle the difference."

William Hinkley turned upon the speaker. The latter
had laid down the violin, having, in the course of the argument, broken all its strings; and he stood now, unjack-
eted, and still in the chamber, where the two young men
had been sleeping, almost in the attitude of one about to
grapple with an antagonist. The serious face of him whose
voice had been for war — his startling position — the unwonted eagerness of his eye, and the ludicrous importance
which he attached to the strange principle which he had
been asserting — conquered for a moment the graver mood
of his love-sick companion, and he laughed outright at his
pugnacious cousin. The latter seemed a little offended.

"It's well you can laugh at such things, Bill Hinkley,
but I can't. There was a time when every mother's son
in Kentucky was a man, and could stand up to his rack

with the best. If he couldn't keep the top place, he went a peg lower; but he made out to keep the place for which he was intended. Then, if a man disliked his neighbor he crossed over to him and said so, and they went at it like men, and as soon as the pout was over they shook hands, and stood side by side, and shoulder to shoulder, like true friends, in every danger, and never did fellows fight better against Indians and British than the same two men, that had lapped muscles, and rolled in the grain together till you couldn't say whose was whose, and which was which, till the best man jumped up, and shook himself, and gave the word to crow. After that it was all peace and good humor, and they drank and danced together, and it didn't lessen a man in his sweetheart's eyes, though he was licked, if he could say he had stood up like a man, and was downed after a good hug, because he couldn't help it. Now, there's precious little of that. The chap that dislikes his fellow, hasn't the soul to say it out, but he goes aside and sneers and snickers, and he whispers things that breed slanders, and scandals, and bad blood, until there's no trusting anybody; and everything is full of hate and enmity — but then it's so peaceful! Peaceful, indeed! as if there was any peace where there is no confidence, and no love, and no good feeling either for one thing or another."

"Really, Ned, it seems to me you're indignant without any occasion. I am tempted to laugh at you again."

"No, don't. You'd better not."

"Ha! ha! ha! I can not help it, Ned; so don't buffet me. You forced me into many a fight when I was a boy, for which I had no stomach; I trust you will not pummel me yourself because the world has grown so hatefully pacific. Tell me, in plain terms, who I am to fight now."

"Who! who but Stevens? — this fellow Stevens. He's your enemy, you say — comes between you and your sweetheart — between you and your own mother — seems to look down upon you — speaks to you as if he was wiser, and

better, and superior in every way — makes you sad and
sulky to your best friends — you growl and grumble at him
— you hate him — you fear him—"

"Fear him!"

"Yes, yes, I say fear him, for it's a sort of fear to skulk
off from your mother's house to avoid seeing him—"

"What, Ned, do you tell me that — do you begrudge me
a place with you here, my bed, my breakfast?"

"Begrudge! dang it, William Hinkley, don't tell me
that, unless you want me to lay heavy hand on your shoulder!" — and the tears gushed into the rough fellow's eyes
as he spoke these words, and he turned off to conceal them.

"I don't mean to vex you, Ned, but why tell me that I
skulk — that I fear this man?"

"Begrudge!" muttered the other.

"Nay, forgive me; I didn't mean it. I was hasty when
I said so; but you also said things to provoke me. Do you
suppose that I fear this man Stevens?"

"Why don't you lick him then, or let him lick you, and
bring the matter to an ending? Find out who's the best
man, and put an end to the growling and the groaning. As
it now stands you're not the same person — you're not fit
company for any man. You scarcely talk, you listen to
nobody. You won't fish, you won't hunt: you're sulky
yourself and you make other people so!"

"I'm afraid, Ned, it wouldn't much help the matter even
if I were to chastise the stranger."

"It would cure him of his impudence. It would make
him know how to treat you; and if the rest of your griev-
ance comes from Margaret Cooper, there's a way to end
that too."

"How! you wouldn't have me fight her?" said William
Hinkley, with an effort to smile.

"Why, we may call it fighting," said the advocate for
such wholesale pugnacity, "since it calls for quite as much
courage sometimes to face one woman as it does to face

three men. But what I mean that you should do with her
is to up and at her. Put the downright question like a
man, 'will you?' or 'won't you?' and no more beating about
the bush. If she says 'no!' there's no more to be said, and
if I was you after that, I'd let Stevens have her or the
d—l himself, since I'm of the notion that no woman is
fit for me if she thinks me not fit for her. Such a woman
can't be worth having, and after that I wouldn't take her
as a gracious gift were she to be made twice as beautiful.
The track's before you, William Hinkley. Bring the stranger to the hug, and Margaret Cooper too, if she'll let you.
But, at all events, get over the grunting and the growling,
the sulky looks, and the sour moods. They don't become
a man who's got a man's heart, and the sinews of a man."

William Hinkley leaned against the fireplace with his
head resting upon his hand. The other approached him.

" I don't mean to say anything, Bill, or even to look anything, that'll do you hurt. I'm for bringing your trouble
to a short cut. I've told you what I think right and reasonable, and for no other man in Kentucky would I have taken
the pains to think out this matter as I have done. But you
or I must lick Stevens."

" You forget, Ned. Your eagerness carries you astray.
Would you beat a man who offers no resistance?"

" Surely not."

" Stevens is a non-combatant. If you were to slap John
Cross on one cheek he'd turn you the other. He'd never
strike you back."

" John Cross and Stevens are two persons. I tell you
the stranger *will* fight. I'm sure of it. I've seen it in his
looks and actions."

" Do you think so?"

" I do; I'm sure of it. But you must recollect besides,
that John Cross is a preacher, already sworn in, as I may
say. Stevens is only a beginner. Besides, John Cross is
an old man; Stevens, a young one. John Cross don't care

a straw about all the pretty girls in the country. He works in the business of souls, not beauties, and it's very clear that Stevens not only loves a pretty girl, but that he's over head and heels in love with your Margaret——"

"Say no more. If he will fight, Ned Hinkley, he shall fight!"

"Bravo, Bill—that's all that I was arguing for—that's all that I want. But you must make at Margaret Cooper also."

"Ah! Ned, there I confess my fears."

"Why, what are you afraid of?"

"Rejection!"

"Is that worse than this suspense—this anxiety—this looking out from morning till night for the sunshine, and this constant apprehension of the clouds—this knowing not what to be about—this sulking—this sadding—this growling—this grunting—this muling—this moping—this eternal vinegar-face and ditchwater-spirit?"

"I don't know, Ned, but I confess my weakness—my want of courage in this respect!"

"Psho! the bark's worse always than the bite. The fear worse than the danger! Suspense is the very d—l! Did you ever hear of the Scotch parson's charity? He prayed that God might suspend Napoleon over the very jaws of hell—but 'Oh, Lord!' said he, 'dinna let him fa' in!' To my mind, mortal lips never uttered a more malignant prayer!"

CHAPTER XVIII.

TRAILING THE FOX.

THIS dialogue was broken by a summons to the breakfast-table. We have already intimated that while the hateful person of Stevens was an inmate of his own house William Hinkley remained, the better portion of his time, at that of his cousin. It was not merely that Stevens was hateful to his sight, but such was the devotion of his father and mother to that adventurer, that the young man passed with little notice from either, or if he incurred their attention at all, it was only to receive their rebuke. He had not been able to disguise from them his dislike to Stevens. This dislike showed itself in many ways—in coldness, distance, silence —a reluctance to accord the necessary civilities, and in very unequivocal glances of hostility from the eyes of the jealous young villager.

Such offences against good-breeding were considered by them as so many offences against God himself, shown to one who was about to profess his ministry ; and being prepared to see in Brother Stevens an object of worth and veneration only, they lacked necessarily all that keenness of discrimination which might have helped somewhat to qualify the improprieties of which they believed their son to be guilty. Of his causes of jealousy they had no suspicion, and they shared none of his antipathies. He was subject to the daily lecture from the old man, and the nightly exhortation and expostulation of the old woman

The latter did her spiriting gently. The former roared
and thundered. The mother implored and kissed — the
father denounced and threatened. The one, amidst the
faults of her son which she reproved, could see his virtues;
she could also see that he was suffering — she knew not
why — as well as sinning; the other could only see an insolent, disobedient boy who was taking airs upon himself,
flying in the face of his parents, and doomed to perish like
the sons of Eli, unless by proving himself a better manager
than Eli, he addressed himself in time to the breaking in
of the unruly spirit whose offences promised to be so heinous. It was not merely from the hateful sight of his rival,
or the monotonous expostulation of his mother, that the
poor youth fled; it was sometimes to escape the heavily
chastening hand of his bigoted father.

These things worked keenly and constantly in the mind
of William Hinkley. They acquired additional powers of
ferment from the coldness of Margaret Cooper, and from
the goadings of his cousin. Naturally one of the gentlest
of creatures, the young man was not deficient in spirit.
What seemed to his more rude and elastic relative a token
of imbecility, was nothing more than the softening influence
of his reflective and mental over his physical powers. These,
under the excitement of his blood were necessarily made
subject to his animal impulses, and when he left the house
that morning, with his Blackstone under his arm, on his way
to the peaceful cottage of old Calvert, where he pursued
his studies, his mind was in a perfect state of chaos. Of
the chapter which he had striven to compass the previous
night, in which the rights of persons are discussed with
the usual clearness of style, but the usual one-sidedness of
judgment of that smooth old monarchist, William Hinkley
scarcely remembered a solitary syllable. He had read
only with his eyes. His mind had kept no pace with his
proceedings, and though he strove as he went along to recall the heads of topics, the points and principles of what

he had been reading, his efforts at reflection, by insensible but sudden transitions, invariably concluded with some image of strife and commotion, in which he was one of the parties and Alfred Stevens another; the beautiful, proud face of Margaret Cooper being always unaccountably present, and seeming to countenance, with its scornful smiles, the spirit of strife which operated upon the combatants.

This mood had the most decided effect upon his appearance; and the good old man, Calvert, whose attention had been already drawn to the condition of distress and suffering which he manifested, was now more than ever struck with the seemingly sudden increase of this expression upon his face. It was Saturday — the saturnalia of schoolboys — and a day of rest to the venerable teacher. He was seated before his door, under the shadows of his paternal oak, once more forgetting the baffled aims and profitless toils of his own youthful ambition, in the fascinating pages of that historical romancer the stout Abbé Vertôt. But a glance at the youth soon withdrew his mind from this contemplation, and the sombre pages of the present opened upon his eye, and the doubtful ones of the future became, on the instant, those which he most desired to peruse.

The study of the young is always a study of the past with the old. They seem, in such a contemplation, to live over the records of memory. They feel as one just returning from a long and weary journey, who encounters another, freshly starting to traverse the same weary but inviting track. Something in the character of William Hinkley, which seemed to resemble his own, made this feeling yet more active in the mind of Mr. Calvert; and his earnest desire was to help the youth forward on the path which, he soon perceived, it was destined that the other should finally take. He was not satisfied with the indecision of character which the youth displayed. But how could he blame it harshly? It was in this very respect that his own character had failed, and though he felt that all his counsels were to be addressed to this point, yet he knew not where, or in what manner, to begin. The volume of Blackstone which the youth carried suggested to him a course, however. He bade the young man bring out a chair, and taking the book in his hand, he proceeded to examine him upon parts of the volume which he professed to have been reading

This examination, as it had the effect of compelling the mind of the student to contract itself to a single subject of thought, necessarily had the further effect of clearing it somewhat from the chaos of clouds which had been brooding over it, obscuring the light, and defeating the warmth of the intellectual sun behind them ; and if the examination proved the youth to have been very little of a student, or one who had been reading with a vacant mind, it also proved that the original powers of his intellect were vigorous and various — that he had an analytical capacity of considerable compass ; was bold in opinion, ingenious in solution, and with a tendency to metaphysical speculation, which, modified by the active wants and duties of a large city-practice, would have made him a subtle lawyer, and a very logical debater. But the blush kept heightening on the youth's cheeks as the examination proceeded. He had answered, but he felt all the while how much his answer had sprung from his own conjectures and how little from his authorities. The examination convinced him that the book had been so much waste-paper under his thumb. When it was ended the old man closed the volume, laid it on the sward beside him, and looked, with a mingled expression of interest and commiseration, on his face. William Hinkley noted this expression, and spoke, with a degree of mortification in look and accent, which he did not attempt to hide : —

"I am afraid, sir, you will make nothing of me. I can make nothing of myself. I am almost inclined to give up in despair. I will be nothing — I can be nothing. I feared as much from the beginning, sir. You only waste your time on me."

"You speak too fast, William — you let your blood mingle too much with your thoughts. Let me ask you one question. How long will you be content to live as you do now — seeking nothing — performing nothing — being nothing?"

The youth was silent.

"I, you see, am nothing," continued the old man — "nay, do not interrupt me. You will tell me, as you have already told me, that I am much, and have done much, here in Charlemont. But, for all that I am, and have done here, I need not have gone beyond my accidence. My time has been wasted; my labors, considered as means to ends, were unnecessary; I have toiled without the expected profits of toil; I have drawn water in a sieve. It is not pleasant for me to recall these things, much less to speak of them; but it is for your good that I told you my story. You have, as I had, certain defects of character — not the same exactly, but of the same family complexion. To be something, you must be resolved. You must devote yourself, heart and mind, with all your soul and with all your strength, to the business you have undertaken. Shut your windows against the sunshine, your ears to the song of birds, your heart against the fascinations of beauty; and if you never think of the last until you are thirty, you will be then a better judge of beauty, a truer lover, a better husband, a more certain candidate for happiness. Let me assure you that, of the hundred men that take wives before they are thirty, there is scarcely one who, in his secret soul, does not repent it — scarcely one who does not look back with yearning to the days when he was free."

There was a pause. The young man became very much agitated. He rose from his chair, walked apart for a few moments, and then, returning, resumed his seat by the old man.

10

" I believe you are right, sir—nay, I know you are ; but I can not be at once—I can not promise—to be all that you wish. If Margaret Cooper would consent, I would marry her to-morrow."

The old man shook his head, but remained silent. The young one proceeded :—

" One thing I will say, however : I will take to my studies after this week, whatever befalls, with the hearty resolution which you recommend. I will try to shut out the sunshine and the song. I will endeavor to devote soul and strength, and heart and mind, to the task before me. I *know* that I can master these studies—I think I can"—he continued, more modestly, modifying the positive assertion—" and I know that it is equally my interest and duty to do so. I thank you sir, very much for what you have told me. Believe me, it has not fallen upon heedless or disrespectful ears."

The old man pressed his hand.

" I know *that*, my son, and I rejoice to think that, having given me these assurances, you will strive hard to make them good."

" I will, sir !" replied William taking up his cap to depart.

" But whither are you going now ?"

The youth blushed as he replied frankly :—

" To the widow Cooper's. I'm going to see Margaret."

" Well, well !" said the old man, as the youth disappeared, " if it must be done, the sooner it's over the better. But there's another moth to the flame. Fortunately, he will be singed only ; but she !—what is left for her—so proud, yet so confiding—so confident of strength, yet so artless ? But it is useless to look beyond, and very dismal."

And the speaker once more took up Vertôt, and was soon lost amid the glories of the knights of St. John. His stud-

ies were interrupted by the sudden and boisterous saluta
tion of Ned Hinkley :—

"Well, gran'pa, hard at the big book as usual? No end
to the fun of fighting, eh? I confess, if ever I get to love
reading, it'll be in some such book as that. But reading's
not natural to me, though you made me do enough of it
while you had me. Bill was the boy for the books, and I
for the hooks. By-the-way, talking of hooks, how did those
trout eat? Fine, eh? I haven't seen you since the day of
our ducking."

"No, Ned, and I've been looking for you. Where have
you been?"

"Working, working! Everything's been going wrong.
Lines snapped, fiddle-strings cracked, hooks missing, gun
rusty, and Bill Hinkley so sulky, that his frown made a
shadow on the wall as large and ugly as a buffalo's. But
where is he? I came to find him here."

While he was speaking, the lively youth squatted down,
and deliberately took his seat on the favorite volume which
Mr. Calvert had laid upon the sward at his approach.

"Take the chair, Ned," said the old man, with a smaller
degree of kindness in his tone than was habitual with him.
"Take the chair. Books are sacred things — to be worshipped and studied, not employed as footstools."

"Why, what's the hurt, gran'pa?" demanded the young
man, though he rose and did as he was bidden. "If 'twas
a fiddle, now, there would be some danger of a crash, but
a big book like that seems naturally made to sit upon."

The old man answered him mildly :—

"I have learned to venerate books, Ned, and can no
more bear to see them abused than I could bear to be
abused myself. It seems to me like treating their writers
and their subjects with scorn. If you were to contemplate
the venerable heads of the old knights with my eyes and
feelings, you would see why I wish to guard them from
everything like disrespect."

"Well, I beg their pardon—a thousand pardons! I meant no offence, gran'pa—and can't help thinking that it's all a notion of yours, your reverencing such old Turks and Spaniards that have been dead a thousand years. They were very good people, no doubt, but I'm thinking they've served their turn; and I see no more harm in squatting upon their histories than in walking over their graves, which, if I were in their country of Jericho—that was where they lived, gran'pa, wa'n't it?—I should be very apt to do without asking leave, I tell you."

Ned Hinkley purposely perverted his geography and history. There was a spice of mischief in his composition, and he grinned good-naturedly as he watched the increasing gravity upon the old man's face.

"Come, come, gran'pa, don't be angry. You know my fun is a sort of fizz—there's nothing but a flash—nothing to hurt—no shotting. But where's Bill Hinkley, gran'pa?"

"Gone to the widow Cooper's, to see Margaret."

"Ah! well, I'm glad he's made a beginning. But I'd much rather he'd have seen the other first."

"What other do you mean?" demanded the old man; but the speaker, though sufficiently random and reckless in what he said, saw the impolicy of allowing the purpose of his cousin in regard to Stevens to be understood. He contrived to throw the inquirer off.

"Gran'pa, do you know there's something in this fellow Stevens that don't altogether please me? I'm not satisfied with him."

"Ah, indeed! what do you see to find fault with?"

"Well, you see, he comes here pretending to study. Now, in the first place, why should he come here to study? why didn't he stay at home with his friends and parents?"

"Perhaps he had neither. Perhaps he had no home. You might as well ask me why I came here, and settled down, where I was not born—where I had neither friends nor parents."

"Oh, no, but you told us why," said the other. "You gave us a reason for what you did."

"And why may not the stranger give a reason too?"

"He don't, though."

"Perhaps he will when you get intimate with him. I see nothing in this to be dissatisfied with. I had not thought you so suspicious, Ned Hinkley—so little charitable."

"Charity begins at home, gran'pa. But there s more in this matter. This man comes here to study to be a parson. How does he study? Can you guess?"

"I really can not."

"By dressing spruce as a buck—curling his hair backward over his ears something like a girl's, and going out, morning, noon, and night, to see Margaret Cooper."

"As there is no good reason to suppose that a student of divinity is entirely without the affections of humanity, I still see nothing inconsistent with his profession in this conduct."

"But how can he study?"

"Ah! it may be inconsistent with his studies though not with his profession. It is human without being altogether proper. You see that your cousin neglects his studies in the same manner. I presume that the stranger also loves Miss Cooper."

"But he has no such right as Bill Hinkley."

"Why not?"

"Why not? Why, Bill is a native here, has been loving her for the last year or more. His right certainly ought to be much greater than that of a man whom nobody knows —who may be the man in the moon for anything we know to the contrary—just dropped in upon us, nobody knows how, to do nobody knows what."

"All that may be very true, Ned, and yet his right to seek Miss Cooper may be just as good as that of yourself or mine. You forget that it all depends upon the young lady herself whether either of them is to have a right at all in her concerns."

" Well, that's a subject we needn't dispute about, gran pa, when there's other things.   Now, isn't it strange that this stranger should ride off once a week with his valise on his saddle, just as if he was starting on a journey — should be gone half a day — then come back with his nag all in a foam, and after that you should see him in some new cravat, or waistcoat, or pantaloons, just as if he had gone home and got a change ?"

" And does he do that ?" inquired Mr. Calvert, with some show of curiosity.

" That he does, and he always takes the same direction ; and it seems — so Aunt Sarah herself says, though she thinks him a small sort of divinity on earth — that the day before, he's busy writing letters, and, according to her account, pretty long letters too.   Well, nobody sees that he ever gets any letters in return.   He never asks at the post-office, so Jacob Zandts himself tells me, and that's strange enough, too, if so be he has any friends or relations anywhere else."

Mr. Calvert listened with interest to these and other particulars which his young companion had gathered respecting the habits of the stranger ; and he concurred with his informant in the opinion that there was something in his proceedings which was curious and perhaps mysterious. Still, he did not think it advisable to encourage the prying and suspicious disposition of the youth, and spoke to this effect in the reply which finally dismissed the subject.   Ned Hinkley was silenced not satisfied.

" There's something wrong about it," he muttered to himself on leaving the old man, " and, by dickens ! I'll get to the bottom of it, or there's no taste in Salt-river.   The fellow's a rascal ; I feel it if I don't know it, and if Bill Hinkley don't pay him off, I must.   One or t'other must do it, that's certain."

With these reflections, which seemed to him to be no less moral than social, the young man took his way back to the village, laboring with all the incoherence of unaccustomed thought, to strike out some process by which to find a solution for those mysteries which were supposed to characterize the conduct of the stranger. He had just turned out of the gorge leading from Calvert's house into the settlement, when he encountered the person to whom his meditations were given, on horseback, and going at a moderate gallop along the high-road to the country. Stevens bowed to him and drew up for speech as he drew nigh. At first Ned Hinkley appeared disposed to avoid him, but moved by a sudden notion, he stopped and suffered himself to speak with something more of civility than he had hitherto shown to the same suspected personage.

"Why, you're not going to travel, Parson Stevens," said he—"you're not going to leave us, are you?"

"No, sir—I only wish to give myself and horse a stretch of a few miles for the sake of health. Too much stable, they say, makes a saucy nag."

"So it does, and I may say, a saucy man too. But seeing you with your valise, I thought you were off for good."

Stevens said something about his being so accustomed to ride with the valise that he carried it without thinking.

"I scarcely knew I had it on!"

"That's a lie all round," said Ned Hinkley to himself as the other rode off. "Now, if I was mounted, I'd ride after him and see where he goes and what he's after. What's to hinder? It's but a step to the stable, and but five minutes to the saddle. Dang it, but I'll take trail this time if I never did before."

CHAPTER XIX.

THE DOOM.

WITH this determination our suspicious youth made rapid progress in getting out his horse. A few minutes saw him mounted, and putting some of his resolution into his heels, he sent the animal forward at a killing start, under the keen infliction of the spur. He had marked with his eye the general course which Stevens had taken up the hills, and having a nag of equal speed and bottom, did not scruple, in the great desire which he felt, to ascertain the secret of the stranger, to make him display the qualities of both from the very jump. Stevens had been riding with a free rein, but in consequence of these energetic measures on the part of Hinkley, the latter soon succeeded in overhauling him. Still he had already gone a space of five miles, and this, too, in one direction. He looked back when he found himself pursued, and his countenance very clearly expressed the chagrin which he felt. This he strove, but with very indifferent success, to hide from the keen searching eyes of his pursuer. He drew up to wait his coming, and there was a dash of bitterness in his tones as he expressed his "gratification at finding a companion where he least expected one."

"And perhaps, parson, when you didn't altogether wish for one," was the reply of the reckless fellow. "The truth is, I know I'm not the sort of company that a wise, sensible, learned, and pious young gentleman would like to keep, but the truth is what you said about taking a stretch, man and beast, seemed to me to be just about as wise a thing for me and my beast also. We've been lying by so long that I was getting a little stiff in my joints, and Flip-flap, my nag here, was getting stiff in his neck, as they say was the case with the Jews in old times, so I took your idea and put after you, thinking that you'd agree with me that bad company's far better than none."

There was a mixture of simplicity and archness in the manner of the speaker that put Stevens somewhat at fault; but he saw that it wouldn't do to show the dudgeon which he really felt; and smoothing his quills with as little obvious effort as possible, he expressed his pleasure at the coming of his companion. While doing so, he wheeled his horse about, and signified a determination to return.

What! so soon? Why, Lord bless you, Flipflap has scarcely got in motion yet. If such a stir will do for your nag 'twont do for him."

But Stevens doggedly kept his horse's head along the back track, though the animal himself exhibited no small restiffness and a disposition to go forward.

"Well, really, Parson Stevens, I take it as unkind that you turn back almost the very moment I join you. I seem to have scared ride out of you if not out of your creature; but do as you please. I'll ride on, now I'm out. I don't want to force myself on any man for company."

Stevens disclaimed any feeling of this sort, but declared he had ridden quite as far as he intended; and while he hesitated, Hinkley cut the matter short by putting spurs to his steed, and going out of sight in a moment.

"What can the cur mean?" demanded Stevens of him-self, the moment after they had separated. "Can he have any suspicions? Ha! I must be watchful! At all events, there's no going forward to-day. I must put it off for next week; and meanwhile have all my eyes about me. The fellow seems to have as much cunning as simplicity. He

10*

is disposed too, to be insolent. I marked his manner at the lake, as well as that of his bull-headed cousin; but that sousing put anger out of me, and then, again, 'twill scarcely do in these good days for such holy men as myself to take up cudgels. I must bear it for awhile as quietly as possible. It will not be long. She at least is suspicionless. Never did creature so happily delude herself. Yet what a judgment in some things! What keen discrimination! What a wild, governless imagination! She would be a prize, if it were only to exhibit. How she would startle the dull, insipid, tea-table simperers on our Helicon—nay, with what scorn she would traverse the Helicon itself. The devil is that she would have a will in spite of her keeper. Such an animal is never tamed. There could be no prescribing to her the time when she should roar—no teaching her to fawn and fondle, and not to rend. Soul, and eye, and tongue, would speak under the one impulse, in the exciting moment; and when Mrs. Singalongohnay was squeaking out her eternal requiems—her new versions of the Psalms and Scriptures—her blank verse elogiacs—oh! how blank!—beginning, 'Night was upon the hills,'—or, 'The evening veil hung low,' or, 'It slept,'—or after some other equally threatening form and fashion—I can fancy how the bright eye of Margaret would gleam with scorn; and while the Pollies and Dollies, the Patties and Jennies, the Corydons and Jemmy Jesamies, all round were throwing up hands and eyes in a sort of rapture, how she would look, with what equal surprise and contempt, doubting her own ears, and sickening at the stuff and the strange sycophancy which induced it. And should good old Singalongohnay, with a natural and patronizing visage, approach, and venture to talk to her about poetry, with that assured smile of self-excellence which such a venerable authority naturally employs, how she would turn upon the dame and exclaim—'What! do you call that poetry?' What a concussion would follow. How the simperers would sheer off;

the tea that night might as well be made of aqua-fortis. Ha! ha! I can fancy the scene before me. Nothing could be more rich. I must give her a glimpse of such a scene. It will be a very good mode of operation. Her pride and vanity will do the rest. I have only to intimate the future sway—the exclusive sovereignty which would follow—the overthrow of the ancient idols, and the setting up of a true divinity in herself. But shall it be so, Master Stevens? Verily, that will be seen hereafter. Enough, if the delusion takes. If I can delude the woman through the muse, I am satisfied. The muse after that may dispose of the woman as she pleases."

Such was a portion of the soliloquy of the libertine as he rode slowly back to Charlemont. His further musings we need not pursue at present. It is enough to say that they were of the same family character. He returned to his room as soon as he reached his lodging-house, and drawing from his pocket a bundle of letters which he had intended putting in the postoffice at Ellisland, he carefully locked them up in his portable writing-desk which he kept at the bottom of his valise. When the devout Mrs. Hinkley tapped at his door to summon him to dinner, the meritorious young man was to be seen, seated at his table, with the massive Bible of the family conspicuously open before him. Good young man! never did he invoke a blessing on the meats with more holy unction than on that very day.

Meanwhile, let us resume our progress with William Hinkley, and inquire in what manner his wooing sped with the woman whom he so unwisely loved. We have seen him leaving the cottage of Mr. Calvert with the avowed purpose of seeking a final answer. A purpose from which the old man did not seek to dissuade him, though he readily conceived its fruitlessness. It was with no composed spirit that the young rustic felt himself approaching the house of Mrs. Cooper. More than once he hesitated and even halt_d. But a feeling of shame, and the efforts of returning manliness re-resolved him, and he hurried with an unwonted rapidity of movement toward the dwelling, as if he distrusted his own power, unless he did so, to conclude the labor he had begun.

He gathered some courage when he found that Margaret was from home. She had gone on her usual rambles. Mrs. Cooper pointed out the course which she had taken, and the young man set off in pursuit. The walks of the maiden were of course well known to a lover so devoted. He had sought and followed her a thousand times, and the general direction which she had gone, once known, his progress was as direct as his discoveries were certain. The heart of the youth, dilated with better hopes as he felt himself traversing the old familiar paths. It seemed to him that the fates could scarcely be adverse in a region which had always been so friendly. Often had he escorted her along this very route, when their spirits better harmonized — when, more of the girl struggling into womanhood, the mind of Margaret Cooper, ignorant of its own resources and unconscious of its maturer desires, was more gentle, and could rejoice in that companionship for which she now betrayed so little desire. The sheltered paths and well-known trees, even the little clumps of shrubbery that filled up the intervals, were too pleasant and familiar to his eye not to seem favorable to his progress, and with a hope that had no foundation, save in the warm and descriptive colors of a young heart's fancy, William Hinkley pursued the route which led him to one of the most lovely and love-haunted glades in all Kentucky.

So sweet a hush never hallowed the sabbath rest of any forest. The very murmur of a drowsy zephyr among the leaves was of slumberous tendency; and silence prevailed, with the least possible exertion of her authority, over the long narrow dell through which the maiden had gone wandering. At the foot of a long slope, to which his eye was conducted by a natural and lovely vista, the youth beheld the object of his search, sitting, motionless, with her back toward him. The reach of light was bounded by her figure, which was seated on the decaying trunk of a fallen tree. She was deeply wrapped in thought, for she did not observe his approach, and when his voice reached her ears, and she started and looked round, her eyes were full of tears. These she hastily bru hed away, and met the young man with a degree of composure which well might have put the blush upon his cheek, for the want of it.

"In tears!—weeping, Margaret?" was the first address of the lover who necessarily felt shocked at what he saw.

"They were secret tears, sir—not meant for other eyes," was the reproachful reply.

"Ah, Margaret! but why should you have secret tears, when you might have sympathy—why should you have tears at all? You have no sorrows."

"Sympathy!" was the exclamation of the maiden, while a scornful smile gleamed from her eyes; "whose sympathy, I pray?"

The young man hesitated to answer. The expression of her eye discouraged him. He dreaded lest, in offering his sympathies, he should extort from her lips a more direct intimation of that scorn which he feared. He chose a middle course.

"But that you should have sorrows, Margaret, seems very strange to me. You are young and hearty; endowed beyond most of your sex, and with a beauty which can not be too much admired. Your mother is hearty and happy, and for years you have had no loss of relations to deplore. I see not why you should have sorrows."

"It is very likely, William Hinkley, that you do not see. The ordinary sorrows of mankind arise from the loss of wives and cattle, children and property. There are sorrows of another kind; sorrows of the soul; the consciousness of denial; of strife—strife to be continued—strife

without victory—baffled hopes—defeated aims and energies. These are sorrows which are not often computed in
the general account. It is highly probable that none of
them afflict you. You have your parents, and very good
people they are. You yourself are no doubt a very good
young man—so everybody says—and you have health and
strength. Besides, you have property, much more, I am
told, than falls to the lot ordinarily of young people in this
country. These are reasons why you should not feel any
sorrow; but were all these mine and a great deal more,
I'm afraid it would not make me any more contented.
You, perhaps, will not understand this, William Hinkley,
but I assure you that such, nevertheless is my perfect conviction."

"Yes, I can, and do understand it, Margaret," said the
young man, with flushed cheek and a very tremulous voice,
as he listened to language which, though not intended to
be contemptuous, was yet distinctly colored by that scornful estimate which the maiden had long since made of the
young man's abilities. In this respect she had done injustice to his mind, which had been kept in subjection and deprived of its ordinary strength and courage, by the enfeebling fondness of his heart.

"Yes, Margaret," he continued, "I can and do understand it, and I too have my sorrows of this very sort. Do
not smile, Margaret, but hear me patiently, and believe,
that, whatever may be the error which I commit, I have no
purpose to offend you in what I say or do. Perhaps, we
are both of us quite too young to speak of the sorrows which
arise from defeated hopes, or baffled energies, or denial of
our rights and claims. The yearnings and apprehensions
which we are apt to feel of this sort are not to be counted as sorrows, or confounded with them. I had a conversation on this very subject only a few days ago, with old
Mr. Calvert, and this was his very opinion."

The frankness with which William Hinkley declared the

source of his opinions, though creditable to his sincerity, was scarcely politic—it served to confirm Margaret Cooper in the humble estimate which she had formed of the speaker.

"Mr. Calvert," said she, "is a very sensible old man, but neither he nor you can enter into the heart of another and say what shall, or what shall not be its source of trouble. It is enough, William Hinkley, that I have my cares—at least I fancy that I have them—and though I am very grateful for your sympathies, I do not know that they can do me any good, and, though I thank you, I must yet decline them."

"Oh, do not say so, Margaret—dear Margaret—it is to proffer them that I seek you now. You know how long I have sought you, and loved you: you can not know how dear you are to my eyes, how necessary to my happiness! Do not repulse me—do not speak quickly. What I am, and what I have, is yours. We have grown up together; I have known no other hope, no other love, but that for you. Look not upon me with that scornful glance—hear me—I implore you—on my knee, dear Margaret. I implore you as for life—for something more dear than life—that which will make life precious—which may make it valuable. Be mine, dear Margaret——"

"Rise, William Hinkley, and do not forget yourself!" was the stern, almost deliberate answer of the maiden.

"Do not, I pray you, do not speak in those tones, dear Margaret—do not look on me with those eyes. Remember before you speak, that the dearest hope of a devoted heart hangs upon your lips."

"And what have you seen in me, or what does your vain conceit behold in yourself, William Hinkley, to make you entertain a hope?"

"The meanest creature has it."

"Aye, but only of creatures like itself."

"Margaret!" exclaimed the lover starting to his feet.

"Ay, sir, I say it.   If the meanest creature has its hope, it relates to a creature like itself — endowed with its own nature and fed with like sympathies.   But you — what should make you hope of me?   Have I not long avoided you, discouraged you?   I would have spared you the pain of this moment by escaping it myself.   You haunt my steps — you pursue me — you annoy me with attentions which I dare not receive for fear of encouraging you, and in spite of all this, which everybody in the village must have seen but yourself, you still press yourself upon me."

"Margaret Cooper, be not so proud!"

"I am what I am!   I know that I am proud — vain, perhaps, and having little to justify either pride or vanity; but to you, William Hinkley, as an act of justice, I must speak what I feel — what is the truth.   I am sorry, from my very soul, that you love me, for I can have no feeling for you in return.   I do not dislike you, but you have so oppressed me that I would prefer not to see you.   We have no feelings in common.   You can give me no sympathies.   My soul, my heart, my hope — every desire of my mind, every impulse of my heart, leads me away from you — from all that you can give — from all that you can relish.   To you it would suffice, if all your life could be spent here in Charlemont — to me it would be death to think that any such doom hung over me.   From this one sentiment judge of the rest, and know, for good and all, that I can never feel for you other than I feel now.   I can not love you, nor can the knowledge that you love me, give me any but a feeling of pain and mortification."

William Hinkley had risen to his feet.   His form had put on an unusual erectness.   His eye had gradually become composed; and now it wore an expression of firmness almost amounting to defiance.   He heard her with only an occasional quiver of the muscles about his mouth.   The flush of shame and pride was still red upon his cheek

When she had finished, he spoke to her in tones of more dignity than had hitherto marked his speech.

"Margaret Cooper, you have at least chosen the plainest language to declare a cruel truth."

The cheek of the girl became suddenly flushed.

"Do you suppose," she said, "that I found pleasure in giving you pain? No! William Hinkley, I am sorry for you! But this truth, which you call cruel, was shown to you repeatedly before. Any man but yourself would have seen it, and saved me the pain of its frequent repetition. You alone refused to understand, until it was rendered cruel. It was only by the plainest language that you could be made to believe a truth that you either would not or could not otherwise be persuaded to hear. If cold looks, reserved answers, and a determined rejection of all familiarity could have availed, you would never have heard from my lips a solitary word which could have brought you mortification. You would have seen my feelings in my conduct, and would have spared your own that pain, which I religiously strove to save them."

"I have, indeed, been blind and deaf," said the young man; "but you have opened my eyes and ears, Margaret, so that I am fully cured of these infirmities. If your purpose, in this plain mode of speech, be such as you have declared it, then I must thank you; though it is very much as one would thank the dagger that puts him out of his pain by putting him out of life."

There was so much of subdued feeling in this address — the more intense in its effect, from the obvious restraint put upon it, that the heart of the maiden was touched. The dignified bearing of the young man, also — so different from that which marked his deportment hitherto — was not without its effect.

"I assure you, William Hinkley, that such alone was my motive for what else would seem a most wanton harshness. I would not be harsh to you or to anybody; and with my firm rejection of your proffer, I give you my regrets that you ever made it. It gives me no pleasure that you should make it. If I am vain, my vanity is not flattered or quickened by a tribute which I can not accept; and if you never had my sympathy before, William Hinkley, I freely give it now. Once more I tell you, I am sorry, from the bottom of my heart, that you ever felt for me a passion which I can not requite, and that you did not stifle it from the beginning; as, Heaven knows, my bearing toward you, for a whole year, seemed to me to convey sufficient warning."

"It should have done so! I can now very easily understand it, Margaret. Indeed, Mr. Calvert and others told me the same thing. But as I have said, I was blind and deaf. Once more, I thank you, Margaret — it is a bitter medicine which you have given me, but I trust a wholesome one."

He caught her hand and pressed it in his own. She did not resist or withdraw it, and, after the retention of an instant only, he released it, and was about to turn away. A big tear was gathering in his eye, and he strove to conceal it. Margaret averted her head, and was about to move forward in an opposite direction, when the voice of the young man arrested her:—

"Stay, but a few moments more, Margaret. Perhaps we shall never meet again — certainly not in a conference like this. I may have no other opportunity to say that which, in justice to you, should be spoken. Will you listen to me, patiently?"

"Speak boldly, William Hinkley. It was the subject of which you spoke heretofore which I shrunk from rather than the speaker."

"I know not," said he, "whether the subject of which I propose to speak now will be any more agreeable than that of which we have spoken. At all events, my purpose is your good, and I shall speak unreservedly. You have refused the prayer of one heart, Margaret, which, if unworthy

of yours, was yet honestly and fervently devoted to it.
Let me warn you to look well when you do choose, lest you
fall into the snares of one, who with more talent may be
less devoted, and with more claims to admiration, may be
far less honest in his purpose."

"What mean you, sir?" she demanded hurriedly, with
an increasing glow upon her face.

"This stranger — this man, Stevens!"

"What of him? What do you know of the stranger that
you should give me this warning?"

"What does anybody know of him? Whence does he
come — whither would he go? What brings him here to
this lonely village?—"

A proud smile which curled the lips of Margaret Cooper
arrested the speech of the youth. It seemed to say, very
distinctly, that she, at least, could very well conjecture what
brought the stranger so far from the travelled haunts.

"Ha! do you then know, Margaret?"

"And if I did not, William Hinkley, these base insinuations against the man, of whom, knowing nothing, you would
still convey the worst imputations, would never move my
mind a hair's breadth from its proper balance. Go, sir —
you have your answer. I need not your counsel. I should
be sorry to receive it from such a source. Failing in your
own attempt, you would seek to fill my mind with calum-
nious impressions in order to prejudice the prospects of another. For shame! for shame, William Hinkley. I had
not thought this of you. But go! go! go, at once, lest I
learn to loathe as well as despise you. I thought you simple and foolish, but honorable and generous. I was mistaken even in this. Go, sir, your slanderous insinuations
have no effect upon me, and as for Alfred Stevens, you are
as far below him in nobleness and honest purpose, as you
are in every quality of taste and intellect."

Her face was the very breathing image of idealized scorn
and beauty as she uttered these stinging words. Her nos-

trils were dilated, her eyes flashing fire, her lips slightly protruded and parted, her hand waving him off. The young man gazed upon her with wild looks equally expressive of anger and agony. His form fairly writhed beneath his emotions ; but he found strength enough gaspingly to exclaim : —

"And even this I forgive you, Margaret."

"Go! go!" she answered; "you know not what you say, or what you are. Go! go!"

And turning away, she moved slowly up the long avenue before her, till, by a sudden turn of the path she was hidden from the sight. Then, when his eye could no longer follow her form, the agony of his soul burst forth in a single groan, and staggering, he fell forward upon the sward, hopeless, reckless, in a wretched condition of self-abandonment and despair.

CHAPTER XX.

BLOWS — A CRISIS.

But this mood lasted not long. Youth, pride, anger, asserted themselves before the lapse of many minutes. Darker feelings got possession of his mind. He rose to his feet. If love was baffled, was there not revenge? Then came the recollection of his cousin's counsel. Should this artful stranger triumph in everything? Margaret Cooper had scarcely disguised the interest which she felt in him. Nay, had not that exulting glance of the eye declared that she, at least, knew what was the purpose of Stevens in seeking the secluded village? His own wrongs were also present to his mind. This usurper had possessed himself of the affections of all he loved — of all of whose love he had till then felt himself secure — all but the good old schoolmaster, and the sturdy schoolmate and cousin. And how soon might he deprive him even of these? That was a new fear! So rapid had been the stranger's progress — so adroitly had he insinuated himself into this Eden of the wilderness — bringing discontent and suffering in his train — that the now thoroughly-miserable youth began to fancy that nothing could be safe from his influence. In a short time his garden would all be overrun, and his loveliest plants would wither.

Was there no remedy for this? There was! and traversing the solemn recesses of that wood, he meditated the various modes by which the redress of wrong, and slight, and indignity, were to be sought. He brooded over images of strife, and dark and savage ideas of power rioting over its victim, with entirely new feelings — feelings new at least to him. We have not succeeded in doing him justice, nor in our own design, if we have failed to show that he was naturally gentle of heart, rigidly conscientious, a lover of justice for its own sake, and solicitously sensitive on the subject of another's feelings. But the sense of suffering will blind the best judgment, and the feeling of injury will arouse and irritate the gentlest nature. Besides, William Hinkley, though meek and conscientious, had not passed through his youth, in the beautiful but wild border country in which he lived, without having been informed, and somewhat influenced, by those characteristic ideas of the modes and manner in which personal wrongs were to be redressed.

Perhaps, had his cousin said nothing to him on this subject, his feelings would have had very much the same tendency and general direction which they were taking now. A dark and somewhat pleasurable anxiety to be in conflict with his rival — a deadly conflict — a close, hard death-struggle — was now the predominant feeling in his mind; — but the feeling was not *altogether* a pleasurable one. It had its pains and humiliations, also. Not that he had any fears — any dread of the issue. Of the issue he never thought. But it disturbed the long and peaceful order of his life. It conflicted with the subdued tastes of the student. It was at war with that gentle calm of atmosphere, which letters diffuse around the bower of the muse.

In the conflict of his thoughts and feelings, the judgment of the youth was impaired. He forgot his prudence. In fact, he knew not what he did. He entered the dwelling of his father, and passed into the dining-room, at that solemn moment when the grace before meat was yet in course of utterance by our worthy Brother Stevens. Hitherto, old Mr. Hinkley had religiously exacted that, whenever any of the household failed to be present in season, this ceremony should never be disturbed. They were required, hat in hand, to remain at the entrance, until the benediction had been implored ; and, only after the audible utterance of the word " Amen," to approach the cloth.

We have shown little of old Hinkley. It has not been necessary. The reader has seen enough, however, to understand that, in religious matters — at least in the forms and externals of religion — he was a rigid disciplinarian. Upon grace before and after meat he always insisted. His own prayers of this sort might have been unctuous, but they were never short ; and the meats were very apt to grow cold, while the impatience of his hearers grew warm, before he finished. But through respect to the profession, he waived his own peculiar privilege in behalf of Brother Stevens ; and this holy brother was in the middle of his entreaty, when William Hinkley appeared at the door. He paused for an instant without taking off his hat. Perhaps had his father been engaged in his office, William would have forborne, as usual, however long the grace, and have patiently waited without, hat off, until it had reached the legitimate conclusion. But he had no such veneration for Stevens ; and without scruple he dashed, rather hastily, into the apartment, and flinging his hat upon a chair, strode at once to the table.

The old man did not once raise his eyes until the prayer was over. He would not have done so had the house been on fire. But at the close, he looked up at his son with a brow of thunder. The cloud was of serious and very unusual blackness. He had for some time been dissatisfied with his son. He had seen that the youth entertained some aversion for his guest. Besides, he had learned from his worthy consort, that, in an endeavor of Brother Stevens to bestow good counsel upon the youth, he had been repulsed with as little respect as ceremony. There was one thing that the stern old man had not seen, and could not see ;

and that was the altered appearance of the lad. As he knew of no reason why he should be unhappy, so he failed to perceive in his appearance any of the signs of unhappiness. He saw nothing but the violation of his laws, and that sort of self-esteem which produces fanaticism, is always the most rigid in the enforcement of its own ordinances. Already he regarded the youth as in a state of rebellion, and for such an offence his feeling was very much that of the ancient puritan. No one more insists upon duty, than he who has attained authority by flinging off the fetters of obedience. Your toughest sinner usually makes the sourest saint.

" And is this the way, William Hinkley, that you show respect to God ? Do you despise the blessing which Brother Stevens asks upon the food which sustains us ?"

" I presume, sir, that God has already blessed all the food which he bestows upon man. I do not think that any prayer of Brother Stevens can render it more blessed."

" Ha ! you do not, do you ? Please to rise from this table."

" Nay, sir—" began Stevens.

" Rise, sir," continued the old man, laying down knife and fork, and confronting the offender with that dogged look of determination which in a coarse nature is the sure sign of moral inflexibility.

" Forgive him, sir, this time," said Stevens ; " I entreat you to forgive him. The young man knows not what he does."

" I will make him know," continued the other.

" Plead not for me, sir," said William Hinkley, glaring upon Stevens with something of that expression which in western parlance is called wolfish, " I scorn and spurn your interference."

" William, William, my dear son, do not speak so—do not make your father angry."

" Will you leave the table, sir, or not ?" demanded the

father, his words being spoken very slowly, through his teeth, and with the effort of one who seeks to conceal the growing agitation. The eyes of the mother fell upon the youth full of tears and entreaty. His fine countenance betrayed the conflicting emotions of his soul. There was grief, and anger, despair and defiance; the consciousness of being wrong, and the more painful consciousness of suffering wrong. He half started from his chair, again resumed it, and gazing upon Stevens with the hate and agony which he felt, seemed to be entirely forgetful of the words and presence of the father. The old man deliberately rose from the table and left the room. The mother now started up in an agony of fear.

"Run, my son — leave the room before your father comes back. Speak to him, Brother Stevens, and tell him of the danger."

"Do not call upon him, mother, if you would not have me defy you also. If *your* words will not avail with me, be sure that his can not."

"What mean you, my son? You surely have no cause to be angry with Brother Stevens."

"No cause! no cause! — but it matters not! *Brother* Stevens knows that I have cause. He has heard my defiance — he knows my scorn and hate, and he shall feel them!"

"William, my son, how—"

The steps of the father, approaching through the passageway, diverted her mind to a new terror. She knew the vindictive and harsh nature of the old man; and apprehensions for her son superseded the feeling of anger which his language had provoked.

"Oh, my son, be submissive, or fly. Jump out of the window, and leave Brother Stevens and me to pacify him. We will do all we can."

The unlucky allusion to Brother Stevens only increased the young man's obstinacy.

"I ask you not, mother. I wish you to do nothing, and

11

to say nothing. Here I will remain. I will not fly. It will be for my father and mother to say whether they will expel their only son from their home, to make room for a stranger."

"It shall not be said that I have been the cause of this," said Stevens, rising with dignity from his chair; "I will leave your house, Mrs. Hinkley, only regretting that I should be the innocent cause of any misunderstanding or discontent among its members. I know not exactly what can be the meaning of your son's conduct. I have never offended him; but, as my presence does offend him, I will withdraw myself—"

"You shall not!" exclaimed old Hinkley, who re-entered the room at this moment, and had heard the last words of the speaker. "You shall not leave the house. Had I fifty sons, and they were all to behave in the manner of this viper, they should all leave it before you should stir from the threshold."

The old man brought with him a cowskin; and the maternal apprehensions of his wife, who knew his severe and determined disposition, were now awakened to such a degree as to overcome the feeling of deference, if not fear, with which the authority of her liege lord had always inspired her.

"Mr. Hinkley, you won't strike William with that whip —you must not—you shall not!" and, speaking thus, she started up and threw herself in the old man's way. He put her aside with no measured movement of his arm, and approached the side of the table where the young man sat.

"Run, William, run, if you love me!" cried the terrified mother.

"I will not run!" was the answer of the youth, who rose from his seat, however, at the same moment and confronted his father.

"Do not strike me, father! I warn you—do not strike me. I may be wrong, but I have suffered wrong. I did not mean, and do not mean, to offend you. Let that content you, but do not strike me."

The answer was a blow. The whip descended once, and but once, upon the shoulders of the young man. His whole frame was in a convulsion. His eyes dilated with the anguish of his soul; his features worked spasmodically. There was a moment's hesitation. The arm that smote him was again uplifted — the cruel and degrading instrument of punishment a second time about to descend; when, with the strength of youth, and the determination of manhood, the son grasped the arm of the father, and, without any more than the degree of violence necessary to effect his object, he tore the weapon from the uplifted hand.

"I can not strike *you!*" he exclaimed, addressing the old man. "That blow has lost you your son — for ever! The shame and the dishonor shall rest on other shoulders. They are better deserved here, and here I place them!"

With these words, he smote Stevens over the shoulders, once, twice, thrice, before the latter could close with him, or the father interfere to arrest the attempt. Stevens sprang upon him, but the more athletic countryman flung him off, and still maintained his weapon. The father added his efforts to those of Stevens; but he shook himself free from both, and, by this time, the mother had contrived to place herself between the parties. William Hinkley then flung the whip from the window, and moved toward the door. In passing Stevens, he muttered a few words : —

"If there is any skin beneath the cloak of the parson, I trust I have reached it."

"Enough!" said the other, in the same low tone. "You shall have your wish."

The youth looked back once, with tearful eyes, upon his mother; and making no other answer but a glance more full of sorrow than anger to the furious flood of denunciation which the old man continued to pour forth, he proceeded slowly from the apartment and the dwelling.

CHAPTER XXI.

CHALLENGE.

THE whole scene passed in very few minutes. No time was given for reflection, and each of the parties obeyed his natural or habitual impulses. Old Hinkley, except when at prayers, was a man of few words. He was much more prompt at deeds than words—a proof of which has already been shown; but the good mother was not so patient, and made a freer use of the feminine weapon than we have been willing to inflict upon our readers. Though she heartily disapproved of her son's conduct toward Stevens, and regarded it as one of the most unaccountable wonders, the offender was still her son. She never once forgot, or could forget, that. But the rage of the old man was unappeasable. The indignity to his guest, and that guest of a calling so sacred, was past all forgiveness, as it was past all his powers of language fitly to describe. He swore to pursue the offender with his wrath to the end of the world, to cut him off equally from his fortune and forgiveness; and when Brother Stevens, endeavoring to maintain the pacific and forgiving character which his profession required, uttered some commonplace pleading in the youth's behalf, he silenced him by saying that, "were he on the bed of death, and were the offender then to present himself, the last prayer that he should make to Heaven would be for sufficient strength to rise up and complete the punishment which he had then begun."

As for Stevens, though he professed a more charitable spirit, his feelings were quite as hostile, and much more deadly. He was not without that conventional courage which makes one, in certain states of society, prompt enough to place himself in the fields of the duello. To this condition of preparedness it has hitherto been the training of the West that every man, at all solicitous of public life, must eventually come. As a student of divinity, it was not a necessity with Alfred Stevens. Nay, it was essential to the character which he professed that he should eschew such a mode of arbitrament. But he reasoned on this subject, as well with reference to past habits as to future responsibilities. His present profession being simply a *ruse d'amour* (and, as he already began to perceive, a harmless one in the eyes of the beauty whom he sought, and whose intense feelings and unregulated mind did not suffer her to perceive the serious defects of a character which should attempt so impious a fraud), he was beginning to be somewhat indifferent to its preservation; and, with the decline of his caution in this respect, arose the natural inquiry as to what would be expected of him in his former relations to society. Should it ever be known hereafter, at a time when he stood before the people as a candidate for some high political trust, that he had tamely submitted to the infliction of a cowskin, the revelation would be fatal to all his hopes of ambition, and conclusive against all his social pretensions. In short, so far as society was concerned, it would be his social death.

These considerations were felt in their fullest force. Indeed, their force can not well be conceived by the citizen of any community where the sense of individual responsibility is less rigid and exacting. They naturally outweighed all others in the mind of Alfred Stevens; and, though no fire-eater, he not only resolved on fighting with Hinkley, but, smarting under the strokes of the cowskin—heavily laid on as they had been—his resolution was equally firm

that, in the conflict, they should not separate until blood
was drawn. Of course, there were some difficulties to be
overcome in bringing about the meeting, but, where the
parties are willing, most difficulties are surmounted with
tolerable ease. This being the case at present, it followed
that both minds were busy at the same moment in devising
the when, the how, and the where, of the encounter.

William Hinkley went from the house of his father to
that of his cousin ; but the latter had not yet returned from
that ride which he had taken in order to discover the course
usually pursued by Stevens. Here he sat down to dinner,
but the sister of Ned Hinkley observed that he ate little,
and fancied he was sick. That he should come to dine
with his cousin was too frequent a matter to occasion question or surprise. This lady was older than her brother
by some seven years. She was a widow, with an only child,
a girl. The child was a prattling, smiling, good-natured
thing, about seven years old, who was never so happy as
when on Cousin William's knee. Poor William, indeed,
was quite a favorite at every house in the village except
that of Margaret Cooper, and, as he sometimes used bitterly to add, his own. On this occasion, however, the child
was rendered unhappy by the seeming indifference of Cousin
William. The heart of the young man was too full of grief,
and his mind of anxiety, to suffer him to bestow the usual
caresses upon her ; and when, putting her down, he passed
into the chamber of Ned Hinkley, the little thing went
off to her mother, to complain of the neglect she had undergone.

" Cousin William don't love Susan any more, mamma,"
was the burden of her complaint.

" Why do you say so, Susan ?"

" He don't kiss me, mamma ; he don't keep me in his lap.
He don't say good things to me, and call me his little sweetheart. I'm afraid Cousin William's got some other sweetheart. He don't love Susan."

It was while the little prattler was pouring forth her infantile sorrows in her mother's ear, that the voice of William Hinkley was heard, calling her name from the chamber.

"There, he's calling you now, Susan. Run to him and kiss him, and see what he wants. I'm sure he loves you just as much as ever. He's got no other sweetheart."

"I'll run, mamma—that I will. I'm so glad! I hope he loves me!" and the little innocent scampered away to the chamber. Her artless tongue, as she approached, enabled him to perceive what had been her grievances.

"Do you call me to love me, and to kiss me, Cousin William, and to make me your sweetheart again?"

"Yes, Susan, you shall be my only sweetheart. I will kiss nobody but you."

"You'll forget—you will—you'll put me out of your lap, and go away shaking your head, and looking so!—" and here the observant little creature attempted a childish imitation of the sad action and the strange, moody gestures with which he had put her down when he was retiring from the room—gestures and looks which the less quick eyes of her mother had failed utterly to perceive.

"No, no!" said he, with a sad smile; "no, Susan. I'll keep you in my lap for an hour whenever I come, and you shall be my sweetheart always."

"Your *little* sweetheart, your *little* Susan, Cousin William."

"Yes, my dear little Susan, my dearest little sweetheart Susan."

And he kissed the child fondly while he spoke, and patted her rosy cheeks with a degree of tenderness which his sad and wandering thoughts did not materially diminish.

"But now, Susan," said he, "if I am to be your sweetheart, and to love you always, you must do all that I bid you. You must go where I send you."

"Don't I, Cousin William? When you send me to Gran'pa Calvert, don't I go and bring you books, and didn't

I always run, and come back soon, and never play by the way?"

"You're a dear Susan," said he; "and I want you to carry a paper for me now. Do you see this little paper? What is it?"

"A note — don't I know?"

"Well, you must carry this note for me to uncle's, but you mustn't give it to uncle, nor to aunty, nor to anybody but the young man that lives there—young Mr. Stevens."

"Parson Stevens," said the little thing, correcting him.

"Ay, ay, Parson Stevens, if you please. You must give it to him, and him only; and he will give you a paper to bring back to me. Will you go now, Susan?"

"Yes, I'll go: but, Cousin William, are you going to shoot the little guns? Don't shoot them till I come back, will you?"

The child pointed to a pair of pistols which lay upon the table where William Hinkley had penned the billet. A flush of consciousness passed over the young man's cheek. It seemed to him as if the little innocent's inquiry had taken the aspect of an accusation. He promised and dismissed her, and, when she had disappeared, proceeded to put the pistols in some condition for use. In that time and region, duels were not often fought with those costly and powerful weapons, the pistols of rifle bore and sight. The rifle, or the ordinary horseman's pistol, answered the purposes of hate. The former instrument, in the hands of the Kentuckian, was a deadly weapon always; and, in the grasp of a firm hand, and under the direction of a practised eye, the latter, at ten paces, was scarcely less so. This being the case, but few refinements were necessary to bring about the most fatal issues of enmity; and the instruments which William Hinkley was preparing for the field were such as would produce a smile on the lips of more civilized combatants. They were of the coarsest kind of holster-pistols, and had probably seen service in the Revolution.

The stocks were rickety, the barrels thin, the bore almost large enough for grape, and really such as would receive and disgorge a three-ounce bullet with little straining or reluctance. They had been the property of his own grandfather, and their value for use was perhaps rather heightened than diminished by the degree of veneration which, in the family, was attached to their history.

William Hinkley soon put them in the most efficient order. He was not a practised hand, but an American forester is a good shot almost by instinct; he naturally cleaves to a gun, and without instruction learns its use. William, however, did not think much of what he could hit, at what distance, and under what circumstances. Nothing, perhaps, could better show the confidence in himself and weapon than the inattention which the native-born woodman usually exhibits to these points. Let his weapon be such as he can rely upon, and his cause of quarrel such as can justify his anger, and the rest seems easy, and gives him little annoyance. This was now the case with our rustic. He never, for a moment, thought of practising. He had shot repeatedly, and knew what he could do. His simple object was to bring his enemy to the field, and to meet him there. Accordingly, when he had loaded both pistols, which he did with equal care, and with a liberal allowance of lead and powder, he carefully put them away without offering to test his own skill or their capacities. On this subject, his indifference would have appeared, to a regular duellist, the very extreme of obtuseness.

His little courier conveyed his billet to Stevens in due season. As she had been instructed, she gave it into the hands of Stevens only; but, when she delivered it, old Hinkley was present, and she named the person by whom it was sent.

"My son! what does he say?" demanded the old man, half-suspecting the purport of the billet.

"Ah!" exclaimed Stevens, with the readiness of a prac-

11*

tised actor, " there is some hope, I am glad to tell you, Mr.
Hinkley, of his coming to his senses.   He declares his wish
to atone, and invites me to see him.   I have no doubt that
he wishes me to mediate for him."

" I will never forgive him while I have breath !" cried
the old man, leaving the room.   " Tell him that !"

" Wait a moment, my pretty one," said Stevens, as he
was about retiring to his chamber, " till I can write an answer."

The billet of Hinkley he again read.   We may do so
likewise.   It was to the following effect :—

" SIR : If I understood your last assurance on leaving
you this day, I am to believe that the stroke of my whip has
made its proper impression on your soul — that you are
willing to use the ordinary means of ordinary persons, to
avenge an indignity which was not *confined to your cloth.*
If so, meet me at the lake with whatever weapons you choose
to bring.   I will be there, provided with pistols for both, at
any hour from three to six.   I shall proceed to the spot as
soon as I receive your answer.   " W. H."

" Short and sharp !" exclaimed Stevens as he read the
billet.   " ' Who would have thought that the *young* man
had so much blood in him !'   Well, we will not balk your
desire, Master Hinkley.   We will meet you, in verity,
though it may compel me to throw up my present hand and
call for other cards.   *N'importe :* there is no other course."

While soliloquizing, he penned his answer, which was
brief and to the purpose : —

" I will meet you as soon as I can steal off without provoking suspicion.   I have pistols which I will bring with
me.   " A. S."

" There, my little damsel," said he, re-entering the
dining-room, and putting the sealed paper into the hands of

the child, " carry that to Mr. Hinkley, and tell him I will
come and speak with him as he begs me. But the note will
tell him."

" Yes, sir."

" So——"

Mrs. Hinkley entered the room at this moment. Her
husband had apprized her of the communication which her
son had made, and the disposition to atonement and repentance which he had expressed. She was anxious to confirm
this good disposition, to have her son brought back within
the fold, restored to her own affections and the favor of his
father. The latter, it is true, had signified his determined
hostility, even while conveying his intelligence; but the
mother was sanguine—when was a mother otherwise?—
that all things would come right which related to her only
child. She now came to implore the efforts of Stevens; to
entreat, that, like a good Christian, he would not suffer the
shocking stripes which her son, in his madness, had inflicted
upon him to outweigh his charity, to get the better of his
blessed principles, and make him war upon the atoning
spirit which had so lately, and so suddenly wakened up in
the bosom of the unruly boy. She did not endeavor to
qualify the offence of which her son had been guilty. She
was far from underrating the indignity to which Stevens
had been subjected; but the offender was her son—her
only son—in spite of all his faults, follies, and imperfections, the apple of her eye—the only being for whom she
cared to live!

Ah! the love of a mother!—what a holy thing! sadly
wanting in judgment—frequently misleading, perverting,
nay, dooming the object which it loves; but, nevertheless,
most pure; least selfish; truest; most devoted!

And the tears gushed from the old woman's eyes as she
caught the hand of Stevens in her own, and kissed it—
kissed *his* hand—could William Hinkley have seen *that*,
how it would have rankled, how he would have writhed!

She kissed the hands of that wily hypocrite, bedewing them
with her tears, as if he were some benign and blessing
saint; and not because he had shown any merits or practised any virtues, but simply because of certain professions
which he had made, and in which she had perfect faith because of the professions, and not because of any previous
knowledge which she had of the professor. Truly, it be-
hooves a rogue monstrous much to know what garment it is
best to wear; the question is equally important to rogue
and dandy.

Stevens made a thousand assurances in the most Christian spirit—we can not say that he gave her tear for tear
—promised to do his best to bring back the prodigal son
to her embrace, and the better to effect this object, put his
pistols under his belt! Within the hour he was on his way
to the place of meeting.

CHAPTER XXII.

FOOT TO FOOT.

WILLIAM HINKLEY was all impatience until his little messenger returned, which she did with a speed which might deserve commendation in the case of our professional Mercuries — stage-drivers and mail contractors, hight! He did not withhold it from the little maid, but taking her in his arms, and kissing her fondly, he despatched her to her mother, while he wrapped up his pistols and concealing them in the folds of his coat, hurried from the house with the anxious haste of one who is going to seek his prey. He felt somewhat like that broad-winged eagle which broods on the projecting pinnacle of yonder rocky peak in waiting for the sea-hawk who is stooping far below him, watching when the sun's rays shall glisten from the uprising fins of his favorite fish. But it was not a selfish desire to secure the prey which the terror of the other might cause him to drop. It was simply to punish the prowler. Poor William could not exactly tell indeed why he wished to shoot Alfred Stevens; but his cause of hostility was not less cogent because it had no name. The thousand little details which induce our prejudices in regard to persons, are, singly, worth no one's thought, and would possibly provoke the contempt of all; but like the myriad threads which secured the huge frame of Gulliver in his descent upon Lilliput, they are, when united, able to bind the biggest giant of us all.

The prejudices of William Hinkley, though very natural

in such a case as his, seemed to him very much like instincts. It seemed to him, if he once reasoned on the matter, that, as he had good cause to hate the intruder, so there must be justification for shooting him. Were this not so, the policy of hating would be very questionable, and surely very unprofitable. It would be a great waste of a very laudable quantity of feeling—something like omitting one's bullet in discharging one's piece—a profligacy only justifiable in a *feu de joie* after victory, where the bullets have already done all necessary mischief, and will warrant a small subsequent waste of the more harmless material.

Without designing any such child's play, our rustic hero, properly equipped with his antique pistols, well charged, close rammed, three-ounce bullets, or nearabouts, in each, stood, breathing fire but without cooling, on the edge of the lake, perched on an eminence and looking out for the coming enemy. He was playing an unwonted character, but he felt as if it were quite familiar to him. He had none of that nice feeling which, without impugning courage, is natural enough to inexperience in such cases. The muzzles of the pistols did not appear to him particularly large. He never once thought of his own ribs being traversed by his three-ounce messengers. He had no misgivings on the subject of his future digestion. He only thought of that blow from his father's hand—that keen shaft from the lips of Margaret Cooper—that desolation which had fallen upon his soul from the scorn of both; and the vengeance which it was in his power to inflict upon the fortunate interloper to whose arts he ascribed all his misfortunes! and with these thoughts his fury and impatience increased, and he ascended the highest hill to look out for his foe; descended, in the next moment, to the edge of the lake, the better to prepare for the meeting.

In this state of excitement the meekness had departed from his countenance; an entire change of expression had taken place: he stood up, erect, bold, eagle-eyed, with the

look of one newly made a man by the form of indomitable
will, and feeling, for the first time, man's terrible commission to destroy. In a moment, with the acquisition of new
moods, he had acquired a new aspect. Hitherto, he had
been tame, seemingly devoid of spirit—you have not forgotten the reproaches of his cousin, which actually conveyed
an imputation against his manliness?—shrinking, with a
feeling of shyness akin to *mauvaise honte*, and almost sub-
mitting to injustice, to avoid the charge of ill-nature. The
change that we have described in his soul, had made itself
singularly apparent in his looks. They were full of a grim
determination. Had he gazed upon his features, in the
glassy surface of the lake beside him, he had probably recoiled from their expression.

We have seen Mrs. Hinkley sending Stevens forth for
the purpose of recalling her son to his senses, receiving his
repentance, and bringing him once more home into the
bosom of his flock. We have not forgotten the brace of
arguments with which he provided himself in order to bring
about this charitable determination. Stevens was a shot.
He could snuff his candle at ten paces, sever his bamboo,
divide the fingers of the hand with separate bullets without
grazing the skin—nay, more, as was said in the euphuistic
phraseology of his admirers, send his ball between soul and
body without impairing the integrity of either.

But men may do much shooting at candle or bamboo, who
would do precious little while another is about to shoot at
them. There is a world of difference between looking in a
bull's-eye, and looking in the eye of man. A pistol, too,
looks far less innocent, regarded through the medium of a
yawning muzzle, than the rounded and neatly-polished butt.
The huge mouth seems to dilate as you look upon it. You
already begin to fancy you behold the leaden mass—the
three-ounce bullet—issuing from its stronghold, like a relentless baron of the middle ages, going forth under his
grim archway, seeking only whom he may devour. The

sight is apt to diminish the influence of skill. Nerves are
necessary to such sportsmen, and nerves become singularly
untrue when frowned upon through such a medium.

Under this view of the case, we are not so sure that the
excellence of aim for which Alfred Stevens has been so
much lauded, will make the difference very material between the parties; and now that he is fairly roused, there
is a look of the human devil about William Hinkley, that
makes him promise to be dangerous. Nay, the very pistols
that he wields, those clumsy, rusty, big-mouthed ante-revolutionary machines, which his stout grandsire carried at
Camden and Eutaw, have a look of service about them—
a grim, veteran-like aspect, that makes them quite as perilous to face as to handle. If they burst they will blow on
all sides. There will be fragments enough for friend and
foe; and even though Stevens may not apprehend so much
from the aim of his antagonist, something of deference is
due to the possibility of such a concussion, as will make up
all his deficiencies of skill.

But they have not yet met, though Stevens, with praiseworthy Christianity, is on his way to keep his engagements,
as well to mother as to son. He has his own pistols—not
made for this purpose—but a substantial pair of traveller's
babes—big of mouth, long of throat, thick of jaw, keen
of sight, quick of speech, strong of wind, and weighty of
argument. They are rifled bores also, and, in the hands
of the owner, have done clever things at bottle and sapling.
Stevens would prefer to have the legitimate things, but
these babes are trustworthy; and he has no reason to suppose that the young rustic whom he goes to meet can produce anything more efficient. He had no idea of those
ancient bull-pups, those solemn ante-revolutionary barkers,
which our grandsire used upon harder heads than his, at
Camden and the Eutaws. He is scarcely so confident in
his own weapons when his eye rests on the rusty tools of
his enemy.

But it was not destined that this fight should take place without witnesses. In spite of all the precautions of the parties, and they were honest in taking them, our little village had its inklings of what was going on. There were certain signs of commotion and explosion which made themselves understood. Our little maid, Susan Hinkley, was the first, very innocently, to furnish a clue to the mystery. She had complained to her mother that Cousin William had not shot the little guns for her according to his promise.

"But, perhaps, he didn't want to shoot them, Susan."

"Yes, mamma, he put them in his pockets. He's carried them to shoot; and he promised to shoot them for me as soon as I carried the note."

"And to whom did you carry the note, Susan?" asked the mother.

"To the young parson, at Uncle William's."

The mother had not been unobservant of the degree of hostility which her brother, as well as cousin, entertained for Stevens. They had both very freely expressed their dislike in her presence. Some of their conferences had been overheard and were now recalled, in which this expression of dislike had taken the form of threats, vague and purposeless, seemingly, at the time; but which now, taken in connection with what she gathered from the lips of the child, seemed of portentous interest. Then, when she understood that Stevens had sent a note in reply — and that both notes were sealed, the quick, feminine mind instantly jumped to the right conclusion.

"They are surely going to fight. Get my bonnet, Susan, I must run to Uncle William's, and tell him while there's time. Which way did Cousin William go?"

The child could tell her nothing but that he had taken to the hills.

"That brother Ned shouldn't be here now! Though I don't see the good of his being here. He'd only make

matters worse. Run, Susan—run over to Gran'pa Calvert,
and tell him to come and stop them from fighting, while I
hurry to Uncle William's.   Lord save us!—and let me get
there in time."

The widow had a great deal more to say, but this was
quite enough to bewilder the little girl.   Nevertheless, she
set forth to convey the mysterious message to Grand'pa
Calvert, though the good mother never once reflected that
this message was of the sort which assumes the party addressed to be already in possession of the principal facts.
While she took one route the mother pursued another, and
the two arrived at their respective places at about the same
time.   Stevens had already left old Hinkley's when the
widow got there, and the consternation of Mrs. Hinkley
was complete.   The old man was sent for to the fields, and
came in only to declare that some such persuasion had filled
his own mind when first the billet of his son had been received.   But the suspicion of the father was of a much
harsher sort than that of the widow Hinkley.   In her sight
it was a duel only—bad enough as a duel—but still only
a duel, where the parties incurring equal risks, had equal
rights.   But the conception of the affair, as it occurred to
old Hinkley, was very different.

" Base serpent!" he exclaimed—" he has sent for the
good young man only to murder him.   He implores him to
come to him, in an artful writing, pretending to be sorely
sorrowful and full of repentance ; and he prepares the
weapon of murder to slay him when he comes.   Was there
ever creature so base !—but I will hunt him out.   God give
me strength, and grant that I may find him in season."

Thus saying, the old man seized his crab-stick, a knotty
club, that had been seasoned in a thousand smokes, and
toughened by the use of twenty years.   His wife caught
up her bonnet and hurried with the widow Hinkley in his
train.   Meanwhile, by cross-examining the child, Mr. Calvert had formed some plausible conjectures of what was on

foot, and by the time that the formidable procession had reached his neighborhood he was prepared to join it. Events thickened with the increasing numbers. New facts came in to the aid of old ones partially understood. The widow Thackeray, looking from her widow, as young and handsome widows are very much in the habit of doing, had seen William Hinkley going by toward the hill, with a very rapid stride and a countenance very much agitated; and an hour afterward she had seen Brother Stevens following on the same route—good young man!—with the most heavenly and benignant smile upon his countenance—the very personification of the cherub and the seraph, commissioned to subdue the fiend.

"Here is some of your treachery, Mr. Calvert. You have spoiled this boy of mine; turning his head with law studies; and making him disobedient—giving him counsel and encouragement against his father—and filling his mind with evil things. It is all your doing, and your books. And now he's turned out a bloody murderer, a papist murderer, with your Roman catholic doctrines."

"I am no Roman catholic, Mr. Hinkley," was the mild reply—"and as for William becoming a murderer, I think that improbable. I have a better opinion of your son than you have."

"He's an ungrateful cub—a varmint of the wilderness—to strike the good young man in my own presence—to strike him with a cowskin—what do you think of that, sir? answer me that, if you please."

"Did William Hinkley do this?" demanded the old teacher earnestly.

"Ay, that he did, did he!"

"I can hardly understand it. There must have been some grievous provocation?"

"Yes; it was a grievous provocation, indeed, to have to wait for grace before meat."

"Was that all? can it be possible!"

The mother of the offender supplied the hiatus in the story — and Calvert was somewhat relieved. Though he did not pretend to justify the assault of the youth, he readily saw how he had been maddened by the treatment of his father. He saw that the latter was in a high pitch of religious fury — his prodigious self esteem taking part with it, naturally enough, against a son, who, until this instance, had never risen in defiance against either. Expostulation and argument were equally vain with him; and ceasing the attempt at persuasion, Calvert hurried on with the rest, being equally anxious to arrest the meditated violence, whether that contemplated the murderous assassination which the father declared, or the less heinous proceeding of the duel which he suspected.

There was one thing which made him tremble for his own confidence in William Hinkley's propriety of course. It was the difficulty which he had with the rest, in believing that the young student of divinity would fight a duel. This doubt, he felt, must be that of his pupil also: whether the latter had any reason to suppose that Stevens would depart from the principles of his profession, and waive the securities which it afforded, he had of course, no means for conjecturing; but his confidence in William induced him to believe that some such impression upon his mind had led him to the measure of sending a challenge, which, otherwise, addressed to a theologian, would have been a shameless mockery.

There was a long running fire, by way of conversation and commentary, which was of course maintained by these toiling pedestrians, cheering the way as they went; but though it made old Hinkley peccant and wrathy, and exercised the vernacular of the rest to very liberal extent, we do not care to distress the reader with it. It may have been very fine or not. It is enough to say that the general tenor of opinion run heavily against our unhappy rustic, and in favor of the good young man, Stevens. Mrs. Thackeray, the widow, to whom Stevens had paid two visits or more since he had been in the village, and who had her own reasons for doubting that Margaret Cooper had really obtained any advantages in the general struggle to find favor in the sight of this handsome man of God — was loud in her eulogy upon the latter, and equally unsparing in her denunciations of the village lad who meditated so foul a crime as the extinguishing so blessed a light. Her denunciations at length aroused all the mother in Mrs. Hinkley's breast, and the two dames had it, hot and heavy, until, as the parties approached the lake, old Hinkley, with a manner all his own, enjoined the most profound silence, and hushed, without settling the dispute.

Meanwhile, the combatants had met. William Hinkley, having ascended the tallest perch among the hills, beheld his enemy approaching at a natural pace and at a short distance. He descended rapidly to meet him and the parties joined at the foot of the woodland path leading down to the lake, where, but a few days before, we beheld Stevens and Margaret Cooper. Stevens was somewhat surprised to note the singular and imposing change which a day, almost an hour, had wrought in the looks and bearing of the young rustic. His good, and rather elevated command of language, had struck him previously as very remarkable, but this had been explained by his introduction to Mr. Calvert, who, as his teacher, he soon found was very well able to make him what he was. It was the high bearing, the courteous defiance, the superior consciousness of strength and character, which now spoke in the tone and manner of the youth. A choice military school, for years, could scarcely have brought about a more decided expression of that subdued heroism, which makes mere manliness a matter of chivalry, and dignifies brute anger and blind hostility into something like a sentiment. Under the prompting of a good head, a generous temper, and the goodness of a highly-roused, but legitimate state of feeling, William Hink-

ley wore the very appearance of that nobleness, pride, ease,
firmness, and courtesy, which, in the conventional world, it
is so difficult, yet held to be so important, to impress upon
the champion when ready for the field. A genuine son of
thunder would have rejoiced in his deportment, and though
a sneering, jealous and disparaging temper, Alfred Stevens
could not conceal from himself the conviction that there
was stuff in the young man which it needed nothing but
trial and rough attrition to bring out.

William Hinkley bowed at his approach, and pointed to
a close footpath leading to the rocks on the opposite shore.

"There, sir, we shall be more secret. There is a narrow
grove above, just suited to our purpose. Will it please you
to proceed thither?"

"As *you* please, Mr. Hinkley," was the reply; "I have
no disposition to balk your particular desires. But the
sight of this lake reminds me that I owe you my life?"

"I had thought, sir, that the indignity which I put upon
you, would cancel all such memories," was the stern reply.

The cheek of Stevens became crimson — his eye flashed
— he felt the sarcasm — but something was due to his position, and he was cool enough to make a concession to circumstances. He answered with tolerable calmness, though
not without considerable effort.

"It has cancelled the *obligation*, sir, if not the memory!
I certainly can owe you nothing for a life which you have
attempted to disgrace—"

"Which I have disgraced!" said the other, interrupting
him.

"You are right, sir. How far, however, you have shown
your manhood in putting an indignity upon one whose profession implies peace, and denounces war, you are as well
prepared to answer as myself."

"The cloth seems to be of precious thickness!" was the
answer of Hinkley, with a smile of bitter and scornful
sarcasm.

"If you mean to convey the idea that I do not feel the shame of the blow, and am not determined on avenging it, young man, you are in error. You will find that I am not less determined because I am most cool. I have come out deliberately for the purpose of meeting you. My purpose in reminding you of my profession was simply to undeceive you. It appears to me not impossible that the knowledge of it has made you somewhat bolder than you otherwise might have been."

"What mean you?" was the stern demand of Hinkley, uttered in very startling accents.

"To tell you that I have not always been a non-combatant, that I am scarcely one now, and that, in the other schools, in which I have been taught, the use of the pistol was an early lesson. You have probably fancied that such was not the case, and that my profession—"

"Come, sir—will you follow this path?" said Hinkley, interrupting him impatiently.

"All in good time, sir, when you have heard me out," was the cool reply. "Now, sir," he continued, "were you to have known that it would be no hard task for me to mark any button on your vest, at any distance — that I have often notched a smaller mark, and that I am prepared to do so again, it might be that your prudence would have tempered your courage—"

"I regret for your sake," said Hinkley, again interrupting him with a sarcasm, "that I have not brought with me the weapon with which *my* marks are made. You seem to have forgotten that I too have some skill in my poor way. One would think, sir, that the memory would not fail of retaining what I suspect will be impressed upon the skin for some time longer."

"You are evidently bent on fighting, Mr. Hinkley, and I must gratify you!"

"If you please, sir."

"But, before doing so, I should like to know in what

way I have provoked such a feeling of hostility in your
mind? I have not sought to do so. I have on the contrary,
striven to show you my friendship, in part requital of the
kindness shown me by your parents."

"Do not speak of them, if you please."

"Ay, but I must. It was at the instance of your worthy
mother that I sought you and strove to confer with you on
the cause of your evident unhappiness."

"You were the cause."

"I?"

"Yes — you! Did I not tell you then that I hated you;
and did you not accept my defiance?"

"Yes; but when you saved my life! —"

"It was to spurn you — to put stripes upon you. I tell
you, Alfred Stevens, I loathe you with the loathing one
feels for a reptile, whose cunning is as detestable as his
sting is deadly. I loathe you from instinct. I felt this dislike and distrust for you from the first moment that I saw
you. I know not how, or why, or in what manner, you are
a villain, but I feel you to be one! I am convinced of it
as thoroughly as if I knew it. You have wormed yourself
into the bosom of my family. You have expelled me from
the affections of my parents; and not content with this, you
have stolen to the heart of the woman to whom my life was
devoted, to have me driven thence also. Can I do less
than hate you? Can I desire less than your destruction?
Say, having heard so much, whether you will make it necessary that I should again lay my whip over your shoulders."

The face of Stevens became livid as he listened to this
fierce and bitter speech. His eye watched that of the
speaker with the glare of the tiger, as if noteful only of the
moment when to spring. His frame trembled. His lip
quivered with the struggling rage. All his feeling of self-
superiority vanished when he listened to language of so unequivocal a character — language which so truly denounced,

without defining, his villany. He felt, that if the instinct of the other was indeed so keen and quick, then was the combat necessary, and the death of the rustic essential, perhaps, to his own safety. William Hinkley met his glance with a like fire. There was no shrinking of his heart or muscles. Nay, unlike his enemy, he felt a strange thrill of pleasure in his veins as he saw the effect which his language had produced on the other.

"Lead the way!" said Stevens; "the sooner you are satisfied the better."

"You are very courteous, and I thank you," replied Hinkley, with a subdued but sarcastic smile, "you will pardon me for the seeming slight, in taking precedence of one so superior; but the case requires it. You will please to follow. I will show you my back no longer than it seems necessary."

"Lead on, sir — lead on."

12

CHAPTER XXIII.

UNEXPECTED ISSUES.

WILLIAM HINKLEY ascended the narrow path leading to the hills with an alacrity of heart which somewhat surprised himself. The apprehensions of danger, if he felt any, were not of a kind to distress or annoy him, and were more than balanced by the conviction that he had brought his enemy within his level. That feeling of power is indeed a very consolatory one. It satisfies the ambitious heart, though death preys upon his household, one by one; though suffering fevers his sleep; though the hopes of his affection wither; though the loves and ties of his youth decay and vanish. It makes him careless of the sunshine, and heedless of the storm. It deadens his ear to the song of birds, it blinds his eye to the seduction of flowers. It makes him fly from friendship and rush on hate. It compensates for all sorts of loneliness, and it produces them. It is a princely despotism; which, while it robs its slave of freedom, covers him with other gifts which he learns to value more; which, binding him in fetters, makes him believe that they are sceptres and symbols before which all things become what he desires them. His speech is changed, his very nature perverted, but he acquires an "open sesame" by their loss, and the loss seems to his imagination an exceeding gain. We will not say that William Hinkley was altogether satisfied with *his* bargain, but in the moment when he stood confronting his enemy on the bald rock, with a deadly weapon in each hand — when he felt that he stood foot to foot in equal conflict with his foe, one whom he had dragged down from his pride of place, and had compelled to the fearful issue which made his arrogance quail — in that moment, if he did not forget, he did not so much feel, that he had lost family and friends, parents and love ; and if he felt, it was only to induce that keener feeling of revenge in which even the affections are apt to be swallowed up.

Stevens looked in the eye of the young man and saw that he was dangerous. He looked upon the ante-revolutionary pistols, and saw that they were dangerous too, in a double sense.

"Here are pistols," he said, "better suited to our purpose. You can sound them and take your choice."

"These," said Hinkley, doggedly, "are as well suited as any. If you will, you can take your choice of mine ; but if you think yours superior, use them. These are good enough for me."

"But this is out of all usage," said Stevens.

"What matters it, Mr. Stevens? If you are satisfied that yours are the best, the advantage is with you. If you doubt that mine can kill, try them. I have a faith in these pistols which will content me ; but we will take one of each, if that will please you better, and use which we think proper."

Stevens expressed himself better pleased to keep his own.

"Suit yourself as to distance," said Hinkley, with all the coolness of an unmixed salamander. His opponent stepped off ten paces with great deliberation, and William Hinkley, moving toward a fragment of the rock upon which he had placed his "revolutions" for the better inspection of his opponent, possessed himself of the veterans and prepared to take the station which had been assigned him.

"Who shall give the word?" demanded Stevens.

"You may!" was the cool rejoinder.

"If 1 do, 1 kill you," said the other.

"I have no fear, Mr. Stevens," answered William Hinkley with a degree of phlegm which almost led Stevens to fancy he had to deal with a regular Trojan—"I have no fear," he continued, "and if you fancy you can frighten me by this sort of bragging you have very much mistaken your man. Shoot when you please, word or no word."

William Hinkley stood with his back to the woods, his face toward the lake which spread itself, smooth and calm at a little distance. He did not perceive that his position was a disadvantageous one. The tree behind, and that beside him, rendered his body a most conspicuous mark; while his opponent, standing with his back to the uncovered rocks ranged with no other objects of any prominence. Had he even been sufficiently practised in the arts of the duello, he would most probably have been utterly regardless of these things. They would not have influenced his firmness in the slightest degree. His course was quite as much the result of desperation as philosophy. He felt himself an outcast as well from home as from love, and it mattered to him very little, in the morbid excitement of his present mind, whether he fell by the hand of his rival, or lived to pine out a wearisome existence, lonely and uninspired, a gloomy exile in the bitter world. He waited, it may be said, with some impatience for the fire of his antagonist. Once he saw the pistol of Stevens uplifted. He had one in each hand. His own hung beside him. He waited for the shot of the enemy as a signal when to lift and use his own weapon. But instead of this he was surprised to see him drop the muzzle of his weapon, and with some celerity and no small degree of slight of hand, thrust the two pistols under his coat-skirts. A buz reached his ears a moment after—the hum of voices—some rustling in the bushes, which signified confusion in the approach of strangers. He did not wish to look round as he preferred keeping his eye on his antagonist.

"Shoot!" he exclaimed — "quickly, before we are interrupted."

Before he could receive any answer there was a rush behind him — he heard his father's voice, sudden, and in a high degree of fury, mingled with that of his mother and Mr. Calvert, as if in expostulation. From the latter the words distinctly reached his ears, warning him to beware. Such, also, was the purport of his mother's cry. Before he could turn and guard against the unseen danger, he received a blow upon his head, the only thing of which he was conscious for some time. He staggered and fell forward. He felt himself stunned, fancied he was shot, and sunk to the ground in an utter state of insensibility.

The blow came from his father's crab-stick. It was so utterly unexpected by the parties who had attended old Hinkley to the place of meeting, that no efforts were made to prevent it. But the mother of the victim rushed in in time to defeat the second blow, which the father prepared to inflict, in the moment when his son was falling from the effects of the first. Grasping the coat skirts of her spouse, she pulled him back with no scrupulous hand, and effectually baffled his designs by bringing him down, though in an opposite direction, to the same level with the youth. Old Hinkley did not bite the dust, but the latter part of his skull most effectually butted it; and had not his head been quite as tough as his crab-stick, the hurt might have been quite as severe as that which the latter had inflicted on the son.

The latter lay as perfectly quiet as if all had been over with him. So much so, that the impression became very general that such was the case. Under this impression the heart of the mother spoke out in mingled screams of lamentation and reproach. She threw herself down by the side of the youth and vainly attempted to stop the blood which was streaming from a deep gash on his skull. While engaged in this work, her apron and handkerchief being both employed for this purpose, she poured forth a torrent of wrath and denunciation against her spouse. She now forgot all the offences of the boy, and even Alfred Stevens came in for his share of the anger with which she visited the offence and the offender.

"Shame! shame! you bloody-minded man," she cried, "to slaughter your own son — your only son — to come behind him and knock him down with a club as if he had been an inhuman ox! You are no husband of mine. He sha'n't own you for a father. If I had the pick, I'd choose a thousand fathers for him, from here to Massassippi, sooner than you. He's only too good and too handsome to be son of yours. And for what should you strike him? For a stranger — a man we never saw before. Shame on you! You are a brute, a monster, William Hinkley, and I'm done with you for ever.

"My poor, poor boy! Look up, my son. Look up, William. Open your eyes. It's your own dear mother that speaks to you. O my God! you've killed him — he will not open his eyes. He's dead, he's dead, he's dead!"

And truly it seemed so, for the youth gave no sign of consciousness. She threw herself in a screaming agony upon his body, and gave herself up to the unmeasured despair, which, if a weakness, is at least a sacred one in the case of a mother mourning her only son. Old Hinkley was not without his alarms — nay, not altogether without his compunctions. But he was one of that round head *genus* whose self-esteem is too much at all times for fear, or shame, or sensibility. Without seeking to assist the lad, and ascertain what was his real condition, he sought only to justify himself for what he had done by repeating the real and supposed offences of the youth. He addressed himself in this labor chiefly to Mr. Calvert, who, with quite as much suffering as any of the rest, had more consideration, and was now busied in the endeavor to stanch the blood and cleanse the wound of the victim.

" He's only got what he deserved," exclaimed the sullen, stubborn father.

" Do not speak so, Mr. Hinkley," replied Calvert, with a sternness which was unusual with him; " your son may have got his death."

" And he deserves it!" responded the other doggedly.

" And if he has," continued Calvert, " you are a murderer—a cold-blooded murderer—and as such will merit and will meet the halter."

The face of the old man grew livid—his lips whitened with rage; and he approached Calvert, his whole frame quivering with fury, and, shaking his hand threateningly, exclaimed :—

" Do you dare to speak to me in this manner, you miserable, white-headed pedagogue—do you dare ?"

" Dare !" retorted Calvert, rising to his feet with a look of majesty which, in an instant, awed the insolence of the offender. Never had he been faced by such defiance, so fearlessly and nobly expressed.

" Dare !—Look on me, and ask yourself whether I dare or not. Approach me but a step nigher, and even my love for your unfortunate and much-abused but well-minded son will not protect you. I would chastise you, with all my years upon me, in spite of my white head. Yours, if this boy should die, will never become white, or will become so suddenly, as your soul will wither, with its own self-torture, within you. Begone !—keep back—do not approach me, and, above all, do not approach me with uplifted hand, or, by Heaven, I will fell you to the earth as surely as you felled this boy ! You have roused a feeling within me, William Hinkley, which has slept for years. Do not provoke it too far. Beware in season. You have acted the brute and the coward to your son—you could do so with impunity to him—to me you can not."

There was something in this speech, from one whom old Hinkley was accustomed to look upon as a dreaming book-

worm, which goaded the tyrannical father into irrepressible
fury; and, grinding his teeth, without a moment's hesitation he advanced, and was actually about to lay the crab-
stick over the shoulders of the speaker: but the latter was
as prompt as he was fearless. Before Hinkley could conceive his intention, he had leaped over the still unconscious
person of William, and, flinging the old man round with a
sudden jerk, had grasped and wrested the stick from his
hands with a degree of activity and strength which confounded all the bystanders, and the subject of his sudden
exercise of manhood no less than the rest.

"Were you treated justly," said Calvert, regarding him
with a look of the loftiest indignation, "you should yourself receive a taste of the cudgel you are so free to use on
others. Let your feebleness, old man, be a warning to
your arrogance."

With these words, he flung the crab-stick into the lake,
old Hinkley regarding him with looks in which it was
difficult to say whether mortification or fury had prepon-
derance.

"Go," he continued—"your son lives; but it is God's
mercy, and none of yours, which has spared his life. You
will live, I hope, to repent of your cruelty and injustice to
him; to repent of having shown a preference to a stranger,
so blind as that which has moved you to attempt the life of
one of the most gentle lads in the whole country."

"And did he not come here to murder the stranger? did
we not find him even now with pistol ready to murder
Brother Stevens? See the pistols now in his hands—my
father's pistols. We came not a minute too soon. But for
my blow, he had been a murderer."

Such was the justification which old Hinkley now offered
for what he had done.

"I am no advocate for duelling," said Calvert, "but I
believe that your son came with the stranger for this purpose, and not to murder him."

"No, no! do you not see that Brother Stevens has no pistols? Did we not see him trying to escape — walking off — walking almost over the rocks to get out of the way?"

Calvert comprehended the matter much more clearly.

"Speak, sir!" he said to Stevens, "did you not come prepared to defend yourself?"

"You see me as I am," said Stevens, showing his empty hands.

Calvert looked at him with searching eye.

"I understand you, sir," he said, with an expression not to be mistaken; "I understand you now. *This lad I know. He could not be a murderer. He could not take any man at advantage.* If you do not know the fact, Mr. Stevens, I can assure you that your life was perfectly secure from his weapon, so long as his remained equally unendangered. The sight of that lake, from which he rescued you but a few days ago, should sufficiently have persuaded you of this."

Stevens muttered something, the purport of which was, that "he did not believe the young-man intended to murder him."

"Did he not send you a challenge?"

"No!" said old Hinkley; "he sent him a begging note, promising atonement and repentance."

"Will you let me see that note?" said Calvert, addressing Stevens.

"I have it not — I destroyed it," said Stevens with some haste. Calvert said no more, but he looked plainly enough his suspicions. He now gave his attention to William Hinkley, whose mother, while this scene was in progress, had been occupied, as Calvert had begun, in stanching the blood, and trimming with her scissors, which were fortunately at her girdle, the hair from the wound. The son, meanwhile, had wakened to consciousness. He had been stunned but not severely injured by the blow, and, with the promptitude of a border-dame, Mrs. Hinkley, hurrying to a pine-tree, had gathered enough of its resin, which, spread

12*

upon a fragment of her cotton apron, and applied to the hurt, proved a very fair substitute for adhesive plaster. The youth rose to his feet, still retaining the pistols in his grasp. His looks were heavy from the stupor which still continued, but kindled into instant intelligence when he caught sight of Stevens and his father.

"Go home, sir!" said the latter, waving his hand in the prescribed direction.

"Never!" was the reply of the young man, firmly expressed; "never, sir, if I never have a home!"

"You shall always have a home, William, while I have one," said Mr. Calvert.

"What! you encourage my son in rebellion? you teach him to fly in the face of his father?" shouted the old man.

"No, sir; I only offer him a shelter from tyranny, a place of refuge from persecution. When you learn the duties and the feelings of a father, it will be time enough to assert the rights of one. I do not think him safe in your house against your vindictiveness and brutality. He is, however, of full age, and can determine for himself."

"He is not of age, and will not be till July."

"It matters not. He is more near the years of discretion than his father; and, judging him to be in some danger in your house, as a man and as a magistrate I offer him the protection of mine. Come home with me, William."

"Let him go, if he pleases—go to the d—l! He who honors not his father, says the Scriptures—what says the passage, Brother Stevens—does it not say that he who honors not his father is in danger of hell-fire?"

"Not exactly, I believe," said the other.

"Matters not, matters not!—the meaning is very much the same."

"Oh, my son," said the mother, clinging to his neck, "will you, indeed, desert me? can you leave me in my old age? I have none, none but you! You know how I have loved—you know I will always love you."

"And I love you, mother—and love him too, though he treats me as an outcast—I will always love you, but I will never more enter my father's dwelling. He has degraded me with his whip—he has attempted my life with his bludgeon. I forgive him, but will never expose myself again to his cruelties or indignities. You will always find me a son, and a dutiful one, in all other respects."

He turned away with Mr. Calvert, and slowly proceeded down the pathway by which he had approached the eminence. He gave Stevens a significant look as he passed him, and lifted one of the pistols which he still carried in his hands, in a manner to make evident his meaning. The other smiled and turned off with the group, who proceeded by the route along the hills, but the last words of the mother, subdued by sobs, still came to the ears of the youth :—

"Oh, my son, come home! come home!"

"No! no! I have no home—no home, mother!" muttered the young man, as if he thought the half-stifled response could reach the ears of the complaining woman.

"No home! no hope!" he continued—"I am desolate."

"Not so, my son. God is our home; God is our companion; our strength, our preserver! Living and loving, manfully striving and working out our toils for deliverance, we are neither homeless, nor hopeless; neither strengthless, nor fatherless; wanting neither in substance nor companion. This is a sharp lesson, perhaps, but a necessary one. It will give you that courage, of the great value of which I spoke to you but a few days ago. Come with me to my home; it shall be yours until you can find a better."

"I thank you—oh! how much I thank you. It may be all as you say, but I feel very, very miserable."

CHAPTER XXIV.

EXILE.

THE artist in the moral world must be very careful not to suffer his nice sense of retributive justice, to get so much the better of his judgment, as an artist, as to make him forgetful of human probabilities, and the superior duty of preparing the mind of the young reader by sterling examples of patience and protracted reward, to bear up manfully against injustice, and not to despond because his rewards are slow. It would be very easy for an author to make everybody good, or, if any were bad, to dismiss them, out of hand, to purgatory and places even worse. But it would be a thankless toil to read the writings of such an author. His characters would fail in *vraisemblance*, and his incidents would lack in interest. The world is a sort of vast moral lazar-house, in which most have sores, either of greater or less degree of virulence. Some are nurses, and doctors, and guardians; and these are necessarily free from the diseases to which they minister. Some, though not many, are entirely incurable; many labor for years in pain, and when dismissed, still hobble along feebly, bearing the proofs of their trials in ugly seams and blotches, contracted limbs, and pale, haggard features. Others get off with a shorter and less severe probation. None are free from taint, and those who are the most free, are not always the greatest favorites with fortune.

We are speaking of the moral world, good reader. We simply borrow an illustration from the physical. Our interest in one another is very much derived from our knowledge of each other's infirmities; and it may be remarked, passingly, that this interest is productive of very excellent philosophical temper, since it enables us to bear the worst misfortunes of our best friends with the most amazing fortitude. It is a frequent error with the reader of a book—losing sight of these facts—to expect that justice will always be done on the instant. He will suffer no delay in the book, though he sees that this delay of justice is one of the most decided of all the moral certainties whether in life or law. He does not wish to see the person in whom the author makes him interested, perish in youth—die of broken heart or more rapid disaster; and if he could be permitted to interfere, the bullet or the knife of the assassin would be arrested at the proper moment and always turned against the bosom of the wrong-doer.

This is a very commendable state of feeling, and whenever it occurs, it clearly shows that the author is going right in his vocation. It proves him to be a *human* author, which is something better than being a mere, dry, moral one. But he would neither be a human nor a moral author were he to comply with the desires of such gentle readers, and, to satisfy their sympathies, arrest the progress of events. The fates must have their way, in the book as in the lazar-house; and the persons of his drama must endure their sores and sufferings with what philosophy they may, until, under the hands of that great physician, fortune, they receive an honorable discharge or otherwise.

Were it with him, our young friend, William Hinkley, who is really a clever fellow, should not only be received to favor with all parties, but such should never have fallen from favor in the minds of any. His father should become soon repentant, and having convicted Stevens of his falsehood and hypocrisy, he should be rewarded with the hand of the

woman to whom his young heart is so devoted. Such, perhaps, would be the universal wish with our readers; but
would this be fortunate for William Hinkley? Our venerable friend and his, Mr. Calvert, has a very different
opinion. He says:—

"This young man is not only a worthy young man, but
he is one, naturally of very vigorous intellect. He is of
earnest, impassioned temperament, full of enthusiasm and
imagination; fitted for work—great work—public work—
head work—the noblest kind of work. He will be a grea·
lawyer—perhaps a great statesman—if he addresses himself at once, manfully, to his tasks; but he will not address
himself to these tasks while he pursues the rusting and
mind-destroying life of a country village. Give him the
object of his present desire and you deprive him of all
motive for exertion. Give him the woman he seeks and
you probably deprive him even of the degree of quiet which
the country village affords. He would forfeit happiness
without finding strength. Force him to the use of his tools
and he builds himself fame and fortune."

Calvert was really not sorry that William Hinkley's
treatment had been so harsh. He sympathized, it is true,
in his sufferings, but he was not blind to their probable
advantages; and he positively rejoiced in his rejection by
Margaret Cooper.

It was some four or five days after the events with which
our last chapter was closed, that the old man and his young
friend were to be seen sitting together, under the shade of
the venerable tree where we have met them before. They
had conferred together seriously, and finally with agreeing
minds, on the several topics which have been adverted to
in the preceding paragraph. William Hinkley had become
convinced that it was equally the policy of his mind and
heart to leave Charlemont. He was not so well satisfied,
however, as was the case with Mr. Calvert, that the loss
of Margaret Cooper was his exceeding gain. When did

young lover come to such a conclusion? Not, certainly, while he was young. But when was young lover wise? Though a discontent, William Hinkley was not, however, soured nor despairing from the denial of his hopes. He had resources of thought and spirit never tested before, of the possession of which he, himself, knew nothing. They were to be brought into use and made valuable only by these very denials; by the baffling of his hope; by the provocation of his strength.

His resolution grew rapidly in consequence of his disappointments. He was now prepared to meet the wishes of his venerable and wise preceptor — to grapple stoutly with the masters of the law; and, keeping his heart in restraint, if not absolute abeyance, to do that justice to his head, which, according to the opinion of Mr. Calvert, it well-deserved if hitherto it had not demanded it. But to pursue his studies as well as his practice, he was to leave Charlemont. How was this to be done — where was he to go — by what means? A horse, saddle, and bridle — a few books and the ante-revolutionary pistols of his grandsire, which recent circumstances seemed to have endeared to him, were all his available property. His poverty was an estoppel, at the outset, to his own reflections; and thinking of this difficulty he turned with a blank visage to his friend.

The old man seemed to enter into and imagine his thoughts. He did not wait to be reminded, by the halting speech of the youth, of the one subject from which the latter shrunk to speak.

"The next thing, my son," said he, "is the necessary means. Happily, in the case of one so prudent and temperate as yourself, you will not need much. Food and clothing, and a small sum, annually, for contingencies, will be your chief expense; and this, I am fortunately able to provide. I am not a rich man, my son; but economy and temperance, with industry, have given me enough, and to spare. It is long since I had resolved that all I have should be yours; and I had laid aside small sums from time to time, intending them for an occasion like the present, which I felt sure would at length arrive. I am rejoiced that my foresight should have begun in time, since it enables me to meet the necessity promptly, and to interpose myself at the moment when you most need counsel and assistance."

"Oh, my friend, my kind generous friend, how it shames me for my own father to hear you speak thus!"

The youth caught the hands of his benefactor, and the hot tears fell from his eyes upon them, while he fervently bent to kiss them.

"Your father is a good but rough man, William, who will come to his senses in good time. Men of his education — governed as he is by the mistake which so commonly confounds God with his self-constituted representative, religion with its professor — will err, and can not be reasoned out of their errors. It is the unceasing operation of time which can alone teach them a knowledge of the truth. You must not think too hardly of your father, who does not love you the less because he fancies you are his particular property, with whom he may do what he pleases. As for what I have done, and am disposed to do for you, let that not become burdensome to your gratitude. In some respects you have been a son to me, and I send you from me with the same reluctance which a father would feel in the like circumstances. You have been my companion, you have helped to cheer my solitude; and I have learned to look on the progress of your mind with the interest of the philosopher who pursues a favorite experiment. In educating you, I have attempted an experiment which I should be sorry to see fail. I do not think now that it will fail. I think you will do yourself and me ample justice. If I have had my doubts, they were of your courage, not your talent. If you have a weakness, it is because of a defi-

ciency of self-esteem — a tendency to self-disparagement.
A little more actual struggle with the world, and an utter
withdrawal from those helps and hands which in a youth's
own home are very apt to be constantly employed to keep
him from falling, and to save him from the consequences
of his fall, and I do not despair of seeing you acquire that
necessary moral hardihood which will enable you to think
freely, and to make your mind give a fair utterance to the
properties which are in it. When this is done, I have
every hope of you. You will rise to eminence in your profession. I know, my son, that you will do me honor."

"Ah, sir, I am afraid you overrate my abilities. I have
no consciousness of any such resources as you suppose me
to possess."

"It is here that your deficiency speaks out. Be bold,
my son — be bold, bolder, boldest. I would not have you
presumptuous, but there is a courage, short of presumption,
which is only a just confidence in one's energies and moral
determination. This you will soon form, if, looking around
you and into the performances of others, you see how easy
they are, and how far inferior they are to your own ideas
of what excellence should be. Do not look into yourself
for your standards. I have perhaps erred in making these
too high. Look out from yourself — look into others —
analyze the properties of others; and, in attempting, seek
only to meet the exigencies of the occasion, without asking
what a great mind might effect beyond it. Your heart will
fail you always if your *beau ideal* is for ever present to
your mind."

"I will try, sir. My tasks are before me, and I know it
is full time that I should discard my boyhood. I will go
to work with industry, and will endeavor not to disappoint
your confidence; but I must confess, sir, I have very little
in myself."

"If you will work seriously, William, my faith is in this
very humility. A man knowing his own weakness, and work-

ing to be strong, can not fail. He must achieve something
more than he strives for."

"You make me strong as I hear you, sir. But I have
one request to make, sir. I have a favor to ask, sir, which
will make me almost happy if you grant it—which will at
least reconcile me to receive your favors, and to feel them
less oppressively."

"What is that, William? You know, my son, there are
few things which I could refuse you."

"It is that *I may be your son;* that I may call you father,
and bear henceforward your name. If you adopt me, rear
me, teach me, provide me with the means of education and
life, and do for me what a father should have done, you
are substantially more than my father to me. Let me bear
your name. I shall be proud of it, sir. I will not disgrace it—nay, more, it will strengthen me in my desire
to do it and myself honor. When I hear it spoken, it
will remind me of my equal obligations to you and to
myself."

"But this, my son, is a wrong done to your own father."

"Alas! he will not feel it such."

The old man shook his head.

"You speak now with a feeling of anger, William. The
treatment of your father rankles in your mind."

"No, sir, no! I freely forgive him. I have no reference
to him in the prayer I make. My purpose is simply what
I declare. Your name will remind me of your counsels,
will increase my obligation to pursue them, will strengthen
me in my determination, will be to me a fond monitor in
your place. Oh, sir, do not deny me! You have shown
me the affections of a father—let me, I entreat you, bear
the name of your son!"

The youth flung his arms about the old man's neck, and
wept with a gush of fondness which the venerable sire could
not withstand. He was deeply touched: his lips quivered;

his eyes thrilled and throbbed. In vain did he strive to resist the impulse. He gave him tear for tear.

" My son, you have unmanned me."

" Ah, my father, I can not regret, since, in doing so, I have strengthened my own manhood."

" If it have this effect, William, I shall not regret my own weakness. There is a bird, you are aware, of which it is fabled that it nourishes its young by the blood of its own bosom, which it wounds for this purpose. Believe me, my dear boy, I am not unwilling to be this bird for your sake. If to feel for you as the fondest of fathers can give me the rights of one, then are you most certainly my son — my son!"

Long, and fond, and sweet, was their embrace. For a full hour, but few words, and those of a mournful tenderness, were exchanged between the parties. But the scene and the struggle were drawing nigh their close. This was the day when they were to separate. It had been arranged that William Hinkley, or as he now calls himself, William Calvert, was to go into the world. The old man had recalled for his sake, many of the memories and associations of his youth. He had revived that period — in his case one of equal bitterness and pleasure — when, a youth like him he was about to send forth, he had been the ardent student in a profession whose honors he had so sadly failed to reap. In this profession he was then fortunate in having many sterling friends. Some of these were still so. In withdrawing from society, he had not withdrawn from all commerce with a select and sacred few ; and to the friendly counsel and protection of these he now deputed the paternal trusts which had been just so solemnly surrendered to himself. There were long and earnest appeals written to many noble associates — men who had won great names by dint of honorable struggle in those fields into which the feebler temper of Mr. Calvert did not permit him to penetrate. Some of these letters bore for their superscriptions

such names as the Clays, the Crittendens, and the Metcalfs
— the strong men, not merely of Kentucky, but of the Union. The good old man sighed as he read them over, sepa-
rately, to his young companion.

"Once I stood with them, and like them — not the meanest among them — nay, beloved by them as an associate,
and recognised as a competitor. But they are here —
strong, high, glorious, in the eye of the nation — and I am
nothing — a poor white-headed pedagogue in the obscurest
regions of Kentucky. Oh, my son, remember this, and be
strong! Beware of that weakness, the offspring of a miserable vanity, which, claiming too much for itself, can bestow nothing upon others. Strive only to meet the exi-
gency, and you will do more — you will pass beyond it.
Ask not what your fame requires — the poor fame of a solitary man struggling like an atom in the bosom of the great
struggling world — ask only what is due to the task which
you have assumed, and labor to do that. This is the simple, small secret, but be sure it is the one which is of more
importance than all beside."

The departure of William Hinkley from his native village was kept a profound secret from all persons except his
adopted father and his bosom friend and cousin, Fisherman
Ned. We have lost sight of this young man for several
pages, and, in justice equally to the reader and himself, it
is necessary that we should hurriedly retrace our progress,
at least so far as concerns his. We left him, if we remember, having driven Alfred Stevens from his purpose, riding
on alone, really with no other aim than to give circulation
to his limbs and fancies. His ride, if we are to believe his
random but significant words, and his very knowing looks,
was not without its results. He had certainly made some
discoveries — at least he thought and said so; but, in truth,
we believe these amounted to nothing more than some plausible conjectures as to the route which Alfred Stevens was
in the habit of pursuing, on those excursions, in which the

neighbors were disposed to think that there was something very mysterious. He certainly had jumped to the conclusion that, on such occasions, the journey of Stevens was prolonged to Ellisland; and, as such a ride was too long for one of mere pleasure and exercise, the next conclusion was, that such a journey had always some business in it.

Now, a business that calls for so much secrecy, in a young student of theology, was certainly one that could have very little relation to the church. So far as Ned Hinkley knew anything of the Decalogue it could not well relate to that. There was nothing in St. Paul that required him to travel post to Ellisland; though a voyage to Tarsus might be justified by the authority of that apostle; and the whole proceeding, therefore, appeared to be a mystery in which gospelling had very little to do. Very naturally, having arrived at this conclusion, Ned Hinkley jumped to another. If the saints have nothing to do with this journey of Alfred Stevens, the sinners must have. It meant mischief—it was a device of Satan; and the matter seemed so clearly made out to his own mind, that he returned home with the further conviction, which was equally natural and far more easily arrived at, that he was now bound by religion, as he had previously been impelled by instinct, to give Stevens "a regular licking the very first chance that offered." Still, though determined on this measure, he was not unmindful of the necessity of making other discoveries; and he returned to Charlemont with a countenance big with importance and almost black with mystery.

But the events which had taken place in his absence, and which we have already related, almost put his own peculiar purposes out of his mind. That William Hinkley should have cowskinned Stevens would have been much more gratifying to him could he have been present; and he was almost disposed to join with the rest in their outcry against this sacrilegious proceeding, for the simple reason, that it somewhat anticipated his own rigorous intentions to the same effect. He was not less dissatisfied with the next attempt for two reasons.

"You might have known, Bill, that a parson won't fight with pistols. You might have persuaded him to fist or cudgel, to a fair up and down, hand over, fight! That's not so criminal, they think. I heard once of Brother John Cross, himself trying a cudgel bout with another parson down in Mississippi, because he took the same text out of his mouth, and preached it over the very same day, with contrary reason. Everybody said that John Cross served him right, and nobody blamed either. But they would have done so if pistols had been used. You can't expect parsons or students of religion to fight with firearms. Swords, now, they think justifiable, for St. Peter used them; but we read nowhere in Old or New Testament of their using guns, pistols, or rifles."

"But he consented to fight, and brought his own pistols, Ned?"

"Why, then, didn't you fight? That's the next thing I blame you for—that, when you were both ready, and had the puppies in your hands, you should have stood looking at each other without taking a crack. By jingo, had there been fifty fathers and mothers in the bush, I'd have had a crack at him. No, I blame you, William—I can't help it. You didn't do right. Oh! if you had only waited for me, and let me have fixed it, how finely we would have managed. What then, if your father had burst in, it was only shifting the barkers from your hands to mine. I'd have banged at him, though John Cross himself, and all his flock, stood by and kneed it to prevent me. They might have prayed to all eternity without stopping me, I tell you."

William Hinkley muttered something about the more impressive sort of procedure which his father had resorted to, and a little soreness about the parietal bones just at that moment giving a quick impatient air to his manner, had

the effect of putting an end to all further discussion of this
topic. Fisherman Ned concluded with a brief assurance,
meant as consolation, that, when he took up the cudgels,
his cousin need make himself perfectly easy with the conviction that he would balance both accounts very effectually.
He had previously exhorted William to renew the attempt,
though with different weapons, to bring his enemy into the
field; but against this attempt Mr. Calvert had already
impressively enjoined him; exacting from him a promise
that he would not seek Stevens, and would simply abide
any call for satisfaction which the latter might make. The
worthy old man was well assured that in Stevens's situation
there was very little likelihood of a summons to the field
from him.

Still, William Hinkley did not deem it becoming in him
to leave the ground for several days, even after his preparations for departure were complete. He loitered in the
neighborhood, showed himself frequently to his enemy, and,
on some of these occasions, was subjected to the mortification of beholding the latter on his way to the house of Margaret Cooper, with whom, a few moments after, he might
be seen in lonely rambles by the lake-side and in the wood.
William had conquered his hopes from this quarter, but he
vainly endeavored to suppress his pangs.

At length the morning came for his departure. He had
seen his mother for the last time the night before. They
had met at the house of the widow Hinkley, between which
and that of Calvert, his time had been chiefly spent, since
the day of his affair with Stevens. His determination to
depart was carefully concealed from his mother. He dreaded to hear her entreaties, and he doubted his own strength
to endure them. His deportment, however, was sufficiently
fond and tender, full of pain and passion, to have convinced
her, had she been at all suspicious of the truth, of the design he meditated. But, as it was, it simply satisfied her
affections; and the fond "good night" with which he ad-

dressed her ears at parting, was followed by a gush of tears which shocked the more sturdy courage of his cousin, and aroused the suspicions of the widow.

"William Hinkley," she said after the mother had gone home—"you must be thinking to leave Charlemont. I'm sure of it—I know it."

"If you do, say nothing, dear cousin; it will do no good —it can not prevent me now, and will only make our parting more painful."

"Oh, don't fear me," said the widow—"I shan't speak of it, till it's known to everybody, for I think you right to go and do just as Gran'pa Calvert tells you; but you needn't have made it such a secret with me. I've always been too much of your friend to say a word."

"Alas!" said the youth mournfully, "until lately, dear cousin, I fancied that I had no friends—do not blame me, therefore, if I still sometimes act as if I had none."

"You have many friends, William, already—I'm sure you will find many more wherever you go; abler friends if not fonder ones, than you leave behind you."

The youth threw his arms round the widow's neck and kissed her tenderly. Her words sounded in his ears like some melodious prophecy.

"Say no more, cousin," he exclaimed with sudden enthusiasm; "I am so well pleased to believe what you promise me of the future, that I am willing to believe all. God bless you. I will never forget you."

The parting with Calvert was more touching in reality, but with fewer of the external signs of feeling. A few words, a single embrace and squeeze of the hand, and they separated; the old man hiding himself and his feelings in the dimness of his secluded abode, while his adopted son, with whom Ned Hinkley rode a brief distance on his way, struck spurs into his steed, as if to lose, in the rapid motion of the animal, the slow, sad feelings which were pressing

heavily upon his heart. He had left Charlemont for ever.
He had left it under circumstances of doubt, and despon-
dency—stung by injustice, and baffled in the first ardent
hopes of his youthful mind. "The world was all before
him, where to choose." Let us not doubt that the benignant Providence is still his guide.

13

CHAPTER XXV.

CONQUEST.

THE progress of events and our story necessarily brings us back to Charlemont. We shall lose sight of William Hinkley, henceforth Calvert, for some time; and here, *par parenthese*, let us say to our readers, that this story being drawn from veritable life, will lack some of that compactness and close fitness of parts which make our novels too much resemble the course of a common law case. Instead of having our characters always at hand, at the proper moment, to do the business of the artist, like so many puppets, each working on a convenient wire, and waiting to be whistled in upon the scene, we shall find them sometimes absent, as we do in real life when their presence is most seriously desired, and when the reader would perhaps prefer that they should come in, to meet or make emergencies. Some are gone whom we should rather see; some present, whose absence, in the language of the Irishman, would be the best company they could give us; and some, not forthcoming, like the spirits of Owen Glendower, even when most stoutly called for. The vast deeps of human progress do not release their tenants at the beck and call of ordinary magicians, and we, who endeavor to describe events as we find them, must be content to take them and persons, too, only when they are willing. Were we writing the dramatic romance, we should be required to keep William Hinkley always at hand, as a convenient foil to Alfred Stevens. He should watch his progress; pursue his sinuosities of course; trace him out in all his ill-favored purposes, and be ready, at the first act—having, like the falcon, by frequent and constantly-ascending gyrations, reached the point of command—to pounce down upon the fated quarry, and end the story and the strife together. But ours is a social narrative, where people come and go without much regard to the unities, and without asking leave of the manager. William Hinkley, too, is a mere man and no hero. He has no time to spare, and he is conscious that he has already wasted too much. He has work to do and is gone to do it. Let it console the reader, in his absence, to know that he *will* do it—that his promise is a good one—and that we have already been shown, in the dim perspective of the future, glimpses of his course which compensate him for his mishaps, and gladden the heart of his adopted father, by confirming its prophecies and hopes.

The same fates which deny that he should realize the first fancies of his boyhood, are, in the end, perhaps, not a jot kinder to others whom they now rather seem to favor. His absence did not stop the social machine of Charlemont from travelling on very much as before. There was a shadow over his mother's heart, and his disappearance rather aroused some misgiving and self-reproachful sensations in that of his father. Mr. Calvert, too, had his touch of hypochondria in consequence of his increased loneliness, and Ned Hinkley's fighting monomania underwent startling increase; but, with the rest, the wheel went on without much sensible difference. The truth is, that, however mortifying the truth may be, the best of us makes but a very small sensation in his absence. Death is a longer absence, in which our friends either forget us, or recollect our vices. Our virtues are best acknowledged when we are standing nigh and ready to enforce them. Like the argumentative eloquence of the Eighth Harry, they are never effectual until the halberdiers clinch their rivets forcibly.

It does not necessarily impugn the benevolence or wisdom of Providence to show that crime is successful for a season in its purposes. Vice may prevail, and victims perish, without necessarily disparaging the career, or impeding the progress of virtue. To show that innocence may fall, is sometimes to strengthen innocence, so that it may stand against all assailants. To show vice, even in its moments of success, is not necessarily to show that such success is desirable. Far from it! As none of us can look very deeply into the future, so it happens that the boon for which we pray sometimes turns out to be our bane; while the hardship and suffering, whose approach we deprecate in sackcloth and ashes, may come with healing on their wings, and afford us a dearer blessing than any ever yet depicted in the loom of a sanguine and brilliant imagination.

We are, after all, humbling as this fact may be to our clamorous vanity, only so many agents and instruments, blind, and scuffling vainly in our blindness, in the perpetual law of progress. As a soul never dies, so it is never useless or unemployed. The Deity is no more profligate in the matter of souls than he is in that of seeds. They pass, by periodical transitions, from body to body; perhaps from sphere to sphere; and as the performance of their trusts have been praiseworthy or censurable, so will be the character of their trusts in future. He who has shown himself worthy of confidence in one state, will probably acquire a corresponding increase of responsibility in another. He who has betrayed his trusts or impaired them, will share less of the privileges of the great moral credit system.

In all these transitions, however, work is to be done. The fact that there is a trust, implies duty and performance; and the practice of virtue is nothing more than the performance of this work to the best of our abilities. Well, we do not do our work. We fail in our trusts. We abuse them. Such a man as Alfred Stevens abuses them. Such a woman as Margaret Cooper fails in them. What then?

Do we destroy the slave who fails in his duty, or chasten him, and give him inferior trusts? Do you suppose that the Deity is more profligate in souls than in seeds — that he creates and sends forth millions of new souls, annually, in place of those which have gone astray? Hardly so! He is too good an economist for that. We learn this from all the analogies. As a soul can not perish, so it never remains unemployed. It still works, though its labors may be confined to a treadmill.

The mere novel-reader may regard all this as so much unnecessary digression. But let him not deceive himself. It would be the most humiliating and painful thought, indeed, could we believe that the genius which informs and delights us — which guides the bark of state through a thousand storms and dangers to its port of safety — which conquers and commands — which sings in melodies that make melodies in human hearts for thousands of succeeding years — is suddenly to be suspended — to have no more employment — to do no more work — guide no more states — make no more melodies! Nay, the pang would be scarcely less to believe that a fair intellect like that of Alfred Stevens, or a wild, irregular genius, like that of Margaret Cooper — because of its erring, either through perversity or blindness, is wholly to become defunct, so far as employment is concerned — that they are to be deprived of all privilege of working up to the lost places — regaining the squandered talents — atoning, by industry and humble desire, the errors and deficiencies of the past! We rather believe that heaven is a world where the labors are more elevated, the necessities less degrading; that it is no more permanent than what we esteem present life; nay, that it is destined to other transitions; that we may still ascend, on and on, and that each heaven has its higher heaven yet. We believe that our immortality is from the beginning; that time is only a periodical step in eternity — that transition is the true meaning of life — and death nothing more than a sign of progress. It may be an upward or a downward progress, but it is not a toilsome march to a mere sleep. Lavish as is the bounty of God, and boundless as are his resources, there is nothing of him that we do know which can justify the idea of such utter profligacy of material.

We transgress. Our business is with the present doings of our dramatis personæ and not with the future employment of their souls. Still, we believe, the doctrine which we teach not only to be more rational, but absolutely more moral than the conjectures on this subject which are in ordinary use. More rational as relates to the characteristics of the Deity, and more moral as it affects the conduct and the purposes of man himself. There is something grand beyond all things else, in the conception of this eternal progress of the individual nature ; its passage from condition to condition ; sphere to sphere ; life to life ; always busy, working for the mighty Master ; falling and sinking to mere menial toils, or achieving and rising to more noble trusts ; but, at all events, still working in some way in the great world-plantation, and under the direct eye of the sovereign World-Planter. The torture of souls on the one hand, and the singing of psalms on the other, may be doctrines infinitely more orthodox ; but, to our mind, they seem immeasurably inferior in grandeur, in propriety, in noble conception of the appointments of the creature, and the wondrous and lovely designs of the benignant Father.

The defeat of such a soul as that of Margaret Cooper, can surely be a temporary defeat only. It will regain strength, it must rise in the future, it must recover the lost ground, and reassert the empire whose sway it has unwillingly abandoned ; for it is not through will, wholly, by which we lose the moral eminence. Something is due to human weaknesses ; to the blindness in which a noble spirit is sometimes suffered to grow into stature ; disproportioned stature — that, reaching to heaven, is yet shaken down and

overthrown by the merest breath of storm that sweeps suddenly beneath its skies. The very hopelessness of Margaret Cooper's ambition, which led her to misanthropy, was
the source of an ever-fertile and upspringing confidence.
Thus it was that the favoring opinions which Alfred Stevens
expressed — a favoring opinion expressed by one whom she
soon discovered was well able to form one — accompanied
by an assurance that the dream of fame which her wild imagination had formed should certainly be realized, gave him
a large power over her confidence. Her passion was sway
— the sway of mind over mind — of genius over sympathy
— of the syren Genius over the subject Love. It was this
passion which had made her proud, which had filled her
mind with visions, and yielded to her a world by itself, and
like no other, filled with all forms of worship and attraction; chivalrous faith, unflagging zeal, generous confidence,
pure spirits, and the most unquestioning loyalty! Ignorant
of the world which she had not seen, and of those movements of human passion which she had really never felt, she
naturally regarded Alfred Stevens as one of the noble representatives of that imaginary empire which her genius continually brought before her eyes. She saw in him the em-
bodiment of that faith in her intellect which it was the first
and last hope of her intellect to inspire; and seeing thus,
it will be easy to believe that her full heart, which, hitherto,
had poured itself forth on rocks, and trees, and solitary
places, forgetful of all prudence — a lesson which she had
never learned — and rejoicing in the sympathy of a being
like herself, now gushed forth with all the volume of its
impatient fullness. The adroit art of her companion led her
for ever into herself; she was continually summoned to
pour forth the treasures of her mind and soul; and, toiling
in the same sort of *egoisme* in which her life heretofore
had been consumed, she was necessarily diverted from all
doubts or apprehensions of the occult purposes of him who
had thus beguiled her over the long-frequented paths. **As**

the great secret of success with the mere worldling, is to pry into the secret of his neighbor while carefully concealing his own, so it is the great misfortune of enthusiasm to be soon blinded to a purpose which its own ardent nature neither allows it to suspect nor penetrate. Enthusiasm is a thing of utter confidence; it has no suspicion; it sets no watch on other hearts; it is too constantly employed in pouring forth the treasures of its own. It is easy, therefore, to deceive and betray it, to beguile it into confidence, and turn all its revelations against itself. How far the frequency of this usage in the world makes it honorable, is a question which we need not discuss on this occasion.

Alfred Stevens had now been for some weeks in the village of Charlemont, where, in the meantime, he had become an object of constantly-increasing interest. The men shrank from him with a feeling of inferiority; the women—the young ones being understood—shrank from him also, but with that natural art of the sex which invites pursuit, and strives to conquer even in flight. But it was soon evident enough that Stevens bestowed his best regards solely upon Margaret Cooper. If he sought the rest, it was simply in compliance with those seeming duties of his ostensible profession which were necessary to maintain appearances. Whether he loved Margaret Cooper or not, he soon found a pleasure in her society which he sought for in no other quarter of the village. The days, in spite of the strife with William Hinkley, flew by with equal pleasantness and rapidity to both. The unsophisticated mind of Margaret Cooper left her sensible to few restraints upon their ordinary intercourse; and, indeed, if she did know or regard them for an instant, it was only to consider them as necessary restraints for the protection of the ignorant and feeble of her sex—a class in which she never once thought to include herself. Her attachment to Alfred Stevens, though it first arose from the pleasure which her mind derived from its intercourse with his, and not from any of those nice and curious sympathies of temperament and taste which are supposed to constitute the essence and comprise the secret of love, was yet sufficient to blind her judgment to the risks of feeling, if nothing more, which were likely to arise from their hourly-increasing intimacy; and she wandered with him into the devious woods, and they walked by moonlight among the solemn-shaded hills, and the unconscious girl had no sort of apprehension that the spells of an enslaving passion were rapidly passing over her soul.

How should she apprehend such spells? how break them? For the first time in her life had she found intellectual sympathy — the only moral response which her heart longed to hear. For the first time had she encountered a mind which could do justice to, and correspond on anything like equal terms with, her own. How could she think that evil would ensue from an acquisition which yielded her the only communion which she had ever craved? Her confidence in herself, in her own strength, and her ignorance of her own passions, were sufficient to render her feelings secure; and then she was too well satisfied of the superiority and nobleness of his. But, in truth, she never thought upon the subject. Her mind dwelt only on the divine forms and images of poetry. The ideal world had superseded, not only the dangers, but the very aspect, of the real. Under the magic action of her fancy, she had come to dwell

> " With those gay creatures of the element
> That in the colors of the rainbow live,
> And play i' the plighted clouds"—

she had come to speak only in the one language, and of the one topic; and, believing now that she had an auditor equally able to comprehend and willing to sympathize with her cravings, she gave free scope to the utterance of her fancies, and to the headlong impulse of that imagination which had never felt the curb.

The young heart, not yet chilled by the world's denials,

13*

will readily comprehend the beguiling influence of the
dreaming and enthusiastic nature of some dear spirit, in
whose faith it has full confidence, and whose tastes are kindred with its own. How sweet the luxury of moonlight in
commerce with such a congenial spirit! how heavenly the
occasional breath of the sweet southwest! how gentle and
soothing fond the whispers of night—the twiring progress
of sad-shining stars—the gentle sway of winds among the
tree-tops—the plaintive moan of billows, as they gather
and disperse themselves along the shores! To speak of
these delights; to walk hand-in-hand along the gray sands
by the seaside, and whisper in murmuring tones, that seem
to gather sympathies from those of ocean; to guide the eye
of the beloved associate to the sudden object; to challenge
the kindred fancy which comments upon our own; to remember together, and repeat, the happy verse of inspired
poets, speaking of the scene, and to the awakened heart
which feels it; and, more, to pour forth one's own inspira-
tions in the language of tenderness and song, and awaken
in the heart of our companion the rapture to which our own
has given speech—these, which are subjects of mock and
scorn to the worldling, are substantial though not enduring
joys to the young and ardent nature.

In this communion, with all her pride, strength, and confidence, Margaret Cooper was the merest child. Without
a feeling of guile, she was dreaming of the greatness which
her ambition craved, and telling her dreams, with all the artless freedom of the child who has some golden fancy of the
future, which it seeks to have confirmed by the lips of experience. The wily Stevens led her on, gave stimulus to
her enthusiasm, made her dreams become reasonable in her
eyes, and laughed at them in his secret heart. She sung
at his suggestion, and sung her own verses with all that
natural tremor which even the most self-assured poet feels
on such an occasion.

"Beautiful!" the arch-hypocrite would exclaim, as if un-

conscious of utteranee; "beautiful!" and his hand would
possess itself of the trembling fingers of hers. "But beautiful as it is, Margaret, I am sure that it is nothing to what
you could do under more auspicious circumstances."

"Ah! if there were ears to hear, if there were hearts to
feel, and eyes to weep, I feel, I know, what might be done.
No, no! this is nothing. This is the work of a child."

"Nay, Margaret, if the work of a child, it is that of a
child of genius."

"Ah! do not flatter me, Alfred Stevens, do not deceive
me. I am too willing to believe you, for it is so dear a
feeling to think that I too am a poet. Yet, at the first, I
had not the smallest notion of this kind: I neither knew
what poetry was, nor felt the desire to be a poet. Yet I
yearned with strange feelings, which uttered themselves in
that form ere I had seen books or read the verses of others.
It was an instinct that led me as it would. I sometimes
fear that I have been foolish in obeying it; for oh, what has
it brought me? What am I? what are my joys? I am
lonely even with my companions. I share not the sports
and feel not the things which delight my sex. Their
dances and frolics give me no pleasure. I have no sympathy with them or their cares. I go apart—I am here on
the hills, or deep in the forests—sad, lonely, scarcely
knowing what I am, and what I desire."

"You are not alone, nor are your pleasures less acute
than theirs. If they laugh, their laughter ends in sleep.
If you are sad, you lose not the slightest faculty of percep-
tion or sensibility, but rather gain them in consequence.
Laughter and tears are signs neither of happiness nor grief,
and as frequently result from absolute indifference as from
any active emotion. If you are absent from them, you have
better company. You can summon spirits to your communion, Margaret; noble thoughts attend you; eyes that
cheer, lips that assure you, and whispers, from unknown
attendants, that bid you be of good heart, for the good

time is coming. Ah! Margaret, believe me when I tell
you that time is at hand. Such a genius as yours, such
a spirit, can not always be buried in these woods."

It was in such artful language as this that the arch-hypocrite flattered and beguiled her. They were wandering
along the edge of the streamlet to which we have more than
once conducted the footsteps of the reader. The sun was
about setting. The autumn air was mild with a gentle
breathing from the south. The woods were still and meek
as the slumbers of an infant. The quiet of the scene harmonized with the temper of their thoughts and feelings.
They sat upon a fragment of the rock. Margaret was silent,
but her eyes were glistening bright—not with hope only,
but with that first glimmering consciousness of a warmer
feeling, which gives a purple light to hope, and makes the
heart tremble, for the first time, with its own expectations.
It did not escape Alfred Stevens that, for the first time,
her eye sank beneath his glance; for the first time there
was a slight flush upon her cheek. He was careful not to
startle and alarm the consciousness which these signs indicated. The first feeling which the young heart has of its
dependence upon another is one little short of terror; it
is a feeling which wakens up suspicion, and puts all the
senses upon the watch. To appear to perceive this emotion is to make it circumspect; to disarm it, one must wear
the aspect of unconsciousness. The wily Stevens, practised
in the game, and master of the nature of the unsuspecting
girl, betrayed in his looks none of the intelligence which
he felt. If he uttered himself in the language of admiration, it was that admiration which would be natural to a
profound adorer of literature and all its professors. His
words were those of the amateur :—

"I can not understand, Margaret, how you have studied
—how you have learned so much—your books are few—
you have had no masters. I never met in my life with so
remarkable an instance of unassisted endeavor."

"My books were here in the woods—among these old rocks. My teacher was solitude. Ah! there is no teacher like one's own heart. My instinct made me feel my deficiencies—my deficiencies taught me contemplation—and from contemplation came thoughts and cravings, and you know, when the consciousness of our lack is greatest, then, even the dumb man finds a voice. I found my voice in consequence of my wants. My language you see is that of complaint only."

"And a sweet and noble language it is, Margaret; but it is not in poetry alone that your utterance is so distinct and beautiful—you sing too with a taste as well as power which would prove that contemplation was as happy in bringing about perfection in the one as in the other art. Do sing me, Margaret, that little ditty which you sang here the other night?"

His hand gently detained and pressed hers as he urged the request.

"I would rather not sing to-night," she replied, "I do not feel as if I could, and I trust altogether to feeling. I will sing for you some other time when you do not ask, and, perhaps would prefer not to hear me."

"To hear you at all, Margaret, is music to my ears."

She was silent, and her fingers made a slight movement to detach themselves from his.

"No, Margaret, do not withdraw them! Let me detain them thus—longer—for ever! My admiration of you has been too deeply felt not to have been too clearly shown. Your genius is too dear to me now to suffer me to lose it. Margaret—dear Margaret!"

She spoke not—her breathing became quick and hard.

"You do not speak, let me hope that you are not angry with me?"

"No, no!" she whispered faintly. He continued with more boldness, and while he spoke, his arm encircled her waist.

"A blessed chance brought me to your village. I saw you and returned. I chose a disguise in which I might study you, and see how far the treasures of your mind confirmed the noble promise of your face. They have done more. Like him who finds the precious ore among the mountains, I can not part with you so found. I must tear you from the soil. I must bear you with me. You must be mine, Margaret—you must go with me where the world will see, and envy me my prize."

He pressed her to his bosom. She struggled slightly.

"Do not, do not, Alfred Stevens, do not press me—do not keep me. You think too much of me. I am no treasure—alas! this is all deception. You can not—can not desire it?"

"Do I not! Ah! Margaret, what else do I desire now? Do you think me only what I appear in Charlemont?"

"No! no!"

"I have the power of a name, Margaret, in my profession—among a numerous people—and that power is growing into wealth and sway. I am feared and honored, loved by some, almost worshipped by others; and what has led me from this sway, to linger among these hills—to waste hours so precious to ambition—to risk the influence which I had already secured—what, but a higher impulse—a dearer prospect—a treasure, Margaret, of equal beauty and genius."

Her face was hidden upon his bosom. He felt the beating of her heart against his hand.

"If you have a genius for song, Margaret Cooper, I, too, am not without my boast. In my profession, men speak of my eloquence as that of a genius which has few equals, and no superior."

"I know it—it must be so!"

"Move me not to boast, dear Margaret; it is in your ears only that I do so—and only to assure you that, in listening to my love, you do not yield to one utterly obscure, and wanting in claims, which, as yours must be finally, are already held to be established and worthy of the best admiration of the intelligent and wise. Do you hear me, Margaret?"

"I do, I do! It must be as you say. But of love I have thought nothing. No, no! I know not, Alfred Stevens, if I love or not—if I can love."

"You mistake, Margaret. It is in the heart that the head finds its inspiration. Mere intellect makes not genius. All the intellect in the world would fail of this divine consummation. It is from the fountains of feeling that poetry drinks her inspiration. It is at the altars of love that the genius of song first bends in adoration. You have loved, Margaret, from the first moment when you sung. It did not alter the case that there was no object of sight. The image was in your mind—in your hope. One sometimes goes through life without ever meeting the human counterpart of this ideal; and the language of such a heart will be that of chagrin—distaste of life—misanthropy, and a general scorn of his own nature. Such, I trust, is not your destiny. No, Margaret, that is impossible. I take your doubt as my answer, and unless your own lips undeceive me, dearest Margaret, I will believe that your love is willing to requite my own."

She was actually sobbing on his breast. With an effort she struggled into utterance.

"My heart is so full, my feelings are so strange—oh! Alfred Stevens, I never fancied I could be so weak."

"So weak—to love! surely, Margaret, you mistake the word. It is in loving only that the heart finds its strength. Love is the heart's sole business; and not to exercise it in its duties is to impair its faculties, and deprive it equally of its pleasures and its tasks. Oh, I will teach you of the uses of this little heart of yours, dear Margaret—ay, till it grow big with its own capacity to teach. We will inform each other, every hour, of some new impulses and

objects. Our dreams, our hopes, our fears, and our desires,
ah! Margaret—what a study of love will these afford us.
Nor to love only. Ah! dearest, when your muse shall have
its audience, its numerous watching eyes and eager ears,
then shall you discover how much richer will be the strain
from your lips once informed by the gushing fullness of this
throbbing heart."

She murmured fondly in his embrace, "Ah! I ask no
other eyes and ears than yours."

In the glow of a new and overpowering emotion, such
indeed was her feeling. He gathered her up closer in his
arms. He pressed his lips upon the rich ripe beauties of
hers, as some hungering bee, darting upon the yet unrifled
flower which it first finds in the shadows of the forest,
clings to, and riots on, the luscious loveliness, as if appetite could only be sated in its exhaustion. She struggled
and freed herself from his embrace: but, returning home
that evening her eye was cast upon the ground; her step
was set down hesitatingly; there was a tremor in her
heart; a timid expression in her face and manner! These
were proofs of the discovery which she then seems to have
made for the first time, that there is a power stronger than
mere human will—a power that controls genius; that
mocks at fame; feels not the lack of fortune, and is independent of the loss of friends! She now first knew her
weakness. She had felt the strength of love! Ah! the
best of us may quail, whatever his hardihood, in the day
when love asserts *his* strength and goes forth to victory.

Margaret Cooper sought her chamber, threw herself on
the bed, and turned her face in the pillow to hide the burning blushes which, with every movement of thought and
memory, seemed to increase upon her cheek. Yet, while
she blushed and even wept, her heart throbbed and trembled with the birth of a new emotion of joy. Ah! how
sweet is our first secret pleasure—shared by one other only
—sweet to that other as to ourself—so precious to him

also. To be carried into our chamber — to be set up ostentatiously — there, where none but ourselves may see — to be an object of our constant tendance, careful idolatry, keen suspicion, delighted worship!

Ah! but if the other makes it no idol — his toy only — what shall follow this desecration of the sacred thing! What but shame, remorse, humiliation, perhaps death! — alas! for Margaret Cooper, the love which had so suddenly grown into a precious divinity with her, was no divinity with him. He is no believer. He has no faith in such things, but like the trader in religion, he can preach deftly the good doctrines which he can not feel and is slow to practise.

CHAPTER XXVI.

FALL.

WE should speak unprofitably and with little prospect of being understood, did our readers require to be told, that there is a certain impatient and gnawing restlessness in the heart of love, which keeps it for ever feverish and anxious. Where this passion is associated with a warm, enthusiastic genius, owning the poetic temperament, the anxiety is proportionably greater. The ideal of the mind is a sort of classical image of perfect loveliness, chaste, sweet, commanding, but, how cold ! .But love gives life to this image, even as the warm rays of the sun falling upon the sullen lips of the Memnon, compel its utterance in music. It not only looks beauty—it breathes it. It is not only the aspect of the Apollo, it is the god himself ; his full lyre strung, his golden bow quivering at his back with the majesty of his motion ; and his lips parting with the song which shall make the ravished spheres stoop, and gather round to listen.

Hitherto Margaret Cooper had been a girl of strong will ; will nursed in solitude, and by the wrong-headed indulgence of a vain and foolish mother. She was conscious of that bounding, bursting soul of genius which possessed her bosom ; that strange, moody, and capricious god ; pent-up, denied, crying evermore for utterance, with a breath more painful to endure, because of the suppression. This consciousness, with the feeling of denial which attended it, had cast a gloomy intensity over her features not less than her mind. The belief that she was possessed of treasures which were unvalued — that she had powers which were never to be exercised — that with a song such as might startle an empire, she was yet doomed to a silent and senseless auditory of rocks and trees ; this belief had brought with it a moody arrogance of temper which had made itself felt by all around her. In one hour this mood had departed. Ambition and love became united for a common purpose ; for the object of the latter, was also the profound admirer of the former.

The anxious restlessness which her newly-acquired sensations occasioned in her bosom, was not diminished by a renewal of those tender interviews with her lover, which we have endeavored, though so faultily, already to describe. Evening after evening found them together ; the wily hypocrite still stimulating, by his glozing artifices, the ruling passion for fame, which, in her bosom, was only temporarily subservient to love, while he drank his precious reward from her warm, lovely, and still-blushing lips and cheeks. The very isolation in which she had previously dwelt in Charlemont, rendered the society of Stevens still more dear to her heart. She was no longer alone — no longer unknown — not now unappreciated in that respect in which hitherto she felt her great denial. "Here is one — himself a genius — who can do justice to mine."

The young poet who finds an auditor, where he has never had one before, may be likened to a blind man suddenly put in possession of his sight. He sees sun and moon and stars, the forms of beauty, the images of grace ; and his soul grows intoxicated with the wonders of its new empire. What does he owe to him who puts him in possession of these treasures? who has given him his sight ? Love, devotion, all that his full heart has to pay of homage and affection.

Such was very much the relation which Margaret Cooper

bore to Alfred Stevens; and when, by his professions of love, he left the shows of his admiration no longer doubtful, she was at once and entirely his. She was no longer the self-willed, imperious damsel, full of defiance, dreaming of admiration only, scornful of the inferior, and challenging the regards of equals. She was now a timid, trembling girl — a dependant, such as the devoted heart must ever be, waiting for the sign to speak, looking eagerly for the smile to reward her sweetest utterance. If now she walked with Stevens, she no longer led the way; she hung a little backward, though she grasped his arm — nay, even when her hand was covered with a gentle pressure in the folds of his. If she sung, she did not venture to meet his eyes, which she *felt* must be upon hers, and now it was no longer her desire that the village damsels should behold them as they went forth together on their rambles. She no longer met their cunning and significant smiles with confidence and pride, but with faltering looks, and with cheeks covered with blushes. Great, indeed, was the change which had come over that once proud spirit — change surprising to all, but as natural as any other of the thousand changes which are produced in the progress of moments by the arch-magician, Love. Heretofore, her song had disdained the ordinary topics of the youthful ballad-monger. She had uttered her apostrophes to the eagle, soaring through the black, billowy masses of the coming thunder-storm; to the lonely but lofty rock, lonely in its loftiness, which no foot travelled but her own; to the silent glooms of the forest — to the majesty of white-bearded and majestic trees. The dove and the zephyr now shared her song, and a deep sigh commonly closed it. She was changed from what she was. The affections had suddenly bounded into being, trampling the petty vanities under foot; and those first lessons of humility which are taught by love, had subdued a spirit which, hitherto, had never known control.

Alfred Stevens soon perceived how complete was his victory. He soon saw the extent of that sudden change which had come over her character. Hitherto, she had been the orator. When they stood together by the lake-side, or upon the rock, it was her finger which had pointed out the objects for contemplation; it was her voice whose eloquence had charmed the ear, dilating upon the beauties or the wonders which they surveyed. She was now no longer eloquent in words. But she looked a deeper eloquence by far than any words could embody. He was now the speaker; and regarding him through the favoring media of kindled affections, it seemed to her ear, that there was no eloquence so sweet as his. He spoke briefly of the natural beauties by which they were surrounded.

" Trees, rocks, the valley and the hill, all realms of solitude and shade, inspire enthusiasm and ardor in the imaginative spirit. They are beneficial for this purpose. For the training of a great poet they are necessary. They have the effect of lifting the mind to the contemplation of vastness, depth, height, profundity. This produces an intensity of mood — the natural result of any association between our own feelings and such objects as are lofty and noble in the external world. The feelings and passions as they are influenced by the petty play of society, which diffuses their power and breaks their lights into little, become concentrated on the noble and the grand. Serious earnestness of nature becomes habitual — the heart flings itself into all the subjects of its interest — it trifles with none — all its labors become sacred in its eyes, and the latest object of study and analysis is that which is always most important. The effect of this training in youth on the poetic mind, is to the last degree beneficial; since, without a degree of seriousness amounting to intensity — without a hearty faith in the importance of what is to be done — without a passionate fullness of soul which drives one to his task — there will be no truthfulness, no eloquence, no concentrated thought and permanent achievement. With you, dear Margaret, such has already been the effect. You shrink from the ordinary enjoyments of society. Their bald chat distresses you, as the chatter of so many jays. You prefer the solitude which feeds the serious mood which you love, and enables your imagination, unrepressed by the presence of shallow witlings, to evoke its agents from storm and shadow — from deep forest and lonesome lake — to minister to the cravings of an excited heart, and a soaring and ambitious fancy."

" Oh, how truly, Alfred, do you speak it," she murmured as he closed.

" So far, so good ; but, dear Margaret — there are other subjects of study which are equally necessary for the great poet. The wild aspects of nature are such as are of use in the first years of his probation. To grow up in the woods and among the rocks, so that a hearty simplicity, an earnest directness, with a constant habit of contemplation should be permanently formed, is a first and necessary object. But it is in this training as in every other. There are successive steps. There is a law of progressive advance. You must not stop there. The greatest moral study for the poet must follow. This is the study of man in society — in the great world — where he puts on a thousand various aspects — far other than those which are seen in the country — in correspondence with the thousand shapes of fortune, necessity, or caprice, which attend him there. Indeed, it may safely be said, that he never knows one half of the responsibility of his tasks who toils without the presence of those for whom he toils. It is in the neighborhood of man that we feel his and our importance. It is while we are watching his strifes and struggles that we see the awful importance of his destiny ; and the great trusts of self, and truth, and the future, which have been delivered to his hands. Here you do not see man. You see certain shapes, which are employed in raising hay, turnips, and potatoes ; which eat and drink very much as man does ; but which, as they suffer to sleep and rest most of those latent faculties, the exercise of which can alone establish the superiority of the intellectual over the animal nature, so they have no more right to the name of man than any other of those animals who eat as industriously, and sleep as profoundly, as themselves. The contemplation of the superior being, engaged in superior toils, awakens superior faculties in the observer. He who sees nothing but the gathering of turnips will think of nothing but turnips. As we enlarge the sphere of our observation, the faculty of thought becomes expanded. You will discover this wonderful change when you go into the world. Hitherto, your inspirers have been these groves, these rocks, lakes, trees, and silent places. But, when you sit amid crowds of bright-eyed, full-minded, and admiring people; when you see the eyes of thousands looking for the light to shine from yours; hanging, with a delight that still hungers, on the words of truth and beauty which fall from your lips—then, then only, dearest Margaret, will you discover the true sources of inspiration and of fame."

"Ah!" she murmured despondingly—"you daunt me when you speak of these crowds—crowds of the intellectual and the wise. What should I be—how would I appear among them?"

"As you appear to me, Margaret—their queen, their idol, their divinity, not less a beauty than a muse?"

The raptures which Stevens expressed seemed to justify the embrace which followed it; and it was some moments before she again spoke. When she did the same subject was running in her mind.

"Ah! Alfred, still I fear!"

"Fear nothing, Margaret. It will be as I tell you—as I promise! If I deceive you, I deceive myself. Is it not for the wife of my bosom that I expect this homage?"

Her murmurs were unheard. They strolled on—still deeper into the mazes of the forest, and the broad disk of

the moon, suddenly gleaming, yellow, through the tops of
the trees, surprised them in their wanderings.

"How beautiful!" he exclaimed. "Let us sit here,
dearest Margaret. The rock here is smooth and covered
with the softest lichen. A perfect carpet of it is at our
feet, and the brooklet makes the sweetest murmuring as it
glides onward through the grove, telling all the while, like
some silly schoolgirl, where you may look for it. See the
little drops of moonlight falling here and there in the small
openings of the forest, and lying upon the greensward like
so many scattered bits of silver. One might take it for
fairy coin. And, do you note the soft breeze that seems to
rise with the moon as from some Cytherean isle, breathing
of love, love only — love never perishing!"

"Ah! were it so, Alfred!"

"Is it not, Margaret? If I could fancy that you would
cease to love me or I you — could I think that these dear
joys were to end — but no! no! let us not think of it. It
is too sweet to believe, and the distrust seems as unholy as
it is unwholesome. That bright soft planet seems to persuade to confidence as it inspires love. Do you not feel
your heart soften in the moonlight, Margaret? your eye
glistens, dearest — and your heart, I know, must be touched.
It is — I feel its beating! What a tumult, dear Margaret,
is here!"

"Do not, do not!" she murmured, gently striving to disengage herself from his grasp.

"No! no! — move not, dearest," he replied in a subdued tone — a murmur most like hers. "Are we not happy? Is there anything, dear Margaret, which we could
wish for?"

"Nothing! nothing!"

"Ah! what a blessed chance it was that brought me to
these hills. I never lived till now. I had my joys, Margaret — my triumphs! I freely yield them to the past! I
care for them no more! They are no longer joys or tri-

umphs! Yes, Margaret you have changed my heart within me. Even fame which I so much worshipped is forgotten."

"Say not that; oh, say not that!" she exclaimed, but still in subdued accents.

"I must—it is too far true. I could give up the shout of applause—the honor of popular favor—the voice of a people's approbation—the shining display and the golden honor—all, dear Margaret, sooner than part with you."

"But you need not give them up, Alfred."

"Ah, dearest, but I have no soul for them now. You are alone my soul, my saint—the one dear object, desire, and pride, and conquest."

"Alas! and have you not conquered, Alfred?"

"Sweet! do I not say that I am content to forfeit all honors, triumphs, applauses—all that was so dear to me before—and only in the fond faith that I had conquered? You are mine—you tell me so with your dear lips—I have you in my fond embrace—ah! do not talk to me again of fame."

"I were untrue to you as to myself, dear Alfred, did I not. No! with your talents, to forego their uses—to deliver yourself up to love wholly, were as criminal as it would be unwise."

"You shall be my inspiration then, dear Margaret. These lips shall send me to the forum—these eyes shall reward me with smiles when I return. Your applause shall be to me a dearer triumph than all the clamors of the populace."

"Let us return home—it is late."

"Not so!—and why should we go? What is sleep to us but loss? What the dull hours, spent after the ordinary fashion, among ordinary people. Could any scene be more beautiful than this—ah! can any feeling be more sweet? Is it not so to you, dearest? tell me—nay, do not tell me—if you love as I do, you can not leave me—not now—

14

not thus — while such is the beauty of earth and heaven — while such are the rich joys clustering in our hearts. Nay, while, in that hallowing moonlight, I gaze upon thy dark eyes, and streaming hair, thy fair, beautiful cheeks, and those dear rosy lips!"

"Oh! Alfred, do not speak so — do not clasp me thus. Let us go. It is late — very late, and what will they say?"

"Let them say! Are we not blessed? Can all their words take from us these blessings — these sacred, sweet, moments — such joys, such delights? Let them dream of such, with their dull souls if they can. No! no! Margaret — we are one! and thus one, our world is as free from their control as it is superior to their dreams and hopes. Here is our heaven, Margaret — ah! how long shall it be ours! at what moment may we lose it, by death, by storm, by what various mischance! What profligacy to fly before the time! No! no! but a little while longer — but a little while!"

And there they lingered! He, fond, artful, persuasive; she, trembling with the dangerous sweetness of wild, unbidden emotions. Ah! why did she not go? Why was the strength withheld which would have carried out her safer purpose? The moon rose until she hung in the zenith, seeming to linger there in a sad, sweet watch, like themselves — the rivulet ran along, still prattling through the groves; the breeze, which had been a soft murmur among the trees at the first rising of the moon, now blew a shrill whistle among the craggy hills; but they no longer heard the prattle of the rivulet — even the louder strains of the breeze were unnoticed, and it was only when they were about to depart, that poor Margaret discovered that the moon had all the while been looking down upon them.

CHAPTER XXVII.

THE BIRTH OF THE AGONY.

It was now generally understood in Charlemont that Margaret Cooper had made a conquest of the handsome stranger. We have omitted — as a matter not congenial to our taste — the small by-play which had been carried on by the other damsels of the village to effect the same object. There had been setting of caps, without number, ay, and pulling them too, an the truth were known among the fair Stellas and Clarissas, the Daphnes and Dorises, of Charlemont, but, though Stevens was sufficiently considerate of the claims of each, so far as politeness demanded it, and contrived to say pleasant things, *pour passer le temps*, with all of them, it was very soon apparent to the most sanguine, that the imperial beauties and imperious mind of Margaret Cooper had secured the conquest for herself.

As a matter of course, the personal and intellectual attractions of Stevens underwent no little disparagement as soon as this fact was known. It was now universally understood that he was no such great things, after all; and our fair friend the widow Thackeray, who was not without her pretensions to wit and beauty, was bold enough to say that Mr. Stevens was certainly too fat in the face, and she rather thought him stupid. Such an opinion gave courage to the rest, and pert Miss Bella Tompkins, a romp of first-rate excellence, had the audacity to say that he squinted!

—and this opinion was very natural, since neither of his eyes had ever rested with satisfaction on her pouting charms.

It may be supposed that the discontent of the fair bevy, and its unfavorable judgment of himself, did not reach the ears of Alfred Stevens, and would scarcely have disturbed them if it did. Margaret Cooper was more fortunate than himself in this respect. She could not altogether be insensible to the random remarks which sour envy and dark-eyed jealousy continued to let fall in her hearing; but her scorn for the speakers, and her satisfaction with herself, secured her from all annoyance from this cause. Such, at least, had been the case in the first days of her conquest. Such was not exactly the case now. She had no more scorn of others. She was no longer proud, no longer strong. Her eyes no longer flashed with haughty defiance on the train which, though envious, were yet compelled to follow. She could no longer speak in those superior tones, the language equally of a proud intellect, and a spirit whose sensibilities had neither been touched by love nor enfeebled by anxiety and apprehension. A sad change had come over her heart and all her features in the progress of a few days. Her courage had departed. Her step was no longer firm; her eye no longer uplifted like that of the mountain-eagle, to which, in the first darings of her youthful muse, she had boldly likened herself. Her look was downcast, her voice subdued; she was now not less timid than the feeblest damsel of the village in that doubtful period of life when, passing from childhood to girlhood, the virgin falters, as it were, with bashful thoughts, upon the threshold of a new and perilous condition. The intercourse of Margaret Cooper with her lover had had the most serious effect upon her manners and her looks. But the change upon her spirit was no less striking to all.

" I'm sure if I did love any man," was the opinion of one of the damsels, " I'd die sooner than show it to him, as she shows it to Alfred Stevens. It's a guess what he must think of it."

"And no hard guess neither," said another; "I reckon there's no reason why he should pick out Margaret Cooper, except that he saw that it was no such easy matter anywhere else."

"Well! there can be no mistake about it with them; for now they're always together—and Betty, her own maid, thinks—but it's better not to say!"

And the prudent antique pursed up her mouth in a language that said everything.

"What!—what does she say?" demanded a dozen voices.

"Well! I won't tell you that. I won't tell you all; but she does say, among other things, that the sooner John Cross marries them, the better for all parties."

"Is it possible!"

"Can it be!"

"Bless me! but I always thought something wrong."

"And Betty, her own maid, told you? Well, who should know, if she don't?"

"And this, too, after all her airs!"

"Her great smartness, her learning, and verse-making! I never knew any good come from books yet."

"And never will, Jane," said another, with an equivocal expression, with which Jane was made content; and, after a full half-hour s confabulation, in the primitive style, the parties separated—each, in her way, to give as much circulation to Betty's inuendoes as the importance of the affair deserved.

Scandal travels along the highways, seen by all but the victim. Days and nights passed; and in the solitude of lonely paths, by the hillside or the rivulet, Margaret Cooper still wandered with her lover. She heard not the poisonous breath which was already busy with her virgin fame. She had no doubts, whatever might be the event, that the

heart of Alfred Stevens could leave her without that aliment which, in these blissful moments, seemed to be her
very breath of life. But she felt many fears, many misgivings, she knew not why. A doubt, a cloud of anxiety, hung
brooding on the atmosphere. In a heart which is unsophisticated, the consciousness, however vague, that all is
not right, is enough to produce this cloud; but, with the
gradual progress of that heart to the indulgence of the more
active passions, this consciousness necessarily increases, and
the conflict then begins between the invading passion and the
guardian principle. We have seen enough to know what
must be the result of such a conflict with a nature such as
hers, under the education which she had received. It did
not end in the expulsion of her lover. It did not end in the
discontinuance of those long and frequent rambles amid silence, and solitude, and shadow. She had not courage for
this; and the poor, vain mother, flattered with the idea
that her son-in-law would be a preacher, beheld nothing
wrong in their nightly wanderings, and suffered her daughter, in such saintly society, to go forth without restraint or
rebuke.

There was one person in the village who was not satisfied that Margaret Cooper should fall a victim, either to
the cunning of another, or to her own passionate vanity.
This was our old friend Calvert. He was rather inclined
to be interested in the damsel, in spite of the ill treatment
of his *protégé*, if it were only in consequence of the feelings with which she had inspired him. It has been seen
that, in the affair of the duel, he was led to regard the
stranger with an eye of suspicion. This feeling had been
further heightened by the statements of Ned Hinkley,
which, however loose and inconclusive, were yet of a kind
to show that there was some mystery about Stevens—that
he desired concealment in some respects—a fact very
strongly inferred from his non-employment of the village
postoffice, and the supposition—taken for true—that he

employed that of some distant town. Ned Hinkley had
almost arrived at certainty in this respect; and some small
particulars which seemed to bear on this conviction, which
he had recently gathered, taken in connection with the
village scandal in reference to the parties, determined the
old man to take some steps in the matter to forewarn the
maiden, or at least her mother, of the danger of yielding
too much confidence to one of whom so little was or could
be known.

It was a pleasant afternoon, and Calvert was sitting beneath his roof-tree, musing over this very matter, when he
caught a glimpse of the persons of whom he thought, as-
cending one of the distant hills, apparently on their way
to the lake. He rose up instantly, and, seizing his staff,
hurried off to see the mother of the damsel. The matter
was one of the nicest delicacy—not to be undertaken
lightly—not to be urged incautiously. Nothing, indeed,
but a strong sense of duty could have determined him upon
a proceeding likely to appear invidious, and which might
be so readily construed, by a foolish woman, into an impertinence. Though a man naturally of quick, warm feelings,
Calvert had been early taught to think cautiously—indeed, the modern phrenologist would have said that, in the
excess of this prudent organ lay the grand weakness of his
moral nature. This delayed him in the contemplated
performance much longer than his sense of its necessity
seemed to justify. Having now resolved, however, and
secure in the propriety of his object, he did not scruple
any longer.

A few minutes sufficed to bring him to the cottage of the
old lady, and her voice in very friendly tenor commanded
him to enter. Without useless circumlocution, yet without
bluntness, the old man broached the subject; and, without
urging any of the isolated facts of which he was possessed,
and by which his suspicions were awakened, he dwelt simply upon the dangers which might result from such a de-

gree of confidence as was given to the stranger. The long, lonely rambles in the woods, by night as well as day, were commented on, justly, but in an indulgent spirit; and the risks of a young and unsuspecting maiden, under such circumstances, were shown with sufficient distinctness for the comprehension of the mother, had she been disposed to hear. But never was good old man, engaged in the thankless office of bestowing good advice, so completely confounded as he was by the sort of acknowledgments which his interference obtained. A keen observer might have seen the gathering storm while he was speaking; and, at every sentence, there was a low, running commentary, bubbling up from the throat of the opinionated dame, somewhat like rumbling thunder, which amply denoted the rising tempest. It was a sort of religious effort which kept the old lady quiet till Calvert had fairly reached a conclusion. Then, rising from her seat, she approached him, smoothed back her apron, perked out her chin, and, fixing her keen gray eyes firmly upon his own, with her nose elongated to such a degree as almost to suggest the possibility of a pointed collision between that member and the corresponding one of his own face, she demanded—

"Have you done—have you got through?"

"Yes, Mrs. Cooper, this is all I came to say. It is the suggestion of prudence—the caution of a friend—your daughter is young, very young, and—"

"I thank you! I thank you! My daughter is young, very young; but she is no fool, Mr. Calvert—let me tell you that! Margaret Cooper is no fool. If you don't know that, I do. I know her. She's able to take care of herself as well as the best of us."

"I am glad you think so, Mrs. Cooper, but the best of us find it a difficult matter to steer clear of danger, and error and misfortune; and the wisest, my dear madam, are only too apt to fall when they place their chief reliance on their wisdom."

"Indeed! that's a new doctrine to me, and I reckon to everybody else. If it's true, what's the use of all your schooling, I want to know?"

"Precious little, Mrs. Cooper, if—"

"Ah! precious little; and let me tell you, Mr. Calvert, I think it's mighty strange that you should think Margaret Cooper in more need of your advice, than Jane Colter, or Betsy Barnes, or Susan Mason, or Rebecca Forbes, or even the widow Thackeray."

"I should give the same advice to them under the same circumstances, Mrs. Cooper."

"Should you, indeed! Then I beg you will go and give it to them, for if they are not in the same circumstances now, they'd give each of them an eye to be so. Ay, wouldn't they! Yes! don't I know, Mr. Calvert, that it's all owing to envy that you come here talking about Brother Stevens."

"But I do not speak of Mr. Stevens, Mrs. Cooper; were it any other young man with whom your daughter had such intimacy I should speak in the same manner."

"Would you, indeed? Tell that to the potatoes. Don't I know better. Don't I know that if your favorite, that you made so much of—your adopted son, Bill Hinkley— if he could have got her to look at him, they might have walked all night and you'd never have said the first word. He'd have given one eye for her, and so would every girl in the village give an eye for Brother Stevens. I'm not so old but I know something. But it won't do. You can go to the widow Thackeray, Mr. Calvert. It'll do her good to tell her that it's very dangerous for her to be thinking about young men from morning to night. It's true you can't say anything about the danger, for precious little danger she's in; but, lord, wouldn't she jump to it if she had a chance. Let her alone for that. You'd soon have cause enough to give her your good advice about the danger, and much good would come of it. She'd wish, after

14*

all was said, that the danger was only twice as big and twice as dangerous."

Such was the conclusion of Mr. Calvert's attempt to give good counsel. It resulted as unprofitably in this as in most cases; but it had not utterly fallen, like the wasted seed, in stony places. There was something in it to impress itself upon the memory of Mrs. Cooper; and she resolved that when her daughter came in, it should be the occasion of an examination into her feelings and her relation to the worthy brother, such as she had more than once before meditated to make.

But Margaret Cooper did not return till a comparatively late hour; and the necessity of sitting up after her usual time of retiring, by making the old lady irritable, had the effect of giving some additional force to the suggestions of Mr. Calvert. When Margaret did return, she came alone. Stevens had attended her only to the wicket. She did not expect to find her mother still sitting up; and started, with an appearance of disquiet, when she met her glance. The young girl was pale and haggard. Her eye had a dilated, wild expression. Her step faltered; her voice was scarcely distinct as she remarked timidly—

"Not yet abed, mother?"

"No! it's a pretty time for you to keep me up."

"But why did you sit up, mother? It's not usual with you to do so."

"No! but it's high time for me to sit up, and be on the watch too, when here's the neighbors coming to warn me to do so—and telling me all about your danger."

"Ha! my danger—speak—what danger, mother?"

"Don't you know what danger? Don't you know?"

"Know!" The monosyllable subsided in a gasp. At that moment Margaret Cooper could say no more.

"Well, I suppose you don't know, and so I'll tell you. Here's been that conceited, stupid old man, Calvert, to tell me how wrong it is for you to go out by night walking with

Brother Stevens; and hinting to me that you don't know how to take care of yourself with all your learning; and how nobody knows anything about Brother Stevens; as if nobody was wise for anything but himself. But I gave him as good as he brought, I'll warrant you. I sent him off with a flea in his ear!"

It was fortunate for the poor girl that the light, which was that of a dipped candle, was burning in the corner of the chimney, and was too dim to make her features visible. The ghastly tale which they told could not have been utterly unread even by the obtuse and opinionated mind of the vain mother. The hands of Margaret were involuntarily clasped in her agony, and she felt very much like falling upon the floor; but, with a strong effort, her nerves were braced to the right tension, and she continued to endure, in a speechless terror, which was little short of frenzy, the outpourings of her mother's folly which was a frenzy of another sort.

"I sent him off," she repeated, "with a flea in his ear. I could see what the old fool was driving after, and I as good as told him so. If it had been his favorite, his adopted son, Bill Hinkley, it would have been another guess-story — I reckon. Then you might have walked out where you pleased together, at all hours, and no harm done, no danger; old Calvert would have thought it the properest thing in the world. But no Bill Hinkley for me. I'm for Brother Stevens, Margaret; only make sure of him, my child — make sure of him."

"No more of this, dear mother, I entreat you. Let us go to bed, and think no more of it."

"And why should we not think of it? I tell you, Margaret, *you must think of it!* Brother Stevens soon will be a preacher, and a fine speck he will be. There'll be no parson like him in all west Kentucky. As for John Cross, I reckon he won't be able to hold a candle to him. Brother Stevens is something to try for. You must play your cards nicely, Margaret. Don't let him see too soon that you like him. Beware of that! But don't draw off too suddenly as if you didn't like him — that's worse still ; for very few men like to see that they ain't altogether pleasing even at first sight to the lady that they like. There's a medium in all things, and you must just manage it, as if you wa'n't thinking at all about him, or love, or a husband, or any-thing ; only take care always to turn a quick ear to what he says, and seem to consider it always as if 'twas worth your considering. And look round when he speaks, and smile softly sometimes ; and don't be too full of learning and wisdom in what you say, for I've found that men of sense love women best when they seem to talk most like very young children — maybe because they think it's a sign of innocence. But I reckon, Margaret, you don't want much teaching. Only be sure and fix him ; and don't stop to think when he asks. Be sure to have your answer ready, and you can't say 'yes' too quickly now-a-days, when the chances are so very few."

The mother paused to take breath. Her very moral and maternal counsel had fallen upon unheeding ears. But Margaret was sensible of the pause, and was desirous of taking advantage of it. She rose from her chair, with the view of retiring ; but the good old dame, whose imagination had been terribly excited by the delightful idea of having a preacher for her son-in-law who was to take such prece-dence over all the leaders of the other tribes, was not wil-ling to abridge her eloquence.

" Why, you're in a great hurry now, Margaret. Where was your hurry when you were with Brother Stevens? Ah! you jade, can't I guess — don't I know? There you were, you two, under the trees, looking at the moon, and talking such sweet, foolish nonsense. I reckon, Margaret, 'twould puzzle you to tell what *he* said, or what *you* said, I can guess he didn't talk much religion to you, heh ? Ah! I know it all. It's the old story. It's been so with all young people, and will be so till the end. Love is the strangest thing, and it does listen to the strangest nonsense. Ain't it so, Margaret? I know nothing but love would ever dumbfounder you in this way; why, child, have you lost your tongue? What's the matter with you?"

"Oh, mother, let me retire now, I have such a headache."

"Heartache, you mean."

"Heartache it is," replied the other desperately, with an air of complete abandonment.

"Ah! well, it's clear that he's got the heartache quite as much as you, for he almost lives with you now. But make him speak out, Margaret—get him to say the word, and don't let him be too free until he does. No squeezing of hands, no kissing, no—"

"No more, no more, I entreat you, mother, if you would not drive me mad! Why do you speak to me thus—why counsel me in this manner? Leave me alone, I pray you, let me retire—I must—I must sleep now!"

The mother was not unaccustomed to such passionate bursts of speech from her daughter, and she ascribed the startling energy of her utterance now, to an excited spirit in part, and partly to the headache of which she complained.

"What! do you feel so bad, my child? Well, I won't keep you up any longer. I wouldn't have kept you up so long, if I hadn't been vexed by that old fool, Calvert."

"Mr. Calvert is a good man, mother."

"Well, he may be—I don't say a word against that," replied the mother, somewhat surprised at the mildly reproachful nature of that response which her daughter had made, so different from her usual custom:—"he may be very good, but I think he's very meddlesome to come here talking about Brother Stevens."

"He meant well, mother."

"Well or ill, it don't matter. Do you be ready when Brother Stevens says the word. He'll say it before long. He's mighty keen after you, Margaret. I've seen it in his

eyes; only you keep a little off, till he begins to press and
be anxious; and after that he can't help himself. He'll
be ready for any terms; and look you, when a man's ready,
none of your long bargains. Settle up at once. As for
waiting till he gets permission to preach, I wouldn't think
of it. A man can be made a preacher or anything, at any
time, but 'tain't so easy in these times, for a young woman
to be made a wife. It's not every day that one can get a
husband, and such a husband! Look at Jane Colter, and
Betsy Barnes, and Rebecca Forbes, and Susan Mason;
they'll be green again, I reckon, before the chance comes
to them; ay, and the widow Thackeray—though she's had
her day already. If 'twas a short one she's got no reason
to complain. She'll learn how to value it before it begins
again. But, go to bed, my child, you oughtn't to have a
headache. No! no! you should leave it to them that's not
so fortunate. They'll have headaches and heartaches
enough, I warrant you, before they get such a man as
Brother Stevens."

At last, Margaret Cooper found herself alone and in her
chamber. With unusual vigilance she locked and double-
locked the door. She then flung herself upon the bed.
Her face was buried in the clothes. A convulsion of feeling shook her frame. But her eyes remained dry, and her
cheeks were burning. She rose at length and began to
undress, but for this she found herself unequal. She entered the couch and sat up in it—her hands crossed upon
her lap—her face wan, wild, the very picture of hopelessness if not desperation! The words of her weak mother
had tortured her; but what was this agony to that which
was occasioned by her own thoughts.

"Oh God!" she exclaimed at length, "can it be real?
Can it be true? Do I wake? Is it no dream? Am I,
am I what I dare not name to myself—and dread to hear
from any other? Alas! it is true—too true. That shade,
that wood!—oh, Alfred Stevens! Alfred Stevens! What
have you done! To what have you beguiled me!"

CHAPTER XXVIII.

STRENGTH AFTER FALL.

THAT weary night no sleep came to the eyelids of the hapless Margaret Cooper. The garrulous language of the mother had awakened far other emotions in her bosom than those which she labored to inspire; and the warning of Mr. Calvert, for the first time impressed upon herself the terrible conviction that she was lost. In the wild intoxicating pleasures of that new strange dream, she had been wofully unconscious of the truth. So gradual had been the progress of passion, that it had never alarmed or startled her. Besides, it had come to her under a disguise afforded by the customary cravings of her soul. Her vanity had been the medium by which her affections had been won, by which her confidence had been beguiled, by which the guardian watchers of her virtue had been laid to sleep.

What a long and dreadful night was that when Margaret Cooper was first brought to feel the awful truth in its true impressiveness of wo. Alas! how terribly do the pleasures of sin torture us. The worst human foe is guilt. The severest censure the consciousness of wrong doing. Poverty may be endured—nay is—and virtue still be secure; since the mind may be made strong to endure the heaviest toil, yet cherish few desires; the loss of kin may call for few regrets, if we feel that we have religiously performed our duties toward them, and requited all their proper claims upon us. Sickness and pain may even prove benefits and blessings, if it shall so happen that we resign ourselves without complaint, to the scourge of the chastener, and grow patient beneath his stripes. But that self-rebuke of one's own spirit from which we may not fly—that remorseful and ever-vexing presence which haunts us, and pursues with a wing even more fleet than that of fear—which tells clamorously of what we had, and scornfully of what we have lost—lost for ever! that is the demon from whom there is no escape, and beyond whom there is no torture. Vainly would we strive with this relentless enemy. Every blow aimed at its shadowy bosom recoils upon our own. In the crowd, it takes the place of other forms and dogs us with suspicious glances; in the solitude, it stalks boldly to our side, confronts us with its audacious truths and terrible denunciations—leaves no moment secure, waking or sleeping! It is the ghost of murdered virtue, brooding over its grave in that most dark and dismal of all sepulchres, the human heart. And if we cry aloud, as did Margaret Cooper, with vain prayer for the recall of a single day, with what a yell of derisive mockery it answers to our prayer.

The night was passed in the delusive effort of the mind to argue itself into a state of fancied security. She endeavored to recall those characteristics in Alfred Stevens, by which her confidence had been beguiled. This task was not a difficult one in that early day of her distress; before experience had yet come to confirm the apprehensions of doubt—before the intoxicating dream of a first passion had yet begun to stale upon her imagination. Her own elastic mind helped her in this endeavor. Surely, she thought, where the mind is so noble and expansive, where the feelings are so tender and devoted, the features so lofty and impressive, the look so sweet, the language so delicate and refined, there can be no falsehood.

"The devotion of such a man," she erringly thought, "might well sanction the weakness of a woman's heart—

might well persuade to the momentary error which none will seek more readily to repair than himself. If *he* be true to me, what indeed should I care for the scorn of others."

Alas! for the credulous victim. This was the soul of her error. This scorn of others—of the opinions of the world around her, is the saddest error of which woman, who is the most dependant of all beings in the moral world, can ever be guilty. But such philosophy did not now deceive even the poor girl by whom it was uttered. It is a melancholy truth, that, where there is no principle, the passions can not be relied on ; and the love of Alfred Stevens had hitherto shown itself in selfishness. Margaret Cooper felt this, but she did not dare to believe it.

" No! no !" she muttered—" I will not doubt—I will not fear ! He is too noble, too generous, too fond ! I could not be deceived."

Her reliance was upon her previous judgment, not upon his principles. Her self-esteem assisted to make this reference sufficient for the purposes of consolation, and this was all that she desired in this first moment of her doubt and apprehension.

" And if he be true—if he keep for ever the faith that his lips and looks declare—then will I heed nothing of the shame and the sin. The love of such a man is sufficient recompense for the loss of all besides. What to me is the loss of society ? what should I care for the association and opinions of these in Charlemont? And elsewhere—he will bear me hence where none can know. Ah! I fear not: he will be true."

Her self-esteem was recovering considerably. from its first overthrow. Her mind was already preparing to do battle with those, the scorn of whom she anticipated, and whose judgments she had always hitherto despised. This was an easy task. She was yet to find that it was not the only task. Her thoughts are those of many, in like situations, and it is for this reason that we dwell upon them. Our purpose is, to show the usual processes of self-deception.

Margaret Cooper, like a large class of persons of strong natural mind and sanguine temper, was only too apt to confound the cause of virtue with its sometimes uncouth, harsh, and self-appointed professors. She overlooked the fact that public opinion, though a moral object against which woman dares not often offend, is yet no standard for her government; that principles are determinable elsewhere; and that, whatever the world may think of them, and whatever may be their seeming unimportance under existing circumstances, are the only real moral securities of earth. She might fly from Charlemont, either into a greater world, or into a more complete solitude, but she would fly to no greater certainties than she now possessed. Her securities were still based upon the principles of Alfred Stevens, and of these she knew nothing. She knew that he was a man of talent — of eloquence; alas for her! she had felt it; of skill — she had been its victim; of rare sweetness of utterance, of grace and beauty; and as she enumerated to herself these his mental powers and personal charms, she felt, however numerous the catalogue, that none of these afforded her the guaranty she sought.

She arose the next day somewhat more composed, and with a face which betrayed sleeplessness, but nothing worse. This she ascribed to the headache with which she had retired. She had not slept an instant, and she arose entirely unrefreshed. But the stimulating thoughts which had kept her wakeful, furnished her with sufficient strength to appear as usual in the household, and to go through her accustomed duties. But it was with an impatience scarcely restrainable that she waited for the approach of evening which would bring her lover. Him she felt it now absolutely of the last necessity that she should see; that she should once more go with him to those secret places, the very thought of which inspired her with terror, and, laying bare her soul to his eyes, demand of him the only restitution which he could make.

He came. Once more she descended the steps to meet him. Her mother arrested her on the stairway. A cunning leer was in her eye, as she looked into the woful, impassive eyes of her daughter. She grinned with a sort of delight expressive of the conviction that the advice she had given the night before was to be put in execution soon.

"Fix him, Margaret; he's mighty eager for you. You've cut your eye-tooth—be quick, and you'll have a famous parson for a husband yet."

The girl shrunk from the counsellor as if she had been a serpent. The very counsel was enough to show her the humiliating attitude in which she stood to all parties.

"Remember," said the old woman, detaining her—" don't be too willing at first. Let him speak fairly out. A young maiden can't be too backward, until the man offers to make her a young wife!"

The last words went to her soul like an arrow.

"A young maiden!" she almost murmured aloud, as she descended the steps—"O God! how lovely now, to my eyes, appears the loveliness of a young maiden!"

She joined Stevens in silence, the mother watching them with the eyes of a maternal hawk as they went forth together. They pursued a customary route, and, passing through one of the gorges of the surrounding hills, they soon lost sight of the village. When the forest-shadows had gathered thickly around them, and the silence of the woods became felt, Stevens approached more nearly, and, renewing a former liberty, put his arm about her waist. She gently but firmly removed it, but neither of them spoke a word. A dense copse appeared before them. Toward it he would have led the way. But she resolutely turned aside, and, while a shudder passed over her frame, exclaimed—

"Not there — not there!"

Breathlessly she spoke. He well enough understood her. They pursued an opposite direction, and, in the shade of a wood which before they had never traversed, they at length paused. Stevens, conducting her to the trunk of a fallen tree, seated her, and placed himself beside her. Still they were silent. There was a visible constraint upon both. The thoughts and feelings of both were alike active — but very unlike in character. With him, passion, reckless passion, was uppermost; selfish in all its phases, and resolute on its own indulgence at every hazard. In her bosom was regret if not remorse, mingled with doubts and hopes in pretty equal proportion. Yet had she, even then, but little doubt of him. She accused him of no practice. She fancied, foolish girl, that his error, like her own, had been that of blind impulse, availing itself of a moment of unguarded reason to take temporary possession of the citadel of prudence. That he was calculating, cunning — that his snares had been laid beforehand — she had not the least idea. But she was to grow wiser in this and other respects in due season. How little did she then conjecture the coldness and hardness of that base and selfish heart which had so fanned the consuming flame in hers!

Her reserve and coolness were unusual. She had been the creature, heretofore, of the most uncalculating impulse. The feeling was spoken, the thought uttered, as soon as conceived. Now she was silent. He expected her to speak — nay, he expected reproaches, and was prepared to meet them. He had his answer for any reproaches which she might make. But for that stony silence of her lips he was not prepared. The passive grief which her countenance betrayed — so like despair — repelled and annoyed him. Yet, wherefore had she come, if not to complain bitterly, and, after exhaustion, be soothed at last? Such had been his usual experience in all such cases. But the unsophisticated woman before him had no language for such a situation as was hers. Her pride, her ambition—the very intensity of all her moods—rendered the effort at speech a mockery, and left her dumb.

"You are sad, Margaret—silent and very cold to me," he said, at last breaking the silence. His tones were subdued to a whisper, and how full of entreating tenderness! She slowly raised her eyes from the ground, and fixed them upon him. What a speech was in that one look! There was no trace of excitement, scarcely of expression, in her face. There was no flush upon her cheeks. She was pale as death. She was still silent. Her eye alone had spoken; and from its searching but stony glance his own fell in some confusion to the ground. There was a dreary pause, which he at length broke:—

"You are still silent, Margaret—why do you not speak to me?"

"It is for you to speak, Alfred," was her reply. It was full of significance, understood but not *felt* by her companion. What, indeed, had she to say—what could she say—while he said nothing? She was the victim. With him lay the means of rescue and preservation. She but waited the decision of one whom, in her momentary madness, she had made the arbiter of her destiny. Her reply confused him. He would have preferred to listen to the ordinary language of reproach. Had she burst forth into tears and lamentations—had she cried, "You have wronged me— you must do me justice!"—he would have been better pleased than with the stern, unsuggestive character that she assumed. To all this, his old experience would have given him an easy answer. But to be driven to condemn himself—to define his own doings with the name due to his deserts—to declare his crime, and proffer the sufficient atonement—was an unlooked-for necessity.

"You are displeased with me, Margaret."

He dared not meet her glance while uttering this feeble and purposeless remark. It was so short of all that he

should have said — of all that she expected — that her eyes
glistened with a sudden expression of indignation which
was new to them in looking upon him.   There was a glittering sarcasm in her glance, which showed the intensity
of her feelings in the comment which they involuntarily
made on the baldness and poverty of his.   Displeasure, indeed!   That such an epithet should be employed to describe
the withering pang, the vulturous, gnawing torture in her
bosom — and that fiery fang which thought, like some
winged serpent, was momentarily darting into her brain!

" Displeased !" she exclaimed, in low, bitter tones, which
she seemed rather desirous to suppress — " no, no ! sir —
not displeased.   I am miserable, most miserable — anything
but displeased.   I am too wretched to feel displeasure !"

" And to me you owe this wretchedness, dear Margaret
— that — that is what you would say.   Is it not, Margaret ?
I have wronged — I have ruined you !   From me comes
this misery !   You hate, you would denounce me."

He put his arm about her waist — he sank upon his knee
beside her — his eye, now that he had found words, could
once more look courageously into hers.

" Wronged — ruined !" she murmured, using a part of his
words, and repeating them as if she did not altogether realize their perfect sense.

" Ay, you would accuse me, Margaret," he continued —
" you would reproach and denounce me — you hate me — I
deserve it — I deserve it."

She answered with some surprise : —

" No, Alfred Stevens, I do not accuse — I do not denounce
you.   I am wretched — I am miserable.   It is for you to
say if I am wronged and ruined.   I am not what I was — I
know that ! — What I am — what I will be !——"

She paused !   Her hands were clasped suddenly and violently — she looked to heaven, and, for the first time, the
tears, streamed from her eyes like rain — a sudden, heavy
shower, which was soon over.

"Ah, Margaret, you would have me accuse myself—and I do. The crime is mine! I have done you this wrong——"

She interrupted him.

"No, Alfred Stevens, *I* have done wrong! *I feel* that I have done wrong. That I have been feeble and criminal, *I know*. I will not be so base as to deny what I can not but feel. As for your crime, you know best what it is. I know mine. I know that my passions are evil and presumptuous; and though I blush to confess their force, it is yet due to the truth that I should do so, though I sink into the earth with my shame. But neither your self-reproaches nor my confession will acquit us. Is there nothing, Alfred Stevens, tnat can be done? Must I fall before you, here, amidst the woods which have witnessed my shame, and implore you to save me? I do! Behold me! I am at your feet —my face is in the dust. Oh! Alfred Stevens—when I called your eyes to watch, in the day of my pride, the strong-winged eagle of our hills, did I look as now? Save me from this shame! save me! For, though I have no reproaches, yet God knows, when we looked on that eagle's flight together, my soul had no such taint as fills it now. Whatever were my faults, my follies, my weaknesses, Heaven knows, I felt not, feared not this! a thought—a dream of such a passion, then—never came to my bosom. From you it came! You put it there! You woke up the slumbering emotion—you—but no!—I will not accuse you! I will only implore you to save me! Can it be done? can you do it—will you—will you not?"

"Rise, dearest Margaret—let me lift you!" She had thrown herself upon the earth, and she clung to it.

"No, no! your words may lift me, Alfred Stevens, when your hands can not. If you speak a hope, a promise of safety, it will need no other help to make me rise! If you do not!—I would not wish to rise again. Speak! let me hear, even as I am, what my doom shall be? The pride

which has made me fall shall be reconciled to my abase·
ment."

"Margaret, this despair is idle. There is no need for it.
Do I not tell you that there is no danger?"

"Why did you speak of ruin?" she demanded.

"I know not—the word escaped me. There is no ruin.
I will save you. I am yours—yours only. Believe me, I
will do you right. I regard you as sacredly my wife as if
the rites of the church had so decreed it."

"I dare not disbelieve you, Alfred! I have no hope
else. Your words lift me! Oh! Alfred Stevens, you did
not mean the word, but how true it was; what a wreck,
what a ruin do I feel myself now—what a wreck have I
become!"

"A wreck, a ruin! no, Margaret, no! never were you
more beautiful than at this very moment. These large, sad
eyes—these long, dark lashes seem intended to bear the
weight of tears. These cheeks are something paler than
their wont, but not less beautiful, and these lips——"

He would have pressed them with his own—he would
have taken her into his arms, but she repulsed him.

"No, no! Alfred—this must not be. I am yours. Let
me prove to you that I am firm enough to protect your rights
from invasion."

"But why so coy, dearest? Do you doubt me?"

"Heaven forbid!"

"Ah! but you do. Why do you shrink from me—why
this coldness? If you are mine, if these charms are mine,
why not yield them to me? I fear, Margaret, that you
doubt me still?"

"I do not—dare not doubt you, Alfred Stevens. My
life hangs upon this faith."

"Why so cold, then?"

"I am not cold. I love you—I will be your wife; and
never was wife more faithful, more devoted, than I will be
to you; but, if you knew the dreadful agony which I have

felt, since that sad moment of my weakness, you would forbear and pity me."

"Hear me, Margaret; to-morrow is Saturday. John
Cross is to be here in the evening. He shall marry us on
Sunday. Are you willing?"

"Oh, yes! thankful, happy! Ah! Alfred, why did I
distrust you for an instant?"

"Why, indeed! But you distrust me no longer—you
have no more misgivings?"

"No, none!"

"You will be no longer cold, no longer coy, dear Margaret—here in the sweet evening, among these pleasant
shades, love, alone, has supremacy. Here, in the words of
one of your favorites:—

> "'Where transport and security entwine,
> Here is the empire of thy perfect bliss,
> And here thou art a god——'"

concluding this quotation, he would have taken her in his
embrace—he would have renewed those dangerous endear-
ments which had already proved so fatal; but she repulsed
the offered tenderness, firmly, but with gentleness.

"Margaret, you still doubt me," he exclaimed reproach-
fully.

"No, Alfred, I doubt you not. I believe you. I have
only been too ready and willing to believe you. Ah! have
you not had sufficient proof of this? Leave me the consciousness of virtue—the feeling of strength still to assert
it, now that my eyes are open to my previous weakness."

"But there is no reason to be so cold. Remember you
are mine by every tie of the heart—another day will make
you wholly mine. Surely, there is no need for this frigid
bearing. No, no! you doubt—you do not believe me,
Margaret!"

"If I did not believe you, Alfred Stevens," she answered
gravely, "my prayer would be for death, and I should find

15

it. These woods which have witnessed my fault should have witnessed my expiation. The homes which have known me should know me no more."

The solemnity of her manner rather impressed him, but having no real regard for her, he was unwilling to be baffled in his true desires.

"If you doubt me not—if you have faith in me, Margaret, why this solemnity, this reserve? Prove to me, by your looks, by your actions, by the dear glances, the sweet murmurs, and the fond embrace, what these cold assurances do not say."

His hand rested on her neck. She gently raised and removed it.

"I have already proved to you my weakness. I will now prove my strength. It is better so, Alfred. If I have won your love, let me now command your esteem, or maintain what is left me of my own. Do not be angry with me if I insist upon it. I am resolute now to be worthy of you and of myself."

"Ah! you call this love?" said he bitterly. "If you ever loved, indeed, Margaret——"

"If I ever loved—and have I given you no proofs?" she exclaimed in a burst of passion; "all the proofs that a woman can give, short of her blood; and that, Alfred Stevens—that too, I was prepared to give, had you not promptly assured me of your faith."

She drew a small dagger from her sleeve, and bared it beneath his glance.

"Think you I brought this without an object? No! Alfred Stevens—know me better! I came here prepared to die, as well as a frail and erring woman could be prepared. You disarmed the dagger. You subdued the determination when you bid me live for you. In your faith, I am willing to live. I believe you, and am resolved to make myself worthy of your belief also. I have promised to be your wife, and here before Heaven, I swear to be your faithful wife; but, until then, you shall presume in no respect. Your lip shall not touch mine; your arms shall not embrace me; you shall see, dear Alfred, that, with my eyes once opened fully upon my own weakness, I have acquired the most certain strength."

"Give me the dagger," he said.

She hesitated.

"You doubt me still?"

"No, no!" she exclaimed, handing him the weapon— "no, no! I do not doubt you—I dare not. Doubt you, Alfred?—that were death, even without the dagger!"

CHAPTER XXIX.

BULL-PUPS IN TRAINING.

ALFRED STEVENS was sufficiently familiar with the sex to perceive that Margaret Cooper was resolved. There was that in her look and manner which convinced him that she was not now to be overcome. There was no effort or constraint in either her looks or language. The composure of assured strength was there. The discovery of her weakness, which he had so unexpectedly made, had rendered her vigilant. Suspecting herself—which women are not apt to do—she became watchful, not only of the approach of her lover, but of every emotion of her own soul; and it was with a degree of chagrin which he could scarcely refrain from showing, that he was compelled to forego, at least for the present, all his usual arts of seduction.

Yet he knew not how to refrain. Never had Margaret Cooper seemed so lovely in his eyes, so commanding, so eloquent with beauty, as now, when remorse had touched her eyes with an unwonted shadow, and tears and night-watching had subdued the richer bloom upon her cheek. Proud still, but pensive in her pride, she walked silently beside him, still brooding over thoughts which she would not willingly admit were doubts, and grasping every word of assurance that fell from his lips as if it had been some additional security.

These assurances he still suffered to escape him, with sufficient frequency and solemnity, to confirm that feeling

of confidence which his promise of marriage had inspired
in her mind. There was a subdued fondness in his voice,
and an *empressement* in his manner, which was not all practice. The character which Margaret Cooper had displayed
in this last interview — her equal firmness and fear — the
noble elevation of soul which, admitting her own errors,
disdained to remind him of his — a course which would
have been the most ready of adoption among the weaker
and less generous of the sex — had touched him with a degree of respect akin to admiration; and so strong was the
impression made upon him of her great natural superiority
of mind to almost all the women he had ever met, that, but
for her one unhappy lapse, he had sought no other wife.
Had she been strong at first as she proved herself at last,
this had been inevitable.

When in his own chamber that night, he could not help
recalling to his memory the proud elevation of her character as it had appeared in that interview. The recollection
really gave him pain, since along with it arose the memory
also of that unfortunate frailty, which became more prominent as a crime in connection with that intellectual merit
which, it is erroneously assumed, should have made it sure.

"But for that, Margaret Cooper, and this marriage were
no vain promise. But that forbids. No, no — no spousals
for me: let John Cross and the bride be ready or not, there
shall be a party wanting to that contract! And yet, what
a woman to lose! what a woman to win! No tragedy-
queen ever bore herself like that. Talk of Siddons, indeed!
She would have brought down the house in that sudden
prostration — that passionate appeal. She made even me
tremble. I could have loved her for that, if for that only.
To make *me* tremble! and with such a look, such an eye,
such a stern, sweet, fierce beauty! By Heavens! I know
not how to give her up. What a sensation she would
make in Frankfort! Were she my wife — but no, no! bait
for gudgeons   I am not so great a fool as that. She who

is mine on my terms, is yours, sir, or yours—is anybody's, when the humor suits and the opportunity. I can not think of that. Yet, to lose her is as little to be thought of. I must manage it. I must get her off from this place. It need not be to Frankfort! Let me see—there is—hum! —hum!—yes, a ride of a few miles—an afternoon excursion—quite convenient, yet not too near. It must be managed; but, at all events, I must evade this marriage—put it off for the present—get some decent excuse. That's easy enough, and for the rest, why, time that softens all things, except man and woman, time will make that easy too. To-morrow for Ellisland, and the rest after."

Thus, resolving not to keep his vows to his unhappy victim, the criminal was yet devising plans by which to continue his power over her. These plans, yet immature in his own mind, at least unexpressed, need not be analyzed here, and may be conjectured by the reader.

That night, Stevens busied himself in preparing letters. Of these he wrote several. It will not further our progress to look over him as he writes; and we prefer rather, in this place, to hurry on events which, it may be the complaint of all parties, reader not omitted, have been too long suffered to stagnate. But we trust not. Let us hurry Stevens through Friday night—the night of that last interview.

Saturday morning, we observe that his appetite is unimpaired. He discusses the breakfast at Hinkley's as if he had never heard of suffering. He has said an unctuous grace. Biscuits hot, of best Ohio flour, are smoking on his plate. A golden-looking mass of best fresh butter is made to assimilate its luscious qualities with those of the drier and hotter substance. A copious bowl of milk, new from the dugs of old Brindle, stands beside him, patiently waiting to be honored by his unscrupulous but not unfastidious taste. The grace is said, and the gravy follows. He has a religious regard for the goods and gifts of this life. He eats heartily, and the thanks which follow, if not from the bottom of the soul, were sufficiently earnest to have emanated from the bottom of his stomach.

This over, he has a chat with his hosts. He discusses with old Hinkley the merits of the new lights. What those new lights were, at that period, we do not pretend to remember. Among sectarians, there are periodical new lights which singularly tend to increase the moral darkness. From these, after a while, they passed to the love festivals or feasts—a pleasant practice of the methodist church, which is supposed to be very promotive of many other good things besides love; though we are constrained to say that Brother Stevens and Brother Hinkley—who, it may be remarked, had very long and stubborn arguments, frequently without discovering, till they reached the close, that they were thoroughly agreed in every respect except in words —concurred in the opinion that there was no portion of the church practice so highly conducive to the amalgamation of soul with soul, and all souls with God, as this very practice of love-feasts!

Being agreed on this and other subjects, Mr. Hinkley invited Brother Stevens out to look at his turnips and potatoes; and when this delicate inquiry was over, toward ten o'clock in the day, Brother Stevens concluded that he must take a gallop; he was dyspeptic, felt queerish, his studies were too close, his mind too busy with the great concerns of salvation. These are enough to give one dyspepsia. Of course, the hot rolls and mountains of volcanic butter—steam-ejecting—could have produced no such evil effects upon a laborer in the vineyard. At all events, a gallop was necessary, and the horse was brought. Brother Hinkley and our matronly sister of the same name watched the progress of the pious youth, as, spurring up the hills, he pursued the usual route, taking at first the broad highway leading to the eastern country.

There were other eyes that watched the departure of

Brother Stevens with no less interest, but of another kind, than those of the venerable couple. Our excellent friend Calvert started up on hearing the tread of the horse, and, looking out from his porch, ascertained with some eagerness of glance that the rider was Alfred Stevens.

Now, why was the interest of Calvert so much greater on this than on any other previous occasion? We will tell you, gentle reader. He had been roused at an early hour that morning by a visit from Ned Hinkley.

"Gran'pa," was the reverent formula of our fisherman at beginning, "to-day's the day. I'm pretty certain that Stevens will be riding out to-day, for he missed the last Saturday. I'll take my chance for it, therefore, and brush out ahead of him. I think I've got it pretty straight now, the place that he goes to, and I'll see if I can't get there soon enough to put myself in a comfortable fix, so as to see what's a-going on and what he goes after. Now, gran'pa, I'll tell you what I want from you — them pocket-pistols of your'n. Bill Hinkley carried off grandad's, and there's none besides that I can lay hold on."

"But, Ned, I'm afraid to lend them to you."

"What 'fraid of?"

"That you'll use them."

"To be sure I will, if there's any need, gran'pa. What do I get them for?"

"Ah, yes! but I fear you'll find a necessity where there is none. You'll be thrusting your head into some fray in which you may lose your ears."

"By Jupiter, no! No, gran'pa, I'll wait for the necessity. I won't look for it. I'm going straight ahead this time, and to one object only. I think Stevens is a rascal, and I'm bent to find him out. I've had no disposition to lick anybody but him, ever since he drove Bill Hinkley off — you and him together."

"You'll promise me, Ned?"

"Sure as a snag in the forehead of a Mississippi steamer. Depend upon me."

"But there must be no quarrelling with Stevens either, Ned."

"Look you, gran'pa, if I'm to quarrel with Stevens or anybody else, 'twouldn't be your pistols in my pocket that would make me set on, and 'twouldn't be the want of 'em that would make me stop. When it's my cue to fight, look you, I won't need any prompter, in the shape of friend or pistol. Now *that* speech is from one of your poets, pretty near, and ought to convince you that you may as well lend the puppies and say no more about it. If you don't you'll only compel me to carry my rifle, and that'll be something worse to an enemy, and something heavier for me. Come, come, gran'pa, don't be too scrupulous in your old age. *Your having* them is a sufficient excuse for *my having* them too. It shows that they ought to be had."

"You're logic-chopping this morning, Ned—see that you don't get to man-chopping in the afternoon. You shall have the pistols, but do not use them rashly. I have kept them simply for defence against invasion; not for the purpose of quarrel, or revenge."

"And you've kept them mighty well, gran'pa," replied the young man, as he contemplated with an eye of anxious admiration, the polish of the steel barrels, the nice carving of the handles, and the fantastic but graceful inlay of the silver-mounting and setting. The old man regarded him with a smile.

"Yes, Ned, I've kept them well. They have never taken life, though they have been repeatedly tried upon bull's eye and tree-bark. If you will promise me not to use them to-day, Ned, you shall have them."

"Take 'em back, gran'pa."

"Why?"

"Why, I'd feel the meanest in the world to have a we'pon, and not use it when there's a need to do so; and I'm half afraid that the temptation of having such beautiful puppies for myself—twin-puppies, I may say—having just

15*

the same look out of the eyes, and just the same spots and marks, and, I reckon, just the same way of giving tongue —I'm half afraid, I say, that to get to be the owner of them, might tempt me to stand quiet and let a chap wink at me — maybe laugh outright — may be suck in his breath, and give a phew-phew-whistle just while I'm passing! No! no! gran'pa, take back your words, or take back your puppies. Won't risk to carry both. I'd sooner take Patsy Rifle, with all her weight, and no terms at all."

"Pshaw, Ned, you're a fool."

"That's no news, gran'pa, to you or me. But it don't alter the case. Put up your puppies."

"No, Ned; you shall have them on your own terms. Take 'em as they are. I give them to you."

"And I may shoot anybody I please this afternoon, gran'pa?"

"Ay, ay, Ned — anybody —"

Thus far the old man, when he stopped himself, changed his manner, which was that of playful good-humor, to that of gravity, while his tones underwent a corresponding change —

"But, Ned, my son, while I leave it to your discretion, I yet beg you to proceed cautiously — seek no strife, avoid it — go not into the crowd — keep from them where you see them drinking, and do not use these or any weapons for any trifling provocation. Nothing but the last necessity of self-preservation justifies the taking of life."

"Gran'pa — thank you — you've touched me in the very midst of my tender-place, by this handsome present. One of these puppies I'll name after you, and I'll notch it on the butt. The other I'll call Bill Hinkley, and I won't notch that. Yours, I'll call my pacific puppy, and I'll use it only for peace-making purposes. The other I'll call my bull-pup, and him I'll use for baiting and butting, and goring. But, as you beg, I promise you I'll keep 'em both out of mischief as long as I can. Be certain sure

that it won't be my having the pups that'll make me get
into a skrimmage a bit the sooner; for I never was the
man to ask whether my dogs were at hand before I could
say the word, 'set-on!' It's a sort of nature in a man that
don't stop to look after his weapons, but naturally expects
to find 'em any how, when his blood's up, and there's a
necessity to do."

This long speech and strong assurance of his pacific nature and purposes, did not prevent the speaker from making,
while he spoke, certain dextrous uses of the instruments
which were given into his hands. Right and left were
equally busy; one muzzle was addressed to the candle
upon the mantelpiece, the other pursued the ambulatory
movements of a great black spider upon the wall. The
old man surveyed him with an irrepressible smile. Suddenly interrupting himself the youth exclaimed:—

"Are they loaded, gran'pa?"

He was answered in the negative.

"Because, if they were," said he, "and that great black
spider was Brother Stevens, I'd show you in the twinkle of
a musquito, how I'd put a finish to his morning's work.
But I'd use the bull-pup, gran'pa—see, this one—the
pacific one I'd empty upon him with powder only, as a sort
of *feu de joie* —and then I'd set up the song—what's it?
ah! *Te Deum*. A black spider always puts me in mind
of a rascal."

CHAPTER XXX.

THE FOX IN THE TRAP.

THE youth barely stopped to swallow his breakfast, when he set off from the village. He managed his movements with considerable caution ; and, fetching a circuit from an opposite quarter, after having ridden some five miles out of his way, passed into the road which he suspected that Stevens would pursue. We do not care to show the detailed processes by which he arrived at this conclusion. The reader may take for granted that he had heard from some way-side farmer, that a stranger rode by his cottage once a week, wearing such and such breeches, and mounted upon a nag of a certain color and with certain qualities. Enough to say, that Ned Hinkley was tolerably certain of his route and man.

He sped on accordingly — did not once hesitate at turns, right or left, forks and cross-roads, but keeping an inflexible course, he placed himself at such a point on the road as to leave it no longer doubtful, should Stevens pass, of the place which usually brought him up. Here he dismounted, hurried his horse, out of sight and hearing, into the woods, and choosing a position for himself, with some nicety, along the road-side, put himself in close cover, where, stretching his frame at length, he commenced the difficult labor of cooling his impatience with his cogitations.

But cogitating, with a fellow of his blood, rather whets impatience. He was monstrous restiff. At his fishing pond, with a trout to hook, he would have lain for hours, as patient as philosophy itself, and as inflexible as the solid rock over which he brooded. But without an angle at his hand, how could he keep quiet? Not by thinking, surely; and, least of all, by thinking about that person for whom his hostility was so active. Thinking of Stevens, by a natural association, reminded him of the pistols which Calvert had given him. Nothing could be more natural than to draw them from his bosom. Again and again he examined them in fascinated contemplation. He had already charged them, and he amused himself by thinking of the mischief he could do, by a single touch upon the trigger, to a poor little wood-rat, that once or twice ran along a decaying log some five steps from his feet. But his object being secrecy, the rat brushed his whiskers in safety. Still he amused himself by aiming at this and other objects, until suddenly reminded of the very important difference which he had promised Calvert to make between the pistols in his future use of them. With this recollection he drew out his knife, and laid the weapons before him.

"This," said he, after a careful examination, in which he fancied he discovered some slight difference between them in the hang of the trigger — "this shall be my bull-pup — this my peace-maker!"

The latter was marked accordingly with a "P," carved rudely enough by one whose hand was much more practised in slitting the weasand of a buck, than in cutting out, with crayon, or Italian crow-quill, the ungainly forms of the Roman alphabet. Ned Hinkley shook his head with some misgiving when the work was done; as he could not but see that he had somewhat impaired the beauty of the peace-maker's butt by the hang-dog looking initial which he had grafted upon it. But when he recollected the subordinate uses to which this "puppy" was to be put, and considered how unlikely, in his case, it would be exposed to sight in comparison with its more masculine brother, he grew partially reconciled to an evil which was now, indeed, irreparable.

It does not require that we should bother the reader with the numberless thoughts and fancies which bothered our spy, in the three mortal hours in which he kept his watch. Nothing but the hope that he should ultimately be compensated to the utmost by a full discovery of all that he sought to know, could possibly have sustained him during the trying ordeal. At every new spasm of impatience which he felt, he drew up his legs, shifted from one side to the other, and growled out some small thunder in the shape of a threat that "it would be only so much the worse for him when the time came!" *Him*—meaning Stevens.

At last Stevens came. He watched the progress of his enemy with keen eyes; and, with his "bull-pup" in his hand, which a sort of instinct made him keep in the direction of the highway, he followed his form upon the road. When he was out of sight and hearing, the spy jumped to his feet. The game, he felt, was secure now—in one respect at least.

"He's for Ellisland. That was no bad guess then. He might have been for Fergus, or Jonesboro', or Debarre, but there's no turn now in the clear track to Ellisland. He's there for certain."

Ned Hinkley carefully restored his pistols to his bosom and buttoned up. He was mounted in a few moments, and pressing slowly forward in pursuit. He had his own plans which we will not attempt to fathom; but we fear we shall be compelled to admit that he was not sufficiently a gentleman to scruple at turning scout in a time of peace (though, with him, by the way, and thus he justified, he is in pursuit of an enemy, and consequently is at war), and dodging about, under cover, spying out the secrets of the land, and not very fastidious in listening to conversation that does not exactly concern him. We fear that there is some such flaw in the character of Ned Hinkley, though, otherwise, a

good, hardy fellow—with a rough and tumble sort of good
nature, which, having bloodied your nose, would put a
knife-handle down your back, and apply a handful of cob-
webs to the nasal extremity in order to arrest the hæmor-
rhage. We are sorry that there is such a defect in his
character; but we did not put it there. We should prefer
that he should be perfect—the reader will believe us—
but there are grave lamentations enough over the failures
of humanity to render our homilies unnecessary. Ned
Hinkley was not a gentleman, and the only thing to be said
in his behalf, is, that he was modest enough to make no
pretensions to the character. As he once said in a row, at
the company muster:—

"I'm blackguard enough, on this occasion, to whip e'er
a gentleman among you!"

Without any dream of such a spectre at his heels to disturb his imagination, Alfred Stevens was pursuing his way
toward Ellisland, at that easy travelling gait, which is the
best for man and beast, vulgarly called a "dog-trot." Some
very fine and fanciful people insist upon calling it a "jog-
trot." We beg leave, in this place, to set them right.
Every trot is a jog, and so, for that matter, is every canter.
A dog-trot takes its name from the even motion of the
smaller quadruped, when it is seized with no particular
mania, and is yet disposed to go stubbornly forward. It
is in more classical dialect, the *festina lente* motion. It is
regularly forward, and therefore fast—it never puts the
animal out of breath, and is therefore slow. Nobody ever
saw a dog practice this gait, with a tin canister at his tail,
and a huddle of schoolboys at his heels. No! it is *the*
travelling motion, considering equally the health of all parties, and the necessity of getting on.

In this desire, Ned Hinkley pressed too closely on the
heels of Stevens. He once nearly overhauled him; and
falling back, he subdued his speed, to what, in the same
semi-figurative language, he styled "the puppy-trot." Ob-

serving these respective gaits, Brother Stevens rode into
Ellisland at a moderately late dinner-hour, and the pursuer
followed at an unspeakable, but not great, distance behind
him. We will, henceforward, after a brief glance at Ellisland, confine ourselves more particularly to the progress
of Brother Stevens.

Ellisland was one of those little villages to which geog-
raphers scarcely accord a place upon the maps. It is not
honored with a dot in any map that we have ever seen of
Kentucky. But, for all this, it is a place! Some day the
name will be changed into Acarnania or Etolia, Epirus or
Scandinavia, and then be sure you shall hear of it. Already, the village lawyers—there are two of them—have
been discussing the propriety of a change to something
classical; and we do not doubt that, before long, their stu-
pidity will become infectious. Under these circumstances
Ellisland will catch a name that will stick. At present
you would probably never hear of the place, were it not
necessary to our purposes and those of Brother Stevens.

It has its tavern and blacksmith shop—its church—the
meanest fabric in the village—its postoffice and public
well and trough. There is also a rack *pro bono publico*,
but as it is in front of the tavern, the owner of that estab-
lishment has not wholly succeeded in convincing the people
that it was put there with simple reference to the public
convenience. The tavern-keeper is, politically, a quad-
rupled personage. He combines the four offices of post-
master, justice of the peace, town council, and publican;
and is considered a monstrous small person with all. The
truth is, reader—this aside—he has been democrat and
whig, alternately, every second year of his political life.
His present politics, being loco-foco, are in Ellisland considered *contra bonos mores*. It is hoped that he will be
dismissed from office, and a memorial to that effect is in
preparation; but the days of Harrison—" and Tyler too"
—have not yet come round, and Jerry Sunderland, who

knows what his enemies are driving at, whirls his coat-skirts, and snaps his fingers, in scorn of all their machinations. He has a friend at Washington, who spoons in the back parlor of the white-house — in other words, is a member of the kitchen-cabinet, of which, be it said, *en passant*, there never was a president of the United States yet entirely without one — and — there never will be! So much for politics and Ellisland.

There was some crowd in the village on the day of Brother Stevens's arrival. Saturday is a well known day in the western and southern country for making a village gathering; and when Brother Stevens, having hitched his horse at the public rack, pushed his way to the postoffice, he had no small crowd to set aside. He had just deposited his letters, received others in return, answered some ten or fifteen questions which Jerry Sunderland, P. M., Q. U., N. P., M. C., publican and sinner — such were all deservedly his titles — had thought it necessary to address to him, when he was suddenly startled by a familiar tap upon the shoulder; such a tap as leads the recipient to imagine that he is about to be honored with the affectionate salutation of some John Doe or Richard Roe of the law. Stevens turned with some feeling of annoyance, if not misgiving, and met the arch, smiling, and very complacent visage of a tall, slender young gentleman in black bushy whiskers and a green coat, who seized him by the hand and shook it heartily, while a chuckling half-suppressed laughter gurgling in his throat, for a moment, forbade the attempt to speak. Stevens seemed disquieted and looked around him suspiciously.

"What! you here, Ben?"

"Ay, you see me! You didn't expect to see me, War-ham——"

"Hush!" was the whispered word of Stevens, again looking round him in trepidation.

"Oh! ay!" said the other with a sly chuckle, and also

in a whisper, " Mr. Stevens — Brother Stevens — hem! I
did not think.   How is your holiness to-day ?"

" Come aside," muttered Stevens; and, taking the arm
of the incautious speaker, he led him away from the crowd,
and took the way out of the village.   Their meeting and
departure did not occasion much, if any, sensation.   The
visiters in the village were all too busy in discussing the
drink and doctrines, pretty equally distributed, of Jerry
the publican.   But there was one eye that noted the meeting of the friends; that beheld the concern and confusion
of Stevens : that saw their movements, and followed their
departing steps.

" Take your horse — where is he ?" demanded Stevens.

" Here, at hand ; but what do you mean to do ?"

" Nothing, but get out of hearing and sight; for your
long tongue, Ben, and significant face, would blab any secret, however deep."

" Ah ! did I not say that I would find you out ? Did you
get my last letter ?"

" Ay, I did : but I'm devilish sorry, Ben, that you've
come.   You'll do mischief.   You have always been a marplot."

" Never, never !   You don't know me."

" Don't I ? — but get your horse, and let's go into the
woods, while we talk over matters."

" Why not leave the nags here ?"

" For a very good reason.   My course lies in that direction, so that I am in my way ; while yours, if your purpose
be to go back to Frankfort, will lie on the upper side.   Neither of us need come back to the village."

" And you think to shuffle me off so soon, do you ?"

" What would you have me do ?"

" Why, give us a peep at this beauty — this Altamira of
yours — at least."

" Impossible !   Do not think of it, Ben ; you'd spoil all.
But, get the horse.   These billet-heads will suspect mis-

chief if they see us talking together, particularly when they behold your conceited action. This political landlord will surmise that you are a second Aaron Burr, about to beat up recruits to conquer California. Your big whiskers — what an atrocious pair! — with your standing collar, will confirm the impression."

The two were soon mounted, and rode into the adjoining woods. They were only a stone's-throw from the village, when Stevens alighted, followed by his companion. They hitched their horses to some swinging branches of a sheltering tree, and, going aside a few paces beyond, seated themselves upon the grass, as they fancied, in a place of perfect security.

"And now, Ben, what in truth brings you here?" demanded Stevens, in tones of voice and with a look which betrayed anything but satisfaction with the visit.

"Curiosity, I tell you, and the legs of my horse."

"Pshaw! you have some other motive."

"No, 'pon honor. I resolved to find you out—to see what you were driving at, and where. I could only guess a part from your letter to Barnabas, and that costive scrawl with which you honored me. Perhaps, too — and give my friendship credit for the attempt—I came with some hope to save you."

"Save me—from what?"

"Why, wedlock—the accursed thing! The club is in terror lest you should forget your vows. So glowing were your descriptions of your Cleopatra, that we knew not what to make. We feared everything."

"Why, Barnabas might have opened your eyes: he knew better."

"You're not married, then?"

"Pshaw! no."

"Nor engaged?"

The other laughed as he replied :—

"Why, on that head, the least said the better. The roving commission permits you to run up any flag that the occasion requires."

"Ah, you sly dog!—and what success?"

"Come, come, Ben, you must not be so inquisitive. The game's my own, you know; and the rules of the club give me immunity from a fellow-member."

"By Gad, I'll resign! I must see this forest beauty."

"Impossible!"

"Where's she? How will you prevent?"

"By a very easy process. Do you know the bird that shrieks farthest from her young ones when the fowler is at hand? I'll follow her example."

"I'll follow you to the uttermost ends of the earth, Warham!"

"Hush! you forget! Am I not Brother Stevens? Ha! ha! ha! You are not sufficiently reverent, brother. See you no divinity in my look and bearing? Hark you, Ben, I've been a sort of small divinity in the eyes of a whole flock for a month past!"

"You pray?"

"And preach!"

"Ha! ha! ha!—devilish good; but I must see you in order to believe. I must, indeed, Brother Stevens. Why, man, think of it—success in this enterprise will make you head of the fraternity—you will be declared pope: but you must have witnesses!"

"So I think; and hark ye, Ben"—laying a finger on the arm of the other—"I am successful!"

"What! you don't say so! This queen, this princess of Egypt, Cleopatra, Altamira—eh?"

"Is mine—soul and body—she is mine!"

"And is what you say? Come, come, you don't mean that such a splendid woman as you describe—such a genius, poet, painter, musician—beauty too!—you don't mean to say that—"

"I do, every bit of it."

" 'Gad! what a fellow!—what a lucky dog! But you must let me see her, Warham!"

" What! to spoil all—to blurt out the truth?—for, with every disposition to fib, you lack the ability. No, no, Ben: when the game's up—when I'm tired of the sport, and feel the necessity of looking out fresh viands—you shall then know all; I'll give the clue into your own hands, and you may follow it to your heart's content. But not now!"

" But how will you get rid of me, *mon ami*, if my curiosity is stubborn?"

" Do as the kill-deer does—travel from the nest—go home with you, rather than you should succeed in your impertinence, and have you expelled from the club for thrusting your spoon into the dish of a brother-member."

" You're a Turk, with no bowels of compassion. But, at all events, you promise me the dish when you're done with it? you give me the preference?"

" I do!"

" Swear by Beelzebub and Mohammed; by Jupiter Ammon and Johannes Secundus; by the ghost of Cardinal Bembo, and the gridiron of the fraternity!"

" Ay, and by the virginity of Queen Elizabeth!"

" Simulacrum! no! no! no such oath for me! That's swearing by the thing that is not, was not—could not be! You shall swear by the oaths of the club—you must be bound on the gridiron of the fraternity, before I believe you. Swear!"

" You are as tenacious as the ghost of buried Denmark. But you shall be satisfied. I swear by the mystic gridiron of the fraternity, and by the legs thereof, of which the images are Beelzebub, Mohammed, Johannes Secundus, and so forth—nay, by that memorable volume, so revered in the eyes of the club, the new edition of 'The Basiad,' of which who among us has been the true exponent?— that profound mystery of sweets, fathomed hourly, yet unfathomable still—for which the commentators, already legions, are hourly becoming legions more;—by these, and by the mysteries of the mirror that reflects not our own, but the image we desire;—by these things—by all things that among the brotherhood are held potent—I swear to—"

" Give me the preference in the favor of this princess; the clue to find her when you have left her; and the assurance that you will get a surfeit as soon as possible : swear!"

" Nay, nay! I swear not to that last! I shall hold on while appetite holds, and make all efforts not to grow dyspeptic in a hurry. I'll keep my stomach for a dainty, be sure, as long as I can. I were no brother, worthy of our order, if I did not."

" Well, well—to the rest! Swear to the rest, and I am satisfied."

" You go back, then, *instanter?*"

" What! this very day?"

" This hour!"

" The d—l! you don't mean *that*, Warham?" returned the other in some consternation.

" Ay, this very hour! You must swear to that. Your oath must precede mine."

" Ah! man, remember I only got here last night—long ride—hard-trotting horse. We have not seen each other for months. I have a cursed sight to tell you about the boys—girls too—love, law, logic, politics. Do you know they talk of running you for the house?"

" All in good season, Ben; not now. No, no! you shall see me when you least look for me, and there will be time enough for all these matters then. They'll keep. For the present, let me say to you that we must part now within the hour. You must swear not to dog my steps, and I will swear to give you *carte blanche*, and the first privileges at my princess, when I leave her. This is my bargain. I make no other."

"I've a great mind not to leave you," said the other doggedly.

"And what will that resolution bring you, do you fancy? Do you suppose I am to be tracked in such a manner? No, Ben! The effect will be to make me set off for the east instantly, whether you go with me or not; and an equally certain effect will be to make us cut loose for ever."

"You're a d——d hard colt to manage," said the other moodily.

"I sha'n't let myself be straddled by every horse-boy, I assure you."

"Come, come, old fellow, that's too much like horse-play Don't be angry with me. I'll accept your conditions."

"Very good," said Stevens; "if you did not, Ben, it would be no better for you; for, otherwise, you should never even see my beauty!"

"Is she so very beautiful, old boy?"

"A queen, I tell you! a proud, high-spirited, wild beauty of the mountains—a thing of fire and majesty—a glorious woman, full of song and sentiment and ambition—a genius, I tell you—who can improvise like Corinne, and, by the way, continually reminds one of that glorious creature. In Italy, she would have been greater than Corinne."

"And you've won her—and she loves you?"

"Ay—to doting! I found her a sort of eagle—soaring, striving—always with an eye upon the hills, and fighting with the sunbeams. I have subdued her. She is now like a timid fawn that trembles at the very falling of a leaf in the forests. She pants with hope to see me, and pants with tremulous delight when I come. Still, she shows every now and then, a glimmering of that eagle spirit which she had at first. She flashes up suddenly, but soon sinks again. Fancy a creature, an idolater of fame before, suddenly made captive by love, and you have a vain, partial image of my forest-princess."

"What a lucky dog! You'll marry her yet, old boy, in spite of all!"

"Pshaw! You are green to talk so."

"You'll be devilish loath to give her up; I'm afraid I'll have to wait a cursed long time."

"No, not long! Do not despair. Easy won, easy valued."

"And was she easily won?"

"Very! the game was a short one. She is a mere country-girl, you know, but eighteen or thereabouts—suspecting nobody, and never dreaming that she had a heart or passions at all. She thought only of her poetry and her books. It was only necessary to work upon heart and passions while talking of poetry and books, and they carried her out of her depth before she could recover. She's wiser now, Ben, I can assure you, and will require more dexterity to keep than to conquer."

"And she has no brother to worry a body—no d——d ugly Hobnail, who has a fancy for her, and may make a window between the ribs of a gallant, such as nature never intended, with the ounce-bullet of some d——d old-fashioned seven-foot rifle—eh?"

"There was a silly chap, one Hinkley, who tried it on me—actually challenged me, though I was playing parson, and there might have been work for me but for his own bull-headed father, who came to my rescue, beat the boy and drove him from the place. There is nobody else to give me any annoyance, unless it be a sort of half-witted chap, a cousin of the former—a sleepy dog that is never, I believe, entirely awake unless when he's trout-fishing. He has squinted at me, as if he could quarrel if he dared, but the lad is dull—too dull to be very troublesome. You might kiss his grandmother under his nose, and he would probably regard it only as a compliment to her superior virtues, and would thank you accordingly——"

A voice a little to the left interrupted the speaker.

"So he does, my brave parson, for his grandmother's sake and his own," were the words of the speaker. They turned in sudden amaze to the spot whence the sounds issued. The bushes opening in this quarter, presented to the astonished eyes of Brother Stevens, the perfect image of the dull lad of whom he had been speaking. There was Ned Hinkley in proper person—perfectly awake, yet not trout-fishing! A sarcastic grin was upon his visage, and rolling his eyes with a malicious leer, he repeated the words which had first interrupted the progress of the dialogue between the friends.

"I thank you, Brother Stevens, for the compliment to my grandmother's virtues. I thank you, on her account as well as my own. I'm very grateful, I assure you, very grateful, very!"

16

CHAPTER XXXI.

"ABSQUATULATING."

HAD a bolt suddenly flashed and thundered at the feet of the two friends, falling from a clear sky in April, they could not have been more astounded. They started, as with one impulse, in the same moment to their feet.

"Keep quiet," said the intruder; "don't let me interrupt you in so pleasant a conversation. I'd like to hear you out. I'm refreshed by it. What you say is so very holy and sermon-like, that I'm like a new man when I hear it. Sit down, Brother Stevens, and begin again; sit down, Ben, my good fellow, and don't look so scary! You look as if you had a window in your ribs already!"

The intruder had not moved, though he had startled the conspirators. He did not seem to share in their excitement. He was very coolly seated, with his legs deliberately crossed, while his two hands parted the bushes before him in order to display his visage — perhaps with the modest design of showing to the stranger that his friend had grievously misrepresented its expression. Certainly, no one could say that, at this moment, it lacked anything of spirit or intelligence. Never were eyes more keen — never were lips more emphatically made to denote sarcasm and hostility. The whole face was alive with scorn, and hate, and bitterness; and there was defiance enough in the glance to have put wings to fifty bullets.

His coolness, the composure which his position and words

manifested, awakened the anger of Brother Stevens as soon as the first feeling of surprise had passed away. He felt, in a moment, that the game was up with him—that he could no longer play the hypocrite in Charlemont. He must either keep his pledges to Margaret Cooper, without delay or excuse, or he must abandon all other designs which his profligate heart may have suggested in its cruel purposes against her peace.

"Scoundrel!" he exclaimed; "how came you here? What have you heard?"

"Good words, Brother Stevens. You forget, you are a parson."

"Brain the rascal!" exclaimed the whiskered stranger, looking more fierce than ever. The same idea seemed to prompt the actions of Stevens. Both of them, at the same moment, advanced upon the intruder, with their whips uplifted; but still Ned Hinkley did not rise. With his legs still crossed, he kept his position, simply lifting from the sward beside him, where they had been placed conveniently, his two "puppies." One of these he grasped in his right hand and presented as his enemies approached.

"This, gentlemen," said he, "is my peace-maker. It says, 'Keep your distance.' This is my bull-pup, or peace-breaker; it says, 'Come on.' Listen to which you please. It's all the same to me. Both are ready to answer you, and I can hardly keep 'em from giving tongue. The bull-pup longs to say something to you, Brother Stevens—the pacificator is disposed to trim your whiskers, Brother Ben; and I say, for 'em both, come on, you black-hearted rascals, if you want to know whether a girl of Charlemont can find a man of Charlemont to fight her battles. I'm man enough, by the Eternal, for both of you!"

The effect of Hinkley's speech was equally great upon himself and the enemy. He sprang to his feet, ere the last sentence was concluded, and they recoiled in something like indecent haste. The language of determination was even

more strongly expressed by the looks of the rustic than by
his language and action. They backed hurriedly at his approach.

"What! won't you stand?—won't you answer to your
villanies?—won't you fight? Pull out your barkers and
blaze away, you small-souled scamps; I long to have a
crack at you—here and there—both at a time! Aint you
willing? I'm the sleepy trout-fisherman! Don't you know
me? You've waked me up, my lads, and I sha'n't sleep
again in a hurry! As for you, Alfred Stevens—you were
ready to fight Bill Hinkley—here's another of the breed—
won't you fight him?"

"Yes—give me one of your pistols, if you dare, and
take your stand," said Stevens boldly.

"You're a cunning chap—give you one of my puppies
—a stick for my own head—while this bush-whiskered
chap cudgels me over from behind. No! no! none of that!
Besides, these pistols were a gift from a good man, they
sha'n't be disgraced by the handling of a bad one. Get
your own weapons, Brother Stevens. and every man to his
tree."

"They are in Charlemont!"

"Well!—you'll meet me there then?"

"Yes!" was the somewhat eager answer of Stevens, "I
will meet you there—to-morrow morning—"

"Sunday—no! no!"

"Monday, then; this evening, if we get home in season."

"It's a bargain then," replied Hinkley, "though I can
hardly keep from giving you the teeth of the bull! As for
big-whiskered Ben, there, I'd like to let him taste my pacificator. I'd just like to brush up his whiskers with gun-
powder—they look to have been done up with bear's grease
before, and have a mighty fine curl; but if I wouldn't frizzle them better than ever a speckled hen had her feathers
frizzled, then I don't know the virtues of gun-powder. On
Monday morning, Brother Stevens!"

"Ay, ay! on Monday morning!"

Had Ned Hinkley been more a man of the world—had he not been a simple backwoodsman, he would have seen, in the eagerness of Stevens to make this arrangement, something, which would have rendered him suspicious of his truth. The instantaneous thought of the arch-hypocrite, convinced him that he could never return to Charlemont if this discovery was once made there. His first impulse was to put it out of the power of Ned Hinkley to convey the tidings. We do not say that he would have deliberately murdered him; but, under such an impulse of rage and disappointment as governed him in the first moments of detection, murder has been often done. He would probably have beaten him into incapacity with his whip—which had a heavy handle—had not the rustic been sufficiently prepared. The pistols of Stevens were in his valise, but he had no purpose of fighting, on equal terms, with a man who spoke with the confidence of one who knew how to use his tools; and when the simple fellow, assuming that he would return to Charlemont for his chattels, offered him the meeting there, he eagerly caught at the suggestion as affording himself and friend the means of final escape.

It was not merely the pistols of Hinkley of which he had a fear. But he well knew how extreme would be the danger, should the rustic gather together the people of Ellisland, with the story of his fraud, and the cruel consequences to the beauty of Charlemont, by which the deception had been followed. But the simple youth, ignorant of the language of libertinism, had never once suspected the fatal lapse from virtue of which Margaret Cooper had been guilty. He was too unfamiliar with the annals and practices of such criminals, to gather this fact from the equivocal words, and half-spoken sentences, and sly looks of the confederates. Had he dreamed this—had it, for a moment, entered into his conjecturings—that such had been the case, he would probably have shot down the seducer without

a word of warning. But that the crime was other than
prospective, he had not the smallest fancy; and this may
have been another reason why he took the chances of Ste
vens's return to Charlemont, and let him off at the moment.

"Even should he not return," such may have been his
reflection—"I have prevented mischief at least. He will
be able to do no harm. Margaret Cooper shall be warned
of her escape, and become humbler at least, if not wiser,
in consequence. At all events, the eyes of Uncle Hinkley
will be opened, and poor Bill be restored to us again!"

"And now mount, you scamps," said Hinkley, pressing
upon the two with presented pistols. "I'm eager to send
big-whiskered Ben home to his mother; and to see you,
Brother Stevens, on your way back to Charlemont. I can
hardly keep hands off you till then; and it's only to do so,
that I hurry you. If you stay, looking black, mouthing
together, I can't stand it. I will have a crack at you.
My peace-maker longs to brush up them whiskers. My
bull-pup is eager to take you, Brother Stevens, by the muzzle! Mount you, as quick as you can, before I do mischief."

Backing toward their horses, they yielded to the advan-
cing muzzles, which the instinct of fear made them loath to
turn their backs upon. Never were two hopeful projectors
so suddenly abased—so completely baffled. Hinkley, ad-
vancing with moderate pace, now thrust forward one, and
now the other pistol, accompanying the action with a spe-
cific sentence corresponding to each, in manner and form
as follows:—

"Back, parson—back, whiskers! Better turn, and look
out for the roots, as you go forward. There's no seeing your
way along the road by looking down the throats of my
puppies. If you want to be sure that they'll follow till
you're mounted, you have my word for it. No mistake, I
tell you. They're too eager on scent, to lose sight of you
in a hurry, and they're ready to give tongue at a moment's

warning. Take care not to stumble, whiskers, or the pacificator 'll be into your brush."

"I'll pay you for this!" exclaimed Stevens, with a rage which was not less really felt than judiciously expressed. "Wait till we meet!"

"Ay, ay! I'll wait; but be in a hurry. Turn now, your nags are at your backs. Turn and mount!"

In this way they reached the tree where their steeds were fastened. Thus, with the muzzle of a pistol bearing close upon the body of each—the click of the cock they had heard—the finger close to the trigger they saw—they were made to mount—in momentary apprehension that the backwoodsman, whose determined character was sufficiently seen in his face, might yet change his resolve, and with wanton hand, riddle their bodies with his bullets. It was only when they were mounted, that they drew a breath of partial confidence.

"Now," said Hinkley, "my lads, let there be few last words between you. The sooner you're off the better. As for you, Alfred Stevens, the sooner you're back in Charlemont the more daylight we'll have to go upon. I'll be waiting you, I reckon, when you come."

"Ay, and you may wait," said Stevens, as the speaker turned off and proceeded to the spot where his own horse was fastened.

"You won't return, of course?" said his companion.

"No! I must now return with you, thanks to your interference. By Heavens, Ben, I knew, at your coming, that you would do mischief; you have been a marplot ever; and after this, I am half-resolved to forswear your society for ever."

"Nay, nay! do not say so, Warham. It was unfortunate, I grant you; but how the devil should either of us guess that such a Turk as that was in the bush?"

"Enough for the present," said the other. 'It is not

now whether I wish to ride with you or not.   There is no choice.   There is no return to Charlemont."

" And that's the name of the place, is it ?"

" Yes! yes!   Much good may the knowledge of it do you."

" How fortunate that this silly fellow concluded to let you off on such a promise.   What an ass!"

" Yes! but he may grow wiser!   Put spurs to your jade, and let us see what her heels are good for, for the next three hours.   I do not yet feel secure.   The simpleton may grow wiser and change his mind."

" He can scarcely do us harm now, if he does."

"Indeed!" said Stevens—"you know nothing.   There's such a thing as hue and cry, and its not unfrequently practised in these regions, when the sheriff is not at hand and constables are scarce.   Every man is then a sheriff."

" Well—but there's no law-process against us!"

" You are a born simpleton, I think," said Stevens, with little scruple.   He was too much mortified to be very heedful of the feelings of his companion.   " There needs no law in such a case, at least for the *capture* of a supposed criminal; and, for that matter, they do not find it necessary for his punishment either.   Hark ye, Ben—there's a farmhouse ?"

" Yes, I see it!"

" Don't you smell tar ?—They're running it now!"

" I think I do smell something like it.   What of it ?"

" Do you see that bed hanging from yon window ?"

" Yes! of course I see it!"

" It is a feather-bed !"

" Well—what of that ?   Why tell me this stuff ?   Of course I can guess as well as you that it's a feather-bed, since I see a flock of geese in the yard with their necks all bare."

" Hark ye, then!   There's something more than this, which you may yet see!   Touch up your mare.   If this fellow brings the mob at Ellisland upon us, that tar will be run, and that feather-bed gutted, for our benefit. What they took from the geese will be bestowed on us. Do you understand me? Did you ever hear of a man whose coat was made of tar and feathers, and furnished at the expense of the county?"

"Hush, for God's sake, Warham! you make my blood run cold with your hideous notions!"

"That fellow offered to frizzle your whiskers. These would anoint them with tar, in which your bear's oil would be of little use."

"Ha! don't you hear a noise?" demanded the whiskered companion, looking behind him.

"I think I do," replied the other musingly.

"A great noise!" continued Don Whiskerandos.

"Yes, it seems to me that it is a great noise."

"Like people shouting?"

"Somewhat—yes, by my soul, that *does* sound something like a shout!"

"And there! Don't stop to look and listen, Warham," cried his companion; "it's no time for meditation. They're coming! hark!—" and with a single glance behind him—with eyes dilating with the novel apprehensions of receiving a garment, unsolicited, bestowed by the bounty of the county—he drove his spurs into the flanks of his mare, and went ahead like an arrow. Stevens smiled in spite of his vexation.

"D—n him!" he muttered as he rode forward, "it's some satisfaction, at least, to scare the soul out of him!"

16*

CHAPTER XXXII.

THE REVELATION.

HAVING seen his enemy fairly mounted, and under way, as he thought, for Charlemont, Ned Hinkley returned to Ellisland for his own horse. Here he did not suffer himself to linger, though, before he could succeed in taking his departure, he was subjected to a very keen and searching examination by the village publican and politician. Having undergone this scrutiny with tolerable patience, if not to the entire satisfaction of the examiner, he set forward at a free canter, determined that his adversary should not be compelled to wait.

It was only while he rode that he began to fancy the possibility of the other having taken a different course; but as, upon reflection, he saw no other plan which he might have adopted—for lynching for suspected offences was not yet a popular practice in and about Charlemont—he contented himself with the reflection that he had done all that could have been done; and if Alfred Stevens failed to keep his appointment, he, at least, was one of the losers. He would necessarily lose the chance of revenging an indignity, not to speak of the equally serious loss of that enjoyment which a manly fight usually gave to Ned Hinkley himself, and which, he accordingly assumed, must be an equal gratification to all other persons. When he arrived at Charlemont, he did not make his arrival known, but, repairing directly to the lake among the hills, he hitched his horse, and prepared, with what patience he could command, to await the coming of the enemy.

The reader is already prepared to believe that the worthy rustic waited in vain. It was only with the coming on of night that he began to consider himself outwitted. He scratched his head impatiently, not without bringing away some shreds of the hair, jumped on his horse, and, without making many allowances for the rough and hilly character of the road, went off at a driving pace for the house of Uncle Hinkley. Here he drew up only to ask if Brother Stevens had returned.

"No!"

"Then, dang it! he never will return. He's a skunk, uncle—as great a skunk as ever was in all Kentucky!"

"How! what!—what of Brother Stevens?" demanded the uncle, seconded by John Cross, who had only some two hours arrived at the village, and now appeared at the door. But Ned Hinkley was already off.

"He's a skunk!—that's all!"

His last words threw very little light over the mystery, and certainly gave very little satisfaction to his hearers. The absence of Alfred Stevens, at a time when John Cross was expected, had necessarily occasioned some surprise; but, of course, no apprehensions were entertained by either the worthy parson or the bigoted host that he could be detained by any cause whatsoever which he could not fully justify.

The next course of Ned Hinkley was for the cottage of Mr. Calvert. To the old man he gave a copious detail of all his discoveries—not only the heads of what he heard from the conspirators in the wood, but something of the terms of the dialogue. The gravity of Calvert increased as the other proceeded. He saw more deeply into the signification of certain portions of this dialogue than did the narrator; and when the latter, after having expressed his disappointment at the non-appearance of Stevens on the

field of combat, at least congratulated himself at having
driven him fairly from the ground, the other shook his head
mournfully.

"I am afraid it's too late, my son."

"Too late, gran'pa! How? Is it ever too late to send
such a rascal a-packing?"

"It may be for the safety of some, my son."

"What! Margaret you mean? You think the poor fool
of a girl's too far gone in love of him, do you?"

"If that were all, Ned—"

"Why, what more, eh? You don't mean!—"

The apprehensions of the simple, unsuspecting fellow, for
the first time began to be awakened to the truth.

"I am afraid, my son, that this wretch has been in Charlemont too long. From certain words that you have dropped,
as coming from Stevens, in speaking to his comrade, I should
regard him as speaking the language of triumph for successes already gained."

"Oh, hardly! I didn't think so. If I had only guessed
that he meant such a thing—though I can't believe it—
I'd ha' dropped him without a word. I'd have given him
the pacificator as well as the peace-breaker. Oh, no! I
can't think it—I can't—I won't! Margaret Cooper is not
a girl to my liking, but, Lord help us! she's too beautiful
and too smart to suffer such a skunk, in so short a time, to
get the whip-hand of her. No, gran'pa, I can't and won't
believe it!'

"Yet, Ned, these words which you have repeated convey some such fear to my mind. It may be that the villain
was only boasting to his companion. There are scoundrels
in this world who conceive of no higher subject of boast
than the successful deception and ruin of the artless and
confiding. I sincerely hope that this may be the case now
—that it was the mere brag of a profligate, to excite the
admiration of his comrade. But when you speak of the
beauty and the smartness of this poor girl, as of securities

for virtue, you make a great mistake. Beauty is more apt to be a betrayer than a protector; and as for her talent, that is seldom a protection unless it be associated with humility. Hers was not. She was most ignorant where she was most assured. She knew just enough to congratulate herself that she was unlike her neighbors, and this is the very temper of mind which is likely to cast down its possessor in shame. I trust that she had a better guardian angel than either her beauty or her talents. I sincerely hope that she is safe. At all events, let me caution you not to hint the possibility of its being otherwise. We will take for granted that Stevens is a baffled villain."

"I only wish I had dropped him!"

"Better as it is."

"What! even if the poor girl is—"

"Ay, even then!"

"Why, gran'pa, can it be possible *you* say so?"

"Yes, my son; I say so here, in moments of comparative calmness, and in the absence of the villain. Perhaps, were he present, I should say otherwise."

"And *do* otherwise! You'd shoot him, gran'pa, as soon as I."

"Perhaps! I think it likely. But, put up your pistols, Ned. You have nobody now to shoot. Put them up, and let us walk over to your uncle's at once. It is proper that he and John Cross should know these particulars."

Ned agreed to go, but not to put up his pistols.

"For, you see, gran'pa, this rascal may return. His friend may have kept him in long talk. We may meet him coming into the village."

"It is not likely; but come along. Give me that staff, my son, and your arm on the other side. I feel that my eyes are no longer young."

"You could shoot still, gran'pa?"

"Not well."

"What, couldn't you hit a chap like Stevens between

the eyes at ten paces? I'm sure I could do it, blindfolded, by a sort of instinct."

And the youth, shutting his eyes, as if to try the experiment, drew forth one of his pistols from his bosom, and began to direct its muzzle around the room.

"There was a black spider *there*, gran'pa! I'm sure, taking him for Stevens, I could cut his web for him."

"You have cut that of Stevens himself, and his comb too, Ned."

"Yes, yes—but what a fool I was not to make it his gills!"

By this time the old man had got on his spencer, and, with staff in hand, declared himself in readiness. Ned Hinkley lowered his pistol with reluctance. He was very anxious to try the weapon and his own aim, on somebody or something. That black spider which lived so securely in the domicil of Mr. Calvert would have stood no chance in any apartment of the widow Hinkley. Even the "pacificator" would have been employed for its extermination, if, for no other reason, because of the fancied resemblance which it had always worn to Brother Stevens—a resemblance which occurred to him, perhaps, in consequence of the supposed similarity between the arts of the libertine and those for the entrapping of his victims which distinguish the labors of the spider.

The two were soon arrived at old Hinkley's, and the tale of Ned was told; but, such was the bigotry of the hearers, without securing belief.

"So blessed a young man!" said the old lady.

"A brand from the burning!" exclaimed Brother Cross.

"It's all an invention of Satan!" cried old Hinkley, "to prevent the consummation of a goodly work."

"We should not give our faith too readily to such devices of the enemy, Friend Calvert," said John Cross, paternally.

"I never saw anything in him that wasn't perfectly saintlike," said Mrs. Hinkley. "He made the most heartfelt prayer, and the loveliest blessing before meat! I think I hear him now — 'Lord, make us thankful' — with his eyes shut up so sweetly, and with such a voice."

"There are always some people, Brother Cross, to hate the saints of the Lord and to slander them! They lie in wait like thieves of the night, and roaring lions of the wilderness, seeking what they may devour."

"Ah," exclaimed Brother Cross, "how little do such know that they devour themselves; for whoso destroyeth his best friend is a devourer of himself."

"The blindness of Satan is upon them, and they do his work."

And thus — purr, purr, purr — they went on, to the end of the chapter. Poor Ned Hinkley found the whole kennel was upon him. Not only did they deny everything that could by possibility affect the fair fame of the absent brother, but, from defending him, they passed, with an easy transition, to the denunciation of those who were supposed to be his defamers. In this the worthy old man Calvert came in for his share.

"All this comes of your supporting that worthless boy of mine in defiance of my will," said old Hinkley. "You hate Brother Stevens because that boy hated him, and because I love him."

"You are mistaken, Mr. Hinkley," said Calvert, mildly. "I hate nobody; at the same time I suffer no mere prejudices to delude me against sight and reason."

"Ah!" said Brother Cross, gently, "it's that very reason, Brother Calvert, that ruins you worldlings. You must not rely on human reason. Build on faith, and you build on the Rock of Ages."

"I propose to use reason only in worldly matters, Mr. Cross," said the other; "for which use, only, I believe it was given us. I employ it in reference to a case of ordinary evidence, and I beg your regards now, while I draw your attention to the use I make of it in the present instance. Will you hear me without interruption ?"

" Surely, Brother Calvert, but call me not Mr. Cross. I am not a Mister. I am plain John Cross ; by virtue of my business, a brother, if it so please you to esteem me. Call me Brother Cross, or Brother John Cross, or plain John Cross, either of these will be acceptable unto me."

" We are all brothers, or should be," said Calvert ; " and it will not need that there should be any misunderstanding between us on so small a matter."

" The matter is not small in the eye of the Lord," said the preacher. " Titles of vanity become not us, and offend in his hearing."

The old teacher smiled, but proceeded.

" Now, Brother Cross, if you will hear me, I will proceed, according to my reason, to dwell upon the proofs which are here presented to you, of the worthlessness of this man, Alfred Stevens ; and when you consider how much the feelings and the safety of the daughters of your flock depend upon the character of those moral and religious teachers to whom the care of them is intrusted, you will see, I think, the necessity of listening patiently, and determining without religious prejudice, according to the truth and reason of the case."

" I am prepared to listen patiently, Brother Calvert," said John Cross, clasping his hands together, setting his elbows down upon the table, shutting his eyes, and turning his face fervently up to heaven. Old Hinkley imitated this posture quite as nearly as he was able ; while Mrs. Hinkley, sitting between the two, maintained a constant to-and-fro motion, first on one side, then on the other, as they severally spoke to the occasion, with her head deferentially bowing, like a pendulum, and with a motion almost as regular and methodical. The movements of her nephew, Ned Hinkley, were also a somewhat pleasant study, after a fashion of his own. Sitting in a corner, he amused himself by drawing forth his

" puppies," and taking occasional aim at a candle or flower-pot ; and sometimes, with some irreverence, at the curved and rather extravagant proboscis of his worthy uncle, which, cocked up in air, was indeed something of a tempting object of sight to a person so satisfied of his skill in shooting as the young rustic. The parties being thus arranged in a fit attitude for listening, Mr. Calvert began somewhat after the following fashion : —

" Our first knowledge of Alfred Stevens was obtained through Brother John Cross."

" And what better introduction would you have ?" demanded old Hinkley.

" None," said the other, " if Brother Cross knew anything about the party he introduced. But it so happens, as we learn from Brother Cross himself, that the first acquaintance he had with Stevens was made upon the road, where Stevens played a trick upon him by giving him brandy to drink."

" No trick, Brother Calvert ; the young man gave it me as a medicine, took it as a medicine himself, and, when I bade him, threw away the accursed beverage."

" Ordinary men, governed by ordinary reason, Brother Cross, would say that Stevens knew very well what he was giving you, and that it was a trick."

" But only think, Mr. Calvert," said Mrs. Hinkley, lifting her hands and eyes at the same moment, " the blessed young man threw away the evil liquor the moment he was told to do so. What a sign of meekness was that !"

" I will not dwell on this point," was the reply of Calvert. " He comes into our village and declares his purpose to adopt the profession of the preacher, and proceeds to his studies under the direction of Brother Cross."

" And didn't he study them ?" demanded Mrs. Hinkley. " Wasn't he, late and early, at the blessed volume ? I heard him at all hours above stairs. Oh ! how often was he

on his bended knees in behalf of our sinful race, ungrateful
and misbelieving that we are !"

" I am afraid, madam," said Calvert, " that his studies
were scarcely so profound as you think them.   Indeed, I
am at a loss to conceive how you should blind your eyes to
the fact that the greater part of his time was spent among
the young girls of the village."

" And where is it denied," exclaimed old Hinkley, " that
the lambs of God should sport together ?"

" Do not speak in that language, I pray you, Mr. Hinkley," said Calvert, with something of pious horror in his
look ; " this young man was no lamb of God, but, I fear, as
you will find, a wolf in the fold.   It is, I say, very well
known that he was constantly wandering, even till a late
hour of the night, with one of the village maidens."

" Who was that one, Brother Calvert ?" demanded John
Cross.

" Margaret Cooper."

" Hem !" said the preacher.

" Well, he quarrels with my young friend, the worthy son
of Brother Hinkley——"

" Do not speak of that ungrateful cub.   Brother Stevens
did not quarrel with him.   He quarrelled with Brother
Stevens, and would have murdered him, but that I put in
in time to save."

" Say not so, Mr. Hinkley.   I have good reason to believe that Stevens went forth especially to fight with William."

" I would not believe it, if a prophet were to tell me it."

" Nevertheless, I believe it.   We found both of them
placed at the usual fighting-distance."

" Ah ! but where were Brother Stevens's pistols ?"

" In his pocket, I suppose."

" He had none.   He was at a distance from my ungrateful son, and flying that he should not be murdered.   The
lamb under the hands of the butcher.   And would you be-

lieve it, Brother Cross, he had gone forth only to counsel
the unworthy boy—only to bring him back into the fold—
gone forth at his own prayer, as Brother Stevens declared
to Betsy, just before he went out."

"I am of opinion that he deceived her and yourself."

"Where were his pistols then ?"

"He must have concealed them. He told Ned Hinkley,
this very day, that he had pistols, but that they were
here."

"Run up, Betsy, to Brother Stevens's room and see."

The old lady disappeared. Calvert proceeded.

"I can only repeat my opinion, founded upon the known
pacific and honorable character of William Hinkley, and
certain circumstances in the conduct of Stevens, that the
two did go forth, under a previous arrangement, to fight a
duel. That they were prevented, and that Stevens had no
visible weapon, is unquestionably true. But I do not confine myself to these circumstances. This young man writes
a great many letters, it is supposed to his friends, but never
puts them in the post here, but every Saturday rides off, as
we afterward learn, to the village of Ellisland, where he
deposites them and receive others. This is a curious circumstance, which alone should justify suspicion.

"The ways of God are intricate, Brother Calvert," said
John Cross, "and we are not to suspect the truth which
we can not understand."

"But these are the ways of man, Brother Cross."

"And the man of God is governed by the God which is
in him. He obeys a law which, perhaps, is ordered to be
hidden from thy sight."

"This doctrine certainly confers very extraordinary privileges upon the man of God," said Calvert, quietly, "and,
perhaps, this is one reason why the profession is so prolific
of professors now-a-days; but the point does not need discussion. Enough has been shown to awaken suspicion and
doubt in the case of any ordinary person; and I now come

to that portion of the affair which is sustained by the testimony of Ned Hinkley, our young friend here, who, whatever his faults may be, has been always regarded in Charlemont, as a lover and speaker of the truth."

"Ay, ay, so far as he knows what the truth is," said old Hinkley, scornfully.

"And I'm just as likely to know what the truth is as you, uncle!" retorted the young man, rising and coming forward from his corner.

"Come, come," he continued, "you're not going to ride rough shod over me as you did over Cousin Bill. I don't care a snap of the finger, I can tell you, for all your puffed cheeks and big bellied speeches. I don't, I tell you!" and suiting the action to the word, the sturdy fellow snapped his fingers almost under the nose of his uncle, which was now erected heavenward, with a more scornful pre-eminence than ever. The sudden entrance of Mrs. Hinkley, from her search after Stevens's pistols, prevented any rough issue between these new parties, as it seemed to tell in favor of Stevens. There were no pistols to be found. The old lady did not add, indeed, that there was nothing of any kind to be found belonging to the same worthy.

"There! That's enough!" said old Hinkley.

"Did you find anything of Stevens's, Mrs. Hinkley?" inquired Mr. Calvert.

"Nothing, whatever."

"Well, madam," said Calvert, "your search, if it proves anything, proves the story of Ned Hinkley conclusively. This man has carried off all his chattels."

John Cross looked down from heaven, and stared inquiringly at Mrs. Hinkley.

"Is this true? Have you found nothing, Sister Betsy?"

"Nothing."

"And Brother Stevens has not come back?"

"No!"

"And reason for it, enough," said old Hinkley. "Did'nt

you hear that Ned Hinkley threatened to shoot him if he came back ?"

"Look you, uncle," said the person thus accused, "if you was anybody else, and a little younger, I'd thrash you for that speech the same as if it was a lie! I would."

"Peace!" said Calvert, looking sternly at the youth. Having obtained temporary silence, he was permitted at length to struggle through his narrative, and to place, in their proper lights, all the particulars which Ned Hinkley had obtained at Ellisland. When this was done the discussion was renewed, and raged, with no little violence, for a full hour. At length it ceased through the sheer exhaustion of the parties. Calvert was the first to withdraw from it, as he soon discovered that such was the bigotry of old Hinkley and his wife, and even of John Cross himself, that nothing short of divine revelation could persuade them of the guilt of one who had once made a religious profession.

Brother Cross, though struck with some of the details which Calvert had given, was afterward prepared to regard them as rather trivial than otherwise, and poor Ned was doomed to perceive that the conviction was general in this holy family, that he had, by his violence, and the terror which his pistols had inspired, driven away, in desperation, the most meek and saintly of all possible young apostles. The youth was nearly furious ere the evening and the discussion were over. It was very evident to Calvert that nothing was needed, should Stevens come back, but a bold front and a lying tongue, to maintain his position in the estimation of the flock, until such time as the truth *would* make itself known — a thing which, eventually, always happens. That night Ned Hinkley dreamed of nothing but of shooting Stevens and his comrade and of thrashing his uncle. What did Margaret Cooper dream of?

CHAPTER XXXIII.

STORM AND CONVULSION.

WHAT did Margaret Cooper dream of? Disappointment,
misery, death. There was a stern presentiment in her
waking thoughts, sufficiently keen and agonizing to inspire
such dreadful apprehensions in her dreams. The temperament which is sanguine, and which, in a lively mood, inspires hope, is, at the same time, the source of those dark
images of thought and feeling, which appal it with the most
terrifying forms of fear; and when Saturday and Saturday
night came and passed, and Alfred Stevens did not appear,
a lurking dread that would not be chidden or kept down,
continued to rise within her soul, which, without assuming
any real form or decisive speech, was yet suggestive of complete overthrow and ruin.

Her dreams were of this complexion. She felt herself
abandoned. Nor merely abandoned. She was a victim.
In her desolation she had even lost her pride. She could
no longer meet the sneer with scorn. She could no longer
carry a lofty brow among the little circle, who, once having envied, were now about to despise her. To the impatient spirit, once so strong—so insolent in its strength—
what a pang—what a humiliation was here! In her
dreams she saw the young maidens of the village stand
aloof, as she had once stood aloof from them:—she heard
the senseless titter of their laugh; and she had no courage
to resent the impertinence. Her courage was buried in

her shame.   No heart is so cowardly as that which is conscious of guilt.   Picture after picture of this sort did her
fancy present to her that night; and when she awoke the
next morning, the sadness of her soul had taken the color
of a deep and brooding misanthropy.   Such had been the
effect of her dreams.   Her resolution came only from despair; and resolution from such a source, we well know, is
usually only powerful against itself.

It is one proof of a religious instinct, and of a universal
belief in a controlling and benevolent Deity, that all men
however abased, scornful of divine and human law, invariably, in their moments of desperation, call upon God.
Their first appeal is, involuntarily, to him.   The outlaw,
as the fatal bullet pierces his breast—the infidel, sinking
and struggling in the water—the cold stony heart of the
murderer, the miser, the assassin of reputation as of life—
all cry out upon God in the unexpected paroxysms of death.
Let us hope that the instinct which prompts this involuntary appeal for mercy, somewhat helps to secure its blessings.   It is thus also with one who, in the hey-day of the
youthful heart, has lived without thought or prayer—a
tumultuous life of uproar and riot—a long carnival of the
passions—the warm blood suppressing the cool thought,
and making the reckless heart impatient of consideration.
Let the sudden emergency arise, with such a heart—let
the blood become stagnant with disease—and the involuntary appeal is to that God, of whom before there was no
thought.   We turn to him as to a father who is equally
strong to help and glad to preserve us.

Margaret Cooper, in the ordinary phrase, had lived without God.   Her God was in her own heart, beheld by the
lurid fires of an intense, unmethodized ambition.   Her own
strength—or rather the persuasion of her own strength—
had been so great, that hitherto she had seen no necessity
for appealing to any other source of power.   She might
now well begin to distrust that strength.   She did so.   Her

desperation was not of that sort utterly to shut out hope; and, while there is hope, there is yet a moral assurance that the worst is not yet—perhaps not to be. But she was humbled—not enough, perhaps—but enough to feel the necessity of calling in her allies. She dropped by her bed-side, in prayer, when she arose that morning. We do not say that she prayed for forgiveness, without reference to her future earthly desires. Few of us know how to sim-plify our demands upon the Deity to this one. We pray that he may assist us in this or that grand speculation: the planter for a great crop; the banker for investments that give him fifty per cent.; the lawyer for more copious fees; the parson for an increase of salary. How few pray for mercy—forgiveness for the past—strength to sustain the struggling conscience in the future! Poor Margaret was no wiser, no better, than the rest of us. She prayed—silly woman!—that Alfred Stevens might keep his engage-ment!

He did not! That day she was to be married! She had some reference to this in making her toilet that morn-ing. The garments which she put on were all of white. A white rose gleamed palely from amid the raven hair upon her brow. Beautiful was she, exceedingly. How beauti-ful! but alas! the garb she wore—the pale, sweet flower on her forehead—they were mockeries—the emblems of that purity of soul, that innocence of heart, which were gone—gone for ever! She shuddered as she beheld the flower, and meditated this thought. Silently she took the flower from her forehead, and, as if it were precious as that lost jewel of which it reminded her, she carefully placed it away in her toilet-case.

Yet her beauty was heightened rather than diminished. Margaret Cooper was beautiful after no ordinary mould. Tall in stature, with a frame rounded by the most natural proportions into symmetry, and so formed for grace; with a power of muscle more than common among women, which, by inducing activity, made her movements as easy as they were graceful; with an eye bright like the morning-star, and with a depth of expression darkly clear, like that of the same golden orb at night; with a face exquisitely oval; a mouth of great sweetness; cheeks on which the slightest dash of hue from the red, red rose in June, might be seen to come and go under the slightest promptings of the active heart within; a brow of great height and corresponding expansion; with a bust that impressed you with a sense of the maternal strength which might be harbored there, even as the swollen bud gives promises of the full-bosomed luxuriance of the flower when it opens: add to these a lofty carriage, a look where the quickened spirit seems ever ready for utterance; a something of eager solemnity in her speech; and a play of expression on her lips which, if the brow were less lofty and the eye less keenly bright, might be a smile—and you have some idea of that noble and lovely temple on which fires of lava had been raised by an unholy hand; in which a secret worship is carried on which dreads the light, shrinks from exposure, and trembles to be seen by the very Deity whose favor it yet seeks in prayer and apprehension.

These beauties of person as we have essayed, though most feebly, to describe them, were enhanced rather than lessened by that air of anxiety by which they were now overcast. Her step was no longer free. It was marked by an unwonted timidity. Her glance was no longer confident; and when she looked round upon the faces of the young village-maidens, it was seen that her lip trembled and moved, but no longer with scorn. If the truth were told, she now envied the meanest of those maidens that security which her lack of beauty had guarantied. She, the scorner of all around her, now envied the innocence of the very meanest of her companions.

Such was the natural effect of her unhappy experience

17

upon her heart. What would she not have given to be like one of them? She dared not take her place, in the church, among them. It was a dread that kept her back. Strange, wondrous power of innocence! The guilty girl felt that she might be repulsed; that her frailty might make itself known —*must* make itself known; and she would be driven with shame from that communion with the pure to which she had no longer any claim! She sunk into one of the humblest seats in the church, drawing her reluctant mother into the lowly place beside her.

John Cross did not that day address himself to her case: but sin has a family similitude among all its members. There is an unmistakeable likeness, which runs through the connection. If the preacher speaks fervently to one sin, he is very apt to goad, in some degree, all the rest: and though Brother Cross had not the most distant idea of singling out Margaret Cooper for his censure, yet there was a whispering devil at her elbow that kept up a continual commentary upon what he said, filling her ears with a direct application of every syllable to her own peculiar instance.

"See you not," said the demon, "that every eye is turned upon you? He sees into your soul; he knows your secret. He declares it, as you hear, aloud, with a voice of thunder, to all the congregation. Do you not perceive that you sit alone; that everybody shrinks from your side; that your miserable old mother alone sits with you; that the eyes of some watch you with pity, but more with indignation? Look at the young damsels—late your companions—they are your companions no longer! They triumph in your shame. Their titter is only suppressed because of the place in which they are. They ask: 'Is this the maiden who was so wise, so strong—who scorned us—scorned *us*, indeed!—and was not able to baffle the serpent in his very first approaches?' Ha! ha! How they laugh! Well, indeed, they may. It is very laughable, Margaret—not less laughable and amusing than strange!—that *you* should have fallen.

— so easily, so blindly — and not even to suspect what every one else was sure of! O Margaret! Margaret! can it be true? Who will believe in your wit now, your genius, your beauty? Smutched and smutted! Poor, weak, degraded! If there is pity for you, Margaret, it is full of mockery too; it is a pity that is full of bitterness. You should now cast yourself down, and cover yourself with ashes, and cry, ' Wo is me!' and call upon the rocks and the hills to cover you!"

Such was the voice in her soul, which to *her* senses seemed like that of some jibing demon at her elbow. Margaret tried to pray — to expel him by prayer; but the object of his mockery had not been attained. She could not surrender herself entirely to the chastener. She was scourged, but not humbled; and the language of the demon provoked defiance, not humility. Her proud spirit rose once more against the pressure put upon it. Her bright, dazzling eye flashed in scorn upon the damsels whom she now fancied to be actually tittering — scarcely able to suppress their laughter — at her obvious disgrace. On John Cross she fixed her fearless eye, like that of some fallen angel, still braving the chastener, whom he can not contend with. A strange strength — for even sin has its strength for a season — came to her relief in that moment of fiendish mockery. The strength of an evil spirit was accorded her. Her heart once more swelled with pride. Her soul once more insisted on its ascendency. She felt, though she did not say :—

" Even as I am, overthrown, robbed of my treasure, I feel that I am superior to these. I feel that I have strength against the future. If they are pure and innocent, it is not because of their greater strength, but their greater obscurity. If I am overthrown by the tempter, it was because I was the more worthy object of overthrow. In their littleness they live: if I am doomed to the shaft, at least it will be as the eagle is doomed; it will be while soaring aloft —

while aiming for the sun—while grasping at the very bolt
by which I am destroyed!"

Such was the consolation offered by the twin-demons of
pride and vanity. The latter finds its aliment in the heart
which it too completely occupies, even from those circumstances which, in other eyes, make its disgrace and weakness. The sermon which had touched her sin had not subdued it. Perhaps no sermon, no appeal, however powerful
and touching, could at that moment have had power over
her. The paroxysm of her first consciousness of ruin had
not yet passed off. The condition of mind was not yet
reached in which an appeal could be felt.

As in the case of physical disease, so with that of the
mind and heart, there is a period when it is neither useful
nor prudent to administer the medicines which are yet most
necessary to safety. The judicious physician will wait for
the moment when the frame is prepared—when the pulse
is somewhat subdued—before he tries the most powerful
remedy. The excitement of the wrong which she had suffered was still great in her bosom. It was necessary that
she should have repose. That excitement was maintained
by the expectation that Stevens would yet make his appearance. Her eye, at intervals, wandered over the assembly in
search of him. The demon at her elbow understood her quest.

"He will not come," it said; "you look in vain. The
girls follow your eyes; they behold your disappointment;
they laugh at your credulity. If he leads any to the altar,
think you it will be one whom he could command at pleasure without any such conditions—one who, in her wild passions and disordered vanity, could so readily yield to his
desires, without demanding any corresponding sacrifices?
Margaret, they laugh now at those weaknesses of a mind
which they once feared if not honored. They wonder, now,
that they could have been so deceived. If they do not
laugh aloud, Margaret, it is because they would spare your
shame. Indeed, indeed, they pity you!"

The head of the desperate, but still haughty woman, was now more proudly uplifted, and her eyes shot forth yet fiercer fires of indignation. What a conflict was going on in her bosom. Her cheeks glowed with the strife—her breast heaved; with difficulty she maintained her seat inflexibly, and continued, without other signs of discomposure, until the service was concluded. Her step was more stately than ever as she walked from church; and while her mother lingered behind to talk with Brother Cross, and to exchange the sweetest speeches with the widow Thackeray and others, she went on alone—seeing none, heeding none—dreading to meet any face lest it should wear a smile and look the language in which the demon at her side still dealt. *He* still clung to her, with the tenacity of a fiendish purpose. He mocked her with her shame, goading her, with dart upon dart, of every sort of mockery. Truly did he mutter in her ears:—

"Stevens has abandoned you. Never was child, before yourself, so silly as to believe such a promise as he made you. Do you doubt?—do you still hope? It is madness? Why came he not yesterday—last night—to-day? He is gone. He has abandoned you. You are not only alone—you are lost! lost for ever!"

The tidings of this unsolicited attendant were confirmed the next day, by the unsuspecting John Cross. He came to visit Mrs. Cooper and her daughter among the first of his parishioners. He had gathered from the villagers already that Stevens had certainly favored Miss Cooper beyond all the rest of the village damsels. Indeed, it was now generally bruited that he was engaged to her in marriage. Though the worthy preacher had very stoutly resisted the suggestions of Mr. Calvert, and the story of Ned Hinkley, he was yet a little annoyed by them; and he fancied that, if Stevens were, indeed, engaged to Margaret, she, or perhaps the old lady, might relieve his anxiety by accounting for the absence of his *protégé*. The notion of

Brother John was, that, having resolved to marry the
maiden, he had naturally gone home to apprize his parents
and to make the necessary preparations.

But this conjecture brought with it a new anxiety. It
now, for the first time, seemed something strange that
Stevens had never declared to himself, or to anybody else
who his parents were — what they were — where they were
— what business they pursued; or anything about them.
Of his friends, they knew as little. The simple old man
had never thought of these things, until the propriety of
such inquiries was forced upon him by the conviction that
they would now be made in vain. The inability to answer
them, when it was necessary that an answer should be
found, was a commentary upon his imprudence which
startled the good old man not a little. But, in the confident hope that a solution of the difficulty could be afforded
by the sweetheart or the mother, he proceeded to her cottage. Of course, Calvert, in his communication to him,
had forborne those darker conjectures which he could not
help but entertain; and his simple auditor, unconscious
himself of any thought of evil, had never himself formed
any such suspicions.

Margaret Cooper was in her chamber when Brother
Cross arrived. She had lost that elasticity of temper
which would have carried her out at that period among
the hills in long rambles, led by those wild, wooing
companions, which gambol along the paths of poetic contemplation. The old man opened his stores of scandal to
Mrs. Cooper with little or no hesitation. He told her all
that Calvert had said, all that Ned Hinkley had fancied
himself to have heard, and all the village tattle touching
the engagement supposed to exist between Stevens and her
daughter.

"Of course, Sister Cooper," said he, "I believe nothing
of this sort against the youth. I should be sorry to think
it of one whom I plucked as a brand from the burning. I

hold Brother Stevens to be a wise young man and a pious; and truly I fear, as indeed I learn, that there is in the mind of Ned Hinkley a bitter dislike to the youth, because of some quarrel which Brother Stevens is said to have had with William Hinkley. This dislike hath made him conceive evil things of Brother Stevens and to misunderstand and to pervert some conversation which he hath overheard which Stevens hath had with his companion. Truly, indeed, I think that Alfred Stevens is a worthy youth of whom we shall hear a good account."

"And I think so too, Brother Cross. Brother Stevens will be yet a burning and a shining light in the church. There is a malice against him; and I think I know the cause, Brother Cross."

"Ah! this will be a light unto our footsteps, Sister Cooper."

"Thou knowest, Brother Cross," resumed the old lady in a subdued tone but with a loftier elevation of eyebrows and head—"thou knowest the great beauty of my daughter Margaret?"

"The maiden is comely, sister, comely among the maidens; but beauty is grass. It is a flower which blooms at morning and is cut down in the evening. It withereth on the stalk where it bloomed, until men turn from it with sickening and with sorrow, remembering what it hath been. Be not boastful of thy daughter's beauty, Sister Cooper it is the beauty of goodness alone which dieth not."

"But said I not, Brother Cross, of her wisdom, and her wit, as well as her beauty?" replied the old lady with some little pique. "I was forgetful of much, if I spoke only of the beauty of person which Margaret Cooper surely possesseth, and which the eyes of blindness itself might see."

"Dross, dross all, Sister Cooper. The wit of man is a flash which blindeth and maketh dark; and the wisdom of man is a vain thing. The one crackleth like thorns beneath the pot—the other stifleth the heart and keepeth down the soul from her true flight. I count the wit and wisdom of thy daughter even as I count her beauty. She hath all, I think—as they are known to and regarded by men. But all is nothing. Beauty hath a day's life like the butterfly; wit shineth like the sudden flash of the lightning, leaving only the cloud behind it; and oh! for the vain wisdom of man which makes him vain and unsteady—likely to falter—liable to fall—rash in his judgment—erring in his aims—blind to his duty—wilful in his weakness—insolent to his fellow—presumptuous in the sight of God. Talk not to me of worldly wisdom. It is the foe to prayer and meekness. The very fruit of the tree which brought sin and death into the world. Thy daughter is fair to behold—very fair among the maidens of our flock—none fairer, none so fair: God hath otherwise blessed her with a bright mind and a quick intelligence, but I think not that she is wise to salvation. No, no! she hath not yearned to the holy places of the tabernacle, unless it be that Brother Stevens hath been more blessed in his ministry than I!"

"And he hath!" exclaimed the mother. "I tell you, Brother John, the heart of Margaret Cooper is no longer what it was. It is softened. The toils of Brother Stevens have not been in vain. Blessed young man, no wonder they hate and defame him. He hath had a power over Margaret Cooper such as man never had before; and it is for this reason that Bill Hinkley and Ned conspired against him, first to take his life, and then to speak evil of his deeds. They beheld the beauty of my daughter, and they looked on her with famishing eyes. She sent them a-packing, I tell you. But this youth, Brother Stevens, found favor in her heart. They beheld the two as they went forth together. Ah! Brother John, it is the sweetest sight to behold two young, loving people walk forth in amity—born, as it would seem, for each other; both so tall, and young, and handsome; walking together with such smiles, as if there was no sorrow in the world; as if there was nothing but flowers and sweetness on the path; as if they could see nothing but one another; and as if there were no enemies looking on. It did my heart good to see them, Brother Cross; they always looked so happy with one another."

"And you think, Sister Cooper, that Brother Stevens hath agreed to take Margaret to wife?"

"She hath not told me this yet, but in truth, I think it hath very nigh come to that."

"Where is she?"

"In her chamber."

"Call her hither, Sister Cooper; let us ask of her the truth."

Margaret Cooper was summoned, and descended with slow steps and an unwilling spirit to meet their visiter.

"Daughter," said the good old man, taking her hand, and leading her to a seat. "thou art, even as thy mother sayest, one of exceeding beauty. Few damsels have ever met mine eyes with a beauty like to thine. No wonder the young men look on thee with eyes of love; but let not the love of youth betray thee. The love of God is the only love that is precious to the heart of wisdom."

Thus saying, the old man gazed on her with as much admiration as was consistent with the natural coldness of his temperament, his years, and his profession. His address, so different from usual, had a soothing effect upon her. A sigh escaped her, but she said nothing. He then proceeded to renew the history which had been given to him and which he had already detailed to her mother. She heard him with patience, in spite of all his interpolations from Scripture, his ejaculations, his running commentary upon the narrative, and the numerous suggestive topics which took him from episode to episode, until the story seemed interminably mixed up in the digression.

But when he came to that portion which related to the

17*

adventure of Ned Hinkley, to his espionage, the conference of Stevens with his companion — then she started — then her breathing became suspended, then quickened — then again suspended — and then, so rapid in its rush, that her emotion became almost too much for her powers of suppression.

But she did suppress it, with a power, a resolution, not often paralleled among men — still more seldom among women. After the first spasmodic acknowledgment given by her surprise, she listened with comparative calmness. She, alone, had the key to that conversation. She, alone, knew its terrible signification. She knew that Ned Hinkley was honest — was to be believed — that he was too simple, and too sincere, for any such invention; and, sitting with hands clasped upon that chair — the only attitude which expressed the intense emotion which she felt — she gazed with unembarrassed eye upon the face of the speaker, while every word which he spoke went like some keen, death-giving instrument into her heart.

The whole dreadful history of the villany of Stevens, her irreparable ruin — was now clearly intelligible. The mocking devil at her elbow had spoken nothing but the truth. She was indeed the poor victim of a crafty villain. In the day of her strength and glory she had fallen — fallen, fallen, fallen!

"Why am I called to hear this?" she demanded with singular composure.

The old man and the mother explained in the same breath — that she might reveal the degree of intercourse which had taken place between them, and, if possible, account for the absence of her lover. That, in short, she might refute the malice of enemies and establish the falsehood of their suggestions.

"You wish to know if I believe this story of Ned Hinkley?"

"Even so, my daughter."

" Then, I do !"

" Ha! what is it you say, Margaret?"

" The truth."

" What?" demanded the preacher, " you can not surely mean that Brother Stevens hath been a wolf in sheep's clothing — that he hath been a hypocrite."

" Alas!" thought Margaret Cooper — " have I not been my own worst enemy — did I not know him to be this from the first?"

Her secret reflection remained, however, unspoken. She answered the demand of John Cross without a moment's hesitation.

" I believe that Alfred Stevens is all that he is charged to be — a hypocrite — a wolf in sheep's clothing! — I see no reason to doubt the story of Ned Hinkley. He is an honest youth."

The old lady was in consternation. The preacher aghast and confounded.

" Tell me, Margaret," said the former, " hath he not engaged himself to you? Did he not promise — is he not sworn to be your husband?"

" I have already given you my belief. I see no reason to say anything more. What more do you need? Is he not gone — fled — has he not failed——"

She paused abruptly, while a purple flush went over her face. She rose to retire.

" Margaret!" exclaimed the mother.

" My daughter!" said John Cross.

" Speak out what you know — tell us all——"

" No! I will say no more. You know enough already. I tell you, I believe Alfred Stevens to be a hypocrite and a villain. Is not that enough? What is it to you whether he is so or not? What is it to me, at least? You do not suppose that it is anything to me? Why should you? What should he be? I tell you he is nothing to me — nothing — nothing — nothing! Villain or hypocrite, **or** what not — he is no more to me than the earth on which I tread. Let me hear no more about him, I pray you. I would not hear his name! Are there not villains enough in the world, that you should think and speak of one only?"

With these vehement words she left the room, and hurried to her chamber. She stopped suddenly before the mirror.

" And is it thus!" she exclaimed — " and I am——"

The mother by this time had followed her into the room.

" What is the meaning of this, Margaret?—tell me!" cried the old woman in the wildest agitation.

" What should it be, mother? Look at me!—in my eyes — do they not tell you? Can you not read?"

" I see nothing — I do not understand you, Margaret."

" Indeed! but you shall understand me! I thought my face would tell you without my words. *I* see it there, legible enough, to myself. Look again!—spare me if you can — spare your own ears the necessity of hearing me speak!"

" You terrify me, Margaret—I fear you are out of your mind.

" No! no! that need not be your fear; nor, were it true, would it be a fear of mine. It might be something to hope — to pray for. It might bring relief. Hear me, since you will not see. You ask me why I believe Stevens to be a villain. I *know* it."

" Ha! how know it!"

" How! How should I know it? Well, I see that I must speak. Listen then. You bade me seek and make a conquest of him, did you not? Do not deny it, mother — you did."

" Well, if I did?"

" I succeeded! Without trying, I succeeded! He declared to me his love—he did!—he promised to marry me. He was to have married me yesterday—to have met me in church and married me. John Cross was to have performed the ceremony. Well! you saw me there—you saw me in white—the dress of a bride!—Did he come? Did you see him there? Did you see the ceremony performed?"

"No, surely not—you know without asking."

"I know without asking!—surely I do!—but look you, mother—do you think that conquests are to be made, hearts won, loves confessed, pledges given, marriage-day fixed—do these things take place, as matters of pure form? Is there no sensation—no agitation—no beating and violence about the heart—in the blood—in the brain! I tell you there is—a blinding violence, a wild, stormy, sensation—fondness, forgetfulness, madness! I say, madness! madness! madness!"

"Oh, my daughter, what can all this mean? Speak calmly, be deliberate!"

"Calm! deliberate! What a monster if I could be! But I am not mad now. I will tell you what it means. It means that, in taking captive Alfred Stevens—in winning a lover—securing that pious young man—there was some difficulty, some peril. Would you believe it? —there were some privileges which he claimed. He took me in his arms. Ha! ha! He held me panting to his breast. His mouth filled mine with kisses——"

"No more, do not say more, my child!"

"Ay, more! more! much more! I tell you—then came blindness and madness, and I was dishonored—made a woman before I was made a wife! Ruined, lost, abused, despised, abandoned! Ha! ha! ha! no marriage ceremony. Though I went to the church. No bridegroom there, though he promised to come. Preacher, church, bride, all present, yet no wedding. Ha! ha! ha! How

do I know!—Good reason for it, good reason—Ha! ha!
——ah!"

The paroxysm terminated in a convulsion. The unhappy girl fell to the floor as if stricken in the forehead.
The blood gushed from her mouth and nostrils, and she
lay insensible in the presence of the terrified and miserable mother.

CHAPTER XXXIV.

THE FATES FIND THE DAGGER AND THE BOWL.

For a long time she lay without showing any signs of life. Her passions rebelled against the restraint which her mind had endeavored to put upon them. Their concentrated force breaking all bonds, so suddenly, was like the terrific outburst of the boiling lava from the gorges of the frozen mountain. Believing her dead, the mother rushed headlong into the highway, rending the village with her screams. She was for the time a perfect madwoman. The neighbors gathered to her assistance. That much-abused woman, the widow Thackeray, was the first to come. Never was woman's tenderness more remarkable than hers — never was woman's watch by the bed of sickness and suffering — that watch which woman alone knows so well how to keep — more rigidly maintained than by her! From the first hour of that agony under which Margaret Cooper fell to earth insensible, to the last moment in which her recovery was doubtful, that widow Thackeray — whose passion for a husband had been described by Mrs. Cooper as so very decided and evident — maintained her place by the sick bed of the stricken girl with all the affection of a mother. Widow Thackeray was a woman who could laugh merrily, but she could shed tears with equal readiness. These were equally the signs of prompt feeling and nice susceptibility ; and the proud Margaret, and her invidious mother, were both humbled by that spontaneous kindness for which, hitherto, they had given the possessor so very little credit, and to which they were now equally so greatly indebted.

Medical attendance was promptly secured. Charlemont had a very clever physician of the old school. He combined, as was requisite in the forest region of our country, the distinct offices of the surgeon and mediciner. He was tolerably skilful in both departments. He found his patient in a condition of considerable peril. She had broken a blood-vessel ; and the nicest care and closest attendance were necessary to her preservation. It will not need that we should go through the long and weary details which followed to her final cure. Enough, that she did recover. But for weeks her chance was doubtful. She lay for that space of time, equally in the arms of life and death. For a long period, she herself was unconscious of her situation.

When she came to know, the skill of her attendants derived very little aid from her consciousness. Her mind was unfavorable to her cure ; and this, by the way, is a very important particular in the fortunes of the sick. To despond, to have a weariness of life, to forbear hope as well as exertion, is, a hundred to one, to determine against the skill of the physician. Margaret Cooper felt a willingness to die. She felt her overthrow in the keenest pangs of its shame ; and, unhappily, the mother, in her madness, had declared it.

The story of her fall — of the triumph of the serpent — was now the village property, and of course put an end to all further doubts on the score of the piety of Brother Stevens ; though, by way of qualification of his offence, old Hinkley insisted that it was the fault of the poor damsel.

" She," he said, " had tempted him — had thrown herself in his way — had been brazen," and all that, of which so much is commonly said in all similar cases. We, who know the character of the parties, and have traced events from the beginning, very well know how little of this is true. Poor Margaret was a victim before she was well aware of those passions which made her so. She was the victim not of lust but of ambition. Never was woman more unsophisticated — less moved by unworthy and sinister design. She had her weaknesses — her pride, her vanity; and her passions, which were tremendous, worked upon through these, very soon effected her undoing. But, for deliberate purpose of evil — of any evil of which her own intellect was conscious — the angels were not more innocent.

But mere innocence of evil design, in any one particular condition, is not enough for security. We are not only to forbear evil; virtue requires that we should be exercised for the purposes of good. She lacked the moral strength which such exercises, constantly pursued, would have assured her. She was a creature of impulse only, not of reflection. Besides, she was ignorant of her particular weaknesses. She was weak where she thought herself strong. This is always the error of a person having a very decided will. The will is constantly mistaken for the power. She could not humble herself, and in her own personal capacities — capacities which had never before been subjected to any ordeal-trial — she relied for the force which was to sustain her in every situation. Fancy a confident country-girl — supreme in her own district over the Hobs and Hinnies thereabouts — in conflict with the adroit man of the world, and you have the whole history of Margaret Cooper, and the secret of her misfortune. Let the girl have what natural talent you please, and the case is by no means altered. She must fall if she seeks or permits the conflict. She can only escape by flight. It is in consideration of this human weakness, that we pray God, nightly, not to suffer us to be exposed to temptation.

When the personal resources of her own experience and mind failed Margaret Cooper, as at some time or other

they must fail all who trust only in them, she had no further
reliance. She had never learned to draw equal strength
and consolation from the sweet counsels of the sacred volume. Regarding the wild raving and the senseless insanity, which are but too frequently the language of the vulgar
preacher, as gross ignorance and debasing folly, she committed the unhappy error of confounding the preacher with
his cause. She had never been taught to make an habitual
reference to religion ; and her own experience of life, had
never forced upon her those sage reflections which would
have shown her that *true* religion is the very all of life, and
without it life has nothing. The humility of the psalmist,
which was the real source of all the strength allotted to the
monarch minstrel, was an unread lesson with her ; and never
having been tutored to refer to God, and relying upon her
own proud mind and daring imagination, what wonder that
these frail reeds should pierce her side while giving way
beneath her.

It was this very confidence in her own strength—this
fearlessness of danger (and we repeat the lesson here, emphatically, by way of warning)—a confidence which the
possession of a quick and powerful mind naturally enough
inspires—that effected her undoing. It was not by the
force of her affections that she fell. *The affections are not
apt to be strong in a woman whose mind leads her out from
her sex !*

The seducer triumphed through the medium of her vanity.
Her feeling of self-assurance had been thus active from
childhood, and conspicuous in all her sports and employments. *She had never been a child herself. She led always
in the pastimes of her playmates, many of whom were older
than herself.*

She had no fears when others trembled ; and, if she did
not, at any time, so far transcend the bounds of filial duty
as to defy the counsels of her parents, it was certainly no
less true that she never sought for, and seldom seemed to

need them. *It is dangerous when the woman, through sheer confidence in her own strength, ventures upon the verge of the moral precipice. The very experiment, where the passions are concerned, proves her to be lost.*

Margaret Cooper, confident in her own footsteps, soon learned to despise every sort of guardianship. The vanity of her mother had not only counselled and stimulated her own, but was of that gross and silly order, as to make itself offensive to the judgment of the girl herself. This had the effect of losing her all the authority of a parent; and we have already seen, in the few instances where this authority took the shape of counsel, that its tendency was to evil rather than to good.

The arts of Alfred Stevens had, in reality, been very few. It was only necessary that he should read the character of his victim. This, as an experienced worldling—experienced in such a volume—he was soon very able to do. He saw enough to discover, that, while Margaret Cooper was endowed by nature with an extraordinary measure of intellect, she was really weak because of its possession. In due proportion to the degree of exercise to which she subjected her mere mind—making that busy and restless—was the neglect of her sensibilities—those nice *antennæ of the heart.*

"Whose instant touches, slightest pause,"

teach the approach of the smallest forms of danger, however inoffensive their shapes, however unobtrusive their advance. When the sensibilities are neglected and suffered to fall into disrepute, they grow idle first, and finally obtuse! even as the limb which you forbear to exercise loses its muscle, and withers into worthlessness.

When Alfred Stevens discovered this condition, his plan was simple enough. He had only to stimulate her mind into bolder exercise—to conduct it to topics of the utmost hardihood—to inspire that sort of moral recklessness which some people call courage—which delights to sport along the edge of the precipice, and to summon audacious spirits from the great yawning gulfs which lie below. This practice is always pursued at the expense of those guardian feelings which keep watch over the virtues of the tender heart.

The analysis of subjects commonly forbidden to the sex, necessarily tends to make dull those habitual sentinels over the female conduct. These sentinels are instincts rather than principles. Education can take them away, but does not often confer them. When, through the arts of Alfred Stevens, Margaret Cooper was led to discuss, perhaps to despise, those nice and seemingly purposeless barriers which society—having the experience of ages for its authority—has wisely set up between the sexes —she had already taken a large stride toward passing them. But of this, which a judicious education would have taught her, she was wholly ignorant. Her mind was too bold to be scrupulous ; too adventurous to be watchful ; and if, at any moment, a pause in her progress permitted her to think of the probable danger to her sex of such adventurous freedom, she certainly never apprehended it in her own case. Such restraints she conceived to be essential only for the protection of *the weak* among her sex. Her vanity led her to believe that she was strong ; and the approaches of the sapper were conducted with too much caution, with a progress too stealthy and insensible, to startle the ear or attract the eye of the unobservant, yet keen-eyed guardian of her citadel. An eagle perched upon a rock, with wing outspread for flight, and an eye fixed upon the rolling clouds through which it means to dart, is thus heedless of the coiled serpent which lies beneath its feet.

The bold eye of Margaret Cooper was thus heedless. Gazing upon the sun, she saw not the serpent at her feet. It was not because she slept : never was eye brighter, more far-stretching ; never was mind more busy, more active, than that of the victim at the very moment when she fell. It was because she watched the remote, not the near — the region in which there was no enemy, nothing but glory — and neglected that post which is always in danger. Her error is that of the general who expends his army upon some distant province, leaving his chief city to the assault and sack of the invader.

We have dwelt somewhat longer upon the moral causes which, in our story, have produced such cruel results, than the mere story itself demands ; but no story is perfectly moral unless the author, with a wholesome commentary, directs the attention of the reader to the true weaknesses of his hero, to the point where his character fails ; to the causes of this failure, and the modes in which it may be repaired or prevented. In this way alone may the details of life and society be properly welded together into consistent doctrine, so that instruction may keep pace with delight, and the heart and mind be informed without being conscious of any of those tasks which accompany the lessons of experience.

To return now to our narrative.

Margaret Cooper lived ! She might as well have died. This was *her* thought, at least. She prayed for death. Was it in mercy that her prayer was denied ? We shall see ! Youth and a vigorous constitution successfully resisted the attacks of the assailant. They finally obtained the victory. After a weary spell of bondage and suffering, she recovered. But she recovered only to the consciousness of a new affliction. All the consequences of her fatal lapse from virtue have not yet been told. She bore within her an indelible witness of her shame. She was destined to be a mother without having been a wife !

This, to *her* mother at least, was a more terrible discovery than the former. She literally cowered and crouched beneath it. It was the *written* shame, rather than the

actual, which the old woman dreaded. She had been so
vain, so criminally vain, of her daughter—she had made
her so constantly the subject of her brag—that, unwitting
of having declared the whole melancholy truth, in the first
moment of her madness, she shrunk, with an unspeakable
horror, from the idea that the little world in which she
lived should become familiar with the whole cruel history
of her overthrow. She could scarcely believe it herself,
though the daughter, with an anguish in her eyes that left
little to be told, had herself revealed the truth. Her pride,
as well as her life, was linked with the pride and the beauty
of her child. She had shared in her constant triumphs over
all around her; and overlooking, as a fond, foolish mother
is apt to do, all her faults of temper or of judgment, she
had learned to behold nothing but her superiority. And
now to see her fallen! a thing of scorn, which was lately a
thing of beauty!—the despised, which was lately the worshipped and the wondered at! No wonder that her weak,
vain heart was crushed and humbled, and her head bowed
in sorrow to the earth. She threw herself upon the floor,
and wept bitter and scalding tears.

The daughter had none. Without sob or sigh, she stooped
down and tenderly assisted the old woman to rise. Why
had she no tears? She asked herself this question, but in
vain. Her external emotions promised none. Indeed, she
seemed to be without emotions. A weariness and general
indifference to all things was now the expression of her features. But this was the deceitful aspect of the mountain,
on whose breast contemplation sits with silence, unconscious
of the tossing flame which within is secretly fusing the stubborn metal and the rock. Anger was in her breast—feelings of hate mingled up with shame—scorn of herself,
scorn of all—feelings of defiance and terror, striving at
mastery; and, in one corner, a brooding image of despair,
kept from the brink of the precipice only by the entreaties
of some fiercer principle of hate. She felt life to be insup-

portable. Why did she live? This question came to her
repeatedly. The demon was again at work beside her.

"Die!" said he. "It is but a blow—a moment's pang
—the driving a needle into an artery—the prick of a pin
upon the heart. Die! it will save you from exposure—the
shame of bringing into the world an heir of shame! What
would you live for? The doors of love, and fame, even of
society, are shut against you for ever. What is life to you
now? a long denial—a protracted draught of bitterness-
the feeling of a death-spasm carried on through sleepless
years; perhaps, under a curse of peculiar bitterness, carried
on even into age! Die! you can not be so base as to wish
for longer life!"

The arguments of the demon were imposing. His suggestions seemed to promise the relief she sought. Hers
seemed the particular case where the prayer is justified
which invokes the mountains and the rocks upon the head
of the guilty. But the rock refused to fall, the mountain
to cover her shame, and its exposure became daily more
and more certain. Death was the only mode of escape
from the mountain of pain which seemed to rest upon her
heart. The means of self-destruction were easy. With a
spirit so impetuous as hers, to imagine was to determine.
She did determine. Yet, even while making so terrible a
resolve, a singular calm seemed to overspread her soul.
She complained of nothing—wished for nothing—sought
for nothing—trembled at nothing. A dreadful lethargy,
which made the old mother declaim as against a singular
proof of hardihood, possessed her spirit. Little did the
still-idolizing mother conjecture how much that lethargy
concealed!

The moment that Margaret Cooper conceived the idea of
suicide, it possessed all her mind. It became the one only
thought. There were few arguments against it, and these
she rapidly dismissed or overcame. To leave her mother
in her old age was the first which offered itself; but this

became a small consideration when she reflected that the latter could not, under any circumstances, require her assistance very long; and to spare her the shame of public exposure was another consideration. The evils of the act to herself were reduced with equal readiness to the transition from one state to another by a small process, which, whether by the name of stab or shot, was productive only of a momentary spasm; for, though as fully persuaded of the soul's immortality as the best of us, the unhappy girl, like all young free-thinkers, had persuaded herself that, in dying by her own hands, she was simply exercising a discretionary power under the conviction that her act in doing so was rendered by circumstances a judicious one. The arguments by which she deceived herself are sufficiently commonplace, and too easy of refutation, to render necessary any discussion of them here. Enough to state the fact. She deliberately resolved upon the fatal deed which was to end her life and agony together, and save her from that more notorious exposure which must follow the birth of that child of sin whom she deemed it no more than a charity to destroy.

There was an old pair of pistols in the house, which had been the property of her father. She had often, with a boldness not common to the sex, examined these pistols. They were of brass, well made, of English manufacture, with common muzzles, and a groove for a sight instead of the usual drop. They were not large, but, in a practised hand, were good travelling-pistols, being capable of bringing down a man at twelve paces, provided there was anything like deliberation in the holder. Often and again had she handled these weapons, poising them and addressing them at objects as she had seen her father do. On one occasion she had been made to discharge them, under his own instructions; she had done so without terror. She recalled these events. She had seen the pistols loaded. She did not exactly know what quantity of powder was necessary for a charge, but she was in no mood to calculate the value of a thimbleful.

Availing herself of the temporary absence of her mother, she possessed herself of these weapons. Along with them, in the same drawer, she found a horn which still contained a certain quantity of powder. There were bullets in the bag with the pistols which precisely fitted them. There, too, was the mould—there were flints—the stock was sufficiently ample for all her desires; and she surveyed the prize, in her own room, with the look of one who congratulates himself in the conviction that he holds in his hand the great medicine which is to cure his disease. In her chamber she loaded the weapons, and, with such resignation as belonged to her philosophy, she waited for the propitious moment when she might complete the deed.

18

CHAPTER XXXV.

FOLDING THE ROBES ABOUT HER.

IT was the sabbath and a very lovely day. The sun never shone more brightly in the heavens; and as Margaret Cooper surveyed its mellow orange light, lying, like some blessed spirit, at sleep upon the hills around her, and reflected that she was about to behold it for the last time, her sense of its exceeding beauty became more strong than ever. Now that she was about to lose it for ever, it seemed more beautiful than it had ever been before.

This is a natural effect, which the affections confer upon the objects which delight and employ them. Even a temporary privation increases the loveliness of the external nature. How we linger and look. That shade seems so inviting; that old oak so venerable! That rock—how often have we sat upon it, evening and morning, and mused strange, wild, sweet fancies! It is an effort to tear one's self away—it is almost like tearing away from life itself; so many living affections feel the rending and the straining —so many fibres that have their roots in the heart, are torn and lacerated by the separation.

Poor Margaret! she looked from her window upon the bright and beautiful world around her. Strange that sorrow should dwell in a world so bright and beautiful! Stranger still, that, dwelling in such a world, it should not dwell there by sufferance only and constraint! that it should have such sway—such privilege. That it should invade every sanctuary and leave no home secure. Ah! but the difference between mere sorrow and guilt! Poor Margaret could not well understand that! If she could—but no! She was yet to learn that the sorrows of the innocent have a healing effect. That they produce a holy and ennobling strength, and a juster appreciation of those evening shades of life which render the lights valuable and make their uses pure. It is only guilt which finds life loathsome. It is only guilt that sorrow weakens and enslaves. Virtue grows strong beneath the pressure of her enemies, and with such a power as was fabled of the king of Pontus, turns the most poisonous fruits of earth into the most wholesome food.

But, even in the heart of Margaret Cooper, where the sense of the beautiful was strong, the loveliness of the scene was felt. She drank in, with strange satisfaction —a satisfaction to which she had long been a stranger —its soft and inviting beauties. They did not lessen her sense of suffering, perhaps, but they were not without their effect in producing other moods, which, once taken in company with the darker ones of the soul, may, in time, succeed in alleviating them. Never, indeed, had the prospect been more calm and wooing. Silence, bending from the hills, seemed to brood above the valley even as some mighty spirit, at whose bidding strife was hushed, and peace became the acknowledged divinity of all. The humming voices of trade and merriment were all hushed in homage to the holy day; and if the fitful song of a truant bird, that presumed beside the window of Margaret Cooper, did break the silence of the scene, it certainly did not disturb its calm. The forest minstrel sung in a neighboring tree, and she half listened to his lay. The strain seemed to sympathize with her sadness. She thought upon her own songs, which had been of such a proud spirit; and how strange and startling seemed the idea that with her, song would soon cease for ever. The song of the bird would be silent in her ears, and her own song! What song would be hers? What strain would she take up? In what abode —before what altars?

This train of thought, which was not entirely lost, however, was broken, for the time, by a very natural circumstance. A troop of the village damsels came in sight, on their way to church. She forgot the song of birds, as her morbid spirit suggested to her the probable subject of their meditations.

"They have seen me," she muttered to herself as she hastily darted from the window. "Ay, they exult. They point to me—me, the abandoned—the desolate—soon to be the disgraced! But, no! no! that shall never be. They shall never have that triumph, which is always so grateful a subject of regale to the mean and envious!"

The voice of her mother from below disturbed these unhappy meditations. The old lady was prepared for church, and was surprised to find that Margaret had not made her toilet.

"What! don't you mean to go, Margaret?"

"Not to-day, mother."

"What, and the new preacher too, that takes the place of John Cross! They say he makes a most heavenly prayer."

But the inducement of the heavenly prayer of the new preacher was not enough for Margaret. The very suggestion of a new preacher would have been conclusive against her compliance. The good old lady was too eager herself to get under way to waste much time in exhortation, and hurrying off, she scarcely gave herself time to answer the inquiry of the widow Thackeray, at her own door, after the daughter's health.

"I will go in and see her," said the lighthearted but truehearted woman.

"Do, do, ma'am--if you please! She'll be glad to see you. I'll hurry on, as I see Mrs. Hinkley just ahead."

The widow Thackeray looked after her with a smile, which was exchanged for another of different character when she found herself in the chamber of Margaret. She put her arms about the waist of the sufferer; kissed her cheeks, and with the tenderest solicitude spoke of her health and comfort. To her, alone, with the exception of her mother—according to the belief of Margaret—her true situation had been made known.

" Alas !" said she, " how should I feel—how should I be ! You should know. I am as one cursed—doomed, hopeless of anything but death."

" Ah ! do not speak of death, Margaret," said the other kindly. " We must all die, I know, but that does not reconcile me any more to the thought. It brings always a creeping horror through my veins. Think of life—talk of life only."

" They say that death is life."

" So it is, I believe, Margaret; and now I think of it, dress yourself and go to church where we may hear something on this subject to make us wiser and better. Come, my dear—let us go to God."

" I can not—not to-day, dear Mrs. Thackeray."

" Ah, Margaret, why not? It is to the church, of all places, you should now go."

" What! to be stared at? To see the finger of scorn pointing at me wherever I turn? To hear the whispered insinuation? To be conscious only of sneer and sarcasm on every hand? No, no, dear Mrs. Thackeray, I can not go for this. Feeling this, I should neither pray for myself, nor find benefit from the prayers of others. Nay, *they* would not pray. They would only mock."

" Margaret, these thoughts are very sinful."

" So they are, but I can not think of any better. They can not but be sinful since they are mine."

But you are not wedded to sin, dearest. Such thoughts

can give you no pleasure. Come with me to church! Come and pray! Prayer will do you good."

"I would rather pray here. Let me remain. I will try to go out among the hills when you are all engaged in church, and will pray there. Indeed I must. I must pray then and pray there, if prayer is ever to do me good."

"The church is the better place, Margaret. One prays better where one sees that all are praying."

"But when I *know* that they are not praying! When I know that envy is in their hearts, and malice, and jealousy and suspicion — that God is not in their hearts, but their fellow; and not him with friendly and fond, but with spiteful and deceitful thoughts!"

"Ah! Margaret, how can you know this? Judge not lest ye be judged."

"It matters not, dear Mrs. Thackeray. God is here, or there. He will be among the hills if anywhere. I will seek him there. If I can command my thoughts anywhere, it will be in the woods alone. In the church I can not. Those who hate me are there — and their looks of hate would only move my scorn and defiance."

"Margaret, you do our people wrong. You do yourself wrong. None hate you — none will point to you, or think of your misfortune; and if they did, it is only what you might expect, and what you must learn patiently to bear, as a part of the punishment which God inflicts on sin. You must submit, Margaret, to the shame as you have submitted to the sin. It is by submission only that you can be made strong. The burden which you are prepared to bear meekly, becomes light to the willing spirit. Come, dear Margaret, I will keep with you, sit by you — show you, and all, that I forget your sin and remember only your suffering."

The good widow spoke with the kindest tones. She threw her arms around the neck of the desolate one, and kissed her with the affection of a sister. But the demon of pride was uppermost.   She withstood entreaty and embrace.

"I can not go with you.   I thank you, truly thank you, dear Mrs. Thackeray, but I can not go.   I have neither the courage nor the strength."

"They will come—the courage and the strength—only try.   God is watchful to give us help the moment he sees that we really seek his assistance.   By prayer, Margaret—"

"I will pray, but I must pray alone.   Among the hills I will pray.   My prayer will not be less acceptable offered among his hills.   My voice will not remain unheard, though no chorus swells its appeal."

"Margaret, this is pride."

"Perhaps!"

"Ah! go with me, and pray for humility."

"My prayer would rather be for death."

"Say not so, Margaret—this is impiety."

"Ay, death!—the peace, the quiet of the grave—of a long sleep—an endless sleep—where the vulture may no longer gnaw the heart, nor the fire burn within the brain! For these I must pray."

And, thus speaking, the unhappy woman smote her throbbing head with violent hand.

"Shocking thought!   But you do not believe in such a sleep?   Surely, Margaret, you believe in life eternal?"

"Would I did not!"

"O Margaret!—but you are sick; you are very feverish.   Your eyeballs glare like coals of fire; your face seems charged with blood.   I am afraid you are going to have another attack, like the last."

"Be not afraid.   I have no such fear."

"I will sit with you, at least," said the kind-hearted woman.

"Nay, that I must positively forbid, Mrs. Thackeray; I will not suffer it.   I will not sit with *you*.   Go you to church. You will be late. Do not waste your time on me. I mean to ramble among the hills this morning. *That*, I think, will do me more good than anything else. There, I am sure—there only—I will find peace."

The worthy widow shook her head doubtfully.

" But I am sure of it," said Margaret. " You will see. Peace, peace—the repose of the heart—the slumber of the brain!—I shall find all there!"

Mrs. Thackeray, finding her inflexible, rose to depart, but with some irresoluteness.

" If you would let me walk with you, Margaret—"

" No! no!—dear Mrs. Thackeray—I thank you very much; but, with a mood such as mine, I shall be much better alone."

" Well, if you are resolved—"

" I am resolved! never more so."

These words were spoken in tones which might have startled a suspicious mind. But the widow was none.

" God bless you!" she said, kissing her at parting. " I will see you when I come from church."

" Will you?" said Margaret, with a significant but sad smile. Then, suddenly rising, she exclaimed:—

" Let me kiss you, dear Mrs. Thackeray, and thank you again, before you go. You have been very kind to me, very kind, and you have my thanks and gratitude."

Mrs. Thackeray was touched by her manner. This was the first time that the proud spirit of Margaret Cooper had ever offered such an acknowledgment. It was one that the gentle and unremitting kindnesses of the widow amply deserved. After renewing her promise to call on her return from church, Mrs. Thackeray took her departure.

Margaret Cooper was once more alone. When she heard the outer door shut, she then threw herself upon the bed, and gave way to the utterance of those emotions which, long restrained, had rendered her mind a terrible anarchy. A few tears, but very few, were wrung from her eyes; but she groaned audibly, and a rapid succession of shivering-fits passed through her frame, racking the whole nervous system, until she scarcely found herself able to rise from the couch where she had thrown herself. A strong, determined will alone moved her, and she rose, after a lapse of half an hour, to the further prosecution of her purpose. Her temporary weakness and suffering of frame had no effect upon her resolves. She rather seemed to be strengthened in them. This strength enabled her to sit down and dictate a letter to her mother, declaring her intention, and justifying it by such arguments as were presented by the ingenious demon who assists always in the councils of the erring heart.

She placed this letter in her bosom, that it might be found upon her person. It was curious to observe, next, that she proceeded to tasks which were scarcely in unison with the dreadful deed she meditated. She put her chamber in nice order. Her books, of which she had a tolerably handsome collection for a private library in our forest-country, she arranged and properly classed upon their shelves. Then she made her toilet with unusual care. It was for the last time. She gazed upon the mirror, and beheld her own beauties with a shudder.

"Ah!" she thought, though she gave no expression to the thought, "to be so beautiful, yet fail!"

It was a reflection to touch any heart with sorrow. Her dress was of plain white; she wore no ornament—not even a riband. Her hair, which was beautifully long and thick, was disposed in a clubbed mass upon her head, very simply but with particular neatness; and, when all was done, concealing the weapon of death beneath a shawl which she wrapped around her, she left the house, and stole away unobserved along the hills, in the seclusion and sacred silence of which she sought to avoid the evil consequences of one crime by the commission of another far more heinous.

18*

CHAPTER XXXVI.

SUSPENSE AND AGONY.

At the risk of seeming monotonous, we must repeat the reflection made in our last chapter, that the things we are about to lose for ever seem always more valuable in the moment of their loss. They acquire a newer interest in our eyes at such a time, possibly under the direction of some governing instinct which is intended to render us tenacious of life to the very last. Privation teaches us much more effectually than possession the value of all human enjoyments; and the moralist has more than once drawn his sweetest portraits of liberty from the gloom and the denials of a dungeon. How eloquent of freedom is he who yearns for it in vain! How glowing is that passion which laments the lost!

To one dying, as we suppose few die, in the perfect possession of their senses, how beautiful must seem the fading hues of the sunlight, flickering along the walls of a chamber! how heavenly the brief glimpses of the blue sky through the half-opened window! how charming the green bit of foliage that swings against the pane! how cheering and unwontedly sweet and balmy the soft, sudden gust of the sweet south, breathing up from the flowers, and stirring the loose drapery around the couch! How can we part with these without tears? how reflect, without horror, upon the close coffin, the damp clod, the deep hollows of the earth in which we are to be cabined? Oh, with what earnestness, at such a moment, must the wholly conscious spirit pray for life! how greedily will he drink the nauseous draught in the hope to secure its boon! how fondly will he seize upon every chimera, whether of his own or of another's fancy, in order to gain a little respite—in order still to keep within the grasp of mind and sight, these lovely agents of earth and its Master, which, in our day of strength and exultation, we do not value at one half their worth! And how full of dread and horror must be that first awful conviction which assures him that the struggle is in vain—that the last remedy is tried—that nothing is left him now but despair—despair and death! Then it is that Christianity comes to his relief. If he believes, he gains by his loss. Its godlike promise assures him then that the things which his desires make dear, his faith has rendered immortal.

The truth of many of these reflections made their way into the mind of Margaret Cooper, as she pursued the well-known path along the hills. She observed the objects along the route more narrowly than ever. She was taking that path for the last time. Her eyes would behold these objects no more. How often had she pursued the same route with Alfred Stevens! But then she had not seen these things; she had not observed these thousand graces and beauties of form and shadow which now seemed to crowd around, challenging her regard and demanding her sympathies. Then she had seen nothing but him. The bitterness which this reflection occasioned made her hurry her footsteps; but there was an involuntary shudder that passed through her frame, when, in noting the strange beauty of the path, she reflected that it would be trodden by her for the last time. Her breathing became quickened by the reflection. She pressed forward up the hills. The forests grew thick around her—deep, dim, solemn, and inviting. The skies above looked down in little blessed blue tufts, through the crowding tree-tops. The long vista of the woods led her onward in wandering thoughts.

To fix these thoughts—to keep them from wandering! This was a difficulty. Margaret Cooper strove to do so, but she could not. Never did her mind seem such a perfect chaos—so full of confused and confusing objects and images. Her whole life seemed to pass in review before her. All her dreams of ambition, all the struggles of her genius! Were these to be thrown away? Were these all to be wasted? Was her song to be unheard? Was her passionate and proud soul to have no voice? If death is terrible to man, it is terrible, not as a pang, but as an oblivion; and to the soul of genius, oblivion is a soul-death, and its thought is a source of tenfold terror.

"But of what avail were life to me now? Even should I live," said the wretched woman, "would it matter more to the ambition which I have had, and to the soul which flames and fevers within me? Who would hearken to the song of the degraded? Who, that heard the story of my shame, would listen to the strains of my genius? Say that its utterance is even as proud as my own vanity of heart would esteem it—say that no plaint like mine had ever touched the ear or lifted the heart of humanity! Alas! of what avail! The finger of scorn would be uplifted long before the voice of applause. The sneer and sarcasm of the worldling would anticipate the favoring judgment of the indulgent and the wise. Who would do justice to my cause? Who listen? Alas! the voice of genius would be of little avail speaking from the lips of the dishonored.

"To the talent which I have, and the ambition which still burns within me, life then can bring nothing—no exercise—no fruition. Suppose, then, that the talent is left to slumber—the ambition stifled till it has no further longings! Will life yield anything to the mere creature of society—to my youth—to my beauty—to my sense of delight—if still there be any such sense left to me? Shall I be less the creature of social scorn, because I have yielded my ambition—because I have forborne the employment of those glorious gifts which Heaven in its bounty has allotted me?

"Alas! no! am I not a woman, one of that frail, feeble sex, whose name is weakness?—of whom, having no strength, man yet expects the proofs of the most unyielding —of a firmness which he himself can not exercise—of a power of self-denial and endurance of which he exhibits no example. If I weep, he smiles at my weakness. If I stifle my tears, he denounces my unnatural hardihood. If I am cold and unyielding, I am masculine and neglected—if I am gentle and pliant, my confidence is abused and my person dishonored. What can society, which is thus exacting, accord to me, then, as a mere woman? What shame will it not thrust upon me—a woman—and as I am?

"Life then promises me nothing. The talent which I have, lies within me idle and without hope of use. The pure name of the woman is lost to me for ever. Shame dogs my footsteps. Scorn points its finger. Life, and all that it brings to others—love, friends, fame, fortune— which are the soul of life—these are lost to me for ever. The moral death is here already. The mere act of dying, is simply the end of a strife, and a breathing and an agony. That is all!"

The day became overcast. A cloud obscured the sunlight. The blue tufts of sky no longer looked downward through the openings of the trees. The scene, dim and silent before, became unusually dark. The aspect of nature seemed congenial with the meditated deed. She had reasoned herself into its commission, and she reproached herself mentally with her delay. Any self-suggestion of an infirmity of purpose, with a nature such as hers, would have produced precipitation. She turned down a slight gorge among the hills where the forest was more close. She knelt beneath a tree and laid down her pistol at its foot.

She knelt—strange contradiction!—she knelt for the purposes of prayer. But she could not pray. It would seem that she attributed this effort to the sight of the pistols, and she put them behind her without changing her position. The prayer, if she made any, was internal; and, at all events it did not seem to be satisfactory. Yet, before it was ended, she started with an expression of painful thought upon her face. The voice of her reason had ceased its utterance. The voice of her conscience, perhaps, had been unheard; but there was yet another voice to be heard which was more potent than all.

It was the mother's voice!

She placed her hand upon her side with a spasmodic effort. The quickening of a new life within her, made that new voice effectual. She threw herself on the ground and wept freely. For the first time she wept freely. The tears were those of the mother. The true fountain of tears had been touched. That first throb of the innocent pledge of guilty passion subdued the fiend. She could have taken her own life, but dared not lift the deadly weapon against that. The arm of the suicide was arrested. She groaned, she wept, bitterly and freely. She was at once feebler and more strong. Feebler, as regarded her late resolution; stronger as regarded the force of her affections, the sweet humanities, not altogether subdued within her heart. The slight pulsation of that infant in her womb had been more effectual than the voice of reason, or conscience, or feminine dread. The maternal feeling is, perhaps, the most imperious of all those which gather in the heart of woman.

Margaret Cooper, however, had not altogether resolved against the deed. She only could not do it there and then. Her wretched determination was not wholly surrendered, but it was touched, enfeebled; and with the increasing powers of reflection, the impetuosity of the will became naturally lessened. Those few glimpses along the roadside which had made her sensible to the beauties she was about to lose, had prepared her mind to act in counteraction of her impulse; and the event which had brought into play the maternal instinct, naturally helped the cause of reason in her soul.

Still, with the erring pride of youth she reproached herself with her infirmity of purpose. She resolved to change .her ground, as if the instinct which had been awakened in one spot would not everywhere pursue her. Time was gained, and in such cases, to gain time is everything. Perhaps no suicide would ever take place if the individual would wait ten minutes. The soul takes its color from the cloud, and changes its moods as often. It is one of the best lessons to the young, to wait! wait! wait! One of the surest signs of strength is where the individual waits patiently and makes no complaint.

Margaret Cooper changed her ground. The spot was a wild one. A broken ledge of rock was at her feet, and just below it ran a dark, narrow winding footpath half-obscured by the undergrowth. Here she once more proceeded to nerve her mind for the commission of the deed, but she had not been there an instant when she was surprised to hear the sound of voices.

This was unusual. Who could they be? The villagers were not apt to stray from church-service whenever a preacher was to be found, and there was a new one, and consequently a new attraction, that day, for the spiritual hungry of Charlemont. The path below was seldom trodden except by herself and an occasional sportsman. The idea that entered her mind was, that her purpose had been suspected, and that she was pursued.

With this idea, she placed the pistol to her breast. She had already cocked the weapon. Her finger was on the trigger. But the tones of another voice reached her ears from below. They were those of a woman — sweet, musical, and tender.

A new light broke in upon her mind. This was the language of love. And who were these new lovers in Charlemont? Could it be that the voice of the male speaker was that of Stevens? Something in the tone sounded like it. Involuntarily, with this impression, the weapon was turned from her own bosom, and addressed in the direction in which the persons below were approaching. A sudden, joyous feeling touched her soul. The thought to destroy the criminal by whom she had been destroyed was a source of exultation. She felt that she could do it. Both pistols were in her hand. The pathway was not more than twenty paces distant; and her nerves, for the first time, braced to an unusual tension, trembled with the new excitement in her soul.

The intruders continued to approach. Their voices became more distinct, and Margaret Cooper was soon undeceived as to one of them being that of Alfred Stevens. She was compelled to lie close, that she might not betray her position and purpose. The male speaker was very urgent; the voice seemed that of a stranger. That of the female was not so clearly distinguishable, yet it seemed more familiar to the unintentional listener.

Something of feminine curiosity now entered the bosom of Margaret Cooper. Crouching where she was, she deposited the pistols at her feet. She remained breathlessly, for the slightest movement would have revealed her to the persons who were now just below. They passed close beneath the place of her concealment, and she soon discovered that they were lovers; and what their language was, even if she had not heard it, might have been conjectured.

The girl was a very pretty brunette of Charlemont—a sweet, retiring damsel of her own age, named Rivers—whom she knew only slightly. She was a shy, gentle, unpresuming girl, whom, for this reason, perhaps, Margaret had learned to look upon without dislike or scorn. Her companion was a youth whom Margaret had known when a lad, but who had been absent on the Mississippi for two years. His tall and masculine but well-made and graceful person sufficiently accounted for, while it justified, the taste

of the maiden.   He was a youth of fine, frank, manly countenance.   His garb was picturesque, that of a bold border-
hunter, with hunting-frock of yellow buckskin, and Indian
leggings.

The girl looked up to him with an expression at once of
eagerness and timidity.   Confidence and maiden bashful-
ness spoke equally in the delight which glowed upon her
features.   The bright eyes and sun-burned features of the
youth were flushed with the feeling of happy triumph and
assuring love.   The relation of the two was sufficiently evident from their looks, even had they no other language.

What were the emotions of Margaret Cooper, as she
looked down upon this pair?   At first she thought, as will
most persons: " Surely there is nothing in nature so lovely
as the union of two fond, devoted hearts.   The picture is
one equally of moral and physical beauty.   The slight,
fragile, depending damsel, hanging in perfect confidence on
the arm of the manly, lofty, and exulting youth — looking
up into his eyes in hope, while he returns the gaze with
pride and fondness!   Unconscious of all things but the love
which to them is life and all things besides, they move along
the forest way and know not its solitude; they linger and
loiter along its protracted paths, and see not their length;
they cling together through the lengthened hours, and fancy
they have lost no time; they hear each other's voices, and
believe that life is all music and delight."

While Margaret Cooper looked down and heard the
pleadings and promises of the youth, and beheld the sweet
emotions of his companion, engaged in a pleasant struggle
between her hopes and misgivings, she scarcely restrained
herself from rising where she was and crying aloud — like
another Cassandra, not to be believed: " Beware! beware!"

But the warning of Margaret Cooper would have been
unnecessary.   The girl was not only free from danger, but
she was superior to it.   She had the wholesome fear of
doing wrong too strongly impressed upon her by education

—she had too little confidence in herself—was too well
assured of her own weakness—to suffer herself, even for a
moment, to depart, in either thought or deed, from those
quiet but stern proprieties of conduct which are among the
best securities of the young. While she looked in her lover's face with confidence, and held his arm with the grasp
of one who is sure of a right to do so, there was an air of
childish simplicity in her manner which was wholly at variance with wild passions and improper fancies. While the
hunter maintained her on his arm, and looked down into her
eyes with love, his glance was yet as respectful, as unex-
pressive of presumption, as her own. Had the eyes of all
Charlemont been looking on, they would have beheld nothing in the conduct of either which could have incurred the
censure of the most becoming delicacy.

Keen was the emotion and bitter was the thought which
worked in the mind of Margaret Cooper. She looked on
the deportment of that young maiden, whose intellect at
another day she would have despised, with envy and regret.
Truer thoughts and feelings came to her as she listened to
the innocent but fond dialogue between the unconscious
pair. The hunter was pursuing an erratic life of enterprise
and industry, then very common among the western youth.
He had been down upon the Mississippi, seeking his fortune in such adventures as make border-life in our country
something like the more civilized life of the middle ages.
He had returned after a long absence, to claim the bride
whose affections he had won long before he had departed.
Never had knight-errant been more true to his mistress.
Her image had been his talisman as well against danger
from without, as against the demon within. It had never
left his mind, and he now returned for his reward. He
had returned to Charlemont just before the church service
had begun, and, being unprepared to go thither, had found
no difficulty in persuading his sweetheart to give the hour
of morning service to himself.

Mixed up with his professions of love was the story of his wanderings. Never were adventures more interesting to any auditor. Never was auditor more easily moved by the transitions of the tale from tears to smiles, and from smiles again to tears. His risks and rewards; his defeats and successes; his wild adventures by fell and flood—not perhaps so perilous as those of Othello, but such as proved he had the soul to encounter the worst in Othello's experience, and maintain himself as well—drew largely on the maiden's wonder and delight, increased her tenderness and tremors, and made her quite as devoted to her hero as ever was Desdemona to her dusky chief. As they went from hearing below, the manner in which the hunter concluded his narrative provided a sufficient test for the faith of his companion.

"And now, Selina, you see all the risks and the dangers. There's work and perhaps trouble for you to go down with me along the Choctaw borders. But if there's work, I am the man to do my own share, and help you out in yours; and, if there's trouble, here's the breast to stand it first, and here's the arm to drive it back, so that it'll never trouble yours. No danger shall come to you, so long as I can stand up between it and you. If so be that you love me as you say, there's one way to show it: you'll soon make up your mind to go with me. If you don't, why—"

"But you know I do love you, John—" murmured the girl.

"Don't I believe it? Well, if what you say means what it should, you're ready. Here's my hand, and all that it's good for. It can work for you and fight for you, Selina, and it's yours eternally, with all that I have."

The hand of the girl was silently put into that of the speaker. The tears were in her eyes; but, if she made any other answer, it was unheard by Margaret Cooper. The rustic pair moved from sight even as they spoke, and the desolate woman once more remained alone!

CHAPTER XXXVII.

SHAME AND DEATH — THE OATH.

MARGARET COOPER was at length permitted to emerge from the place of her concealment. The voices of the lovers were lost, as well as their forms, in the wooded distance. Dreaming, like children as they were, of life and happiness, they had wandered off, too happy to fancy for a moment that the world contained, in its wide, vast bosom, one creature half so wretched as she who hung above them, brooding, like some wild bird of the cliff, over the storm which had robbed her of her richest plumage.

She sank back into the woods. She no longer had the heart to commit the meditated crime. This purpose had left her mind. It had given place to another, however, scarcely less criminal. We have seen her, under the first impression that the stranger whose voice she heard was Alfred Stevens, turning the muzzle of the pistol from her breast to the path on which he was approaching. Though she discovered her error, and laid the weapon down, the sudden suggestion of her mind, at that moment, gave a new direction to her mood.

Why should she not seek to avenge her wrong? Was he to escape without penalty? was she to be a quiescent victim? True, she was a woman, destined it would seem to suffer — perhaps with a more than ordinary share of that suffering which falls to her sex. But she had also a peculiar strength — the strength of a man in some respects; and in her bosom she now felt the sudden glow of one of his fiercest passions. Revenge might be in her power. She might redress her wrong by her own hand. It was a weapon of death which she grasped. In her grasp it might be made a weapon of power. The suggestion seemed to be that of justice only. It was one that filled her whole soul with a triumphant and a wild enthusiasm.

"I shall not be stricken down without danger to mine enemy. For *this*—this, at least—strength is allotted me. Let him tremble! In his place of seeming security let him tremble! I shall pursue his steps. I will find him out. There shall be a day of retribution! Alfred Stevens, there is a power within me which tells me you are no longer safe!

"And why may I not secure this justice—this vengeance? Why? Because I am a woman. Ha! We shall see. If I am a woman, I can be an enemy—and such an enemy! An enemy not to be appeased, not to be overcome. War always with my foe—war to the knife—war to the last!"

Such a nature as that of Margaret Cooper needed some such object to give it the passionate employment without which it must recoil upon itself and end either in suicide or madness. She brooded upon this new thought. She found in it a grateful exercise. From the moment when she conceived the idea of being the avenger of her own wrong, her spirit became more elastic—she became less sensible to the possible opinions upon her condition which might be entertained by others. She found consolation, in retreating to this one thought, from all the rest. Of the difficulties in the way of her design, it was not in her impetuous character to think. She never once suspected that the name of Alfred Stevens had been an assumed one. She never once asked how she was to pursue and hunt him up. She thought of a male disguise for herself, it is true; but of the means and modes of travel—in what direction to go, and after what plan to conduct her pursuit, she had not the most distant idea.

She addressed herself to her new design, however, in one respect, with amazing perseverance. It diverted her from other and more oppressive thoughts. Her pistols she carried secretly to a very distant wood, where she concealed them in the hollow of a tree. To this wood she repaired secretly and daily. Here she selected a tree as a mark. A small section of the bark, which she tore away, at a given height, she learned to regard as the breast of her seducer. This was the object of her aim. Without any woman fears, she began her practice and continued it, day by day, until, as we are told by one of the chroniclers of her melancholy story, "she could place a ball with an accuracy, which, were it universally equalled by modern duellists, would render duelling much more fatal than it commonly is."

In secret she procured gunpowder and lead, by arts so ingenious as to baffle detection. At midnight when her mother slept she moulded her bullets. Well might the thoughts and feelings which possessed her mind, while engaged in this gloomy labor, have endowed every bullet with a wizard spell to make it do its bidding truly. Bitter, indeed, were the hours so appropriated; but they had their consolations. Dark and terrible were the excited moods in which she retired from her toils to that slumber which she could not always secure. And when it did come, what were its images! The tree, the mark, the weapon, the deep, dim forest, all the scenes and trials of the day, were renewed in her sleep. A gloomy wood filled her eyes — a victim dabbled in blood lay before her; and, more than once, her own fearful cry of vengeance and exultation awakened her from those dreams of sleep, which strengthened her in the terrible pursuit of the object which occasioned them.

Such thoughts and practices, continued with religious

pertinacity, from day to day, necessarily had their effect upon her appearance as well as her character. Her beauty assumed a wilder aspect. Her eye shot forth a supernatural fire. She never smiled. Her mouth was rigid and compressed as if her heart was busy in an endless conflict. Her gloom, thus nurtured by solitude and the continual presence of a brooding imagination of revenge, darkened into something like ferocity. Her utterance became brief and quick—her tones sharp, sudden, and piercing. She had but one thought which never seemed to desert her, yet of this thought no ear ever had cognizance. It was of the time when she should exercise the skill which she had now acquired upon that destroyer of herself, whom she now felt herself destined to destroy.

Of course we are describing a madness—one of those peculiar forms of the disease which seems to have its origin in natural and justifiable suggestions of reason. Not the less a madness for all that.

Succeeding in her practice at one distance, Margaret Cooper changed it. From one point to another she constantly varied her practice, until her aim grew certain at almost any distance within the ordinary influence of the weapon. To strike her mark at thirty feet became, in a little while, quite as easy as to do so at five; and, secure now of her weapon, her next object—though there was no cessation of her practice—was how to seek and where to find the victim.

In this new object she meditated to disguise herself in the apparel of a man. She actually commenced the making up of the several garments of one. This was also the secret labor of the midnight hour, when her feeble-minded mother slept. She began to feel some of the difficulties lying in the way of this pursuit, and her mind grew troubled to consider them, without however, relaxing in its determination. That seemed a settled matter.

While she brooded over this new feature of her purpose

—as if fortunately to arrest the mad design—her mother fell seriously sick, and was for some time in danger. The duty of attending upon her, put a temporary stop to her thoughts and exercises; though without having the effect of expelling them from her mind.

But another event, upon her mother's recovery, tended to produce a considerable alteration in her thoughts. A new care filled her heart and rendered her a different being, in several respects. She was soon to become a mother. The sickness of soul which oppressed her under this conviction, gave a new direction to her mood without lessening its bitterness; and, in proportion as she found her vengeance delayed, so was the gratification which it promised, a heightened desire in her mind.

For the humiliating and trying event which was at hand, Margaret Cooper prepared with a degree of silent firmness which denoted quite as strongly the resignation of despair as any other feeling.

The child is born.

Margaret Cooper has at length become a mother. She has suffered the agony, without being able to feel the compensating pride and pleasure of one. It was the witness of her shame—could she receive it with any assurances of love? It is doubtful if she did.

For some time after its birth, the hapless woman seemed to be unconscious, or half-conscious only, of her charge. A stupor weighed upon her senses. When she did awaken, and her eyes fell upon the face and form of the infant with looks of recognition, one long, long piercing shriek burst from her lips. She closed her eyes—she turned away from the little unoffending, yet offensive object with a feeling of horror.

Its features were those of Alfred Stevens. The likeness was indelible; and this identity drew upon the child a share of that loathing hatred with which she now remembered the guilty father.

It may very well be supposed that the innocent babe suffered under these circumstances. The milk which it drew from the mother's breast, was the milk of bitterness, and it did not thrive. It imbibed gall instead of nutriment. Day after day it pined in hopeless misery; and though the wretched mother strove to supply its wants and soothe its little sorrows, with a gradually increasing interest which overcame her first loathing, there was yet that want of sweetest sympathy which nothing merely physical could well supply.

Debility was succeeded by disease—fever preyed upon its little frame, which was now reduced to a skeleton. One short month only had elapsed from its birth, and it lay, in the silence of exhaustion upon the arm of its mother. Its eyes, whence the flickering light was escaping fast, looked up into hers, as she fancied, with an expression of reproach. She felt, on the instant, the pang of the maternal conscience. She forgot the unworthy father, as she thought of the neglectful mother. She bent down, and, for the first time, imprinted on its little lips the maternal kiss.

A smile seemed to glimmer on its tiny features; and, from that moment, Margaret Cooper resolved to forget her injuries, for the time, at least, in the consideration of her proper duties. But her resolution came too late. Even while her nipple was within its boneless gums, a change came over the innocent. She did not heed it. Her eyes and thoughts were elsewhere; and thus she mused, gazing vacantly upon the wall of her chamber until her mother entered the room. Mrs. Cooper gave but a single glance at the infant when she saw that its little cares were over.

"Oh, Margaret!" she exclaimed, "the child is dead."

The mother looked down with a start and shudder. A big tear fell from her eyes upon the cold cheek of the innocent. She released it to her mother, turned her face upon the couch, and uttered her thanks to Heaven that had so

19

decreed it—that had left her again free for that darker
purpose which had so long filled her mind.

"Better so," she murmured to her mother. "It is at
peace. It will neither know its own nor its mother's griefs.
It is free from that shame for which I must live!"

"Come now, Margaret, no more of that," said the mother
sharply. "There's no need of shame. There are other
things to live for besides shame."

"There are—there are!" exclaimed the daughter, with
spasmodic energy. "Were there not, I should, indeed, be
desperate."

"To be sure you would, my child. You have a great
deal to live for yet; and let a little time blow over, and
when everything's forgotten, you will get as good a husband as any girl in the country."

"For Heaven's sake, mother, none of this?"

"But why not! Though you are looking a little bad just
now—quite pale and broken—yet it's only because you
have been so ill; and this nursing of babies, and having
'em too, is a sort of business to make any young woman
look bad; but in spite of all, there's not a girl in the village, no matter how fresh she may be looking, that can hold
a candle to you."

"For mercy, mother!——"

"Let me speak, I tell you! Don't I know? You're
young, and you'll get over it. You will get all your beauty
and good looks back, now that the baby's out of the way,
and there's no more nursing to be done. And what with
your beauty and your talents, Margaret——"

"Peace! mother! Peace—peace! You will drive me
to madness if you continue to speak thus."

"Well, I'm sure there's no knowing what to say to please
you. I'm sure, I only want to cheer you up, and to convince you that things are not so bad as you think them now
The cloud will blow over soon, and everything will be for
gotten, and then, you see——"

The girl waved her hand impatiently.

"Death — death !" she exclaimed. "Oh ! child of shame, and bitterness, and wrath !" she murmured, kneeling down beside the infant, "thou art the witness that I have no future but storm, and cloud, and wrath, and—— Vengeance !"

The last word was inaudible to her mother's ears.

"It is an oath !" she cried ; "an oath !" And her hands were uplifted in solemn adjuration.

"Come — come, Margaret ! none of this swearing. You frighten me with your swearing. There's nothing that you need to swear about ! What's done can't be helped now, by taking it so seriously. You must only be patient, and give yourself time. Time's the word for us now ; after a little while you'll see the sky become brighter. It's a bad business, it's true ; but it needn't break a body's heart. How many young girls I've known in my time, that's been in the same fix. There was Janet Bonner, and Emma Loring, and Mary Peters—I knew 'em all, very well. Well, they all made a slip once in their lives, and they never broke their hearts about it, and didn't look very pale and sad in the face either ; but they just kept quiet and behaved decent for awhile, and every one of 'em got good husbands. Janet Bonner, she married Dick Pyatt, who came from Massachusetts, and kept the school down by Clayton's Meadow ; Emma Loring married a baptist-preacher from Virginia, named Stokes. I never saw him to know him ; and as for Mary Peters, there never was a girl that had a slip that was ever so fortunate, for she's been married no less than three times since, and as she's a widow again, there's no telling what may happen to her yet. So don't you be so downcast. You're chance is pretty nigh as good as ever, if you will only hold up your head, and put the best face on it."

"Oh ! torture—torture ! Mother, will you not be silent ?

Let the dead speak to me only. I would hear but the voice of this one witness——"

And she communed only with the dead infant, sitting or kneeling beside it. But the communion was not one of contrition or tears—not of humility and repentance—not of self-reproach and a broken spirit. Pride and other passions had summoned up deities and angels of terror and of crime, before the eyes and thoughts of the wretched mourner, and the demon who had watched with her and waited on her, and had haunted her with taunt and bitter mockeries, night and day, was again busy with terrible suggestions, which gradually grew to be divine laws to her diseased imagination.

" Yes !" she exclaimed unconsciously.

" I hear ! I obey ! Yet speak again. Repeat the lesson. I must learn it every syllable, so that I shall not mistake —so that I can not fail !"

" Who are you talking to, Margaret ?" asked the mother anxiously.

" Do you not see them, where they go ? There—through the doors ; the open windows—wrapped in shadows, with great wings at their shoulders, each carrying a dart in his bony grasp."

" Lord, have mercy ! She's losing her senses again !" and the mother was about to rush from the apartment to seek assistance ; but with the action, the daughter suddenly arose, wearing a look of singular calmness, and motioning to the child, she said : —

" Will you not dress it for the grave ?"

" I'm going about it now. The poor lovely little creature. The innocent little blossom. We must put it in white, Margaret—virgin white—and put white flowers in its little hands and on its breast, and under its head. Oh ! it will look so sweet in its little coffin !"

" God ! I should go mad with all this !" exclaimed the daughter. " were it not for that work which is before me !

I must be calm for that—calm and stern! I must not
hear—I must not think—not feel—lest I forget myself,
and the deed which I have to do. That oath—that oath!
It is sworn! It is registered in heaven, by the fatal angels
of remorse, and wrath, and vengeance!"

And again, a whisper at her ears repeated:—

"For this, Margaret, and for this only, must thou live?"

"I must! I will!" she muttered, as it were in reply,
and her eye glared upon the opened door, as she heard a
voice and footsteps without; and the thought smote her:—

"Should it be now! Come for the sacrifice! Ha!"

CHAPTER XXXVIII.

THE PALL UPON THE COFFIN.

THE noise which arrested the attention of Margaret
Cooper, and kindled her features into an expression of wild
and fiery ferocity, was of innocent origin. The widow
Thackeray was the intruder. Her kindness, sympathy,
and unweared attentions, so utterly in conflict with the esti-
mates hitherto made of her heart and character, by Mrs.
Cooper, had, in some degree, disarmed the censures of that
excellent mother, if they had not wholly changed her sentiments. She professed to be very grateful to Thackeray's
attentions, and, without making any profession, Margaret
certainly showed her that she felt them. She now only
pointed the widow to the corpse of the child, in that one
action telling to the other all that was yet unknown. Then
she seated herself composedly, folded her hands, and, beside the corpse, forgot its presence, forgot the presence of
all—heard no voice, save that of the assiduous demon
whom nothing could expel from her companionship.

"Poor little thing!" murmured the widow Thackeray,
as she proceeded to assist Mrs. Cooper in decking it for the
grave.

The duty was finally done. Its burial was appointed for
the morrow.

A village funeral is necessarily an event of some importance. The lack of excitements in small communities, in-

vests even sorrow and grief and death with a peculiar interest in the eyes of curiosity. On the present occasion, all the villagers attended. The funeral itself might have sufficed to collect them with few exceptions; but now there was a more eager influence still, working upon the gossippy moods of the population. To see Margaret Cooper in her affliction—to see that haughty spirit humbled and made ashamed—was, we fear, a motive, in the minds of many, much stronger than the ostensible occasion might have awakened. Had Margaret been a fashionable woman, in a great city, she might have disappointed the vulgar desire, by keeping to her chamber. Nay, even according to the free-and-easy standards prevailing at Charlemont, she might have done the same thing, and incurred no additional scandal.

It was, indeed, to the surprise of a great many, that she made her appearance. It was still more a matter of surprise—nay, pious and virgin horror—that she seemed to betray neither grief nor shame, surrounded as she was by all whom she knew, and all, in particular, whom, in the day of her pride, she had kept at a distance.

"What a brazen creature!" whispered Miss Jemima Parkinson, an interesting spinster of thirty-six, to Miss Ellen Broadhurst, who was only thirty-four; and Miss Ellen whispered back, in reply:—

"She hasn't the slightest bit of shame!"

Interesting virgins! they had come to gloat over the spectacle of shame. To behold the agonizing sense of degradation declare itself under the finger-pointing scorn of those who, perhaps, were only innocent from necessity, and virtuous because of the lack of the necessary attractions in the eyes of lust.

But Margaret Cooper seemed quite as insensible to their presence as to their scorn and her own shame. She, in truth, saw none of them. She heard not their voices. She conjectured none of their comments. She had anticipated all of them; and having, in consequence, reached a point of intensity in her agony which could bear no addition, she had been relieved only by a still more intense passion, by which the enfeebling one, of mere society, stood rebuked and almost forgotten.

They little dreamed the terrible thoughts which were working, beneath that stolid face, in that always eager-working brain. They never fancied what a terrible demon now occupied that fiery heart which they supposed was wholly surrendered to the consciousness of shame. Could they have heard that voice of the fiend whispering in her ears, while they whispered to one another—heard his terrible exhortations—heard her no less terrible replies—they would have shrunk away in horror, and felt fear rather than exultation.

Margaret Cooper was insensible to all that they could say or do. She knew them well—knew what they would say, and feel, and do; but the very extremity of her suffering had placed it out of their power any longer to mortify or shame.

Some few of the villagers remained away. Ned Hinkley and his widowed sister were absent from the house, though they occupied obscure places in the church when the funeral-procession took place. An honorable pity kept them from meeting the eyes of the poor shame-stricken but not shame-showing woman.

And Margaret followed the little corpse to its quiet nook in the village graveyard. In that simple region the procession was wholly on foot; and she walked behind the coffin as firmly as if she knew not what it held. There was a single shiver that passed over her frame, as the heavy clods fell upon the coffin-lid—but that was all; and when her mother and the widow Thackeray took each of them one of her arms, and led her away from the grave, and home, she went quietly, calmly, it would seem, and with as firm a step as ever!

"She has not a bit of feeling!" said Miss Jemima to Miss Ellen.

"That's always the case with your very smart women," was the reply. "It's all head with 'em; there's no heart. They can talk fine things about death, and sorrow, and affliction, but it's talk only. They don't feel what they say."

Ned Hinkley had a juster notion of the state of the poor victim — of her failings and her sensibilities, her equal strength and weakness.

"Now," said he to his sister, "there's a burning volcano in that woman's heart, that will tear her some day to pieces. For all that coldness, and calmness, and stateliness, her brain is on fire, and her heart ready for a convulsion. Her thoughts now, if she thinks at all, are all desperate. She's going through a very hell upon earth! When you think of her pride — and she's just as proud now as the devil himself — her misfortune hasn't let her down — only made her more fierce — you wonder that she lets herself be seen; you wonder that she lives at all. I only wonder that she hasn't thrown herself from the rocks and into the lake. She'll do it yet, I'm a-thinking.

"And just so she always was. I knew her long ago. She once told me she was afraid of nothing — would do as she pleased — she could dare anything! From that moment I saw she wasn't the girl for Bill Hinkley. I told him so, but he was so crazy after her, he'd hear to nothing. A woman — a young woman — a mere girl of fifteen — boasting that she can dare and do things that would set any woman in a shiver! I tell you what, sis, the woman that's bolder than her sex is always in danger of falling from the rocks. She gets such a conceit of her mind, that the devil is always welcome. Her heart, after that, stands no sort of chance!

"Protect me, say I, from all that class of women that pride themselves on their strongmindedness! They get

19*

insolent upon it. They think that mind can do everything. They're so vain, that they never can see the danger, even when it's yawning at their feet. A woman's never safe unless she's scary of herself, and mistrusts herself, and never lets her thoughts and fancies get from under a tight rein of prudence. For, after all, the passions will have their way some day, and then what's the use of the mind? I tell you, sis, that the passions are born deaf—they never listen to any argument.

"But I'm sorry for her—God knows I'm sorry for her! I'd give all I'm worth to have a fair shot or clip at that rascal Stevens. Brother Stevens! Ain't it monstrous, now, that a sheep's cover should be all that's sufficient to give the wolf freedom in the flock?—that you've only to say, 'This is a brother—a man of God'—and no proof is asked! nobody questions! The blind, beastly, bigoted, blathering blockheads! I feel very much like setting off straight, and licking John Hinkley, though he's my own uncle, within an inch of his life! He and John Cross—the old fools who are so eager to impose their notions of religion upon everybody, that anybody may impose upon them—they two have destroyed this poor young creature. It's at their door, in part, this crime, and this ruin! I feel it in my heart to lick 'em both out of their breeches!

"Yet, as I'm a living sinner, they'll stand up in the congregation, and exhort about this poor girl's misfortune, just as if they were not to blame at all who brought the wolf into the farmyard! They'll talk about her sins, and not a word, to themselves or anybody else, about their own stupidities! I feel it in my heart to lather both of them right away!"

The sister said little, and sorrowfully walked on in silence homeward, listening to the fierce denunciations of Ned Hinkley. Ned was affected, or, rather, he showed his sympathies, in a manner entirely his own. He was so much for fight, that he totally forgot his fiddle that night, and amused himself by putting his two "barking-pups" in order —getting them ready, as he said, "in case he ever should get a crack at Brother Stevens!"

The cares of the child's burial over, and the crowd dispersed, the cottage of the widow Cooper was once more abandoned to the cheerlessness and wo within. Very dismal was the night of that day to the two, the foolish mother and wretched daughter, as they sat brooding together, in deep silence, by the light of a feeble candle. The mother rocked a while in her easy-chair. The daughter, hands clasped in her lap, sat watching the candlelight in almost idiotic vacancy of gaze. At length she stood up and spoke —slowly, deliberately, and apparently in as calm a mood as she had ever felt in all her life :—

"We must leave this place, mother. We must go hence —to-morrow if we can."

"Go ?—leave this place ? I want to know why! I'm sure we're very comfortable here. I can't be going just when you please, and leaving all my company and friends."

"Friends!"

"Yes, friends! There's the widow Thackeray—and there's—"

"And how long is it since Mrs. Thackeray was such a dear friend, mother?" asked the daughter, with ill-suppressed scorn.

"No matter how long: she's a good friend now. She's not so foolish as she used to be. She's grown good; she's got religion; and I don't consider what she was. No!— I'm willing—"

"Pshaw, mother! tell me nothing of your friendships. You'll find, wherever you go, as many friends as you please, valued quite as much as Mrs. Thackeray."

"Well, I do say, Margaret, it's very ungrateful of you to speak so disrespectfully of Mrs. Thackeray, after all her kindness and attention."

"I do not speak disrespectfully of Mrs. Thackeray. I *never* did speak ill of her, even when it was your favorite practice to do so. I only speak of your newly-acquired appreciation of her. But this is nothing to the purpose. I repeat, mother, we can not remain here. I will depart, whether you resolve to go or not. I can not, I will not, exist another week in Charlemont."

"And where would you go?"

"Back—back to that old farm, from which you brought me in evil hour! It is poor, obscure, profitless, unsought, unseen: it will give me a shelter—it may bring me peace. I must have solitude for a season; I must sleep for months."

"Sleep for months! La me, child, what a notion's that!"

"No matter—thither let us go. I seem to see it, stretching out its hands, and imploring us to come."

"Bless me, Margaret! a farm stretching out its hands! Why, you're in a dream!"

"Don't wake me, then! Better I should so dream! Thither I go. It is fortunate that you have not been able to sell it. It is a mercy that it still remains to us. It was my childhood's home. Would it could again receive me as a child! It will cover my head for a while, at least, and that is something. We must leave this place. Here every thing offends me—every spot, every face, every look, eve-y gesture."

"It's impossible, Margaret!—"

"What! you suppose it an honorable distinction, do you, when the folks here point to your daughter, and say—ha! ha!—listen what they say! It is the language of compliment! They are doing me honor, with tongue and finger! Repeat, mother; tell me what they say—for it evidently gives you great pleasure."

"O Margaret! Margaret!—"

"You understand, do you? Well, then, we go. We can not depart too soon. If I stay here, I madden! And I must not madden. I have something which needs be done

—which must be done.   It is an oath ! an oath in heaven !
The child was a witness.   She heard all — every syllable !"

"What all ? what did you hear ?"

"No matter ! I'm sworn to be secret.   But you shall
hear in time.   We have no time for it now.   It is a very
long story.   And we must now be packing.   Yes, we must
go.   *I* must go, at least.   Shall I go alone ?"

"But you will not leave your mother, Margaret !"

"Father and mother—all will I leave, in obedience to
that oath.   Believe me or not, mother—go with me or not
—still I go.   Perhaps it is better that I should go alone."

The strong will naturally swayed the feebler, as it had
ever done before.   The mother submitted to an arrangement
which she had not the resolution to oppose.   A few days
were devoted to necessary arrangements, and then they left
Charlemont for ever.   Margaret Cooper looked not once
behind them as they traversed the lonely hills looking down
upon the village—those very hills from which, at the opening of this story, the treacherous Alfred Stevens and his
simple uncle beheld the lovely little settlement.   She recognised the very spot, as they drove over it, where Stevens
first encountered her, and the busy demon at her ears whispered :—

"It was here !   You remember !"

And she clinched her teeth firmly together, even though
she shuddered at her memories ; and she renewed her oath
to the demon, who, thereupon, kept her company the rest of
the journey, till she reached the ancient and obscure farmstead in which she was born.

"She retired," says the rude chronicle from which we
have borrowed many of the materials for this sombre history, "to a romantic little farm in ——, there to spend in
seclusion, with her aged mother and a few servants, the
remainder of her days."

Our simple chronicler takes too much for granted.   Margaret Cooper retired with no such purpose.   She had pur-

poses entirely at conflict with any idea of repose or quiet. She thought nothing of the remainder of her days. Her mother was not so aged but that she could still think, six months afterward, of the reported marriage of the widow Thackeray with repining, and with the feeling of one who thinks that she has suffered neglect and injustice at the hands of the world. Touching the romance of the ancient farmstead, we are more modestly content to describe it as sterile, lonely, and unattractive; its obscurity offering, for the present, its chief attractions to our desolate heroine, and the true occasion for that deep disgust with which her amiable mother beheld it.

Our chronicle of Charlemont is ended. We have no further object or interest within its precincts. William Hinkley is gone, no one knows whither, followed by his adopted father, the retired lawyer, whose sensibilities were fatal to his success. It was not long before Ned Hinkley and his widowed sister found it their policy to depart also, seeking superior objects in another county; and at this moment Charlemont is an abandoned and deserted region. It seemed to decline from the moment when the cruel catastrophe occurred which precipitated Margaret Cooper from her pride of place. Beautiful as the village appeared at the opening of our legend, it was doomed to as rapid a decay as growth. " Something ails it now — the spot is cursed !"

But *our* history does not finally conclude with the fate of Charlemont. That chronicle is required now to give place to another, in which we propose to take up the sundered clues, and reunite them in a fresh progress. We shall meet some of the old parties once more, in new situations. We shall again meet with Margaret Cooper, in a new guise, under other aspects, but still accompanied by her demon — still inspired by her secret oath — still glowing with all the terrible memories of the past — still laboring with unhallowed pride; and still destined for a dark catastrophe. Our scene, however, lies in another region, to which the reader, who has thus far kept pace with our progress, is entreated still to accompany us. The chronicle of "CHARLEMONT" will find its fitting sequel in that of "BEAUCHAMPE"—known proverbially as "THE KENTUCKY TRAGEDY."

END OF CHARLEMONT.